GUARDIAN OF DEFIANCE

A NYX FORTUNA NOVEL

MICHELLE MANUS

1

Nyx Fortuna stood just outside the boundary of her Station, portal magic humming around her in a lazy, serpentine loop. A map of planets was splayed like an interactive hologram in the surrounding air, silver dots shimmering against an ocean of velvet black. There were more dots—more planets—than there had been when she'd started bringing up the map for practice several months ago.

The first time she'd tried, wearing the four portal magic bracelets that were her minimum number to feel safe, she'd only been able to bring up those planets and moons that were within the bounds of Earth's solar system. Now, there were multitudes of dots beyond those, enough that she had to walk through the map if she actually wanted to see them all.

"Have you had any luck with the navigation?" Griff asked. He'd walked up a minute or so ago, stopping just within the Station's boundary, as Kaliaris required either Griff or Nyx to remain connected to them at all times.

"No," Nyx said glumly. By "navigation" he meant not only manipulating the map, but also identifying the planets the dots represented.

Seth had once told her that when Jevryn had been looking for Nyx when she'd been lost on Amentia Furor, he had been able to make the map smaller—in effect like zooming out on a computer screen—so that he could see more planets at once without having to physically walk through the points. So far, she'd been unable to do it herself. She'd tried various hand motions—including drawing her middle finger and thumb together, as Seth told her Jevryn had done —and attempting to imbue both her magic and her intention into the movement, but nothing had worked.

She had no idea how he'd done it. Just like she had no idea how he'd been able to tell which planets were which. She could identify those within Earth's solar system, obviously, because she could relate where she was standing—Earth—to the orbits of the other planets. But outside of that she had no idea. She'd toyed with the thought of trekking into Dead Earth for some books on astronomy that detailed various planetary systems—which she still might do at some point—but had ultimately decided they wouldn't do anything but sate her curiosity. They wouldn't help her actually navigate when—*if*—she went somewhere new. She couldn't carry an astronomy book around with her every time she portaled. She couldn't memorize every system in the universe. Also, those systems were not all mapped, so all it would take was one slip into uncharted territory for her mostly useless book to become completely useless.

How Jevryn had pulled up this very map, in nearly this very spot—though his map had, certainly, included far more planets than hers did—and identified Lehine and then Amentia Furor as the planets Nyx had been on, she didn't know. And it was driving her to distraction.

"This would be so much easier if you could just explain it all to me," she told Griff, not for the first time. Unfortunately, Kiev had magically tied Griff's tongue on all things related to portal magic when he'd bound Griff to the Station. Griff could creatively talk around the subject, but he couldn't tell her anything instructive.

Stars, she really hated her uncle. And to think, she'd only met the man once. Yet somehow, Kiev's foul touch seemed to be bound up in all the important aspects of—and people in—her life.

"I am sorry for that," Griff said.

"You have nothing to apologize for. For one, it's not your fault, and for another, if I were more of a natural, I'd be able to under-stand this."

"Given what you have managed to do in your limited uses of the ability thus far, I can assure you that you *are*, in fact, a natural. As much as Jevryn was when he began."

"And yet he can understand all this"—she waved at the silver points—"and I can't."

"He couldn't always."

She bestowed upon him her most skeptical look.

"You cannot truly think that he discovered—" Griff's beak clicked shut, a sound of irritation issuing from his throat instead of whatever he'd intended to say. Kiev's underhandedness at work. Griff stretched out his wings, resettled them. "That is to say, whenever a person discovers something that is entirely new to them, be it a skill or a subject of study, they cannot be expected to be as knowledgable about it as someone who is possessed of several hundred years of practice."

"I know that," Nyx said, still frustrated with herself. "But he *discovered* portaling. Him and everyone who's now a councilor. They were pioneers in the field. So if they figured out how to navigate this"—she waved a hand at the map—"then I should be able to as well."

Griff's head canted at that angle that said he was considering his words carefully, in order to find ones that could slip around the magic binding his speech. "He did learn, more or less on his own, how to do the very thing you are now attempting to do. But he was also doing one thing that you, crucially, are not. And he was doing it often and at frequent risk to himself."

"Actually portaling places?" she guessed.

Griff nodded. "Though I must beg you not to get it into your head to take the same approach. It is a statistical miracle that Jevryn —and the other councilors—survived. The skies alone only know how many others with their abilities died alone and forever forgotten in inhospitable locales."

Nyx shivered, remembering her nearly fatal attempts to leave the prison on Lehine. Somehow, she'd never given much thought to the number of portal witches who must have simply died on their first or second trip out.

She let the map fade and shook her wrist with its stacked bracelets, all imbued with portal magic. "I'm not exactly swimming in enough magic to take planet-leaping risks." She'd been practicing short-distance, on-planet portaling with an eye towards improving her efficiency in regards to magic usage. If the way her map's range had expanded—despite her only having access to the same amount of magic—was any indication, her efficiency *was* improving. That didn't mean she was planning to go planet-hopping any time soon.

Griff sighed. "Yes, well, I expect that limitation will persuade you towards caution for precisely as long as there is no pressing need for you to go elsewhere. You have an insatiable curiosity, much like your—" He cut off abruptly.

Nyx very much wanted to pretend he had done so because magic had caught his tongue. Realistically, he'd been about to say *much like your father* and stopped himself. She smiled at him. "It's okay, you can say the "F" word. It's not like it's a secret."

Except for that part where she hadn't told anyone. At first, she hadn't known how. Then Morgen and Evra had left on an ultimate Dead Earth vacation for a few months and only returned three weeks ago. All of which added up to it having been six months since she'd learned her heritage and not said a word, so how was she supposed to admit to it now?

"It may not be a secret as such," Griff said, "but that does not mean it is easy for you to hear."

No, it wasn't easy to hear, but not for the reasons Griff thought. He was under the impression that after the way Jevryn had treated her—essentially telling her he wanted nothing to do with her and that she was better off without him—that she now also wanted nothing to do with him. The truth was far worse. The truth was that she still wanted to know him, she just didn't want to be the one asking for him to remember she existed. After nearly six months of complete silence from him, she still wanted to wake up one morning to find that the companion journal, which had remained void of new entries since she'd last seen him, was filled with a lengthy apology and a request for reconciliation.

It was as bad as her childhood fantasies where she'd hoped her father would show up and rescue her from the misery of her life. Except this was actually worse, because she was an adult now, and where her childhood self had envisioned her father as a perfect hero who could do no wrong, the adult her knew Jevryn was, at best, living in a moral shade of dark gray.

"Just as," Griff continued, "it may not be easy for you to hear that I think we should request his help."

She tried and failed to keep her reaction off her face. "I'm not asking him for anything," she said flatly. "Unless it's related to the Harvester." They had a business arrangement where that was concerned.

"You do not have to. I can."

She started to protest that Griff shouldn't have to talk to him either. But Griff's relationship with Jevryn wasn't her own, and whatever footing the two of them were on, Jevryn was one of the few people in the universe who could understand Griff. Jevryn was the only person who had both known Griff before he'd become Kaliaris' Avatar and would happily talk to him about it now. So if it didn't hurt Griff to engage with him, that was his business. But she didn't want him going to Jevryn on her behalf.

"I don't need his help."

Griff rustled his feathers like a sigh. Gently, and choosing his words with careful vagueness, he said, "You *do*. The book I wrote is not an instruction manual. I wish to the skies it was."

So did she. She could only suppose no one else had written an actual instruction manual, since Jevryn hadn't sent her one.

Griff continued. "The book is an exploration of magical theory, of the uses and limitations of the ability. It was somewhat of a love letter to the ability itself, and to the man I knew who possessed it. What it is not, is useful for someone who does not understand the basics of the ability because they have never been taught it, nor have they garnered the experience on their own.

"However repulsive you may find the idea of Jevryn's tutelage, he is the only person both qualified and able to help you. Furthermore, he has a responsibility to do so. It is—"

"I don't want his help," she stated again. "And it's not as if I have an abundance of opportunities to need it." She held up her left hand, showing the number three tattooed between her thumb and forefinger, indicating the remaining trips she was allowed to take away from Earth, in accordance with her and Kaliaris' bargain. "I also don't have enough portal magic to risk going anywhere. I have enough to practice on-planet, and soon I'm going to have to quit even that, because I need to make sure I have enough to get myself back here, in the event I'm stranded somewhere again."

Returning to her anchors, like the one embedded in a tree ten feet away, was something she had at least proved herself adept at doing. And she only needed to do that in the event she was stuck somewhere unknown. Seth still had enough portal stones to Earth that could return them here from all of the ley-line-connected planets. It was only the unknown ones that might require more magic than the stones possessed. Unfortunately, those were also the planets she tended to find herself stranded on.

If she had toyed with the idea of accessing more portal magic on her own, she'd talked herself out of it. She only knew of two places where it could be found: Lehine, and the Shadow Market. She had no idea how to find Lehine on her map, not to mention that returning to a prison where all of the inmates had been abandoned and left to die in their cells was not a life experience she was keen on having again. As for the Shadow Market, the portal magic there was controlled by the Keeper of Shadows. And though Evra was still in contact with Bryn Morrigan—the two had settled into a long-distance friendship that appeared to be based mostly on bickering with each other via the written word—Nyx doubted even Evra could get access to the portal magic well without an explanation of *why*. Even if she could, it would still tell Bryn what Nyx was, as only a portal witch was capable of manipulating portal magic, and therefore only a portal witch would have any reason to need access to the well.

Long story short, Nyx was staring down the barrel of an extended life trapped within the bounds of Kaliaris, with few opportunities to leave, and no portal magic to do it with even if she wanted to. She was well aware that she was playing with an ability she would essentially lose soon, and it killed her a little bit. Because the ability was a part of who she was, and discovering it had felt like finding something lost. Being without it—never flexing that muscle again—would be like cutting off a piece of herself.

"If you do not wish me to ask," Griff eventually relented, "then I will not."

"Thank you."

"But I must note—for the record, as you say here on Earth—that I disagree with the decision."

Nyx hugged him, squeezing gently so as not to dislodge any feathers. "Consider it noted."

They turned, walking toward the Station building, when a flicker of movement in her peripheral vision caught her attention. She jerked her head to the right, just in time to see a slip of black disappearing behind a tree trunk, just outside the Station boundary.

Griff halted, making her realize she'd done so as well. "Are you all right?" he asked.

"Fine," she reassured him, and started walking again before he could question it. This wasn't the first time she'd caught flashes of shadowy black out of the corner of her eye in the last few weeks. The first few times, the glimpses she'd seen had made her think maybe it was a stray dog. But she knew from experience, now, that if she were to investigate the tree where she'd seen the shadow disappear, she would find nothing. No stray dog, no paw prints, no disturbances of any kind.

If she was being honest with herself, she wasn't certain she was seeing anything at all. Her mind wasn't exactly quiet these days—stars alone knew what phantoms might be running through it.

She walked into the Station, passing a sunbathing Temerex on her way, the unicorn-dragon conked out on her side, legs twitching every now and then like a dreaming cat. It might be winter in Dead Earth—and therefore extra-wintery on the Station grounds, because Nyx and cold weather were fast friends—but Temerex was a creature of warmth. She could survive in colder weather, but she didn't like it, which meant the area containing her heated-rock stall and her private paddock lived in perpetual summer.

Nyx stepped inside, where sounds of merriment drew her to the recently added billiards room. Or, as Nyx privately thought of it, the bar. Because it was a bar, and a dive bar at that, albeit one that was hygienically clean and only had the outer trappings of grunge.

Evra had apparently fallen in love with the places on her and Morgen's international Dead Earth adventure. She claimed there was something "delightfully freeing" in both the atmosphere and the anonymity. Morgen had cheerfully informed Nyx the Amazon had gotten into no less than thirteen bar fights—which, truthfully, Nyx viewed as a sign of great restraint on Evra's part—and had fallen in love with bar games.

Nyx stopped several feet from the doorway, observing. The pool table was abandoned for the moment, but Evra, Morgen, and Seth were involved in an animated darts tournament, with Evra and Seth facing off against each other. Seth stood behind the throwing line, flipping a dart and catching it, so quickly and economically she could barely see his fingers moving as he repeated the movement.

"It does not have to be a production every time you throw the dart," Evra growled, surlier than usual, no doubt because the scoreboard indicated she was losing. That was what she got for playing darts with Seth. The man had never met a sharp, properly-weighted projectile he couldn't throw with near-perfect accuracy.

"Of course it does." Seth caught the dart and blew on it like he was blowing out a candle. "Life's a production. Otherwise, what's the point?" He threw all three of his darts in rapid succession. The first hit directly in the red bullseye, the other two landing next to it on either side in the green surrounding circle, forming a horizontal line. If Nyx put a level on those darts, she had no doubt it would come back perfectly even.

Evra groaned and pushed Morgen forward. "It's your turn. Lose quickly so he can stop showing off."

Morgen grinned at her. "I could win. I do have a persuasive voice. I'm sure if I whisper sweet nothings in his ear at the pivotal moment, he might fumble a throw."

Evra folded her arms across her chest. "I told you no more whispering sweet nothings after that bar in Kansas City."

What happened in Kansas City? The question was on the tip of her tongue. She could ask it, walk in, and join them all. She *wanted* to. Instead, she found herself taking careful, silent steps back.

Seth was the only one to see her, flashing her a grin and beckoning with his hand for her to come join them. She shook her head and mouthed *work*. To which he mouthed back *come on*. She just gave him what felt like a sad excuse for a smile and turned away, heading for the Archives, her chest tight. Breathing felt…not difficult, exactly, but simply as if her normal breaths did not deliver the requisite amount of oxygen, and her heart beat fast and short.

The feeling was customary now, though when it had first started happening, she'd thought she was having heart problems, or inexplicably developing asthma. But anxiety, it turned out, had one hell of an effect on the body, and hers seemed to be a near constant companion these days.

There was no rational reason for it. She finally had the ordinary life she'd always wanted. Or at least, as close to an ordinary life as she could ever hope to come. She had the things she'd never thought she would get to have, when she'd been memory-less in Dead Earth: a stable job, a home, friends, a father figure. Seth.

Sure, the stable job involved being bonded to a sentient Station that doubled as her home, her friends were from far-flung planets that she would probably never get to visit, and her father-figure was a nine-hundred-year-old man trapped in the body of a griffin, whom she needed to free from his own bond to her Station, but... beggars couldn't be choosers, right?

And Seth was *Seth*. The one thing she'd never stopped wanting. She'd loved him since she was a kid. First, it had been in that way kids idolize those who are slightly older than them. Then it had simply been a feeling she couldn't categorize, until she'd grown up enough for it to turn into something more. She'd missed him in Dead Earth, when she hadn't remembered who she was missing. And when she'd seen him again for the first time, still not remembering who he was, she'd been drawn to him in a way she never had been to anyone else.

Because beating underneath their history, from childhood to now, was a bone-deep certainty that he was *hers*. That he always had been, and he always would be.

But having him—safe, in this place that was so idyllic, as only a home that morphed to suit one's every whim could be—had come with an unexpected complication. She was terrified, every second of every day, of losing him. Of losing Evra and Morgen, Griff and Kaliaris.

If she couldn't solve the problem of the Harvester and free Griff and Kaliaris, would they eventually come to hate her? Would Evra and Morgen move on, needing to grow and change in a way life in the Station couldn't allow? If Nyx did solve the Harvester problem, Kaliaris would be gone forever. With the Station gone and Griff no longer bound to it, would he choose to stay near her? Or would he be gone, needing to experience everything centuries of imprisonment hadn't allowed him?

And Seth... Well, there was still that part of her that was waiting for him to get bored. He'd been trapped with her almost his entire life. He said that he didn't mind and she believed him. For now. But if she couldn't fix this, if she stayed bound to the Station, how would he feel in twenty years? A hundred? A thousand? Or what if she did fix everything and they discovered they didn't know how to exist when they weren't isolated together?

What if, what if, *what if?* That was where the anxiety came from. It made her want to never solve the issue of the Harvester. Because being here, in the Station, was a kind of stasis and she selfishly wanted everything to remain exactly as it was.

She *wanted* to free Griff and Kaliaris. But she also wanted more time. More time here, with her friends, and Griff, and Seth. Because the problems that might arise from that future would at least take a few years to get to, and in the meantime, she could keep what she had.

She'd confessed as much to Griff on one of the many nights she couldn't sleep, expecting him to be disappointed in her. But he'd only said, "Kaliaris and I have waited centuries, Nyx. A few weeks or months or years would hardly mean anything more to us, after so long. Take your time. Live your life. Neither they nor I will judge you for it."

His lack of judgment had only made her judge herself more harshly. So the very next day she'd started dedicating four hours, five days a week, to scouring the universe's archives for the name she'd gotten from Laiveran: Gharew. The person who might well have been the Harvester's maker.

As she walked into the Den now, her anxiety dulled to a kind of weary resignation. Thus far, her searches had yielded nothing, and she couldn't help but wonder if she was failing to make any progress because the problem wasn't an easy one to solve, or because she didn't *want* to find an answer.

The universe has a causality to it, Calista had once told her, after Laiveran woke. *Power speaks to power, and those powers which have been entangled before often find themselves drawn back to each other.*

She'd thought it amusing, then, that the sapient Station believed in destiny. Now she was more than a little worried it was right, and she'd find out who Gharew was precisely when she didn't want to.

She took her now-customary perch on one side of the Den's formal dining table—the one that was safe to sit at so long as no more than twelve people were seated at it for a formal dinner—and cracked open the Archives book with a sigh. If past history was any indicator of future performance, it was going to be a long four hours.

2

After four hours of research that had netted Nyx nothing more than a few more Gharews who were definitely *not* the one she was looking for, she'd wandered upstairs and found Seth in his room. He'd basically converted the space to a game room, because it was her bed—theirs now—that he slept in each night.

She was lying on the couch, her feet on his lap and a book propped open on her stomach while he played a video game. It had something to do with zombies but mostly just appeared to involve a lot of blood spraying all over the screen. The moment was one that shouldn't have really been special, because it was so mundane. But it was that very mundanity that made it special to *her*. They'd come close to moments like this as teenagers, when they'd run away for a few days or weeks, but those moments had always been overshadowed by the knowledge that they were made on stolen time.

Maybe that was why she couldn't stop thinking of this moment as being made on stolen time too. And because that fear kept intruding, the special perfection of the moment was ruined by her inability to be present in it. Instead of reading and relaxing, she kept watching the side profile of Seth's face, memorizing the contours of it, marveling at the way his expression could change half-a-dozen times in less than a minute because he was so caught up in what he was doing.

She thought she was being covert in her observations, until he glanced over at her and said, "You're thinking too hard." He tossed the controller onto the floor. Honestly, for a man who could play video games for hours, he had no problem dropping them mid-fight to pay attention to something else—usually her.

He shifted to face her. "What's going on?"

"Nothing is going on. I'm reading." She waved the book. "It requires focus."

"You haven't flipped a page in ten minutes because you've been staring at me. You're worried about something."

She shrugged, not wanting to talk about the screwed up mental space that was her brain. She had to spend enough time with her anxiety—she didn't figure he needed to be dragged into it.

"Is it the lack of progress on the Gharew search?" he pressed. "Because that is like looking for a needle in a haystack the size of the universe."

"It's...not going well," she admitted, happy to let him believe that explanation for her behavior. Both Jevryn and Griff had said Gharew's name sounded familiar, but neither of them had been able to determine where that familiarity stemmed from.

At least, she knew Griff hadn't. Presumably Jevryn hadn't either, though he would have had to actually communicate with her in some way for her to be sure of that. She found herself thinking of the last time she'd spoken to him, the day her mother had left Earth's Station. The day they'd agreed it was best to continue their relationship as it had been before she'd learned he was her biological father.

She wondered how oblivious he had to be to believe she'd meant it. Oblivious, or selfishly content to *choose* to believe that a woman who had begged him to know her would change her mind so easily.

Maybe that was why she still checked the companion journal every evening, as he'd once told her to. Even after everything, she just couldn't stop herself from trying to be the good daughter she'd always imagined her real father would want. The good daughter she'd tried so hard to be growing up, when she'd invented an idea of what kind of man her father would be, and what he would want *her* to be.

If she'd never gotten those memories back, it would have been easier to deal with Jevryn's indifference. The Nyx who had first come to the Station, who hadn't remembered anything, had only wanted a place to belong, and for people to see her. She had wondered about her family, but she hadn't known if she had one, so she hadn't pinned her hopes on them finding her.

Now she had eighteen years' worth of memories of longing. Eighteen years she'd spent knowing that somewhere out there she had a father. Eighteen years of desperately wanting him to want her. So no matter how cold Jevryn was, no matter that he never would have told her who he was to her had Elena not outed him, she couldn't simply flip a switch and stop herself from wanting a relationship with him. Wanting him to want to know her. Even if she let Griff believe she didn't, so he wouldn't try to force Jevryn into it on her behalf. Even if she told herself it was better that Jevryn didn't want to know her. He was, as he'd once told her, not a good man.

"I don't mean to be the messenger of despair," Seth said, drawing her from her thoughts, "but you know you may never find them, right?" At her blank look he added, "Gharew."

"Oh. Right."

He shook his head, a small smile on his face, and started massaging her left foot. "It's a single name several centuries old, and you don't even know if this person came from a planet that still exists. And it was given to you by someone of questionable sanity." Did he sound almost...happy about how difficult this was?

"I know," she said. "I'm not working myself to the bone on it, but I do have to try."

"There's trying, and then there's trying too hard. You know you can just be here for a little while, right?" His fingers tightened as his thumbs dug into the arch of her foot. "That you can be here with me?"

She set aside the book she wasn't reading and pushed herself onto her elbows. "Do you feel like I'm not?" She wasn't—she *knew* she wasn't—being present enough. Emotionally or mentally. But she'd thought she'd been faking it well enough to fool everyone.

"I don't know. You've been off. You aren't sleeping much and you don't talk about it." He hesitated, something she couldn't label on his face. "Is it me? Did I do something?"

She sat up and shifted onto his lap, facing him, linking her hands behind his neck. She needed to fix this before she ruined everything. She'd thought she was doing him a favor by keeping her anxiety to herself. Apparently all she'd been doing was making him worry.

"It isn't you. It's my brain, I guess? I can't stop thinking about what happens if the Council discovers Jevryn is the one who killed Koral. If that leads them to us. Or what happens if I can't figure out what to do with the Harvester. What happens if I *do*.

"I've never been responsible for anyone else before. And now everyone in this Station is under *my* protection. What I do affects them, and when it comes to the Harvester, what I do affects *everyone*. I don't want to get anyone hurt."

He relaxed. His hands slid over her hips, tugging her closer. "It doesn't have to be your responsibility." She must have looked as puzzled as she felt because he said, "You could give the Harvester to Jevryn. I know he hasn't earned the title, but he *is* your father. And it is one-hundred percent his fault that you are mixed up in this."

She blew out a breath, not wanting to admit how much that reminder felt like a punch to her heart. She knew Jevryn had meant for the Harvester to go to her mother, not Nyx. But the very fact he hadn't known until long after the fact that it *was* Nyx's problem spoke volumes about how little thought he gave to his accidental daughter.

"You aren't wrong," she answered. "And I'm not saying it wouldn't be nice for this to not be my responsibility."

He slumped back against the couch. "I sense a 'but' coming."

"But however it came to me, the Harvester *is* mine now. And I don't know Jevryn well enough to trust him with something this powerful. He's a part of running the universe and I don't think too highly of how he's managing that.

"If I just give it to him because I don't want to deal with it, I'm partly responsible for what he does with it. And though I know he would try to free Griff, and I don't think he would hurt me"—though, really, she didn't *know*—"past that, I don't know. So I'm stuck with it, and that's a decision too, and I'm worried it'll hurt the people I care about."

For a moment, she thought he was going to argue with her—he had that look in his eyes—though she wasn't sure about what, exactly. Then the looked melted away and his hands stroked up her back, his dark brown eyes uncharacteristically serious. "Everyone here knows all of that, Nyxi. All of us you're so worried about? We don't have to be here. We're here because we want to be. You think Morgen and Evra don't understand the risks they take by staying?

"If they wanted to walk away, they could. They could have never come back from vacation, if that was what they wanted. So stop worrying you're going to get us killed, because every second you spend on that, you aren't here." His mouth curved into a crooked smile. "And I really, really like it when you're here."

The ever-present tightness in her chest eased, her feelings of dread partially alleviated now that she'd shared them. They would build up again—it was inevitable, unless she actually made progress on the Harvester—but for this moment, she felt better. And it *was* nice, being here with him.

"I hate it when you're right about things," she told him.

His eyes widened. "I had no idea you've been living your life in a state of constant hatred. That seems emotionally unhealthy."

"Shut up," she said. And since kissing him was the only foolproof way *to* shut him up, she did. His mouth met hers and she lost herself in the taste of him, familiar in a way that was sweet and bitter at the same time. Sweet, because every time she touched him it knit a few more of the broken pieces inside her back together. Bitter, because it felt like they'd never been together without a specter of doom hanging over them.

He drew back long enough to say "You're thinking again" before diving back in. His hands slipped under her shirt, and she'd just decided that thinking was highly overrated, perhaps even the detriment of all humankind, when someone pounded on the door.

Seth broke from her with a groan and yelled, "Go away."

"I would," Morgen called, "but then I'd have to tell everyone you're too busy making out to come to game night. It's your turn to pick."

"Fuck," she muttered, "I forgot it was Saturday." She was starting to think everyone in this Station played too many games, even if this particular night's gaming was her fault. After Evra and Morgen had come back from vacation, Nyx had decreed that Saturday night was game night, informed everyone living in the Station that they were required to attend, and created a rotation for when each person was responsible for choosing that week's game. Tonight was Seth's night.

"We could skip," Seth suggested, kissing his way down the side of her neck.

"We really can't, so stop distracting me."

"I'm going to pick poker. I know how much you hate poker."

She groaned. She was miserable at poker. She couldn't bluff for shit.

He tried to kiss her again and she valiantly shoved him back. He grinned, holding his hands out to either side of her, palms up, as if weighing invisible items on a scale. He lifted his left hand. "Poker, or"—he lifted his right hand—"me...distracting you for the next hour."

She snorted. "I think the last time you 'distracted me' for a full hour was back when we had no goddamn idea what we were doing."

He grinned. "Yeah, but it was fun though."

"You kids okay in there?" Morgen called.

She yelled back, "We're coming!"

"I wish," Seth muttered.

She punched him on the shoulder.

"Ow." He rubbed his shoulder. "You know, you've got everyone fooled. They think you're so sweet, but it's only because I bear the brunt of all your violent tendencies."

"That's because you *bring out* all of my violent tendencies. But I'm not a complete monster." She kissed his shoulder. "All better."

"Yeah, that's not where it hurts."

She rolled her eyes and shoved off the couch, heading for the door. "Don't make me hit you again."

"Violent tendencies," he called after her. "I think this is what therapy is for."

3

Nyx really, truly, deeply hated poker. Supposedly, the ability to play the game well equated to the ability to play *people* well, and to bluff without any easily discernible tell. She didn't like playing people and she couldn't bluff convincingly if her life depended on it. She could count on her fingers the number of hands she'd ever won against Seth, and they had played a *lot* of poker growing up.

Suffice it to say, she'd hated the game *before* she'd met Morgen, who counted cards in his sleep and won most games that could be benefited by having an eidetic memory and the ability to do complex math in one's head in seconds. She'd lost all of her money —they were playing the equivalent of penny poker—ages ago, as had Evra, Kalvar, and Griff. The only three left in the game were Morgen, Seth, and Liya, the last of whom was proving to be a card shark, quite at odds with the shy, attention-averse persona she typically presented.

They played their hands and this time Morgen lost what had been an all-in bet. He was…fuming was not the right word, as she'd only ever seen him truly angry once, but he was definitely confused. She could practically see him re-running calculations in his head, trying to understand how this had happened to him.

Nyx knew precisely how it had happened, and the answer was

Seth Connor Hawthorne. Like any good Illusionist, he didn't only do tricks with his magic. His sleight of hand was excellent, and that was what he'd been using on Morgen. Now that it was just Liya left in the game, Seth had switched back to illusion magic. He was good at reading people and he'd determined that Morgen had a better eye for catching magical subterfuge, while Liya had a better one for the physical kind.

Liya, who still had yet to give up a last name, was more than a little bit of an enigma. Her early days in the Station had been spent almost entirely in her rooms—Kalvar had said she was recovering from a medical procedure—and whenever someone *had* seen her, she'd tended to duck her head and disappear.

The first time she'd spent more than a handful of minutes in public had been at Nyx's first inaugural Neighborhood Barbecue Day. Nyx had been absolutely certain there was something different about her then from when she'd first met her, but she'd never managed to figure out what it was, because she hadn't wanted to be That Weirdo Staring at People. She hadn't asked, because it was rude to pry into someone's personal life, even though this felt like a Secret with a capital "S" and she was drawn to secrets like a moth to the flame.

Since the barbecue, though, Liya had quit hiding in her rooms. She was cordial to everyone, but the only person she was truly friends with was Kalvar. That was clearly the way she wanted things to remain, and Nyx was doing her level best to allow them to remain so, even if the Hidden side of her nature that was obsessed with secrets very much wanted to know Liya's.

She kept getting this odd feeling that wherever the woman went, any nearby shadows perked up and took notice. More than a few times, Nyx would swear a tendril or two of them had wrapped lovingly around Liya's wrist as she passed. And once, Nyx would wager her entire year's salary that the shadows had whispered to the woman. It made her wonder if the not-quite-dog shadow she kept catching glimpses of belonged to Liya. Except she'd only ever seen it out of the corner of her eye, and off the Station's grounds at that, so it seemed unlikely that Liya would be responsible.

Not to mention, there was a high likelihood the not-quite-dog was an anxiety-induced figment of Nyx's imagination. And since

Liya hadn't broken Nyx's cardinal rule for justifying prying—meaning she hadn't hurt anyone—it was another of those things Nyx bit her tongue on and didn't ask about. Liya was not a part of what Nyx thought of as her Station "family". Mostly because the young woman had kept a polite but careful distance, as if recognizing that Nyx was the type of person who would adopt every stray soul if given the opportunity, and Liya did not wish to be adopted.

Only a week ago she had quietly told Nyx that she was grateful to have been given refuge in the Station to recover medically, and to think, but she had done both and would be leaving once Kalvar had taken his Proficiency Exam for Universal Merit. She bore a fierce loyalty to Kalvar for bringing her here and—Nyx suspected—convincing her that whatever had happened in her life prior to her arrival here did not make her a terrible person. As such, she was staying to continue helping him prepare for the exam, after which she had only said she had, "A life to return to and things to fix."

This simple phrase had been said with complete neutrality, the kind Liya still wore as she glanced occasionally over the top of her cards to study Seth. Seth studied her back. His expression was very much not neutral. His face was a masterpiece of constantly moving micro-expressions, the kind that concealed even as they pretended to reveal. Looking at him you might think him careless, happy, over-confident.

He could be all three, when the occasion called for it. But he only appeared to be all three of them now because it was a combination that had a tendency to make people underestimate him. To think he was just a playboy devil having a good time, not capable of being serious long enough to actually amount to anything.

What was more interesting was that Liya, for all she really didn't know Seth that well, appeared to understand precisely what he was doing. She hadn't reacted once to him the entire game, and Nyx suspected she could have won more hands than she had so far.

"Are you two ever going to make a decision?" Evra grumbled. The Amazon, Nyx had noted, quickly ran out of patience for game night once she became eliminated from whatever they were playing.

"Decisions," Seth said, "are like wine. You really have to let them breathe to appreciate the full effect."

Nyx recognized the moment he split, an illusion of himself flawlessly taking his place in the chair. She couldn't put her finger on what, precisely, the tell was that gave it away. It wasn't the glimmer she'd seen on that rooftop in the Shadow Market, when Seth had made so many copies of himself. That had been a sloppy tell, one he'd only made then because he'd been in a hurry, and tired, and hadn't thought she'd remember enough to catch him.

No, this was something *else*. A feeling that was second nature, some ineffable quality that was just *Seth*. Something that told her that the facsimile of him sitting in the chair, no matter how convincing, wasn't *him*. She didn't need to tap into the Station's senses, the ones Seth still couldn't fool, to prove to herself that she was right. She'd already proved her infallible Seth radar far more conclusively the night she'd played the find-the-real-Seth drinking game with Morgen and Evra. They'd done it just outside the Station's grounds, so she couldn't be accused of cheating, and after she'd found the invisible version of him a dozen times without fail, her friends were convinced. And also very drunk.

That night, it had flummoxed even Seth. She had been able to identify when his facsimiles weren't actually him since she was nine. It had been a skill gained out of a sense of self-preservation, really. Living with a practical joker who had nothing but spare time on his hands and a wealth of budding illusion magic was a recipe for disaster, so she had adapted. But pinpointing his true location when he wasn't visible to the naked eye was a new development. Another one she couldn't quite explain, save that since he couldn't fool Kaliaris' senses, she'd picked up on that *something else* that was still Seth even when his magic covered him.

After the final time Nyx had successfully identified Seth's location during that drinking game, Morgen had devolved into the kind of theoretical ramble that had probably been one-hundred percent brilliant, but no one else had been able to follow his logic while intoxicated. Near as she could tell, it had boiled down to this: if two people practiced magic together long enough, they gained a feel for the other person's use of it. An instinctual attunement, so to speak.

It was that instinctual attunement that told Nyx Seth was currently peering over Liya's shoulder at her cards, even though she couldn't see him. Nyx could feel him there, feel the thing that drew her to him whenever they were in the same room, that intrinsic quality that was just *Seth*. But just to prove it to herself again, because she found it oddly comforting, she sank back in to Kaliaris' senses and found the real Seth right where she expected him to be.

No one else noticed. Not even Liya, against whose ankle Nyx would swear a tendril of shadow brushed. Just like she would swear the shadow on the wall behind Illusion Seth shifted in a way it shouldn't have. Nyx felt through Kaliaris, but she didn't *feel* anything different about those shadows.

"Decisions may be like wine," Liya said, responding to him, "but no matter how you let a poor vintage breathe, it is still a poor vintage."

Seth's illusion opened its mouth. Evra glared at it. "If you continue this wine analogy, I am flipping this table and ending the game."

He *tsked*, as if disappointed, the real him seamlessly replacing his illusion in the chair. "You really shouldn't play *directly* into the barbarian stereotype. Save a little room for mystery."

Kalvar snickered. Griff gave both him and Seth a look of fatherly disapproval, while Morgen wisely chose not to involve himself in the interchange. Evra appeared to be contemplating murder.

A tremor abruptly ran through Nyx, one that originated from the Station. She knew instinctively what it was—a request for an immediate, unscheduled Arrival—even though she'd never felt it before. The only other such request during her tenure had gone through to Griff, as she had been dropped out of the Station's senses at the time.

Her eyes met his golden eagle ones, her uneasiness no doubt displayed on her face. The one and only previous time she'd had an unscheduled Arrival, Beauregard had come through the ley lines nearly dead. So she couldn't stop her thoughts from immediately jumping to the worry that something was wrong.

Griff answered her unspoken question with a slight shake of his head.

"What's wrong?" Seth asked it quietly, but given that everyone else had already noticed her suddenly go rigid, they heard clearly enough.

"Nothing." She stood. "Just an emergency Arrival request, that's all."

"Who is it?" Evra demanded, hand drifting to her knife hilt. "How many people?"

Griff answered, his eyes going distant as he searched for that answer. "I am not sure, and five."

Seth frowned. "How can you not be sure?"

"The party has requested anonymity until they are in the Station's landing bay."

"Are you expecting trouble?" Liya asked.

Nyx gave Liya what she hoped was a reassuring smile. "No. We just don't get many emergency requests. I'd guess it's someone with more money than sense." Because that pretty much described anyone purchasing immediate fare to Earth Between, as they almost always had vacancies in their normal schedule at very affordable rates.

When she stood up, Seth tossed his cards on the table, face down. "I'm afraid I have to forfeit."

Seth never forfeited. Unless, apparently, he was determined to follow her out of a room. His mouth was set in a grim line, indicating that he might have recently given her a reassuring speech about how she shouldn't worry all the time, but when circumstances gave him cause, he could worry as much as she did. Usually, though, he hid it better.

"It's not the Council," she reassured him, trying to guess where his thoughts were as they walked to the Arrival Room. "They wouldn't send an unplanned Arrival request, even an anonymous one. They'd just show up."

He nodded, but his expression didn't lighten.

"So," she said, pointedly dragging out the word, "there's no need for you to come with me."

He stopped abruptly, one arm snagging her waist and pulling her in. "What if it's your mother?"

Nyx blinked. She supposed "more money than sense" *did* describe Elena Fortuna. But there was a glaring problem with that. "She couldn't run away from this place fast enough." Couldn't run away from *Nyx* fast enough. "What do you possibly think could prompt her to come back here? Or to send someone else here?"

He hesitated.

"Spit it out."

"She hates being humiliated. Jevryn humiliated her. She also likes power, which he has. If she wants to do something about both of those things, going through you is the clearest path."

Nyx thought about it, then shook her head. "She tried that, remember? It's ninety-percent of the reason I was born." The other ten percent had been Elena needing another Hidden for her magical network, needing the feedback she'd grown up having from other Hidden. It was a network Nyx could feel, now that she knew what to look for—two points in the darkness calling back to her: her mother, Elena, and her half-sister, Serenity.

Her mother had been desperate to recreate that feedback in the only way she could—through offspring—but not so desperate that she hadn't been strategic about it. Nyx had been born to lessen Elena's sense of isolation, yes, but Nyx specifically had been born because of Jevryn. Because her mother had erroneously thought Jevryn would actually care about his own child. "It didn't work out so well for her, and whatever else she is, Elena's not stupid. I don't think she's likely to try again."

"It didn't work out for her because Jevryn convinced her he didn't care about you."

Nyx snorted. "He *doesn't* care about me." The sting of that hadn't lessened any with time. That he didn't want to know anything about her, that he didn't want to have anything to do with her if it didn't involve the Harvester and its relation to potentially freeing Griff from the Station.

While it was true that she hadn't reached out to him via the companion journal, he also hadn't reached out to her. And since she was the one who had practically begged him to talk to her after she'd found out about their connection, she was relatively certain it wasn't *her* job to try and renew any attempts at a relationship. If he wanted there to be a relationship, he could talk to her. Suffice it to say she wasn't surprised he hadn't.

Seth looked less convinced than she was that Dear Old Dad gave zero fucks about his unwanted child.

"Trust me," she said, "this isn't my mother."

"But you won't mind if I come with you, just in case?"

"I do mind. You don't work here." She was not going to start engaging in Bring Your Boyfriend to Work Day.

"But—"

"Seth." She cupped his face in her hands. "You are my favorite person in the entire universe. But you are not following me around every second of every day just because somewhere, sometime, something might happen to me. Because you know if you do that, I will slowly go insane and murder you, right?"

He sighed. "Right."

"Good." She kissed him. "Then I'll see you after the non-dangerous travelers have exited the Station."

4

G riff slipped into the Arrival Room just as Nyx granted the Station permission to bring the waiting travelers in from the ley line. She could already hear Seth complaining that Griff got to be here and he didn't, but the Station *was* Griff's job, and his presence as Avatar wouldn't elicit the same curiosity from travelers that Seth's presence would. Travelers tended to treat the Avatars like Dead Earthers treated machines: there to be useful, not to be recognized. It infuriated Nyx but it would, in this one instance, work to her advantage.

Griff took up a post slightly behind Nyx and to her right as the arriving group rose up through the portal floor. The ley dust sloughed off, revealing five persons in total, all base Human. One stood slightly off to the side of the group, a man with pale skin in his late sixties who was impeccably dressed, obviously irritated to be here, and who finally made Nyx understand what the phrase "had his nose stuck in the air" meant. She had the distinct impression he thought he was the most important member of the group, despite no one else agreeing with him.

This was clear by the fact that three of the remaining four members—all women, Nyx noted—had "bodyguard" written all over them, and their point of focus was the individual at their center. A young man of perhaps nineteen or twenty, he had warm brown skin and matching eyes that contrasted sharply with an unusual defining feature: his hair. Brushing the tops of his shoulders in thick waves, it was pure blue. And not just any blue. Oh, no, it was the exact shade of blue as Liya's.

Nyx and Griff took action at the same time, both moving to lock everyone into the private sections of the Station so no one would have any accidental interactions with their new Arrivals. Nyx stared at the stranger's blue hair while trying to avoid looking like she was staring. Not long after Liya had come to the Station, Nyx—not entirely able to quell her curiosity—had tried to narrow down where she was from. Given how seamlessly Liya's hair color fit her —and, okay, given *aliens*—Nyx had assumed it was natural. She'd been quickly disabused of the notion when she'd discovered that the only known race that had blue hair were Sirens, who also had blue skin. The blue hair and skin color never expressed in those of mixed Siren descent.

So, while it wasn't impossible that someone else out in the universe had decided to dye their hair and eyebrows the same blue as Liya's, the fact that that someone was standing in Nyx's Station with Very Important Person written all over him raised a certain level of suspicion in Nyx. The young man in question stood for a moment, grappling with the confusion she'd come to learn some people experienced when they traveled the ley lines. She would guess his guards had been chosen, in part, because they did not suffer from it. Only once his confusion finally broke, and he shook himself like a dog flinging off water, did his guards relax a fraction.

His gaze searched the room, landed on Nyx, and a smile that could only be termed Charming with a capital "C" claimed his face. It was almost dazzling in its brilliance, to the extent she wanted to tell him to tone it down a bit. He made his way across the room, guards in step, and handed her his identification papers. At the edge of the room, off by himself, Mr. Self Important remained where he was.

A quick glance at the information she'd been handed identified her blue-haired traveler as Valedan Tekhar, home planet Alzherra.

"I appreciate your quick response to our last-minute request," Valedan said smoothly. "I understand they can be quite inconvenient for Guardians."

He'd either met a lot of cranky Guardians, or he was trying to butter her up. Or both. "It was no trouble." She began filling out the requisite information on her form, while trying to determine how best to uncover his motivations for being here. "Earth doesn't usually see a lot of unplanned Arrivals. We aren't typically considered an interesting location to visit."

The dazzling smile grew impossibly wider and Nyx found herself blinking rapidly, trying to shake off the sudden insistent feeling that she should trust this person unconditionally.

"Anywhere can be interesting, if it holds the proper attraction," Valedan replied.

That charming magnetism grew heavier, weighing on her, and she had the desperate need to say something—anything—in reply. Even something inane like: "Earth has a lot of attractions."

Off to the side, Mr. Self Important looked like the only reason he hadn't rolled his eyes was because he found the reaction too undignified. Griff shifted, as if he was trying to unobtrusively get her attention, but she couldn't imagine why. Valedan was so nice.

"So many attractions," Valedan agreed, leaning closer to her, as if to share a secret. "But I'm looking for a very specific one. Approximately this tall"—he held out his hand, indicating a height that would hit his shoulder if he was standing fully straight—"hair this color." He tugged at a lock of long blue hair.

For a moment, Nyx was unbearably happy because she knew the answer to his question: Liya! He was asking about Liya, and *she* could be the one to tell him that yes, she did know where Liya was, and Liya was in fact right here in this Station, and—

Griff knocked into her at the exact same time her Hidden magic snapped angrily inside her. The two jolts—one physical, one magical—screamed loudly that something wasn't right. Valedan—nice though he was—wanted to know about Liya. But Nyx had promised to protect Liya, who was obviously hiding from someone, and Nyx's magic was insistently reminding her that she did not break her promises. Even when someone else's magic really, really wanted her to. Now that her own ability had recognized the threat, it provided a buffer to Valedan's magic—she could still *feel* the desire to please him, but it was muted, no longer holding full sway over her.

"Is something the matter with your Avatar?" one of the guards asked, her voice dark with suspicion.

Nyx tried to reproduce the slightly drunk feeling she'd had

under the thrall of Valedan's influence. "Oh, he's just clumsy," she said cheerfully, reaching out to pat Griff on the shoulder. "Sometimes I think he can't tell where his feet are." She turned wide eyes on Valedan. "Oh I hope you don't think less of Earth for it. I promise, he's really a very good Avatar."

Mr. Self Important sighed. Two of the guards rolled their eyes. Valedan flashed her another one-thousand-megawatt smile. The force of it rolled over her like a tidal wave. "I promise you," he said, "I *love* Earth. Now, do you recall that attraction I was asking you about? Yea tall, blue hair?"

Despite the buffer of her own magic, his was potent enough that genuine disappointment laced her voice when she said, "I'm sorry. I can't tell you where anyone like that is."

Valedan's eyes narrowed slightly, but his smile never wavered. "Are you sure?" Another cascade of magic poured out of him, drowning her.

Hidden magic was, by its nature, subtle, so he wouldn't feel it when her magic grew as his did, strengthening the barrier between Nyx and him. Still, she responded with the sadness she was certain she would feel if in its full thrall. "I'm sorry I can't tell you what you want to hear." Fearing that wouldn't be enough, she added, "I could tell you other things. There must be something else you'd like to see."

Valedan blew out a frustrated breath, dragging a hand through his hair. "No, that's quite all right, thank you."

Mr. Self Important stepped up to Valedan's side, speaking low, but not so low that Nyx couldn't hear. "Are you quite convinced *now*, Your Highness? Not on this planet, not on any of the others. It is time for you to return home. You have responsibilities to—"

"I am *not* going home alone," Valedan said icily. "Not without an explanation. And this is the one. I know it is." He turned back to Nyx, magic still pulsing off him in waves. "This is an odd conversation you'd do well to simply forget."

Nyx did her best to look vacant and desirous of pleasing him. "Of course."

He beamed at her. "Wonderful. And could you perhaps recommend the best place in town for lodging? And the best place for gossip."

She pulled one of the Earth Between travel guides from beneath her podium. "Personally, I'd recommend the Wanderer's Inn." She circled it under the lodging section. "And if it's gossip you want, I'd try Cain's Confections." She circled that under the cafe section.

There was, unfortunately, nothing she could do to stop him from talking to people, and people *did* have a tendency to gossip at Cain's. But Earth Between's gossip was, on the whole, fairly harmless. Most people who came here were either running away from something, looking for a fresh start somewhere they could easily be forgotten, or just didn't want to be bothered by others. All of it meant that they were unlikely to respond to someone fishing for information on a specific individual.

Hopefully, that natural lack of trust would give them some immunity to whatever Valedan's charm was. And if not, she at least trusted that there were very few people in Earth Between who had actually seen Liya before she'd come to the Station. With any luck, it would take Valedan a day or two to figure out where Liya was. Enough time for Nyx to understand what she was dealing with and properly safeguard against it.

She checked in Mr. Self Important and the guards, and didn't breathe easily until they were all off the Station grounds.

"'I promise he's really a very good Avatar'?" Griff said dryly.

Nyx winced. "Sorry about that. I was trying to sound ditzy and dazzled."

"I would say you quite succeeded."

"Hey, you were the one who decided knocking into me was a smooth move."

"I feared you were *dazzled*."

"And you weren't?"

"No. I am nine-hundred and thirty-two years old. I am immune to handsome twenty-year-olds."

"I'm almost twenty-seven, I'm also immune to handsome twenty-year-olds. His smile was literal magic."

"Yes," Griff said casually, "I am sure it was."

There was something in the tone of his voice, the glint of his eye… "Are you seriously messing with me right now?"

He stretched his wings, resettled them. "I am certain I have no idea what you mean."

He was. He was totally messing with her. It made her smile. Griff was studious and serious by nature, and she was only just starting to discover that he *did* have a sense of humor, it was just ridiculously easy to miss. "Uh-huh. Sure. Perhaps, instead of teasing me, you could be a *very good Avatar* and tell me what you know about Alzherra and how much trouble we are or aren't in."

He took off his glasses, polishing them on his feathers. "I could tell you, but then I might bear the brunt of your displeasure. I will, however, direct you to the relevant Archive entry."

Nyx didn't have to read more than a paragraph before wanting to tilt her head to the skies and ask *why me?* She made herself read the rest of it anyway, then turned back to Griff.

"I have to go talk to her."

"Yes."

"Do you want to come?"

He shook his head. "She is still shy and I fear she would not do well if confronted by both of us."

Nyx agreed. "Okay, can you let Morgen and Evra know who Valedan is and that he's looking for Liya? Just so they don't let anything slip if they run into Valedan in Earth Between? I'm sure Liya will tell Kalvar, and I'll talk to Seth."

"Of course."

Nyx stood, and went to find out why the heir to the Blood Throne of Alzherra was on her planet.

5

A search of the Station's senses showed Liya had retired to her room after the conclusion of poker night, so Nyx made her way there, knocking gently but firmly. It was a testament to how far the woman had come that, rather than sit still and ignore the knock, Liya came to the door and answered it.

There was no delicate way to put this. "Do you want to tell me why Valedan Tekhar is looking for someone yea tall"—she indicated Liya's height—"with blue hair?"

Liya's eyebrows shot up to her hairline. "Valedan is *on Earth?*"

"Yes."

Liya pushed onto her toes, looking over Nyx's shoulder, as if expecting to find him in the hallway. Nyx couldn't tell if it was relief or disappointment in Liya's eyes when she found that hallway empty. "I am surprised he didn't insist on coming up here with you."

"He doesn't know you're in the Station."

"You…didn't tell him?" Liya asked slowly.

"No."

"He didn't smile at you?"

"Oh, he did. What is that, by the way?" It had felt similar but distinct from Morgen's Siren ability. Morgen's ability had been seduction, of a sort. Not necessarily the romantic kind, but the simple allure of safety, of the conviction that he could be trusted.

Valedan's ability had felt more like...adoration. An all-consuming need to please him, to give him whatever he wanted.

Liya shrugged. "That's just...Valedan." She shook her head. "I can't believe you managed not to tell him."

"Well, I get the feeling a good number of Earth Between's inhabitants won't be so fortunate. Which means he's going to discover you're here eventually. When that happens, I need to know what to be prepared for." She tried to be as gentle as possible with her next question. "Kalvar said when you first came here that you were recovering from a medical procedure. Is Valedan the reason you needed medical treatment?"

"I—what? No, of course not." She sounded defensive. Because it was the truth, or because she was scared?

"Look, I understand why you might be wary of saying anything against someone that powerful. But I promise you that this is a safe space." Dear stars, she'd actually just said "safe space". She forged ahead. "Anything you tell me won't go beyond me. If you're afraid of retaliation—"

"It's nothing like that. Valedan would never hurt me. *Ever*. He loves me."

"Okay." Nyx tried to puzzle this through to some logical conclusion, since Liya wasn't offering any further information. "But you... don't love him?"

Liya bit her lip. "I'm not getting out of this conversation, am I?"

"Not if I'm worried you're being stalked across the universe by some guy who doesn't know how to take 'no' for an answer."

"It isn't like that. I love him, too. We were supposed to be married."

"So you love each other, but you...what? Ran away from your wedding?"

Liya nodded.

This was giving Nyx a headache. "Please explain."

Liya picked at a loose thread on her shirt. "I've known Valedan since we were kids. He *knows me*, better than anyone, but...there's a part of me I never showed him. I needed to find that part of me and I thought—I *know*—that if I'd stayed, if I'd married him first, I'd have been too afraid of losing him to do it. And I needed to do it.

"So I left before the wedding. I told him I had something I needed to figure out and that I'd come back once I had."

"How did he take that?"

"I don't know. Probably not well."

Nyx's nascent headache inched closer to full realization. "You didn't tell him in person?"

"I...might have sent a letter."

Nyx had a bad feeling. "Did that letter arrive at your wedding in place of you?"

Liya winced. "It might have."

Well, that explained why everyone in Valedan's party had looked so *enthused* to be here. Liya had stood up the heir to something called the *Blood Throne* on their wedding day. "That was... gutsy."

"It was stupid." Liya crossed the room and dropped heavily onto her bed. "I acted impulsively. I *never* act impulsively. The second I left I wanted to go back, but I think if I ruined a royal wedding for a less-than-one-day disappearance, Rothbert might finally have tried to kill me." She did not say this last bit like someone from Earth would, like she was joking. "He never did like me much."

"Is that the older guy that constantly looks like he's constipated?" She already knew from his papers that it was, but she was hoping Liya would expand on the subject, and wasn't disappointed.

"That's him. He's Valedan's advisor, appointed by Valedan's mother, and he's never liked me. So I did what I needed to do, and I thought I would wait to return until things calmed down." She sighed. "Except by then it had been long enough that I didn't know how to go back. It wasn't my intention, but I publicly humiliated Vale. It did occur to me that he probably hates me now."

Nyx bit down on her instinctual response of *I'm sure he didn't travel across the universe looking for you because he hates you.* Because she did not know this man, and furthermore did not know his cultural customs. Sure, Liya had said he would never hurt her, but for all Nyx knew, if a member of the royal family got jilted at the altar, they were honor bound to track their runaway fiancée across the universe. If there was one thing she'd learned in her life, it was that reassuring statements not born of fact were never actually helpful.

"I'm sure he's hurt," she said honestly. "But you won't know the rest until you talk to him."

Liya shook her head. "How am I supposed to do that?"

"However you feel comfortable doing it. I promise the Station won't let any harm come to you here."

Liya gave her an exasperated look. "I told you there's no need to worry about that."

"And yet, I worry. I have to ask—that charm thing he does. Are you susceptible to it?" If Valedan could trick Liya into making a decision that wasn't her own, Nyx was not letting her leave this Station with him.

Liya laughed. "No. It's why we became friends, initially. It drove him up the wall that I wouldn't just do whatever he wanted the second he smiled at me."

"And his guards and advisor?"

"You can build up an immunity to him, once you understand what he's doing. All of his inner circle are required to develop it before The Blood Matron assigns them."

His mother's title was "Blood Matron". Delightful. Still, it was good to know that if his guards ended up being fanatically loyal to him, at least it wouldn't be a fanaticism born of magic. Meaning she could, in theory, hold them fully accountable for their own actions. "When he realizes you're here and comes back"—and Nyx had a feeling that would happen sooner rather than later—"are you going to talk to him?"

"I…want to."

Which wasn't a yes. So Nyx said, "I'll let you know when he inevitably shows back up."

She was at the door when Liya said, "Nyx? Thank you for letting me stay here. And for not prying until you had to."

"You're still welcome to stay as long as you want. And I won't pry any more if I can help it."

Nyx walked into her room—well, hers and Seth's, now—to find Seth lounging on the bed, lazily flipping a throwing knife. He tossed it up by the blade, caught it by the hilt, tossed, caught it by the flat of the blade, repeated.

"Careful," she said, "or I might decide the Station needs a carnival and you should be the star attraction."

"Please, I'm the star attraction anywhere." He flipped the knife a final time, then set it aside. "How were the non-dangerous travelers?"

"They might be here looking for Liya."

He arched an eyebrow and sat up. "Really?"

"You've had slightly more experience with the universe than I have. What do you know about the Blood Throne of Alzherra?"

"That you don't want to fuck with it."

"Thank you, that was highly enlightening."

"Seriously. Think court politics on steroids. Think alliances and betrayals and scheming and infighting, all amped up to the nth degree, and that's Alzherra. It's currently a matriarchal society—it switches depending on who's in charge—so it's ruled by the Blood Matron. She has *a lot* of kids by her many consorts, and while in theory her chosen heir will succeed her, in practice I understand that whichever one lives the longest will."

"Her chosen heir just came through my Station."

Seth scanned the room.

She rolled her eyes. "I didn't bring him with me."

"Wasn't looking for him."

"Then what *are* you looking for?"

"The nearest hard surface to bang my head against. How do you always do this?"

"Do what?"

"Attract trouble."

"It's not my trouble, it's Liya's trouble."

He gave her a look. "Oh, so since it's Liya's trouble, you definitely won't be getting in the middle of it then?"

She crossed her arms and took refuge in the power of silence.

He snorted. "That's what I thought."

"What am I supposed to do? Leave her to the mercy of her ex-fiancé? Whom she jilted on their wedding day?"

Seth's eyes widened. "She stood up the heir to the Blood Throne *on* the wedding day?"

"Apparently, an apologetic letter arrived in her place."

Seth decided the nearest hard surface was the one behind him and thunked the back of his head against the wall. "So you told this guy Liya didn't want to talk to him and he went home?" he asked hopefully.

"No, I told him I couldn't tell him where she was, so he went to the Wanderer's Inn, where he will no doubt use his charming smile to find out exactly where Liya is and then come back here demanding to see her."

His eyes narrowed. "How charming was the smile?"

"Magically so. Similar to how Morgen's ability feels but not quite the same. Liya claims she's not susceptible."

"Were you?"

"At first. But you know how I feel about being asked to give up secrets." She grinned at him. "It pissed me off."

"Nyx," he began carefully, his failure to turn her name into *Nyxi* indicating the level of his seriousness, "I know you like Liya—"

"Don't even think about asking me to kick her out, you know I won't."

"—but maybe you should consider learning something more about her."

Nyx frowned. "She doesn't exactly like to talk about herself."

"No shit. And maybe that was fine before the heir to the Blood Throne showed up looking for her, but it's not good enough anymore. You need to know what you're dealing with."

"I'm dealing with a messy breakup complicated by political factors."

He gave her a pointed look. "As far as she's told you. Look"—he held up his hands, forestalling her instinctual defense—"I'm not saying she's lying. I *am* saying that it doesn't hurt anything to search the Alzherran news to confirm that she's a runaway bride as opposed to being wanted for murder or something. Because Stations are not no-extradition zones for the universe. She's an Alzherran citizen subject to Alzherran law, and while you can physically prevent him from taking her out of here, if she's wanted for a crime, or if he can spin this as *you* endangering *her*, he's one petition away from an Enforcer team showing up here to remove her. And that's exactly the kind of attention you're trying to avoid."

He…might have a point. "Fine. I'll look into it in the morning."

"So she *can* be made to see reason."

"Keep talking like that and I'm going to punch you."

"You know I love it when you're violent." He patted the bed next to him. "Come be violent closer."

Seth was, as usual, a master of getting what he wanted.

6

The next morning, Seth took his life into his hands and woke Nyx early. That was, early by her standards, not his. He'd already been up for an hour. She responded to his initial attempts to rouse her by grabbing the nearest pillow and dragging it over her face. He took the pillow away and she rolled over, burying her face in *his* pillow.

In the end, he had to resort to tickling her, which was where his near-death came in. He took a foot to the ribs, dodged the next angry strikeout, and succeeded in getting her out of the bed by retreating to the opposite side of the room. She followed, spitting mad, until he clamped her in a hug that might also conveniently serve as a martial arts hold, and kissed her.

"Good morning, Nyxi darling."

She groaned. "I hate you."

"You know, it's these sweet nothings that really make me feel valued in this relationship. Cherished, even."

"Seth." She drew out his name like a complaint. "Why am I awake?"

"Well," he said patiently, "for centuries now on Earth, when the sun rises, humanity does too." Only his tight hold on her prevented a retaliatory punch.

"Why am I awake?" she repeated.

"I was thinking—no, don't die of shock, I do think sometimes—

that it would be nice to spend some time with my girlfriend before she buries herself in research and the problems of other people."

"You could help with the research if it bothers you that much."

"I *could*, but I've recently been informed I don't work here."

She leaned back in his arms, studying his face. "Are you sore about that?"

"No." He wasn't *sore*, precisely. He had no desire to either play Guardian of the Station *or* follow his girlfriend around twenty-four hours a day. But the remark had been a reminder that he did not, at present, have a purpose, and everyone else did. Morgen was catching up on a lifetime of lab experiments that Seth had neither the patience nor the foundational science knowledge to understand, and Griff spent a fair amount of time helping him. Evra was happy dedicating her days to physical training and studying martial strategy. Kalvar, in preparation of taking his academy exams, hadn't surfaced from a book—or Liya's tutelage—for longer than an hour in the last five months.

And Nyx was so thoroughly locked in her quest for answers on the Harvester—and now would no doubt shift her focus to Liya and Valedan—that he'd been very much aware that during the quote-unquote "working hours" of the day, he was the one at loose ends. It wasn't that he didn't have ideas on what he'd like to do with his life, it was that all of the things he *wanted* to do involved putting down roots. And given the fervor with which Nyx was dedicating herself to figuring out the Harvester—an end goal that would mean there would be no more Station here, and any roots he grew would wither —he found himself stuck in limbo.

They needed to talk about it. He'd kept waiting for the conversation to happen organically, but after the brief understanding he'd gained last night on *why* she was so obsessed with the Harvester, it had become apparent to him that the conversation he wanted to have was never going to happen on its own. So he'd dragged her out of bed early in order to steal her time before she gave it to someone else. That said, despite his love of living dangerously, not even he was foolish enough to have the let's-discuss-the-future talk with an uncaffeinated Nyx.

"Come on," he coaxed. "I made you breakfast. There will be coffee."

"Well, when you put it that way, how can I resist?"

Nyx frowned at Seth's back as she followed him downstairs to the cafe. Something was going on with him, and she wasn't sure what. He was being a little too Seth. Too sarcastic, too devil-may-care, and definitely too serious under the facade of being the opposite.

She had, in general, a bad feeling about it all, and she didn't like having bad feelings. It re-upped all the anxiety she'd managed to tamp down when she'd talked to him yesterday. But then, he'd said he wanted her to be more present, so maybe that was all this was?

She observed him for clues as he plated up slices of bacon and servings of spinach and mushroom frittata. He was…not quite avoiding her as he moved on to latte production, but he was definitely avoiding eye contact. Kind of like he was gearing himself up for something.

It's fine, she assured herself. *Everything is fine.* It was so fine that she checked in on where everyone else in the Station was to determine the likelihood that her and Seth's perfectly fine breakfast would be interrupted. Griff was with Morgen in his laboratory, the two of them clearly overachieving. It was too early to be awake, much less *doing science*. Liya was, as usual, in her room. Kalvar was passed out on one of the library couches, and Nyx took the liberty of locking all the doors so no one would walk in and accidentally wake him up. The kid needed sleep in the worst way, and no one seemed to be able to convince him of that fact. If his body had mutinied and forced him to finally rest, she intended to enable the process.

Evra was in the gym. This wasn't exactly unusual behavior, but Nyx thought the Amazon might be working out a little more than was normal even for her. Nyx made a mental note to check in on her, and the very fact she had to make a mental note to check in on her own best friend, who lived in the same building as her, made her understand that Seth had had more of a point about her lack of presence than she'd realized. Clearly, Nyx needed to get her shit together.

Seth slid a plate and mug across the counter to her. "Could you disconnect from the Station? Just for breakfast?" he asked.

"Yeah, of course." She did so. Seth was making eye contact now. That was a positive sign, right?

They ate breakfast. They talked about things that didn't matter and bickered in that comforting way they always did. She had just about convinced herself that any weird vibes she was getting from him were in her head when he reached across the counter, took her hands in his and said, "So. I wanted to talk to you about something."

She suddenly felt unwell. "Okay."

"Since you got your memories back," he began carefully, "and since we became *us* again, we haven't really talked about—"

The Station's front door opened. Despite it being a very normal, non-violent opening, it still startled Nyx into jumping straight up. She'd always been easy to startle, much to Viktor's constant disappointment, and it had only gotten worse with her connection to the Station. She was so accustomed to being forewarned about everything from Kaliaris that, when she wasn't connected to the Station's senses, she spooked twice as easily as she had before.

Diana and Tobi walked in.

"Is something wrong?" Nyx asked. It was pretty early in the morning for a kid to be out of bed, right? She welcomed the Station's senses back in, checking to make sure no one had suffered a life-threatening injury in the last twenty minutes, failed to tell her about it, and somehow summoned Tobi for help without her knowing.

Yeah, put that way...

"No," Diana said. "I'm here to spar with Evra." For a moment, she looked like she was going to say something else to Nyx, and for that moment Nyx hoped that maybe the Warlock had sent her with a message. She'd seen her in passing in the last few months. Their interactions had been carefully neutral, and Nyx was still sad that what could have been a friendship had been cut short. But, given how it had happened, she wasn't willing to be the person taking the initiative to mend that rift. If the Warlock wanted to reach out, though...

But Diana turned from Nyx to Seth, her hands landing on Tobi's shoulders. "Did you want to ask?" Tobi ducked his head, shaking it *no*. Apparently, he was feeling shy this morning. "He said the last time you were in town, you promised to show him how to use the Station of Play."

It took Nyx a moment to figure out she meant "play games on the *Playstation*".

"Oh, right." Seth looked between the hopeful eight-year-old and Nyx, clearly torn.

Diana gave Seth an apologetic smile. "I did explain that it's polite to ask in advance, but he was very excited."

"It's okay if you can't," Tobi said. Unfortunately, when a very hopeful kid said he understood if you didn't have time for him, there was no way to say *no* and not feel like a monster.

Seth was clearly feeling this, and yet what terrified Nyx was that she thought he was actually going to say *no* anyway. Which meant he thought the conversation with *her* was more important, and she didn't want to be more important right now, because what if it was important in a way she wasn't going to like?

"Seth would love to," she answered for him. "I should get to work." She leaned across the counter and kissed Seth's cheek.

He didn't say a word as she left and that, frankly, told her exactly how much trouble she was going to be in when they talked about this later. And truth be told, she regretted running away from the conversation the moment she did it. Because she was forcefully reminded of Jevryn walking away from her, when she'd wanted so desperately for him to just listen to her.

Stars, she did not want to turn out to be just like her father. It wasn't fair when the man hadn't even been around to influence her behavior growing up. She would fix this with Seth. But...later. What was done was already done, and she really did have work to do.

_7_

Nyx reflected, as she walked into the Station's Den, that she had become far better acquainted with the Station's Archives than she'd ever intended, and yet still didn't fully understand how they worked. The universe's archives were strangely like and unlike Earth's computers and internet database. A person could purchase private systems for personal storage, and Nyx thought of those systems like local computer drives for the sake of her sanity, even though it wasn't a direct corollary. Mostly because computers had physical drives where data was stored, and Nyx still hadn't been able to determine where the information put into an archives system actually went.

Beauregard's private archives had been accessed via tokens he'd kept on a necklace chain, like charms on a charm bracelet. But they were just that—a means of access. If the tokens had been destroyed, the information they allowed access to could, apparently, be retrieved. Which put the system more in line with internet cloud storage except, again, she didn't know where the information actually was.

Of course, now that she thought about it, she couldn't explain precisely where the information stored in the cloud was, either. None of which actually mattered, since she was capable of using both systems without understanding the precise mechanisms by which they functioned.

As she sat down to access the magical version, she couldn't shake the sense that she was being disloyal to Liya by prying into her past. Nyx had considered going to Kalvar instead of the Archives, but hadn't for two reasons. One, he was still passed out on the library couch, and he really did need sleep. Two, Nyx knew that Kalvar felt like he owed her for letting him stay at the Station, and for getting his identification papers sorted out. While she'd tried to make it clear that he didn't, she was afraid if she asked him about Liya, he would feel like he *had* to tell her. Nyx didn't want to get between their friendship.

Besides, Kalvar wasn't likely to know anything except what Liya had told him, and wasn't Nyx down here doing independent research for the sole purpose of finding out if public record matched Liya's personal account of events? The key words to soothing Nyx's conscience, she figured, were "public record". This wasn't any different than doing an internet search. A person might not be happy you'd done one on them, but it wasn't as if you'd broken into their house and gone through their personal files.

She tugged the Archives book closer and searched for Liya's name in conjunction with Valedan's, Alzherra, and "royal wedding". The first thing she noticed was that every hit that came back listed Liya's name as Liyan. If the girl been trying to lie low by dropping a single letter from her name, it wasn't the most inventive means of hiding.

As Nyx scrolled through the headlines, she had the added bonus of feeling like she was seeking out celebrity gossip. She avoided articles with titles like PRINCE VALEDAN SET TO MARRY CHILDHOOD BEST FRIEND and EVERYTHING YOU WANT TO KNOW ABOUT LIYAN ASHERAN. Those felt like the literal definition of prying into Liya's life, and wouldn't tell her anything about what had happened *after* Liya had run away. When Nyx came to the articles about the wedding day itself, she chose the one with the least sensational headline she could find.

LIYAN ASHERAN MISSING AT ROYAL WEDDING. FOUL PLAY, OR SECOND THOUGHTS? by LITTICA VIN RAYNE

The scene of Prince Valedan Tekhar's royal wedding to childhood best friend Liyan Asheran was set with the perfection and ostentation one has come to expect whenever one of the Blood Matron's children takes it into their foolish heads to marry.

The royal balcony dripped with a veritable abundance of blood flowers, and there at the focal point stood our young Prince Valedan, resplendent in lilac finery and an interesting change—his hair dyed the exact blue Liyan has been frequently ridiculed for, a clear and perhaps overly sweet gesture of solidarity from the Blood Prince to his betrothed on this monumental day.

Unfortunately, it was a gesture destined to go unnoticed by its intended recipient. As the sun crested the horizon, Liyan did not emerge from the betrothed's chamber. After sufficient time and embarrassment passed, the royal guard entered the chamber, emerging moments later not with Liyan, but with a letter, taken directly to His Highness Valedan.

No doubt those of you not in attendance have heard stories of his reaction as he read this letter—the exact contents of which have still not been released despite multiple requests by this author—but let me assure you that whatever you have heard cannot do justice to the stricken expression that crossed our ordinarily stoic prince's face. Even to call it anguish would be to cheapen the depth of the emotion seen that day.

His guard removed him immediately from public sight, shortly after which the public was given the official statement that Liyan Asheran had gone missing, and Prince Valedan would not rest until his betrothed was found. Given the frequency with which new spouses of the Blood Matron's children tend to die, we have all taken this announcement to mean that Liyan Asheran has been taken for use as leverage against the prince.

But, after speaking with several persons close to the prince, this author would like to propose another possibility—that Liyan Asheran ran away rather than marry Prince Valedan. That the letter was written, not by Liyan's abductors, but by Liyan, and the anguish on our dear prince's face was that of a man abandoned by both his true love and his best friend on what ought to have been the happiest day of his life.

One source close to the prince, who wishes to remain anonymous, stated that "Liyan has ever been what one might call fickle, and ill-suited to shoulder the burdens expected of a royal partner. The Blood Matron herself had doubts about the match, but she is ever reluctant to deny her children their heart's desires, when their lives are otherwise fraught with so much peril.

"As Prince Valedan has allowed no one to read the letter he received, I cannot say anything for certain, save that it is my personal opinion the letter was from Liyan, who found the pressure of the wedding too great, and ran away to escape it."

While this author cannot, of course, reveal the source of this statement, I can assure you, with utmost sincerity, its issuer has no reason to have anything but our prince's best interests at heart. If the contents of Prince Valedan's letter were truly those of a threat against Liyan's life, would not he have divulged its contents to someone?

This author must suppose that only time will answer these questions...and fears that, whichever is the case, our young prince's heart may be irrevocably shattered.

Nyx snorted. Clearly, she hadn't succeeded in picking the least sensationalized article after all. Or she had, and the standards were low. If the rest of the articles were like this one, there was nothing to indicate that Liya was anything other than what she herself had admitted to being—a runaway bride. Nyx was further encouraged by the fact that Valedan appeared to have done everything possible to smother suspicions that Liya had gotten cold feet.

A cynic might claim that he'd only done so because making it appear as if his bride had been abducted made the entire affair look less embarrassing for him. While that might be the case, it also meant that if Liya wanted to come home, she could do so without enduring the scathing public backlash she would no doubt suffer if everyone knew she'd left of her own volition. Maybe Nyx was a romantic, but she wanted to believe this situation could have a happy ending.

She scanned a few more articles, just to be thorough, but all she really learned was that humanity the universe over was obsessed with celebrities. One particular piece, ostensibly on Liyan's failure to show up on the big day, segued into a lament over the fact that no one would ever get to see the wedding gifts if the marriage didn't take place. By Alzherran tradition, if a marriage was called off, the wedding gifts were burned in a symbolic torching of the future that would never come.

Deciding she didn't need to read an exhaustive list of every important person on Alzherra who had sent a gift for the royal wedding, Nyx was closing the Archives book when a name caught her eye and she froze.

> This author will be particularly distressed if the gift from famed metalworker Riven Gare Ru should melt on a magical pyre, unseen and unappreciated. For this reason alone, I must express my whole-hearted hope for the safe return of Liyan Asheran.

Dread was a twisting thing in Nyx's stomach. Gare Ru. It could be the name Laiveran had spoken. She had guessed at the spelling, settling on G-H-A-R-E-W, but she'd searched by alternate versions of it too, of course. Even trying to accommodate for various other spellings hadn't seemed like enough, seeing as how not all written languages on Earth, let alone the rest of the universe, were letter-based. The translator spells did their best, attempting to find close matches in character or symbol-based written languages, but she'd known it wasn't foolproof. And she'd never thought of this partic-ular variation—two names instead of one.

As Seth had said, it was like looking for a needle in a haystack the size of the universe, and she'd grown semi-comfortable with the knowledge that it might take her years to ever find Gharew. If indeed she even could.

She pressed a hand to her stomach, trying to calm her sudden nausea. This Gare Ru wouldn't be the right one any more than any of the other Gharews she'd searched for who had ties to metal-working had been the right one. Names changed over time, took on new spellings, reinvented themselves. They died out as people married into different names, chose new ones for themselves, or as family lines ended for lack of children. The odds that this particular name had been around for nine or so centuries and thus could be from the same family line that might have helped build the Harvester was slim.

Nyx made herself search the Archives for the name anyway, in conjunction with Alzherra. The results it returned were sparse, only six entries, including the one from the article she'd just read. But six entries was enough to tell her that, while Riven Gare Ru was a reclu-sive figure whose family worked exclusively for the Alzherran royals, they were known for two specialties: an unparalleled talent for imbuing metals with magic, and the ability to make those metals expand and collapse.

Expand and collapse, like the rings of the Harvester had expanded when she—and later Laiveran—had used its power. Like—oh shit. Her gaze dropped to her thigh, where her bo staff rested in its holster. Expand and collapse, like her bo staff did.

Griff and Jevryn had both thought they recognized Gare Ru's name. Turning away from the Station's Archives, she found the private archives where she and Griff had painstakingly inventoried all the items in the Den. Each item in the Den had a corresponding intake form—or at least, was supposed to have one—that detailed why the item had been confiscated, along with everything that was known about it. They had completed the inventory project primarily for the sake of organizing and identifying everything, in order to turn the jumbled heaps of dangerous objects into neatly sorted and stored objects whose dangers could be easily avoided.

Nyx found the intake form for the bo staff. It hadn't been labeled as a staff, specifically, upon its arrival, only as a "metal weapon of changeable nature, alloy unknown". The reason for its confiscation had been listed as: "Traveler refused to put it away. Removed by force. Unknown magical properties." Clearly, the Guardian who had taken it had been a loquacious sort. They'd written only one other line on the intake form, but it was the one she needed. "Traveler objected to confiscation on the grounds of weapon being a 'Gare-ruin original'. Failed to elaborate satisfactorily."

Nyx set the form aside and unclipped her bo staff. It was in its compact state, only a foot long, and she turned it over in her hands, searching the smooth surface as if she could find the answer she was looking for etched there. Naturally, she didn't. After a moment of hesitation, she tugged her necklace chain over her head.

Three items were strung on it. The first was Jevryn's ring, the one he'd given her what seemed like a lifetime ago, so she could contact him. He'd never asked for it back. She didn't know if it still worked, and supposed it didn't really matter, now that she had the companion journal to contact him through. If she'd thought about it, she would have given it back the last time she'd seen him, but she'd been dealing with a lot at the time, and he'd been a wall of silence ever since. Writing to ask if he wanted his ring back felt like a flimsy excuse to contact him, and she was pretty sure no matter what she wrote it would come out sounding like, "Hey, Dad, remember me? Your daughter?"

The second item was in the same vein as the first, the anchor stone Jevryn had given her. A thin, flat black rock spiderwebbed with blue, tied to one of Jevryn's homes, so she could portal there without preparation should she fine herself in dire straits. Somehow, his giving it to her had managed to make her feel like he was fulfilling an obligation rather than expressing actual care.

The final item was the one she was looking for, though it didn't elicit any cheerier thoughts than the first two had. The Harvester pulsed faintly against her palm, its four overlapping rings forming a sphere the size of a marble. She had seen it expand in size, both during the single time she'd used it, and the time when Laiveran had started to.

She ran her fingers over the rings, but like her bo staff, there was no segmentation in the metal or other indication of how it might be extended by physical means. There was also the fact that the metal hadn't thinned as the rings expanded. It hadn't been as if the same amount of metal was being stretched further, weakening and compromising the integrity. It was as if the rings simply grew proportionally, without feeling the need to obey the laws of physics. Precisely the same way her bo staff did.

She extended the staff out to its full length with barely a thought. But if she'd hoped the use of whatever magic fueled its transformation would somehow speak to the Harvester, or give her some sign that the two had indeed been made by similar hands, she was disappointed.

Sighing, she collapsed the bo staff and tucked it back into its holster, then slipped the Harvester back over her neck. She would have to tell Griff. She *should* tell Jevryn. There were many reasons she didn't want to do the latter, not the least of which was that she was certain this development would have him portaling back to Earth in a blink and she was resentful of the fact.

She didn't want to care. She wanted to pack Jevryn neatly into a file labeled People Not Worth Caring About and leave him there. She wanted to accept the fact that he was never going to even notice her, much less love her, so she could stop being hurt by it.

But she couldn't. It would be one thing if she could believe that

Jevryn couldn't love. But he loved Griff. He was capable of the emotion—just not for her.

She shook her head. She would tell Griff and let him talk her into writing to Jevryn. But before she did that, she was hoping a certain prince might be able to confirm whether the bo staff, at least, had been created by his family's favorite metalworker. That task was going to be a little tricky, since she doubted Valedan was going to be kindly disposed toward her once he figured out she'd hidden Liya from him.

But that was a problem for Future Nyx.

8

As fate would have it, the problem Nyx had shunted off onto Future Nyx came due in a mere two hours. Diana had just left with Tobi, so Nyx was on her way to the cafe to find Seth and work harder at being an adult, when Valedan crossed the border onto the Station's grounds. Judging by his fast, lengthened stride, she suspected he knew precisely where Liya was, and he wasn't happy about it.

Griff met her in the hallway on the way down. "He knows."

"Yep," she agreed. They reached the cafe a few seconds before Valedan did. She barely had time to give Seth a sorry-I-ran-out-on-you-earlier glance before the Alzherran prince walked in. Valedan was alone, and she wondered if he'd slipped his guards and his advisor, or if they were waiting at the Station's border. She bet on the former, mostly because the average person didn't know the Stations extended anywhere beyond the physical buildings where the Arrival Rooms resided. Or, for that matter, that the Stations were sentient.

Valedan stopped just inside the door, observing her coolly before turning to take in Seth and Griff.

Nyx put on her brightest, most chipper voice. "What brings you back to the Station so soon? Don't tell me you're planning on leaving already."

"Hardly." His tone was as cool as his expression. "I'm finding Earth fascinating."

"Fascinating isn't the word most people use to describe us." She slipped behind the counter. "Coffee?"

He stared at her, as if he was trying to figure out if she really was as oblivious to his mood and reason for being here as she was pretending to be. "No, thank you," he said finally. "As for my ability to find this place fascinating where others do not, I imagine it is because most people do not come here looking for lost things. Though they really should, as there seem to be *so many* lost things here."

"Oh?" she asked, enough false innocence in her voice that Seth let go of his irritation with her long enough to snort. He covered it badly with a fake cough.

The brief flick of Valedan's eyes to Seth told her the Blood Prince hadn't missed the reaction. He turned back to Nyx. "Yes. I've hardly been here a day and already I've found a missing royal, the castle of the universe's most paranoid ex-Enforcer, and a shocking number of people bearing the Shadow Market's slave marks."

Nyx did her best to look confused. "I didn't know we had any royalty in residence." How had *he* spotted Diana so easily? Yes, he'd probably passed her on the way in, but she doubted all the royalty on Earth could recognize each other on sight, much less the royalty of the universe recognize all the *rest* of the universe's royalty.

"Ah," Valedan said. "So Dianara Kormadin eludes you, but the castle and the escaped slaves come as no surprise?"

"Lord Beauregard isn't in hiding, and I'm not sure what you mean by the rest of it." She put on her best confused expression. "I didn't think slavery was legal."

Seth's absolute rigidity, combined with his stone-faced expression, told her he was a few seconds away from bursting into laughter. Honestly, if he couldn't maintain a little dignity while she attempted to lie, he could have the decency to leave.

"Oh, it isn't. Still happens, though. One has to wonder how so many of them all found their way here."

She didn't miss the implied threat in the words, but she pretended to, furrowing her brow. "Maybe it's part of some kind of relocation program? Do you guys have those? I haven't even been

here a year so most of this is all still really new to me. You know"—
she waved her hand—"aliens, and all that."

"Earth's general ignorance of the rest of the universe *is*
appalling. However, I would have to think even your culture must
be advanced enough to understand the rudeness of lying directly to
someone's face."

"You didn't like the Wanderer's Inn?" she asked innocently. "I
really do think it's the best in Earth Between."

He drummed his fingers on the countertop. "I asked you if Liyan
was here and you said no."

"Technically, I said that I couldn't tell you what you wanted to
hear. Even though you asked so *charmingly.*"

"Hmm." He turned his attention to Seth, smiling at him, that
compulsive wave of magic wafting off him. "And I don't suppose
you answer any more truthfully when asked charmingly?"

Seth didn't even blink. "As I consider myself the most charming
person in existence, I find it impossible to be charmed by anyone
else."

Valedan sighed. He ignored Griff—because he recognized that a
Station's Avatar would be immune, or because he thought the
Stations' Avatars were beneath his notice? A shame she couldn't
know the answer, as it would tell her a lot about him.

"Very well." Valedan turned back to Nyx. "Let us dispense with
the pleasantries. You are holding my betrothed here." He sounded
so certain about the "holding" part, as if convinced Liya couldn't
possibly be here of her own volition. What exactly had she written
in that letter she'd left him?

Seeing as how Liya did not bear Valedan any ill will, and the guy
had kind of been ditched at the altar, Nyx tried to be gentle. "I don't
hold people against their will. Liyan"—she used the full name she'd
read, since it was what he was using—"needed a place to disappear,
from *everyone,* and I offered it."

Valedan's jaw clenched, uncertainty passing over his face, like
she was confirming something he'd been denying. Something,
perhaps, other people had been trying to convince him of. But then
his resolve firmed and he shook his head. "No. If Liyan felt he
needed to disappear, it would not be from *me.* I won't pretend to
understand what threat caused him to flee Alzherra, but you will
take me to him immediately so I may rectify it."

Everything Liya had told Nyx met that sentence and clicked into place. She chose her next words carefully, because Liya's secrets weren't Nyx's to share. "I won't override their wishes," she said carefully, "but I'll ask if they're willing to see you now."

She could see Valedan's desire to argue with her on his face.

"You have my word that no one is keeping them here against their will. And this might be difficult to hear, but they left Alzherra of their own free will."

She stood. A quick glance at Seth and Griff confirmed they would stay and keep an eye on their guest. Nyx had made it to the cafe exit when Valedan said, "Wait."

She turned. His shoulders were slumped, the court bearing gone from his posture and his words. "Tell him that whatever it is—whatever he thinks I can't handle—I can. Whatever he needs, he can have. I would never deny him anything. I thought he knew that."

Nyx hoped that was true. Because Liya had already taken what she needed, and Nyx didn't want her to get her heart broken.

She made her way to Liya's room and knocked.

"Yes?" Liya's soft voice called.

"Hey, it's me."

She heard the shuffle of footsteps and then the door opened. Liya's face was resigned, her eyes red and puffy, like she'd spent most of the last night crying. "He's here, then?"

"You don't seem surprised."

Liya smiled a little. "I might not be ready to talk to him, but he wouldn't be Valedan if it had taken him any longer to find me."

"He asked to talk to Liyan," she said gently.

Liya flinched, obviously putting together that Nyx had put things together. "Did you tell him?"

"Of course not," Nyx said, and Liya relaxed. "I guess that answers the question of whether you left him any indication of why you were leaving?"

Liya shook her head. "I...didn't know how. I still don't." She looked to the left, where her reflection stared back from a long mirror, and said, "But then, I guess I don't have to say anything anymore, do I? That was the whole point."

Nyx didn't know what to say to that, and before she could figure it out, something in the Station's senses caught her attention. Kalvar was awake. He'd taken one step into the cafe, seen Valedan, and turned and sprinted for Liya's room. He arrived in a sliding skid, lines marked into one side of his face where he'd clearly fallen asleep on a book, his tiger stripes prominently displayed against his skin. He saw Nyx and froze, looking between her and Liya.

Nyx raised her eyebrows at him. "When I asked if I needed to be on the lookout for anything, you didn't think running from the Blood Throne of Alzherra warranted a mention?" She smiled, to let him know she wasn't actually angry.

He scuffed the toe of his boot on the floor. "Technically, you asked about angry spouses or parents. Temporarily jilted royal fiancés weren't brought up." Looking past her to Liya, he said, "You okay?"

She nodded, then halfway through changed her mind and shook her head. Kalvar crossed to her, pulling Liya into a hug. "It'll be all right."

"What if it isn't?" she asked.

"Then fuck him." He lowered his voice, but Nyx still heard his next words. "Trust me, trying to be what you think someone wants, trying to be only the parts of yourself you think they can love? It's…" He trailed off.

"Like dying every day?" Liya suggested.

"Yeah. And living is better, even if it hurts more at first."

With a rough laugh she said, "Maybe one day I'll believe that." She gave him a final squeeze and stepped back. "Thank you for being my friend. I really needed one."

"So did I." He grinned at her. "I'm here if he needs sense knocked into him at any point."

Liya's eyes widened. "For the love of the blood on which the throne is built, do *not* get into a fight with Valedan."

He lifted his hands. "No promises."

"I am serious, Kalvar, he only looks harmless."

He winked at her. "So do I." Then he left.

Liya rounded on Nyx, that wide look still in her eyes.

"Don't worry," Nyx reassured her, "Valedan's under Seth and Griff's watch. They won't let Kalvar near him. But for the record, I think Kalvar's just teasing you. There's only one idiot in this Station who likes to pick fights with people, and he's my idiot."

"Right." Liya gave her a strange look, indicating that statement might not have come across in the affectionate way Nyx had meant it. Liya bit her lower lip. "Did Valedan say anything else to you?"

Nyx hesitated. "He asked me to tell you that he can handle any change you needed."

Liya smiled, a little bitterly. "People say that, but it's only because they're imagining the change is something they *can* handle."

Sadness twisted inside Nyx. She'd honestly hoped the rest of the universe would be a little more enlightened about this matter. "Is Alzherra not very accepting?"

Liya's eyebrows furrowed. "Accepting? Of what?"

"Transitioning?"

"Transitioning." Liya repeated the word, and Nyx wondered if it had translated properly. But then she said, "That is an interesting description of it, I suppose."

"What do you call it?"

"Alignment. You're simply coming into agreement with yourself. What do you mean by 'accepting'?"

Well, maybe the rest of the universe was enlightened after all. "Ah, some people on Earth can be a little...angry when people choose to transition."

Liya's bafflement was clear. "Why would anyone begrudge a person becoming the true reflection of who they are?"

Nyx had no good answer for that, because there wasn't one, Since she didn't feel like repeating bigoted talking points, she shrugged and pointed out the obvious. "You seem to be worried Valedan will."

Liya sighed. "Valedan won't be angry about the alignment. He'll be hurt I never told him this was what I needed. He'll feel responsible for me waiting this long. And, well, probably a little angry that I left him standing in front of half of Alzherra alone."

"Why didn't you tell him?" If Alzherra didn't have Earth's problems with transitioning, then where was the problem?

Liya hugged herself. "I don't know if he's romantically interested in women. We just...belonged to each other, from the beginning. He never looked at anyone else like he looked at me. So I never knew. I still don't." She sighed. "But it's time I found out. Can you ask him to come up here?"

Nyx nodded. She walked one step, paused and pointed at the

wall, where a bright red circle had appeared. "Hit that if you need anything."

"What is it?"

"A panic button." At Liya's blank look, Nyx elaborated, "You know, in case you feel unsafe. Hit it and we'll come help."

"Valedan would never hurt me." Liya sounded offended on his behalf.

Nyx held up her hands. "It's there if you need it."

She went to the cafe to retrieve Valedan, who now looked a little sick. Griff had on his most fatherly expression, and Seth had apparently coaxed the Blood Prince into trying coffee. Not that it appeared to be having any impact on his glumness.

He shot to his feet the second she entered the room. "Is he..." Valedan trailed off.

"Willing to see you," Nyx finished for him. "Come on." She led him to Liya's room, pausing a few feet from the door, though the twisting shadows on the wall made Nyx suspect Liya would hear everything despite the distance. "Can I offer you some unsolicited advice?"

"I have found when people ask that, there is rarely any stopping them."

"Is that a yes or a no?"

He made a go-on gesture with his hand. "By all means."

"How you feel and how you love isn't something anyone can ask you to change. All I ask is that you aren't cruel."

Valedan's eyes narrowed. "I would never hurt him. I love him."

Nyx sighed. "We hurt people we love all the time when *we're* already hurt. Or when we're scared and we can't handle something." She really had to apologize to Seth, she reflected, as she led Valedan to the door. "Knock whenever you're ready."

Then she left, desperately hoping this had a happy ending.

9

Nyx returned to the cafe, finding Seth and Griff where she'd left them. She must have had some kind of look on her face, because Seth said, "If he breaks her heart, we can always kill him."

She arched her eyebrows. "Just like that? We casually off visiting royalty now?"

"Sure."

"We can't kill him."

"*Can't* is a strong word. Shouldn't, maybe, but—"

"Can't. I think we need him."

Seth frowned. "Did that charming smile get to you after all? Do I need to submerge you in an ice bath to shock you back to your senses?"

"Put me anywhere near an ice bath, and you'll be the one going in it," she warned.

"Children," Griff said mildly. "Might I suggest we forego both murder and ice baths?"

"In favor of what?" Seth asked.

"Whatever it is Nyx clearly needs to tell us but doesn't want to."

Nyx sighed. She hated being easy to read. "Who says I have anything to tell?"

"Your face does." Seth drew a circle in the air with his finger, indicating said face. "It's in the eyes. They look guilty. Of course, they could look guilty for other reasons."

Nyx winced. She deserved that. "Maybe they look guilty for multiple reasons." She dropped into one of the cafe chairs, resting her forearms on the counter, and just spit it out. "I think I found Gare Ru."

The still silence that greeted her was not encouraging. She didn't know *what* it was.

Finally, Griff asked, "What did you find?"

"It was in one of the articles I read this morning when I looked into Liya." Here, Griff's feathers rustled in mild disapproval, so Nyx pointed a finger at Seth. "He said I should make sure she wasn't an escaped convict or something, it's the only reason I looked."

"You agreed it was a good idea," Seth retorted.

Griff lifted a wing, forestalling further argument. "I understand. Continue."

"One of the articles mentioned a metalworker named Gare Ru whose family has been employed by Valedan's family for centuries. They have two specialties—imbuing metal with magic, and making metal expand and collapse without compromising its structural integrity."

Griff canted his head. "That sounds like—"

"My bo staff," she finished. "And something else." She tapped her chest, where the Harvester rested beneath her shirt. "Somehow I never thought of them as operating in the same manner before. I don't *know* that they were made by this particular family, but I think the bo staff at least was." She explained about what she'd read on the weapon's intake form.

"I knew I'd run across the name *somewhere*," Griff said, sounding irritated with himself, "and recently. I never thought of the inventory."

"We catalogued over one-thousand items in the Den, I think you can be forgiven for not remembering a random name on an intake form."

Seth looked like he'd bitten into something bitter. "So someone in this Gare Ru family probably made your bo staff. That doesn't mean they made the Harvester." He sounded almost...defensive. "There have to be thousands of magical metalworkers in the connected worlds."

"There are," Nyx said slowly. "Too many for me to have sorted through them all yet. But the thing is, before I figured out how to keep the staff from getting stuck to my hand every fifteen minutes, I looked into having one similar to it made. I asked Laila—the blacksmith in Earth Between—if she or anyone she knew could replicate it. She'd never seen anything like it."

"So?" The single word from Seth's mouth was uncharacteristically grumpy.

"So," she answered, dragging the word out, "if she'd never heard of it, I'm guessing it isn't a common ability, and the Gare Ru family is very secretive. They don't make things that are for sale to the general public, and in the wealth of the universe's archives there is a whopping total of six whole articles on them. Articles I never would have found if I hadn't already known who I was looking for.

"So even if they didn't make the Harvester, don't you think the odds are good that they might know who did?"

Seth didn't answer. His mouth was pressed in a thin line.

"It would seem likely," Griff said mildly. "I take it you intend to ask Valedan for an introduction?"

"Something like that."

"What exactly is the plan?" Seth asked. "Even if this is the right person, you can't just show them the Harvester and ask them how it works."

"Why not?"

He stared at her.

"Why not?" she repeated. "It was wiped from public knowledge centuries ago. Long enough that everyone who originally knew about it died off except for the councilors. I could stroll through any planet marketplace with the Harvester on display and no one would even recognize it. As far as Gare Ru needs to know, it's just a metal sphere designed to contain magic, and I want to know how it works."

"That's your brilliant plan?"

His tone made her lose her temper. "Yes, Seth, that is my brilliant plan. Do you have a better one?" Why was he being so contrary all of the sudden? Yesterday he'd been all reassurances and *take your time* and *it's practically an impossible task so don't feel bad for not solving it*. Now she might have solved it and he wasn't happy.

Oh. She might have solved it. And solving it came with a host of complications and dangers and work that needed to be done, and she was already doing a bad job of *being present,* and she'd run out on him this morning to find this piece of information, and... Her "ands" could probably fill a book.

"No," he said tightly. "I guess I don't have a better one."

His words from yesterday came back to her. *You know you can just be here, for a little while, right? That you can be here with me?*

She hadn't meant to set the hourglass spinning so soon. She'd thought that even if she found the right name there would be...well, she didn't know what, exactly, but more impediments. More steps. More time. She hadn't expected the answer to be so immediate. "Seth..."

He shook his head. "I'm going for a walk."

She didn't try to stop him. They'd grown up without anyone ever teaching them how to deal with their emotions, so as they'd gotten older they'd had to figure it out for themselves. They'd only really known that they hadn't wanted to be like Elena or Viktor. The first had been cruel, the second empty.

So when Nyx had been too upset or angry to discuss something rationally, she'd gone to see the horses. When Seth was in that state, he went for a walk. They each knew better than to interrupt the other during this asked-for space if they didn't want their head bitten off.

It had worked for them, maybe in part because they'd had nothing but time. There hadn't really been any urgency to fixing a problem. There hadn't been any outside people or forces requiring that the problem *be* fixed.

Now... It was a little harder to let him go, now. Especially after this morning. As a kid she'd known that if he went for a walk he'd come back anywhere from fifteen minutes to four hours later to calmly tell her exactly what was bothering him and why, and they would sort it out. But she hadn't given him that courtesy this morning. She hadn't listened to him and told him she'd needed time to think. She'd broken the rules first. What if, this time, he didn't come back in four hours?

Unlike their isolated childhood, they now lived lives where people and events could tear them apart. It had never occurred to her, when they were kids, that anything could happen to either of them. If she needed to spend six hours with the horses before she was capable of speaking civilly to him, it hadn't felt like wasted time. Hadn't felt like a risk.

She didn't like that it felt that way now. And if it weren't for her ability to sink into the Station's senses, to feel his every footfall on the ground, she probably would have gone after him and forced an argument.

As it was, she turned back to Griff, only to find he didn't look any happier than Seth had. Though Griff, being less volatile, hid it better. Even if he wasn't the slightest bit convincing when he said, "This is…wonderful news."

"What's wonderful news?" Evra asked, striding into the room.

The words stuck in Nyx's throat, so it was just as well when Griff answered, "Nyx may have found Gare Ru."

"Oh? Are you certain?"

"Not entirely." Nyx explained about Liya and Valedan, and how it had led to what she'd found concerning Gare Ru.

"I see," Evra said, once Nyx finished. "Liya certainly has dangerous tastes if she intends to marry a prince of the Blood. As for the other… Well, I should tell Morgen. He is still quite frustrated in his attempts to decipher Laiveran's journal, and it seems as if there might not be much point now. I am sure it will be a great relief to him."

The Amazon exited the room, looking anything but relieved, and a heavy feeling spread through Nyx's stomach. She'd been feeling so much pressure—all of it self-imposed—to find Gare Ru. Because it *had* seemed like an impossible task, one that might take years to complete. Because she'd felt so guilty for *wanting* it to take years, had thought that if she wasn't working to find Gare Ru, everyone would think she hadn't found them yet because she didn't want to. Because she wasn't trying hard enough.

She'd been so wrapped up in her own anxiety—her own shame for wanting to stop thinking about problems beyond her control and just enjoy her life—that she had missed what was rapidly becoming obvious to her: everyone else in her Station had wanted a little time to enjoy life too.

10

Physical fitness was Evra al'Daemon's personal god, and the Amazon worshipped daily and with the strictest of devotion. It was due to this devotion that Nyx, seeking the company of her best friend after an unproductive hour spent with her own thoughts, found herself stretching in preparation for her least favorite activity: running.

She'd wanted to talk to Evra, but she wasn't quite sure how or about what. Mostly because one thing having the entirety of her memories back had done for Nyx was to make her more awkward rather than less. When she'd first come to the Station, she'd had years of being mostly alone, not interacting normally with anyone. But those years had been filled with a wealth of observation when it came to human interaction.

She'd known, more or less, how she was supposed to act should she ever be fortunate enough to run into anyone who could notice her. Any hesitation she might have had at attempting never-before-performed social interactions had been easily overwhelmed by her exuberant excitement at having the opportunity to attempt them.

Now she remembered the first eighteen years of her life, wherein the very sight of people other than her mother, Seth, and Viktor had been overwhelming. As a child, she'd been acutely conscious of the fact that the way she lived was not normal, and that *she* was therefore not normal. It had affected her so much that when she and Seth started sneaking into Dead Earth, she'd Hidden herself half the time. It wasn't until she was older that she'd developed a desperate desire to make a friend outside of him. Even then, it had taken her until she was fourteen to finally work up the courage to approach a group of girls at the mall. They had probably been a year or two older than her, which would have been a first sign that she was unlikely to be successful in her friendship quest, though she hadn't had the life experience to know it at the time.

Nor would it have mattered. She'd been *awkward.* She'd waited until Seth was distracted looking at the sunglasses stand—okay, shoplifting at the sunglasses stand—and walked up to a trio of girls. It wasn't until she'd actually reached them that she'd realized she had no idea what to say. They'd seemed unreal to her, so pretty and carefree, their hair styled and their outfits so much more brightly colored and interesting than her baggy black t-shirt and worn jeans.

She *still* couldn't remember what she'd said, but she could remember the way they'd gone from laughter to dead silence, the way they'd stared at her like she was a giant insect slowly filling them with horror. The way the most sleekly polished of the three had looked Nyx over from head to toe, her nose wrinkling, and said, "I think you have a tree in your hair." At which point Nyx's hand had flown up to said hair to find a stray pine needle was indeed stuck there. "And what is with those boots? Is that a *knife?* What are you, like, some kind of forest girl?"

The other two had laughed, and Nyx hadn't needed prior experience to understand it wasn't nice laughter. She should have just walked away then—it wasn't like she knew these girls or ever had to see them again—but her stupid feet had been frozen to the floor, even as the girls continued to make fun of her and her face grew red as her eyes pricked with tears.

Then there had been a familiar weight at her back and Seth had shoved a pair of sunglasses into her hand saying, "Here, I got you the glasses you wanted. We should go."

And even though she hadn't asked for sunglasses, she'd put them on in the middle of the mall so no one could see her cry. Not that any of the girls would have noticed, as the second Seth had walked up, their attention had instantly diverted. He'd actually been their age and, having shoplifted much nicer clothing for himself the last time they'd been in Dead Earth—Nyx had refused everything he'd tried to get for her prior to the sunglasses, on account of a firm belief, gained from reading, that theft was wrong —he looked like one of them.

She hadn't thought her humiliation could deepen any more until the one who'd called her a forest girl had looked him over like he was edible and said, "Are you taking your little sister shopping? That's so sweet. She's a little…challenged, I take it?"

Seth had never gotten a chance to respond—which was probably a good thing since he'd had that particular energy that said he was riding the razor's edge of his irritation—because Nyx had been overcome by what Seth would later term one of her "possessive rages". Though she hardly thought snapping *he's not my brother* and dragging him away from the other teenagers actually counted as a rage.

That first experience had left a mark on her, one that had formed the foundation of how she saw herself in relation to other people— especially other women—and now that the memory and all related ones were once again firmly a part of her, Nyx found it affecting her at times like this. Six months ago, she wouldn't have hesitated to dramatically drop onto her back on the gym floor and tell Evra she needed friend time, and that Evra was obliged to comply because she was Nyx's best friend.

Now, past experience formed an insidious voice that whispered that Nyx was more trouble than she was worth. That she'd lived a bizarre life even by the standards of aliens, and she should keep her mouth shut and be grateful that anyone put up with her. Rationally, she knew it wasn't true. But old scars meant that when Evra had suggested they go for a run, Nyx had just said, "Okay."

She finished stretching and followed Evra outside, the Amazon setting the pace at what she called a "light jog" and Nyx called a "moderate run" when she was feeling charitable. She'd put physical distance markers up around the perimeter of the Station after Evra had taken an interest in Nyx's cardiovascular health, so she knew they were a little over three-point-five miles in when Evra said, "All right, what is it?" Her voice was perfectly even—practically cheerful, for Evra—her breathing steady an unlabored.

Nyx could speak without gasping which, given the pace they were going at, she considered a testament to how much Evra's efforts had increased Nyx's lung capacity. "What is what?"

"The thing that is wrong with you."

"That's a long list, we could be here all day." Mentally, she kicked herself. A habit of self-deprecation was another thing she wasn't excited to discover was once more a part of her.

"You could begin with the thing that is bothering you right now," Evra suggested.

"Who says anything's bothering me?"

They entered a steep descent immediately followed by an equally steep ascent, during which time Nyx was exceptionally pleased with herself for not skidding on the downhill dirt portion, though it was a short-lived victory since her quads screamed as she immediately began the slog uphill.

Evra maintained perfect running form while verbally ticking off the list of evidence for why Nyx was bothered. "You came to the gym but barely greeted me. You agreed to come running without a single token protest. You have yet to curse, whine, or bemoan what you frequently refer to as the 'evil necessity of cardio'. I can only conclude, given this highly irregular behavior, that something is wrong."

It took Nyx several gasping breaths to get her words out as she crested the hill. "Okay, fine, something's wrong with me. But I could say the same about you."

"There is nothing the matter with me," Evra said.

Nyx took a few breaths on level ground to recover, and managed to maintain adequate, borderline poor, running form while verbally ticking off her own list of evidence for why Evra was bothered. "In the last week, you've increased your cardio sessions from two a day to three, and you've quit taking your rest day. You've been an unusually sore loser at games but haven't once remarked on how late I get up in the mornings." Evra loved commenting on that. But, by far, the most damning piece of evidence in Nyx's arsenal was: "Two days ago Seth made jalapeno poppers and you didn't eat them. You didn't even eat *one*. I can only conclude, given this highly irregular behavior, that something is wrong."

Evra stopped running. Actually stopped running in the middle of a planned workout. Nyx stopped with her, more grateful than she would admit for the break.

"Tamrin wrote to Bryn."

Nyx waited. Evra hadn't talked much about her sister since

they'd parted ways in the Shadow Market. The girl had been angry at being sent home, and had wanted to go with the Moors and Kalvar.

"Before she wrote to Bryn, she wrote to Kalvar, and before she wrote to him, she wrote to Kaden and Maruca. I only know this because Horace found the latter three letters in her room, all returned undeliverable, and because Bryn informed me of the one she received."

It took Nyx a moment to remember that Horace was the name of Evra's brother. "What did Bryn's letter say?"

Evra waved her hand. "You know Tamrin reaches the age of majority soon? Apparently, since she doesn't know how to find the Moors to become a mercenary, she's decided she wants to go work for Bryn the second her life is legally her own responsibility."

"Would that be the worst thing?" Nyx asked carefully. "I know you don't necessarily approve of Bryn's operation, but it does sound like she's done *some* good things in the Shadow Market, now that she has the Keep under full control." Keeping the slave trade from operating had to count for something, right? "Bryn could keep an eye on Tamrin while she figures things out."

"I have not explained fully. Tamrin asked Bryn if she could come work for her *as an assassin.*"

"Oh."

"Indeed." Evra swiped her hand across her face. "I do not know what my sister went through on Arkadia before Kaden found her. She refused to talk about it. I wrote to Maruca, since Morgen knows where to find her, but she doesn't know either. Kaden might, but no one knows where to find him.

"And even if I get the answer, I don't know if it will help. Before Arkadia, Tamrin was...unusually sweet for a girl in the al'Daemon bloodline. She isn't anymore. Horace informs me that even Mother is concerned, and Moriana al'Daemon is never concerned about her children."

"Evra...you know if you need to go home I would never hold that against you, right?"

"I do. Unfortunately, my mother might be 'concerned' but it is not to such an extent that she will allow me to visit." Evra gave her a tight smile. "You forget, after all, that all of Tamrin's problems are entirely my fault."

"Tamrin ending up on Arkadia was *not* your fault."

"Wasn't it?" For the first time Nyx could remember, Evra looked lost. "If I had only reacted a little faster…"

Suddenly, Nyx understood where all of Evra's extra workouts were coming from. She was trying to hone herself into some idealized physical perfection, as if becoming the perfect Amazon could retroactively prevent everything that had happened to her sister.

"It wasn't your fault," Nyx said again, "and you nearly killed yourself getting her out of there."

Evra sighed. "Yes, and since I have forced her to return home, she refuses to speak to me. Before Arkadia, we were close. Now Horace says she does not even open the letters I send."

"I'm sorry. What are you going to do? About the whole assassin thing."

"I do not know. I am sure if I run another mile or thousand, it will come to me. Now, we have discussed *me* far more than I prefer. What is your problem?"

Nyx's problem was a multitude of problems, but the most pressing one kept circling back to the person she needed to reach out to for help and didn't want to. She *meant* to try and frame her difficulties around the subject in the vague, general way two individuals might have issues with each other but still need to work together.

Instead, she blurted out, "Jevryn's my father." Nyx clapped a hand over her mouth as Evra's eyes went wide. *Shit. Shit, shit, shit.*

"Jevryn is your father," Evra repeated. "Jevryn, as in, Councilor Jevryn A-Morridahn?"

"Do you know another Jevryn?" At Evra's glare, Nyx confirmed, "Yes, that Jevryn."

Evra thought for a moment. "In retrospect, it makes so much sense. You have known this for how long?"

"Since my mother was here."

"Six months. You have kept this information to yourself for *six* months?"

Guilt surged through Nyx. She nodded.

"I am impressed."

Nyx nodded. "Of course you're angry, I—wait, what?"

"Impressed," Evra repeated. "I would not have thought you capable of keeping a secret for such a length of time."

"Hey, I've been keeping a lot of secrets, quite successfully, for a while now."

Evra waved her hand dismissively. "Not from me. Who else have you told?"

"Technically? You're the first."

The corner of Evra's lip twitched. "I am honored. Yet I cannot believe Seth does not know."

"He does," Nyx admitted. "So does Griff. Elena kind of outed Jevryn in front of them."

"Is Griff all right?" There was genuine concern in the Amazon's voice, and it made Nyx smile. Evra had come a long way from referring to Griff as *the Avatar,* as she'd done when she'd first arrived at the Station.

"He is. It's complicated and I can't explain it."

Evra nodded. Unlike Nyx, who had to push until she learned every little detail, Evra tended to take *I can't talk about this* in stride, so long as the guarded information didn't affect her safety or anyone else's. "So Griff is all right. Are you?"

"I..." She shook her head. "No. I know I should be, by now. Jevryn doesn't want me. He never did, and I get it, I do. He's important and busy. I just thought..." Her lungs constricted, and she told herself it was from the run.

Evra's voice didn't quite soften, but it came close. "I am sorry, Nyx. I know how much you had hoped for something more, when you found your father. Perhaps, given time, he will feel differently."

"He won't." Nyx ruthlessly weeded out the hope that sprang roots at Evra's suggestion. "He never would have told me if Elena hadn't done it. And she only told me to hurt me—and him—as much as possible."

"It would seem she succeeded."

Nyx laughed bitterly. "Only with me. All she did to Jevryn was inconvenience him. He basically told me not to bother him until I had news on the Harvester. He hasn't spoken to me since."

Understanding registered on Evra's face. "And now you have news, and must be the first to reach out.

Nyx's eyes narrowed. "When did you get so good at diagnosing emotional problems? What happened to my stoic Amazon who couldn't even figure out Morgen *liked her* liked her?"

"I have far more experience with being a disappointment to

one's parents than I do with being liked by potential romantic partners."

Didn't everyone? "What if I...don't reach out?"

Evra hesitated. "I do not pretend to understand Councilor A-Morridahn. However, I cannot imagine he would take it well if you embarked on the next step regarding the Harvester without informing him."

No, he wouldn't, but that wasn't exactly what Nyx had meant. "I'll have to tell him once I contact Gare Ru. I know that. But what if I don't reach out to Gare Ru yet?"

Evra frowned. "Why would you not?"

"Because no one seems to want me to?" Nyx blew out a frustrated breath. "Because *I* don't want to? I thought I was being selfish, hoping it would take me years to find an answer, but Griff and Seth weren't happy I might have, and you didn't seem to be either, when you found out."

"I wasn't," Evra agreed. "And I was surprised by the fact. This place"—she made a gesture that encompassed the Station—"has a way of making time seem unimportant. I do not know if that is a facet of it being a Nexus, and its literal suspension of time, or if it is because of what you have made it into—a home.

"Whichever it is, it is...difficult to feel the urgency of the issue. Perhaps that is only because the Harvester has been in existence so very long, and your Hiding of it makes the matter feel less pressing. Regardless, do not let my momentary reluctance sway you. Do what you feel you must."

Nyx blew out a breath. "That's the problem—I don't know what I feel I should do. How do I figure that out?"

"You will not like my answer."

"I'll take it anyway."

"Running. Physical exercise is an excellent way to clear the mind."

"Is your mind constantly in a jumble that needs untangling?" Nyx asked. "Is that why you're in entirely too good a shape?"

"I value clarity for clarity's sake. And I have an older brother who was always insufferably good at pleasing my mother in shows of physical adeptness. It was motivating. Now come"—she clapped Nyx on the shoulder—"we have a run to finish."

Evra sprinted away and Nyx groaned, jogging after her. The

Amazon was already way too far ahead. If Nyx were to slightly change the distance between mile markers—like, say, by shrinking the space between them by a quarter mile—what were the odds Evra would notice?

"And no using your control of the Station to shorten the distances!" Evra called back.

"Is she a mind reader?" Nyx muttered. But she refrained from making any geographical adjustments, even if the physical exertion didn't seem to be having the promised effect of clearing her mind. Especially when they jogged past the absolute ugliest wall Nyx had been able to make.

Behind it lay Seth's project of the last five months. She knew it was the garden he was working on, but past that general idea, she hadn't seen it. Or felt it through the Station's senses. She'd promised to let him have his privacy until he was ready for her to see it, hence the ugly wall.

Ugly, because if she'd made it pretty, or even ancient-crumbling-ruin mysterious, she'd have been unable to resist the urge to see what lay on the other side. The hideous eyesore that was the current wall made her shrink away from it in horror, which was precisely the point.

It was also enough of a motivator for her to finally sprint to catch up to Evra. "Have you seen what he's doing behind there?" she gasped out.

"Are you worried it is of a dangerous nature?"

"No, Kaliaris and Griff would be on that."

"Then why are you trying to find out the answer from me, when I believe you agreed not to look for it?"

"I'm not asking you to tell me, I'm just asking if you know. Five months seems like a long time for decorative gardening or whatever." Not that he worked on it every day, though he was in there now —she'd felt him walk up to the door, then disappear from her senses, as she was dutifully blocking out that portion of the Station.

Evra shook her head. "I have not seen it. I think Morgen has."

Nyx did not have the proper amount of air in her lungs to sigh, but she did so mentally. He hadn't asked for too much space—only roughly half an acre—so the question she was trying valiantly to ignore was *what the hell is he doing back there?* The curiosity was eating at her daily. She had never, in the entirety of her now fully remembered life, managed to go this long without ferreting out a secret.

She was beginning to wonder if he was *ever* going to show her what lay on the other side of the wall. *Gosh, Nyx, maybe he was going to do that this morning before you literally ran away from him. Did you ever think of that?*

Nyx decided her inner voice was a bitch as the end of the seven-mile course came into sight, and she struggled across it. She gladly came to a full stop—mostly so she could see Evra's immediate glare at the inaction—before she began walking again to cool down.

Her brain did not feel particularly de-jumbled. "What do you do if the mental clarity doesn't kick in?" she asked.

Evra gave her a rare smile, albeit one that had a diabolical cast to it, and said, "I run again later."

11

Nyx was in the shower, washing away the sweat from the run, when she felt Seth's footsteps emerge onto the ground outside his walled garden. She was tempted—so tempted—to peak behind that wall. Just a tiny glimpse, just to know. But she didn't.

She did track him as he walked across the grounds, into the Station, up the stairs to their room. He paused just inside, as if listening, then turned and walked to the bathroom door. She'd closed it, to keep the steam and heat of the shower in, and she felt through the air as he raised a fist to knock, stopped short and opened his hand, placing his palm against the wood.

She didn't know if he knew she was keyed into the Station's senses right this moment, if the gesture was a silent question or not. But she answered it anyway, reaching out through the Station to swing the door open. She didn't turn to face him as he stepped through.

He closed the door and then there was the rustle of clothing being discarded, the brief rush of cooler air entering the shower before he tugged her back against the warmth of his chest. His arms wrapped around her stomach and he buried his face in the curve of her neck.

For a minute, he only held her, and for a minute, she only let him. "I'm sorry," she said softly.

"I know."

He didn't say anything else. Whatever he'd been going to say that morning, he'd either changed his mind, or there was something new in the way of it now. Easy enough to guess what that might be. "You're upset with me about Gare Ru."

"Not *with* you, exactly." He sighed, then kissed her neck, just below her ear. "I didn't expect you to find an answer so soon. Maybe not ever. And don't get your pride pricked," he said when she bristled, "it's not because I didn't think you were capable, it's because you were looking for an answer that might not have been discoverable."

"We don't know that I *have* found it," she pointed out. "This might not be the right person, or if it is, they might not talk to us. If we do get to talk to them, they might not be able or willing to tell us what we need to know."

"Doesn't matter if they do or don't." His fingers dragged lazily across her stomach, the slow, familiar teasing at odds with his melancholic tone. "Either way, we have to find out. Which means we'll be leaving here again."

"And you don't want to go," she realized.

"I don't want us to *have* to go," he corrected, turning her to face him, his eyes searching hers. "This was never what we wanted out of life."

Her stomach dropped, and she felt her throat closing up. Was this what he'd been going to say this morning? That this—the Station—wasn't what he'd wanted? "You said you didn't feel trapped with me. You said you *wanted* to be here." Her mind raced through the last few months, trying to find the place where that could have changed, looking for signs she'd missed and only coming up with that damned area of her Station he disappeared to that she'd never seen. Maybe there was nothing behind it at all. Maybe what he'd wanted to build, he didn't want to anymore.

"I want to be here," he said. "I want to be right here, with you. But you haven't really been here with me. You've been with this." He tapped the Harvester. "And I wanted to talk to you this morning about—" He broke off. "I just wanted to talk to you."

She fell back against the wall of the shower, the tiles warm from an unending supply of hot water. "And now you don't?"

"I'm not sure." He shut his eyes briefly. "It occurred to me that we're in very different places."

"What do you mean?" She interlaced her fingers behind his neck, tugging him closer, trying to calm the sudden pounding in her chest. "We're both here. You say this isn't the life we wanted, but we have a home. We have *us*. We have friends." Those were the things they'd always dreamed of. Simple things, to most people, but ones they'd never taken as a given.

He tapped the Harvester again. "*This* isn't the life we wanted. Safety, stability—maybe we didn't think of it in terms of those words when we were kids, but that's what we wanted. That's what's *here*, in the Station." He swallowed. "That's what we come closer to losing every step you come closer to solving the Harvester."

"We don't have to lose it this moment," she whispered. "Even if this is the answer we need, we don't have to act on it right now."

He was holding something else back, she could see it in his face. And he confirmed it when he said, "Why do you have to be the one to act on it at all? I understand everything you said last night, why you feel you're responsible for it because it dropped in your lap. But Nyx—your father will be far more responsible for what happens because of that thing than you will ever be.

"I *just* got you back. I don't want to lose you again. And maybe it's selfish but I don't want to see what *being responsible* for this thing will do to you." His hands settled on her waist, his fingers flexing into her skin. "I want you to give it to Jevryn because I want to *live* with you. I want—" He cut off abruptly.

"You want what?" she asked softly. This was what he'd wanted to say to her this morning, what she'd run away from. He had the same look in his eyes now that he'd had then.

"I want to build a life the Harvester isn't in. One where I can get an actual job and be involved in the community here because I'm not thinking it's pointless because we might not be here long enough for it to matter. I want to ask you to marry me in two years and I want you to say yes."

He drew in a rough breath. "I want to have a family with you, Nyxi. I want to have kids. Not today, not tomorrow, but when we're ready. I want to be so good of a father they'll never even guess how fucked up we had it. I want to be a family and not worry about whether we're going to make it to the next day, or—"

She cut him off with a kiss. Her fingers and her toes buzzed with a restless energy she couldn't shake, and she poured all of it into the way her mouth claimed his. She felt him respond against her and she arched her hips, needing him closer, needing the familiar press of his body.

The picture he'd painted wouldn't leave her mind's eye. She'd never thought far enough in her life-planning to reach the kids-and-family stage. To find out if that was something she was even interested in. Her sole focus in her youth had been getting away from her mother and not getting separated from Seth. In her identity-less years, there hadn't been any reason to ever think she could have *anything*, and thinking about the possibilities had hurt too much.

And since she'd gotten her memories back... Well, Seth was right. She *had* been with the Harvester more than him. At least in her focus. Because it had felt like something that needed to be dealt with before she could have a life.

But Seth had done that thinking and now that he'd said it out loud...she wanted it. Not for a few years, on the kids, but she *wanted it.*

Seth drew back, his breathing ragged. "Nyx..."

He was going to ask her to give the Harvester to Jevryn, to wipe her hands of the matter altogether. And no matter how much she wanted that pretty future he'd dangled in front of her, she didn't think she could do it—give the Harvester up. She certainly couldn't promise it now, without thinking it through. So she dragged her fingernails down his back. A little pain had always been his catnip, and that hadn't changed.

His mouth crashed against hers, and once she hitched her leg over his hip, aligning their bodies, they both forgot he'd started a sentence he never finished.

Nyx lay in bed, drawing lazy circles on the bare skin of Seth's back while he slept. She'd always envied the way sex left him sleepy. He could drop into a power nap effortlessly, while all the happy chemicals working their way through her system always amped up her energy.

Her brain was racing. She'd delayed the continuation of their conversation to give herself time to think, but she couldn't delay it forever. She didn't want to, either. She wasn't running away again, like she had this morning, she was just…thinking.

She hadn't realized how much the underlying tension they'd both been carrying had been bothering her the last few months. It had seemed like such a minor thing, because it wasn't as if they'd been fighting or unhappy. But that small dissonance neither of them had brought up had chafed until it caused a small hurt, and she wasn't stupid enough to go back to letting it do so again.

"You're thinking," Seth said, cracking one eye open.

"How perceptive of you."

"What are you thinking about?"

"That you're right—"

"Tell me something I don't know."

"—about where my thoughts have been," she finished with a glare. "I never thought past getting my memories back so we could be *us* again. And since I've done that, all I've been thinking about is the Harvester. I never thought about…any of the things you mentioned."

He pushed onto his elbow. "And now?"

"I want it. I want everything you want." The happiness that lit his eyes dimmed a second later when she said, "But I can't give Jevryn the Harvester."

"Why?" The question wasn't accusatory, only a simple request for an explanation.

She picked at a loose thread on the bedspread. "A lot of reasons. I don't trust him. Even if I did, I made a promise to Kaliaris. To all of the Stations, really. That I'd fix what was done to them. I can't keep that if I wipe my hands of all this.

"Jevryn might initially agree to keep that promise on my behalf, but the first time it comes down to a hard choice, I don't think he'll have any qualms about breaking it. And even if he did all of that right, what if he doesn't destroy the Harvester?

"I can't just settle down and have a happy life knowing all of that is out there. I can't have *kids* knowing I'm bringing them into a world where I willfully abnegated responsibility for possibly the most dangerous thing in the universe, something that could easily end or upset their entire existence."

"Counterpoint," he said. "The universe is always going to be dangerous. There are probably thousands of things that could end or upset their entire theoretical existences."

"But not ones *I've* directly been involved with. Not things I've started and left unfinished that are likely to blow back on them. Seth—our kids will be Hidden. The ability is fully dominant, it will pass on to them. And the Hidden were hunted to the brink of extinction over the Harvester.

"Jevryn has no qualms about using me to continue keeping it Hidden, and I'm his daughter. Do you really think he would hesitate to use our children? And he would know exactly where to find them because unless he did make good on freeing the Stations, I will be tied here *forever*.

"And I don't—" She closed her eyes. Opened them. "I don't want to have kids and know there's every possibility that they will grow up before I solve this problem. Because they will leave and they will age and they will die while we still look just like we do now. And I couldn't live with that. Could you?"

She could see on his face that he hadn't worked it all through that far. That he'd conveniently forgotten the parts of the narrative that didn't fit with what he wanted. That was Seth to a *T*. She'd often thought it was part of why he was so good with illusion—he could make anything the way he wanted it in his head, and his magic could spin out the facsimile of it.

"No," he said finally. "I couldn't." She could see him thinking about it, watched his expression clear as he came to a decision. "The Harvester's our problem then."

"My problem."

"*Our* problem," he repeated, "and that's not changing." He dragged a hand through his hair. "So I guess this is the part where I stop being a hindrance and start being a help."

She arched her eyebrows. "I wouldn't have called you a hindrance, per se." Though he *had* had a habit of distracting her during the allotment of time she'd set aside each day to search the Archives for Gare Ru. She just hadn't realized until now that it might have been intentional, for the purposes of slowing down her finding of that answer.

She linked her fingers with his. "I wanted more time, too," she told him softly. "And I felt guilty for wanting it so I didn't enjoy any of it while we had it. I'm sorry."

He raised up and brushed his nose against hers. "It only means we're closer to the rest of it, right?"

"Right." She hoped she sounded more convincing than she felt. Her anxiety was already shoving at her the many things that could go wrong. This wouldn't be the right Gare Ru. If it was the right one, they wouldn't talk to her. If they did talk to her, they would tell her there wasn't a way to disassemble the Harvester.

Just focus on the step you have to do next. Ask Valedan about Gare Ru. "So," she said casually, "since it's *our* problem, want to go have a chat with the heir apparent to the Blood Throne?"

"Not if I'm walking in on whatever stage of fighting or making up he and Liya are in."

She smiled. "They went downstairs fifteen minutes ago. Judging by how close they're sitting next to each other on the library couch, I'd say they've finished with both the fighting and the making up." Griff was with them, and so was Kalvar, so she hadn't felt bad about not checking in the moment she'd realized they'd come out of Liya's room. And since Griff hadn't come to retrieve her, she guessed that Liya and Valedan weren't in an immediate rush to leave.

"All right." Seth brushed a kiss to her cheek and rolled out of bed, hunting for his jeans. "Let's go talk."

12

Only once Nyx laid eyes on Liya did the knot of worry in her chest fully unravel. The young woman was smiling, her bare feet tucked underneath her on the couch, while Valedan was animatedly describing something to Griff and Kalvar that involved a great many hand gestures for emphasis. He finished as they walked in, sending Griff and Kalvar into a fit of laughter.

Who would have guessed someone called the Blood Prince would be so cheer-inducing? His eyes landed on her and he rose, offering her a short bow. "Guardian. I must offer my apologies for my earlier rudeness. Though it is no excuse, I fear I was at the end of a long search and my limited patience had been exhausted. I hope you can forgive me."

"You do know," Seth said, answering before she could, "that attempting to influence a Guardian via magical or non-magical means is illegal, right?"

Valedan smiled. Widely, oh-so-very charmingly. "Of course. But surely, as my motives were pure, no one would dream of reporting me to the proper authorities?"

Seth crossed his arms. "I'd dream of it, but I'm guessing it wouldn't do any good, would it?"

"Not in the legal sense, though my mother would certainly be cross with me. As she is, in all likelihood, already exceptionally cross with me, I doubt the addition of another infraction would tip the scales overmuch."

"No one is reporting you," Nyx said.

He lowered his eyes in a show of demureness. "Your generosity is humbling."

Seth and Liya rolled their eyes.

"To be perfectly serious," Valedan continued, "I am grateful for everything you have done for Liya. It comforts me to know she was safe during her time here."

Nyx looked at Liya. "You're going back to Alzherra then?"

Liya nodded. "You have a lovely Station, and Earth is...diverting," she said diplomatically, "but I miss home. Though as I've told Valedan, I do have obligations here for another three weeks."

Kalvar spoke up. "I've already told you not to stay on my account."

Liya looked affronted. "I promised I would help you pass your proficiency exam, and I mean to do just that."

"You've been tutoring me non-stop for months. If the knowledge hasn't sunk in by now, I don't think a few weeks is going to change that."

Hah. Nyx was going to remind him he'd said that the next time she found him falling asleep over a textbook.

"Nonetheless," Liya said, "when I make promises, I keep them. Valedan understands that."

Liya's prince nodded. "Indeed I do. And the extra time will hardly make any difference, as I am on a...leave of absence of unspecified length."

"I think the descriptor you were looking for was un*sanctioned* leave of absence," Liya said smoothly. "I can't believe you went to *every* planet."

"I can't believe you came to Earth, of all places." To Nyx he said, "Begging your pardon."

"Are you two going to have difficulties when you go home?" Nyx had been counting on Valedan's status as the Blood Matron's favored son to smooth over any issues. But if he was on the outs with her right now...

Valedan waved an elegant hand dismissively. "Oh, I am certain it will be fine. I will be clever and charming, and so long as I am clever and charming enough, it's unlikely Mother will order me executed for insubordination."

"She would order the execution of her own child?" Nyx felt a rising sense of alarm.

Valedan was unbothered. "She only did it the one time."

"And Hinden truly was a liability," Liya said, also unbothered. "Though I don't think Alicie ever forgave the Blood Matron for it. He was her only child."

"He tried to murder mother in her sleep and he wasn't even *clever* about it. What did Alicie expect?"

"It would have made a difference if he'd been clever?" Nyx asked.

"Oh, undoubtedly. Mother values cleverness—and usefulness— above all else. If he'd had a decent plan and come close to executing it, she would have been proud. Furious, of course, but proud. She'd have shipped him off somewhere for a few years until she cooled down, and everything would have been fine.

"Which is why," he said to Kalvar, "a few weeks here isn't a terrible idea. It will give us time to set our stories straight about precisely what happened and…plot."

Just then, four sets of footsteps crossed over the border onto Station grounds, prompting Nyx to ask, "Are your guards and your advisor going to be on board with this plan? Because they're approaching the building as we speak." She subtly added more ground between their approach and the Station building, giving Valedan and Liya more time before their arrival.

Valedan's eyebrows crept up. "Someone in that group clearly has more intelligence than I gave them credit for. I thought it would take them until nightfall, at least, to discover where I'd gone."

"So they won't be a problem?"

"Oh no, they will. But for all Rothbert enjoys blustering, there's very little he can actually do. The guards answer directly to me, and Mother doesn't value Rothbert's opinion half as much as he thinks she does. Still, she could be angry enough with me to actually listen to him, for once." Valedan rolled his bottom lip between his thumb and his forefinger. "I suppose I could always threaten to leave him here." He snapped his fingers, grinning at Liya. "Frame him for your abduction? Now that would be good."

"I have a better idea." Liya stood and placed one hand on Valedan's shoulder, leaning in to whisper in his ear.

He listened, then a smile curved his lips. "Oh, that *is* good. Precisely the right leverage to ensure compliance without losing his usefulness." His hand covered Liya's. "I've been positively wretched without you, only half as clever as usual. It's a good thing I haven't been home for the decline to be noticed. Marishka's cohort would have me looking practically incompetent."

"What is the state of things with the other heirs?" Liya asked.

Valedan shrugged. "The usual. Though I did leave Risha, Mayala, and Daine fending off some particularly nasty machinations from Tilda and Vessor, and who knows what happened if the twins decided to get involved."

Nyx blinked, assuming these were all names of his brothers and sisters. "How many siblings do you have?"

"Seventeen still living," Valedan replied cheerfully.

"Seventeen?"

Liya nodded. "All the Matron's consorts have to do is give her sad eyes and the next thing you know, she's signing another pairing agreement. Then again, if it's the *other* women going through the messy business of childbirth, I suppose it doesn't inconvenience her too much."

The front door opened in the adjoining room, and Rothbert and the guards stepped into the cafe. Rothbert wasted no time in ringing the bell labeled *Please ring for service.* Repeatedly.

"Does your plan involve coming with me to greet Rothbert?" Nyx asked Valedan and Liya.

"If you wouldn't mind going out ahead?" Valedan's eyes practically sparkled with mirth. "I'll only be along shortly after you."

"Anything I should avoid mentioning?"

"No. In fact, if you could casually mention my betrothed's presence, should the opportunity present itself, I would be grateful."

Nyx walked into the cafe, Seth and Griff on her heels. Rothbert's finger descended once more toward the bell and Nyx, annoyed with the constant sound, melted it into a flat disk, which had the gratifying effect of startling him. He turned on her, a furious scowl consuming his face.

"Guardian," he said, in what could have been a greeting but

sounded more like a reprimand. "I demand to see Prince Valedan at once."

She arched her eyebrows. "Do you?"

He was momentarily taken aback by her response, but recovered quickly enough. "Yes, I do."

"I'm afraid he's occupied at the moment."

"With what?"

"He and his betrothed are working out their relationship."

Rothbert's face took on a stony expression. "Liyan is *here*?"

"Valedan's betrothed is here," Nyx evaded. Not sure of exactly when Valedan intended to make an appearance, she added, "I'll inform them of your arrival, of course, but in the meantime, why don't you sit down and wait? I can offer tea, coffee, water—"

"I am not interested in refreshments." He spoke the last word as if it were worthy of the utmost scorn. "I *demand* to—"

"Your habit of demanding grows increasingly tedious, Rothbert," Valedan said, striding into the room. "The problem is that you do it so often, and rarely with any means of backing it up. Take your most recent one. You're in a Station. She is a Guardian. Under the Waystation sanctuary clause, without a contradictory order from the Council, she is under no obligation to produce me had I not wished to be produced.

"I imagine it would have been quite embarrassing for you had you kept on. A word of advice? If you don't have the means to ensure a demand is met, don't issue it. I myself never do so unless I am certain I can control the outcome."

Rothbert gaped at Valedan for a stunned moment before recovering. "*I* am *your* advisor, young prince. Need I remind you that I have your mother's ear?" Clearly taking strength from having reminded himself of this fact, Rothbert puffed up. "Given your behavior since Liyan's obvious abandonment of you, culminating in your conspiring to send myself and your guards on a pointless search— an action which left your safety in grave question—I fear I have no choice but to inform your mother I no longer think you the best choice for Blood Prince. I rather think one of your siblings may be better suited to the role of heir."

Valedan looked disappointed. It was an excellent disappointed look, one which made him appear to be the elder, experienced advisor, and Rothbert the unruly youth. "First, you make demands you cannot enforce, then you make threats you will not deliver on. None of my siblings is looking for a new advisor, and you enjoy bearing the status of being the Blood Prince's advisor too much. You will not say a thing to Mother to risk having my title removed. After all, a drop in my status is a drop in yours."

Valedan paused a moment to let this sink in. "As for my betrothed, we have reconciled our differences. Therefore *you* have reconciled your differences." It was perhaps the politest way Nyx had ever heard anyone say "My will is law".

Rothbert chose to ignore it. "Your Highness, I expressed my concerns over that boy's unsuitability for life in the monarchy upon your betrothal. I had hoped his disappearing act on your wedding day would make you see some sense, but it did not.

"Instead, your actions have become increasingly more rash, and in the name of what? A meek boy who was never your equal, who hides away in shadows whenever the opportunity presents itself."

Some of those shadows were, even now, twining around Rothbert's and the guards' ankles, creeping up to curl around their weaponry. Nyx was the only one save Valedan who noticed, and she only noticed because she'd felt Liya slip into the room.

"You may think yourself clever," Rothbert continued, "by guessing that I will not petition for your demotion as heir, but I assure you I have no such qualms about imploring your mother to reconsider allowing your marriage. Do you honestly believe your would-be husband will fight overmuch to stay by your side if the Blood Matron orders him away?"

"His would-be *wife* will fight if she needs to," Liya said, stepping gracefully out of the shadows in the corner of the room. The sudden appearance had the guards reaching for swords and finding themselves bafflingly unable to draw them, shadows holding them tight. "I am not *meek*, Rothbert, I am shy. There is an important difference. And if I hide too much in the shadows, it is only because I learn so many interesting things there. Such as the money you've been skimming off Valedan's allowance ever since you were appointed his advisor, the mistress you keep in Bellor, who's a secret from the other mistress in Alenton, but neither of whom are a secret from your wife like you think they are. Oh, and then there's that unfortunate bliss powder habit you have to take the edge off when things get too stressful."

Rothbert paled.

"I could continue, though I do feel this is enough to recommend that you hold your tongue in the future. Else you may find yourself reassigned to the underground annals of the Sixth Library. I hear the historians there do not see the sun for months. Perhaps you will learn something from the experience."

Rothbert stared at Liya like he'd never seen her before. In some ways, Nyx supposed he hadn't. Seth's face had taken on a speculative look that said he suddenly found Liya a lot more interesting, while Griff observed it all with his usual unflappable expression.

Next to Liya, Valedan's eyes were filled with a steady, quiet pride. "Allow me to reintroduce my betrothed, Liya Asheran, formerly but never again known as Liyan Asheran, and the primary reason my siblings find themselves continually incapable of taking off my pretty head."

"As for the Matron," Liya said, sliding smoothly into the gap of silence Valedan's announcement produced, "seeing as she was the one who told me she would be happy to see me marry into the family so long as I came as my true self, I don't expect her to have any problem with my return." She brushed non-existent wrinkles from her shirt. "At least, I don't expect her to have any problem so long as Valedan and I bring her something suitably impressive to make up for the public conjecture we have caused."

Rothbert finally appeared at a complete loss for words. He didn't put up even a token argument when Valedan ordered him and the three guards to return to the Wanderer's Inn and "Stay there until I send for you." He did shudder when Valedan suggested he immerse himself in the local culture.

Nyx wondered if this was because Rothbert found the local culture distasteful, or because he considered other cultures beneath him. Once the door had closed behind him and the guards, Seth asked, "Why do you put up with him?"

"He is extremely manageable," Valedan replied immediately.

"Manageable?" Nyx echoed. Rothbert seemed the opposite of manageable.

"Terribly easy to manipulate," Liya explained. "All the more so because he thinks he is not. And he's so self-important and loud any time we're in public that he draws all of the attention to himself, leaving Valedan and I much more room to maneuver unnoticed."

Valedan nodded enthusiastically. "Truly, I could not have chosen a better distraction to keep at my side if I had invented one myself. I knew Mother was going to name me Blood Prince the day she assigned him to me. She was never so generous with any of my siblings."

Nyx decided she was not cut out for court politics.

"But," Valedan continued, "useful as he is, I do understand he can be a bit tedious to deal with if one has not built up a tolerance. I will do my best to keep him in town for the remainder of our stay. Though if it isn't too much of an imposition, I should like to stay here at the Station with Liya."

Nyx nearly laughed at him asking permission. He did it so sincerely, as if her answer wasn't a foregone conclusion. Either he was the most humble prince a land had ever produced, or he thought getting what he wanted would be easier if she liked him. She decided it was likely the latter, not that his approach was necessary. Her answer would have been the same even if she'd found him as onerous as Rothbert. "Of course."

"Thank you. For this, and for giving Liya a safe place to stay. If there is anything I can do to repay the favor, please let me know."

Nyx wasn't ashamed to admit that this was precisely the kind of opening she'd been hoping for. "There might be, actually. I'm looking for the maker of something. This." She pulled her bo staff from its clip at her belt. If she'd hoped for recognition, she didn't see any on either Valedan's or Liya's faces. Refusing to be discouraged, she continued on. "It's a unique metal," she explained, and extended it from its compact, easily stored shape to its full length.

This time, a glimmer of interest lit Valedan's eyes.

"I couldn't find anyone who knows how this type of metalwork might be done, but then I read about someone who works for your family—someone named Gare Ru."

"May I?" Valedan held out his hand.

Nyx was reluctant to acquiesce. The weapon had an imbued level of awareness, and while she didn't think it thought thoughts or had complex desires, she'd also been capable of anthropomorphizing something as inanimate as a tea cup in her lonelier days. Since the bo staff was far more animate than a tea cup, she'd grown rather attached to it. Especially now that they'd worked through their issues and it had stopped adhering itself to her palm all the time.

She hadn't let anyone else handle it once she'd stopped needing a second person to unstick it from her hand. She'd made it a promise, of sorts, on Amentia Furor—that she wouldn't abandon it if it didn't cling so tightly to her. She didn't want it to feel like she was giving it away.

"Only for a minute," she reassured it.

Valedan's eyebrows lifted, but he otherwise didn't comment as she placed the staff in the palm of his hand. It hummed, a deep vibration that felt like recognition. Nyx tried and failed not to feel jealous.

He turned the weapon over in his hands. "I'd like to try something, with your permission."

Nyx wiped suddenly sweaty palms on her jeans. "Okay." Seth and Griff crowded a little closer to her.

She didn't know what Valedan did, but a ripple went through the staff. Not just the feeling of it but an actual physical ripple, as if the solidity of the metal was a pliant lake surface, little waves cascading along its length. It shivered, that hum growing louder. The metal liquefied, suspended in midair, then crawled over itself, rearranging.

The metal from the lower half of the bo staff traveled up, crawling over the backs of Valedan's fingers. Some of it pooled just above his hand while the rest continued up, thickening what had previously been the other half of the bo staff. She recognized the shape it was taking a second before the metal gave another fluid shiver and solidified into a silver sword.

Valedan grinned and offered it back to her, hilt first.

For a moment, she forgot that she'd had a higher purpose in asking Valedan about the staff, that his doing…whatever it was he'd done was a good sign for her inquiry. She accepted the sword, cradling it in her arms like it was a puppy instead of a now-sharp object.

Seth squeezed her shoulder supportively, but she couldn't keep the horror from her voice when she asked, "What did you do to my bo staff?"

13

"Don't worry, I haven't permanently altered it," Valedan reassured her. "Oh, see there? It's already shifting for you."

The sword in her arms was indeed shifting. It once again turned liquid, stretched, and resolidifed into the bo staff she'd always known it as. She squeezed it to her. Then, conscious that she was hugging a weapon in front of royalty and soon-to-be royalty, she shrank it to its compact length, stored it back in its holster, and tried to once again mimic the behavior of a responsible adult.

"That," Valedan said, "is Constance. The very first thing the Gare Ru family ever made for mine. It can be anything you need it to be, the only drawback being it's a little sensitive, otherwise it couldn't sense your intentions."

She blinked. "It's infinitely mutable but its name is Constance?"

He grinned. "Because it will *always* be whatever you need it to be. It disappeared a few generations ago with one of the family's lesser cousins. How in the stars did it end up with you, if I might ask?"

"It was confiscated by a previous Guardian." Valedan didn't have to know it had gone into the Station's Den, from which things were theoretically irretrievable. She hedged, "It was sort of forgotten in an out-of-the-way corner of the Station and I happened upon it."

"How…unusual." Valedan clearly didn't buy her story, but also didn't push her on it. "So you would like to speak with Riven Gare

Ru because of Constance. Are you having some manner of difficulty with it?"

"No, we've worked out our issues."

"Then do you wish her to make you something else like it? Because I must inform you, she will refuse, and there is nothing I can do to change her mind on that. The Gare Ru family has served mine under a carefully worded, magically binding contract that *they* wrote.

"They are given the money and stability to execute their craft as it calls to them. But anything they make must remain the property of the Blood Throne. It cannot be sold or given away. With regards to weapons, each descendant of the line will make only one, of their own choosing, to also remain the property of the Blood Throne. In return, the Blood Throne ensures they are never required to—and are never able to—make any creation for anyone else. Theft, or confiscation"—he gestured to Constance—"is literally the only way an item can leave my family."

Nyx's heart beat a little faster. "That's…an interesting contract. One I wouldn't think most makers would be willing to sign, much less ask for."

Valedan's eyes narrowed. "Are you asking if I know why they did?"

"If you're willing to answer."

He looked at Liya. When she nodded, he said, "I asked Riven about it once. All she would tell me was that her family once made something terrible, simply to see if it could be done. And after they witnessed what their creation destroyed, they vowed penance for that act, chaining themselves and all their descendants to my family to ensure they could never do anything similar again."

The Harvester warmed against Nyx's chest. It was certainly something terrible. She shared a look with Griff, whose eyes reflected her own certainty. There could be little doubt, now, that they'd found the right Gare Ru, the right metalworker, the right answer. "I understand she won't make anything for me, nor do I wish her to. But if you asked, would she speak with me?"

Valedan studied her with all the wariness she imagined came from a lifetime of growing up with seventeen siblings all engaged in a bloody contest for the same throne. "I appreciate what you have done for Liya. Truly, I do. But Riven's family came to mine to avoid garnering interest. If you have no questions about Constance, and you truly do not intend to trick her into making you something else, I must know, what *do* you want from her? I will not ask her for anything without knowing that."

Nyx's heart thudded against her chest. She felt, with the Harvester, like she was always walking a fine line. It had been Hidden for so long that it had disappeared from public record. As she'd told Seth, she *should* be able to walk around with it showing, for all the universe to see, and not have to worry that anyone outside of a councilor would recognize it.

Valedan and Liya shouldn't have any idea the Harvester existed. If Nyx told them she thought she was in possession of the item that had made Riven Gare Ru's ancestor bind their family line to the Alzherran royals, they might be curious to find out what the item was, but the Harvester shouldn't even be on their list of possibilities.

"That terrible creation Riven's ancestor made? I need her to tell me how to *un*make it."

Nyx stood on the receiving end of twin disbelieving stares. Liya, who'd mostly been listening up to this point, said, "You...think you are in possession of the creation that brought the Gare Ru family to Alzherra?"

"I am relatively certain I am, yes."

"And...what is that item?" Valedan asked.

Nyx shook her head. "I can't tell you that. I *won't*. So don't ask again. But trust me when I say that it's in everyone's best interests for it to not exist anymore."

"At the risk of sounding skeptical, I don't have any proof that you actually have it."

"What reason would she have to lie?" Seth asked.

"The most obvious one would be that you wish to assassinate Riven, in order to destroy the Gare Ru line and rob the Blood Throne of their talents."

Nyx blinked. "You're...serious?"

"Deadly so."

"I'm a *Guardian*. I don't exactly go around assassinating people. Guardians don't leave their Stations." Given Liya's self-imposed isolation during Nyx's most recent trip off-planet, she'd never realized Nyx had been gone and thus wasn't entirely subject to that particular drawback of Guardianship.

"No," Valedan said slowly, "but you wouldn't need to if I brought Riven here."

"I am not trying to assassinate Riven and 'rob the Blood Throne'." She looked at Liya. "Could you perhaps back me up here?"

Liya looked contemplative. "It's not as farfetched as you might think. Guardians *are* susceptible to bribery, and one did once attempt to assassinate a lesser daughter of the throne a few centuries ago. It didn't end well for the Guardian."

Seth snorted. "Of course it didn't end well. A Guardian assassinating someone in their own Station is a terrible idea."

"It is," Liya agreed.

"Not to mention," Nyx interjected, "if I was planning to assassinate Riven, asking you to bring her to me would *also* be a really stupid idea." So stupid, in fact, that she realized Valedan *couldn't* have been seriously worried about it. Which meant... She crossed her arms. "You're just trying to get me to tell you what the object is."

He flashed her a guilty grin.

"I'm not going to. If you won't ask Riven to meet with me, I *do* have a way to guarantee she will, and neither you nor she will like it."

If Nyx had to throw Jevryn A-Morridahn at the problem, she would. If he could extricate Elena Fortuna from the Kormadin royal palace, she was relatively certain he could extricate Riven Gare Ru from Alzherra. But she'd rather avoid that route, as it would mean she'd have to talk to him.

"I don't like being threatened," Valedan said.

"And I don't like being given the runaround. If you aren't willing to ask her, that's fine. Just tell me that now."

Liya put her hand on Valedan's arm. "There really is no harm in asking."

Valedan relaxed a fraction under her touch. "Probably not," he admitted. "But it doesn't matter. Riven is no longer on Alzherra to ask, and I am incapable of getting in touch with her."

Liya frowned. "How is that possible? The contract—"

"Only states they can't metalwork for anyone else, and that the

Blood Throne will protect them on Alzherra. It doesn't forbid them from leaving, they just never have."

"But what would prompt her to leave?" Liya looked genuinely confused. "Riven never expressed any interest in doing so."

"She received a call to arms from her people. Shortly after you left, she left for Kyvren. And neither I nor anyone else has been able to contact her on that planet."

A sinking feeling hit Nyx's stomach. "Valedan," she said slowly. "Is Riven a Dwarf?"

"Yes. Why?"

"That...complicates things." Kyvren, the Meerkin homeworld, was one she'd avoided looking into after her return from Arkadia, because she hadn't wanted to draw attention to herself or it. But in the last few months, she'd started surreptitiously doing so. She'd thought enough time had passed for it to go unnoticed, and she'd wanted to know that the Meerkin were, if not safe, at least not losing the battle to reclaim their homeworld.

Her first searches had been fairly simple—scouring news articles from that sector of the ley line network. She hadn't expected to need to do much more than that. When the Council had arrived in her Station after her return from Arkadia, Kiev had called the Meerkin's homeworld a "valuable planetary asset". Given that descriptor, she'd assumed that information on a war on Kyvren would be front page news.

Instead, she'd failed to find a single article. No news of war, of the Meerkin, of *anything*. She'd had Griff help her look, at which point they'd discovered that nothing was going in or out of Kyvren. Not shipments, not people, not mail delivery.

The planet had been marked as "isolated", meaning that no one save a member of the All Council could open a ley line path to it, the Guardians' access having been revoked. This had happened shortly after Nyx's return from Arkadia, which meant Riven's joining of her people had either been achieved before the lockdown, or via a portal stone.

Valedan stepped closer to her. "Do you know what is happening on Kyvren?"

"Not exactly," she hedged. "But I can find out."

"How?"

Her shoulders slumped. "By talking to someone I really don't want to talk to."

After reassuring Griff that she was fine to write Jevryn—he'd offered to do it—and promising Seth that she didn't need him looking over her shoulder while she wrote—he disagreed but caved —Nyx went upstairs alone and flipped the companion journal open. A tiny spark of hope rushed through her as she opened it, as it did *every* time she opened it, then died as it did each time she realized there was nothing written on the pages that hadn't been there before. Only the simple sentence Jevryn had written last: *Expect my arrival in two days' time.*

She stared at it, trying and failing to sort through her mixed emotions. When she'd read that sentence directly after it had been sent, she'd felt relief. Because it had meant Jevryn was bringing her mother to her, and that was going to fix everything. Now that she knew he was the other half of the equation that had brought her into the universe, his elegant scrawl pissed her off.

She twirled a pen through her fingers. What was she supposed to write? *Dear Dad, thanks for continuing to ignore me, as you successfully managed for the first twenty-six years of my life. By the way, do you happen to know what the situation on Kyvren is?*

She mentally went through a dozen iterations of a similar nature before settling on two short lines:

I might have found something. I need to know what's happening on Kyvren.

Message written, she left the journal open and set it aside on her nightstand. It was late afternoon now. When Jevryn had given her the book, he'd asked her to check it each evening and told her he would do the same. Though she'd had many reasons for not contacting him, one of those reasons was that she hadn't wanted to know if she was the only one still putting in the effort and checking the damn book each night.

Well, that, and the uniquely human stubbornness to not be the first person to reach out. She hadn't truly needed anything from him up to now, so she hadn't been willing to break the silence first. At least with this communication, it could all simply be…business. Yes, business. That was how she would think of it.

But it wasn't business that made her leave the book open all evening, that made her check the page every half hour until Seth came up and she snapped it closed. Jevryn wasn't going to write her back that night, because Jevryn was not checking to see if she'd written him. And that didn't hurt. Not a bit.

14

Mornings at the Station were rarely quiet affairs, which felt woefully unreasonable to Nyx. In her opinion, mornings were for heroically dragging oneself out of bed, drinking coffee, and reading a book while surrounded by the comfort of a cozy library or, weather permitting, the serenity of the back porch.

Griff, being a sensible individual, shared this opinion with Nyx, and if the two of them ever decided to use their powers for evil and lock the rest of the Station's inhabitants in a soundproof room, they might actually get that ideal morning. Currently, she was curled in her papasan chair in the library, cradling a mug of hot coffee with a book open in her lap.

Griff was stretched out on a large, flat sofa that had no back or arms to cramp his wings. His glasses were perched low on his beak as he peered down at a large tome. A cup of steaming tea sat to his right, and he hooked it delicately with his talon, lifting it to his beak for a careful sip.

Nyx still wasn't sure how he managed to drink out of cups without spilling liquid all over himself, but somehow he managed. She had succeeded in reading all of two pages in her book when the library door burst open, admitting Morgen, Seth, and Evra. Morgen liked to spend his mornings discussing magical theories that gave Nyx splitting headaches to even think about, and to this end it was usually Griff's mornings the half-Siren intruded upon most, as Griff was the one who could keep up with him intellectually.

Seth and Evra liked to argue in the mornings. About anything and everything. It was goodnatured arguing and they both took great joy in it, but it was loud and ceaseless. This morning, they appeared to have dragged Morgen from the realm of theory and into the argument with them.

Why they needed to be doing this here, in the sanctity of the library, when she'd only woken up thirty minutes ago, Nyx had no idea. She and Griff lifted their gazes from their books to glare at the disruptors of the morning peace. The scathing glances went unnoticed as the other three continued their heated discussion of—oh, they had to be kidding. She continued following the argument. No, apparently they weren't kidding.

"I'm telling you, you're dead wrong," Seth said firmly.

"You can't even explain how his magic works," Morgen argued. "And if you can't explain that, you can't explain how he would beat a Terminator."

Nyx sighed. Evra and Morgen had watched *a lot* of movies on their Dead Earth vacation.

Seth crossed his arms. "I don't have to explain how his magic works until you explain how a Terminator works."

"Science," Morgen said.

"I do not care how the magic or the science works," Evra said. "He's not beating a Terminator. Clearly, we must appeal to a neutral, informed fourth party." She turned to Nyx. "What do you think?"

Nyx took a long, fortifying drink of her coffee. *Mmm,* caffeine. Sweet, wonderful caffeine that was doing its best to soothe her after all the screeching she'd just listened to. "Let me get this straight. The three of you are having it out over whether Gandalf or a Terminator would win in a fight?"

Three nods answered her. She took another drink and gave her answer: "No."

Evra frowned. "No?"

"No," Nyx repeated. "It's six in the morning. I am not wading into the depths of an argument over which of two fictional beings would be better able to—" She cut off at the same time Griff's head snapped up. Her eyes went out of focus as she slipped wholly into other senses, certain she must be mistaken.

"Nyxi?" Seth was at her side in an instant. His voice held an undercurrent of worry that was still there any time she did anything strange, no matter that five months should have proved her mind was all back in one piece and staying that way. He was allowed his trauma.

"It's okay," she said. "I asked a question. Apparently I'm getting an in-person answer." From multiple people. She looked down at herself. She was wearing black sweatpants, a loose t-shirt, and no bra. She was also relatively certain she hadn't brushed her hair yet this morning. Just how she wanted to meet her father and her ex. She could make them wait long enough for her to change, but that might give them the impression she cared what they thought.

"Try to behave," she told Seth, a second before she felt the cafe door open.

His brow wrinkled in confusion. "What are—" He cut off as Jevryn A-Morridahn and Kaden Moor walked into the library.

Morgen saw Kaden and looked like he'd been sucker punched. Kaden Moor was Morgen's best friend. More like a brother than a friend, as Morgen's mother had taken Kaden and Maruca in after their parents had disappeared. And Nyx knew for a fact that Morgen hadn't seen or heard from him since Kaden had been here to pick up Maruca after she'd nearly died on Nethrayne. Morgen hadn't talked to Nyx about it, for obvious reasons, but he talked to Evra, and Evra talked to Nyx. So she knew he'd written Kaden himself and sent all the letters Tobi asked him too, and never heard a single thing in reply.

And now here Kaden was. His gaze remained resolutely ahead, fixed on some indeterminate point in the distance. Easy evidence that he didn't want to be here, but Jevryn had brought him. He looked...haggard. More than haggard, actually. Everything about him looked toughened and weathered, as if he'd purged every ounce of softness from his body. And his eyes... He had a deadness in his eyes she'd seen only once, after he'd come back from Arkadia and thought he was back in Psionics.

He's not your problem anymore, she reminded herself. She had bigger ones.

Jevryn's gaze went, as it always went first, to Griff. The Station's Avatar pushed his glasses up his beak and gave the councilor a pointed look in response. Jevryn's mouth tightened. Nyx had suspected they were in semi-regular communication, and that silent exchange pretty much confirmed it.

She dropped her voice into her chilliest, most impersonally polite tone. "Councilor A-Morridahn. To what do I owe the honor of this visit?" She had never once called Jevryn "Councilor A-Morridahn". She didn't think she'd ever addressed him directly by any name or title, but when she referenced him to other people, she'd always simply called him Jevryn.

She was aiming for aloof but unbothered, a tone she pretty much never affected, and she must have succeeded by the way Kaden seemed to come alive just a fraction, his brow furrowing. He didn't know, then, who Jevryn was to her. He shot Morgen a barely perceptible, questioning look. Morgen shrugged his shoulders, just as confused as Kaden.

Which meant Evra hadn't shared Nyx's revelation with him. She wasn't really surprised—Evra was a vault when it came to information—but now she felt more than a little bad that Morgen was the only one in her inner circle who didn't know Jevryn was her father.

"You wrote that you had news," Jevryn said, ignoring the coolness in her tone.

"I wrote that I *might* have news, but to determine if I do, I need some in return. I never dreamed you would descend upon my humble dwelling in all your stately glory to answer it in person."

A muscle beneath Jevryn's eye twitched.

"I think," Griff said, rising from the couch with a stretch, "we should give the councilor and Nyx some privacy."

"An excellent idea," Evra said, giving a now even more confused Morgen a shove toward the door. "Moor, you're included in 'we'."

Kaden waited for the dismissive flick of Jevryn's hand before he followed Evra and Morgen to the door, Griff on his heels. But he lingered in the doorway—likely because Seth hadn't yet moved to leave—forcing Griff to wait with him.

Seth glowered at Jevryn. "You have a lot of nerve, showing up like this without an invitation." The words were clipped, and they made Kaden's eyes widen in alarm.

"I do not require an invitation."

"No," Seth agreed, "but if you had a shred of human decency, you would have waited for one."

Nyx tugged on Kaliaris and the floor swallowed Seth, depositing him in the Station's basement. If he'd stayed, he would have really gone off, and she didn't want Jevryn to murder him.

"That one has no manners," Jevryn said.

"That one actually cares about me," Nyx answered, mimicking his tone.

The muscle beneath Jevryn's eye twitched again. He inhaled as if to speak when Griff cleared his throat, drawing the councilor's gaze.

"Try," Griff ordered. "For me." He bumped Kaden with his head, pushing him out of the room, and then he was gone, the library door snicking shut behind him.

15

"The fucking basement, Nyxi?" Seth muttered. He hadn't even realized the Station had a basement. For all he knew, it was a recent addition, created specifically for dropping him into. It certainly looked to be of new construction. The walls were plain gray, and the room contained no furniture.

He found the stairs and jogged up them. He got halfway up and no further, and it wasn't for lack of continuing to climb. "Nyxi," he said, pouring a wealth of exasperation into the nickname. "Come on."

The air rippled like a laugh but the stairs quit multiplying. He soon reached the top, where the steps terminated at a door. Painted on the door in bold block letters were the words *don't antagonize Kaden.*

"Yeah, no promises on that one." He reached for the doorknob and a column of deadbolts appeared on the door, all locked, all without an unlocking mechanism on this side. "Fine, I won't antagonize him if he isn't a dick. Did you leave him a *don't be a dick to Seth* message on the cafe counter?"

The words on the door flashed, little Christmas lights dancing around them. He crossed his arms. "I don't make unqualified promises. I reserve the right to antagonize him if he's a dick."

The black letters swirled together, resolving into a new message: *You're a pain in the ass.*

"Yes, but I'm *your* pain in the ass."

He could feel her rolling her eyes from across the Station as the deadbolts slid open in rapid succession and the door swung out, revealing the cafe where Griff, Evra, Morgen, and—unfortunately—Kaden waited. They all looked over as he walked in, and he met Kaden's eyes.

The guy had always had a thousand-yard stare, but it was more pronounced now. A little more empty, a little more hollow. It begged the question, what could Jevryn have had him doing that was *worse* than spending years on a prison planet he'd thought he would never escape?

"Where did she send you?" Kaden asked. His voice was the equivalent of the look in his eyes. Dull and distant and going through the motions.

"The basement. I was let out on promises of good behavior."

Kaden managed enough emotion to snort at that.

"We have a basement?" Morgen asked.

"I think it's a recent addition," Seth said. "Possibly as recent as five minutes ago. Terrible color scheme, no decor."

Morgen made a noncommittal sound. Casually, he said, "Your banishment to the basement for poor behavior wouldn't have anything to do with why Nyx was being unwisely rude to one of the twelve remaining most powerful people in the universe, would it?"

"Uh…" Guilt wormed its way underneath Seth's skin. He understood why Nyx hadn't told anyone about Jevryn. It wasn't necessarily a safe secret to hand out, either for her or the people who learned it. But Seth hadn't made any real friendships in his life prior to Morgen, and he didn't like having to withhold information.

"Nyx isn't the one who told Jevryn that if he had a 'shred of human decency' he wouldn't have come here without an invitation." Kaden said this to Morgen, but three-quarters of his attention seemed to be on the wall over Morgen's shoulder.

Morgen winced. "You didn't."

Seth shrugged.

Morgen looked at Kaden. "Tell me he didn't."

Sometimes—as in, all the time, since Kaden was never around—it was easy to forget Kaden and Morgen had grown up together. Seth knew there was a rift there—one created first by the Moors leaving in the Shadow Market, then made a little bit deeper when

Morgen had learned Kaden Linked to Nyx without her consent—but they still had a lifetime of friendship and history behind all that that Seth envied.

"He did." Kaden said. His attention was still on that spot over Morgen's shoulder. "Shame Nyx dropped him through the floor when she did. Jevryn's temper has a remarkably short fuse." He stopped staring at nothing long enough to flash Seth a humorless smile. "I'd have found it highly amusing to see what he did with you once you lit it."

Seth decided this met the Kaden-being-a-dick clause and he was now free to engage in antagonizing behaviors. "He wouldn't do anything. You'd know that if Jevryn told you anything, which he clearly doesn't. Is it fun, being at his beck and call constantly and still being in the dark about everything that matters?"

A throat cleared and Seth followed the sound to Griff and the very disappointed look on his face. Seth did not like the rare occasions when he managed to bring out Griff's disappointed face. Unlike Viktor Hawthorne's use of the expression, which had mostly been disapproving-disappointed, Griff's was always I-know-you're-better-than-this disappointed. The problem with people thinking you were actually worth something? It made you want to not let them down.

"Question," Morgen said slowly. "Am I also in the dark about something?" He was looking between Seth, Griff, and Evra, but it was Evra he landed on. Probably because the silent lack of curiosity she'd been exhibiting up to this point indicated, Seth realized, that she already knew what was going on. When had Nyx told her?

"Nyx has cause to be angry with Councilor A-Morridahn." Evra informed Morgen. "Beyond that, the issue is personal."

"Yes. So personal that everyone except—apparently—Kaden knows it."

Seth was pretty sure Kaden was supposed to react to that, if the way Morgen waited expectantly was any indication, but he didn't. He was staring over Morgen's shoulder again, his eyes narrowed. Seth followed his gaze, but there was nothing where Kaden looked. It was just Station wall, painted a stormy gray-blue. No pictures, no hardware, just—

Oh. Morgen's *shadow* fell across the wall.

"Also," Morgen continued, "me. I don't know what's—" He cut

off abruptly as Kaden *moved*. One second the Hound was sitting there, the next he'd drawn a dagger and sent it hurtling at that spot behind Morgen. It sank into the wall, right through the shadow's left shoulder.

An unholy shriek split the air.

16

Nyx looked at her father. She knew she shouldn't think of him that way. He didn't want to *be* her father, and calling him that, even if it was only in her head, was only bound to make her give him leeway he didn't deserve. But the part of her that had spent her entire childhood wishing her dad would show up and rescue her from the misery of her life just couldn't help herself.

She wondered if he knew that, even now, even with everything she'd learned about him, he could have cut through all of her defenses by showing the slightest bit of interest in her. Something as basic as a hesitant "How have you been?" would have softened her immeasurably toward him.

Try, Griff had ordered. It was only too easy to guess what he'd meant.

But she wasn't surprised when Jevryn didn't. He folded his hands together in front of him. "I fail to see how the matter of a civil war on Kyvren can have any relevance to your work with the Harvester."

The man got straight to the point, didn't he? She swallowed down the sharp bite of hurt his impersonal statement caused. *He's never going to be anything more than this to you,* she reminded herself. *And you're never going to let him know that you want him to be.*

Not again. Not after she'd so thoroughly humiliated herself the last time.

She schooled her voice into a mimicry of his. "Your failure to see it doesn't make it impossible."

His face remained impassive. "Perhaps you should open my eyes, then."

Point to Jevryn, she thought, with no small amount of irritation. And though she was typically an open book where her emotions were concerned, she did her best to keep this one off her face. To look as bored and indifferent as he did.

"There is a Dwarven metalworker named Riven Gare Ru who specializes in metals capable of expanding or collapsing without loss of structural integrity. She is currently on Kyvren."

"I assume you have some more significant reason to think she is the correct Gare Ru?"

"Aside from the fact that her family made this?" She reached through the Station and pulled Constance from her room to this one. She extended it to its full length and, after a moment's hesitation, willed a new request to it. One the staff responded to. Sharp, wicked blades sprouted from each end of the staff. "Its metal transition is as seamless as the Harvester's. And"—she paused long enough to make sure Jevryn was paying attention—"Riven's ancestor apparently made something so terrible that he sought to pay penance for the act by binding his descendants to the Blood Throne of Alzherra."

Jevryn held out his hand, palm up. "Let me see it."

Nyx felt the moment Constance's magic decided it didn't like Jevryn's tone. "I thought we were past this," she told it as she tried —and failed—to uncurl her fingers from the metal. "He's not going to keep you." Constance was apparently not reassured. Exasperated, Nyx asked Jevryn, "Look, can you promise it you'll give it back to me in the next five minutes?"

He blinked. "You wish me to promise the weapon that I will return it to you?"

"I want you to promise the magical sort-of-but-not-quite-sentient weapon with abandonment issues that you will return it."

"Abandonment issues," he repeated. Given it was the second time in a row he'd said her words back to her, she was worried she'd broken him.

"It was sort of stolen and then locked in the Den for a really long time. I promised it we'd have a working relationship if it would quit binding itself to me all the time, and it did, but apparently you've scared it."

He pinched the bridge of his nose, eyelids fluttering closed. Nyx waited. Five seconds. Ten. Fifteen. His hand lowered and he opened his eyes. "You have my word the staff will be returned to you within five minutes."

Reluctantly, the magic affixing the staff to her dimmed. She held it out. Jevryn took it, having to pull a little harder than he should have, the staff clinging to her like a cat digging its claws in as someone tried to lift it from a surface it didn't wish to be lifted from.

He held it flat in the palms of both hands. Constance shivered, metal rippling like disturbed water in the wake of a boat. It turned fluid, contracting on itself, until a sphere of liquid metal rested in his cupped palms. It spun, faster and faster. On each revolution it began to take form, only to collapse in on itself having never formed enough of anything for Nyx to determine what it had been thinking of becoming.

Its spinning increased in speed, until the sphere moved so quickly it began to wobble, like a planet tilted off its axis. Its attempts at formation became jerky and uncoordinated, painful to watch, Constance's confusion and panic obvious.

Nyx swiped it from Jevryn's hands, not bothering to ask permission. It shuddered and snapped into the familiar bo staff, magic trembling through it. *Safe,* it seemed to whisper. Nyx was safe, because she knew what she wanted, what she needed. With Jevryn, it hadn't known what to be. As if he needed...nothing. Or *wanted* nothing. Nothing Constance could give him, anyway.

"Well?" Nyx asked.

"I would like to see the Harvester."

"No."

"I cannot accurately compare the two without—"

"No," she repeated. "Take my word for it that they're very similar."

He studied her for a time. "You will, at some point, have to trust me."

"I will *never* trust you." The words came out more vehemently than she meant them to. When he opened his mouth to respond, she cut him off. "Tell me what's happening on Kyvren. Are the Meerkin okay?"

Jevryn stilled. He stood practically like a statue at the best of times, but he somehow went *more* inert. "Am I to understand, from this question, that the Meerkin did not simply happen to escape when you left Arkadia, but that you actively aided them in doing so?"

Well, she'd all but asked for him to make that intuitive leap. She crossed her arms. "Are you going to arrest me if I did?"

He sighed. "Of course I have no intention of arresting you. But you must understand, the Meerkin are a violent race who—"

"*Violent?* You want to call *them* violent? Their homeworld was overrun by invaders, whom they attempted to peacefully coexist with, but who instead stripped their planet of natural resources to the extent the Meerkin couldn't even protect their own children from the planet's environmental dangers. They watched their children die, and when they couldn't fight off the Dwarves they were expelled from their own planet to a *prison planet*, all so the Council's dirty laundry wouldn't be aired universe-wide."

"I am not sure what their descendants led you to believe—"

"Their descendants didn't lead me to believe anything. I spoke with someone who was there." She tapped the chaos thorns in her cheek. "Someone other Meerkin gave years of their lives to so they could ensure that history didn't get rewritten. So that someone who was there in the beginning could be there to someday lead his people home.

"Vorex watched his daughter die because of the Dwarves' greed, and maybe that doesn't mean anything to someone like you, but I saw how much it hurt him, even after all this time. So *don't* lie to me. Don't you dare tell me they're vicious or dangerous or whatever propaganda the Council created to justify what you did."

"Nyx—"

"How could you do that to them?" She was standing, her hands shaking. She hadn't realized how angry she was until this moment. When Vorex had told her what the Meerkin had suffered, she'd been angry, but it had been at the Council. The Council, at that time, had been a distant group she could never hope to influence or hold accountable.

But Jevryn wasn't some remote entity she could blame from a safe distance. He was real to her and worse than that, he was her father. She was *related* to one—two, if she counted Kiev—of the people directly responsible for everything the Meerkin had suffered. And though she didn't blame herself for the actions other people had made centuries before her birth, she still felt tainted by association.

"How could you?" she asked again, softer, desperately wanting some explanation. "You weren't...*this* back then, were you? You were just—how old *were* you?"

He was quiet. So quiet the only sound she heard in the room was her own harsh breathing.

"Twenty-nine," he finally answered. "It seems an unconscionably young age to me now. I never intended to wield the power I now do, Nyx. I am sure you no doubt long to tell me that that does not absolve me of the responsibility for it, and while you would be correct, I was not thinking of any of that at the time the Meerkin conflict occurred.

"I was not even truly aware of just how much power had shifted into my hands, or that the conflict was occurring. My world had been turned upside down and I was aware of one thing and one thing only."

How long ago had Vorex said the Meerkin came to Arkadia? Around nine centuries? It clicked into place. "Griff."

"Yes."

He would have just been bound as the Station's Avatar around that time.

"Arradin was..." Jevryn closed his eyes briefly. "I prefer not to dwell too deeply on that time, but suffice to say it was not pleasant. I did not leave this Station for years for fear that if I did, he would not be here when I returned."

Nyx frowned. "But he couldn't leave."

Jevryn simply waited for her to put it together.

"Oh," she said softly.

He nodded. "Yes. Therefore, the particular events surrounding the Meerkin were ones I learned of secondhand."

"And you just...believed what they told you? After what they did to Griff?"

Jevryn's mouth tightened. "The Council that exists did not do that to him, nor did they have any knowledge, in advance, of its being done. There is a reason the Council numbered thirteen, these last centuries, instead of twenty-seven. There is a reason the other councilors will never fully trust me, just as they will never forget to truly fear me. Because anyone who was involved with Arradin's imprisonment here did not live long enough to regret it."

"Except for one," she challenged. "Why *is* your brother still alive?"

Jevryn's expression cooled, the gray of his eyes shading more towards a silver like ice. "The reasons for his continued existence are my own. Do not doubt that I have them."

Different day, same version of *I don't have to explain myself to you.*

"As for why I believed the others with regard to the Meerkin… Many of them were once my friends. And of those who were not, we were nonetheless all reforged within the same crucible. Not all races are kind. Not all are welcoming to outsiders. As we explored the universe, we left and did not return to those planets which were openly hostile to our arrival, but it was not unusual for a planet's inhabitants to be welcoming on the surface, only for us to turn around and find they simply wished to draw us in. To take what we had to offer, to learn what they could from us, and then seek to do away with us.

"Kyvren was a planet discovered in the aftermath of Laiveran's terror, and which I had no personal interaction with. I had no cause to doubt the version of events I was told. As to the planet's current status, Kyvren falls under Councilor Loclyn's jurisdiction."

"Meaning?"

"Meaning I do not know. But"—he raised a hand, forestalling her protest—"I will find out. Should Loclyn be on the planet personally, retrieving your Riven may prove more difficult, but it is nothing I cannot manage."

"If you're going to Kyvren, I'm coming with you."

"No."

Magic sparked angrily, deep within her. It had been doing that a lot lately—a response she now remembered having frequently in her more turbulent adolescent years, but which had been absent in the fog of her amnesia—a darkness that twisted inside her, wanting to lash out. "I wasn't asking you for permission. When I sent the Meerkin off to their homeworld, alone, I didn't understand very much about how this universe works. Now that I do, I'm worried about them. Especially if what you told me was the truth, because it means that someone on the Council, if not the entire Council, lied to you about what happened."

"Have you considered, Nyx Ilera, that it is you who has been lied to?"

Nyx Ilera. The names curled into her, like they belonged there, as if his speaking them was a comfort, or a gift.

Pull yourself together, she snapped. He'd likely only called her that to throw her off balance. Or because she'd pettily called him Councilor A-Morridahn when he'd arrived. So she didn't outwardly acknowledge his use of her names. "Considering that, of the two of us, I'm the only one who's actually met the people involved, I feel confident in saying that I know which of the two sides I trust. I'm going."

"Are you so eager to rush towards danger again? Need I remind you that the last time you tangled with another councilor, you survived only because *I* arrived to remedy the situation?"

"I didn't intend to end up on Nethrayne. My mind was a little fractured at the time."

"Indeed. Now that it is once more intact, I might have hoped for more rational thought from you, but clearly I have set my expectations too high."

Nyx gritted her teeth. Had he just called her an idiot in councilor speak? Her magic sparked again, writhing and restless. She could feel it rising up in her throat, begging for release. But it wasn't as if Hiding something was going to make her feel better right now. Hiding was not a destructive talent, and what she felt was an overwhelming itch towards destruction.

Jevryn's eyes narrowed, as if he could sense her intent. His all-knowing stare only pissed her off further. He didn't know anything about her, hadn't *wanted* to know anything about her. If he thought he could just waltz in here and—

A blur of gray fur streaked across Nyx's vision, snapping her abruptly from her haze of anger. Her Majesty, the Queen of Wrath, shot for the couch directly behind Nyx, diving beneath its protective bulk mere seconds before Temerex thundered into the room, trumpeting a war cry. The Queen of Wrath, more commonly known as Fangs, issued a long, indignant yowl in response.

Nyx planted herself firmly in Temerex's path and folded her arms across her chest, leveling the unicorn-dragon with her most serious I-am-not-putting-up-with-this-behavior look. Temerex skidded to a halt, hind hooves sliding under her, wickedly sharp unicorn's horn halting a single inch from Nyx's chest.

"How many times have I told you not to chase your sister?"

Tem turned big, mournful eyes on Nyx, peering around her with a soft whicker. At the same time, she sent Nyx an image of the gray cat sitting on Tem's back.

"I know you want to make friends with her, but you're large and impressive and she can't understand human speech in the same capacity you can. If you want her to get used to you, you're going to have to try taking a less aggressive approach. Like *not* chasing."

Nyx sent her an image of Fangs walking by and Temerex calmly waiting. Not that she had any hope of it actually sticking this time. Fangs and Temerex's little hunt and chase game had been going on for months.

Fangs was technically Laiveran the Mass Murderer's emotional support cat. As such, she spent most of her time in the Station's Heart, which seemed to suit her preferences. But as Kaliaris had grown inordinately fond of the feline, they'd taken to ferrying her out of the Heart for what they called "excursions", and she'd developed a system of pawing at the Heart's pedestal when she wanted to take a jaunt up top.

Temerex had been overjoyed at meeting this new friend, and had promptly expressed that joy by engaging in a rousing game of chase-the-kitty. Which she repeated frequently. Fangs did not take the same level of joy in this activity as Temerex, and Nyx had had more than one stern conversation with the unicorn-dragon about it. But so far nothing, including threatening to take away Tem's favorite weekly treat of Qualtez fish, could dissuade her from her actions. If Fangs left the Heart and neither Griff nor Nyx realized it in time to intervene, Temerex went a-chasing.

Tem let out a long sigh that fluttered her lips.

Knowing the situation wasn't entirely Tem's fault, Nyx turned, willing the couch to slide back and the floor to hold Fangs precisely where she was. The big gray cat let out a shriek befitting a mountain lion, her claws shooting out.

Nyx pointed a finger at her. "And you—don't think I don't realize you're taunting her. It's a big Station and cats understand territory. You *don't* have to go past her to take a walk in the wide

wide world. Tone it down or I'm confining your outdoor activities to a catio instead of the Station boundary."

Fangs hissed.

"I think I've made my point." Nyx flicked her wrist and the floor opened up, transporting Fangs from the library to the Station's portal. It opened, Kaliaris ferrying Fangs back into their Heart.

Nyx turned back to Tem. "You *have* to stop chasing her, okay? I don't know how many more ways I can send you images of you behaving before it gets through your adorable reptilian-equine skull."

A throat cleared. "Would you like me to try?"

Nyx and Tem shifted their attention to Jevryn in a rapid tandem that would have been amusing had it not meant that Nyx had literally forgotten he was there.

"I don't think she wants—" Nyx began, except Tem apparently did want. The unicorn-dragon, who had been cold towards Jevryn ever since he'd left her here—an attitude Nyx fully supported—was thawing. Nyx sighed. "By all means, go ahead."

He clearly already was. Tem's ears had flicked toward him, as if listening. Her big yellow eyes were full of tentative equine trust, and a tremor ran through her. Hesitantly, she stretched her head toward him.

Don't do it girl, he doesn't deserve your forgiveness.

Jevryn petted her muzzle. Temerex trembled again, took one step, two, and dropped her great head onto his shoulder. She looked more content than Nyx had ever seen her as he ran a hand down her scaled neck, and Jevryn—he looked the closest thing to happy she thought he was capable of.

That hot anger that had been building before Tem's interruption returned. Her unicorn-dragon, whom Nyx had comforted through her depression in the wake of Jevryn's abandonment, still preferred him over her. And her father felt more genuine affection for his designer pet than he would ever feel for his own daughter.

She walked away before she could do something stupid. She felt like she was sixteen again, all turbulent emotions and no control. She needed to cool off for five minutes and then she could deal with him rationally.

But he just couldn't let her go. "I will discern the truth of what is happening on Kyvren."

Nyx halted. He was so arrogant, so self-assured, so—so—*Jevryn A-Morridahn.* As if his wisdom was infinite and her acceptance of it inevitable.

She shoved down the part of her that wanted to react childishly —he brought that out in her, but she was an adult, damn it, and she didn't have to let it show—and turned back to him.

He continued, as if there could be no objection to his plans. "Once I have, I will determine the safest method to approach this Riven Gare Ru." The subtext was clear. *He* would figure everything out. She would stay here, far away from Kyvren. She would have to take his word on what was happening with the Meerkin. And there was absolutely nothing she could do about it.

She stared at him for a long moment. When she spoke, she found herself once again reshaping words he'd spoken to her, delivering them in a mimicry of his haughty tone. "Have you ever considered, Councilor A-Morridahn, that you take a risk in coming here? That if you continue to treat me as powerless, I might find myself with the urge to show you I am not?"

The floor turned pliant, swallowing Jevryn to his knees. Temerex nickered uncertainly and lipped at his hair. He patted her in absent reassurance, his attention wholly on Nyx. "I cannot decide whether to be amused or annoyed."

She shrugged. "I don't really care how you feel." He'd certainly never cared how *she* felt.

"And what do you believe you are proving with this little display?"

"Only this—you seem to be under the illusion that I'm going to agree with what you've decided. That I have no choice in agreeing. But I wonder if I could keep you here long enough to make you reconsider."

Some of the icy remoteness around him broke as he bared his teeth in an expression no one would ever mistake for a smile. "Do you wish to test your will against mine, daughter?"

You have no right to call me that.

The councilors had some control over the Stations. Not as much as an Avatar did—or that she now did—but some. So did she want to test her will against his? "I'd love to, *father.*"

17

The unholy shrieking coming from the shadow made Seth want to plug his ears. Morgen slid sideways and turned, his expression unreadable as he stared at the spot where his shadow was pinned to the wall. It writhed and wailed, shadow hands clawing at the dagger that held it. Morgen's own hand shot out, gripping the shadow by the throat.

The shadow grasped the dagger's hilt, ripped it free, and vanished. Morgen's fist closed on empty air. His shadow was once more behind him, where it belonged, though that didn't stop Morgen from turning three circles, trying to see if he could grab it. He only stopped when Evra's hands latched onto his shoulders and held him still.

Morgen, more than a little wild in the eye, raised his hand. "Question: What the fuck?"

Seth opened his mouth to relay what he'd seen yesterday of Liya and her shadows with Valedan's guards, but never got the chance. Kaden, who'd been standing with his eyes closed ever since the shadow disappeared, suddenly snapped them open and took off. Right in the direction of Liya's room.

"Shit." Seth sprinted after the ex-Enforcer, Morgen, Evra, and Griff following. Kaden moved faster than Seth would have expected for a guy with that much muscle, but it wasn't nearly as fast as Seth could move. He caught up quickly enough and stayed on Kaden's heels, but he didn't try to physically stop him.

Picking a fight with a guy who was in his right mind—like Seth had done the last time Kaden was here—was one thing. Trying to stop a guy in Kaden's current frame of mind got you the kind of response that meant one of you was ending up dead at the end of the scuffle. Griff was the one who could easily stop Kaden without risking damage to any of them, but since he hadn't, Seth had to assume he had a reason.

Kaden flung the door to Liya's room open, and the abruptness with which he stopped on the threshold told Seth that Griff had finally decided to intervene. He had a feeling Griff had allowed this much simply to startle Liya and Valedan, which he succeeded in doing.

Inside the room, Valedan had a towel pressed to Liya's shoulder, which bled profusely from exactly the same place Kaden's dagger had struck the shadow. Valedan's eyes flashed with anger. He pressed Liya's hand to the towel in place of his own and stalked toward them, his eyes fixed on Kaden. "You."

Griff stepped between the two, and the floor suddenly turned sticky for Valedan as well. "If your partner chooses to use unknown magic within this Station to spy on some of its members, she can hardly blame someone trained to react to threats for treating it as one." He looked past Valedan to Liya. "I am grievously disappointed that you would repay our hospitality in this fashion. I—"

Griff suddenly went stock still, his eyes slipping out of focus the way his and Nyx's both did when they were paying attention to something in another area of the Station.

"Oh dear." Griff's fur and feathers went jet black. "None of you will do anything until either I or Nyx return."

He turned and bounded down the hallway. Kaden slid backward into the hall, Liya's door slammed shut, and Seth found himself with his back to the wall, unable to move more than a foot or so. Morgen and Evra were to his left, Kaden across the hall.

"Can any of you move?" Seth asked.

"No." Evra said through clenched teeth.

"Afraid not," Morgen said.

Kaden glared, which was answer enough.

Seth discovered that, while he couldn't walk away, he could slide down the wall to a sitting position. Guess they were all in timeout. Normally, he might find this funny. Normally, Nyx wasn't alone in a room with her father, and Griff hadn't taken off like he was in fear for her life.

Seth looked at Kaden, who was currently the only emotional outlet he had to use to blow off steam. "Your boss hurts her, I'm gonna kill him."

A fraction of emotion flashed across Kaden's face and disappeared. "No," he said flatly, "you won't."

It was easy enough to read that what he meant was *you can't*. Which really begged the question, what had Kaden Moor seen in the last six months?

18

Jevryn reacted the moment Nyx accepted his challenge, but then, so did she. She clamped his legs, trying to drag him deeper into the floor at the exact moment he strained against her. The floor trembled. No, the *room* trembled, the walls shuddering, picture frames falling from their hooks.

Temerex startled, letting out a low, nervous snort.

"It's all right, Tem," they said in unison. Nyx would also bet they both sent Tem images of the unicorn-dragon outside, because she booked it for the freedom of open skies as fast as her hooves could carry her.

Jevryn strained, a mental shove against her control of the Station as he dragged his right leg up, freeing himself an inch. Two inches. Three.

Nyx found the point of resistance where his will met hers and shoved back. It felt like trying to push a one-ton block with nothing but her bare hands while in sock feet on a slick floor. All she did was skid back.

Jevryn lifted his left leg and, despite her grip, slid it free half a foot. Stars above, he was not going to simply *walk* out of her control. Gritting her teeth against an acid rasp of pain, she jerked her arms up. Skeletal wooden hands broke from the floor, long, bony fingers clamping around Jevryn's thighs.

She felt a burst of triumph as she dragged him down, reclaiming the ground he'd won. The victory was short-lived.

Quick as a pouncing cat, he drew the slender sword sheathed at his hip. In a movement almost too fast to follow it flicked in a semi-circle to his right, shearing one of the skeletal hands at the wrist, then flowed in the opposite direction, cleaving the other. Had there been any justice in the world, the force he'd used to make those strikes would have driven the blade to continue right through into his legs. Alas, the world lacked justice.

Agony tore through her, raw and undiluted, as if he'd actually wounded the Station. Because...because he *had*. His sword had severed the hands *from* the Station, the wooden appendages clanking onto the floor, no longer capable of melding into it at will. No longer a part of the Station.

Kaliaris howled with rage.

"What kind of sword is that?" Nyx demanded as sweat trickled down her spine to the small of her back. The Station had been cut many times during her tenure. No blade had ever made the thing which was cut no longer belong to the Station.

"Its make is not currently your concern. Are we finished, or do I need to continue?"

In answer, she envisioned the floor as quicksand, designed to trap him as he moved. Vaguely, she was aware that Griff had arrived at the library door, no doubt drawn by Kaliaris' outrage, and Nyx split her focus, keeping him out. She wasn't finished.

"Continue, then." Jevryn sounded pleased. As if he was enjoying this. He started to walk upward again—slowly, an inch at a time—as if her will was merely a resistant force as opposed to a controlling one.

How was he doing this? He hadn't been able to force his way into Kaliaris' Heart when getting there—getting to Griff—had been the most important thing in the world to him. Granted, the entrance to the Heart was entirely Kaliaris' to control, *their* will he would have needed to overcome, but still. Jevryn, Seth, and Griff combined had barely been enough to contain Nyx when she'd been memory skipping and running the Station on instinct.

Instinct. Of course. The realization was so obvious she immediately felt foolish. Instinct wasn't fettered by things like belief.

Instinct was imagination and all the limitlessness imagination implied.

Jevryn had asked if she wanted to match *her* will to his, and in doing so, he'd set the playing field. He'd convinced her this was a direct contest of wills—could she hold him in the floor while he pushed against it—thus narrowing the scope of her attention. And her resources. And her belief.

Because his age, his arrogance, and his power made it feel impossible that her will should ever be greater than his, no matter how much she wanted it to be otherwise. Maybe it was even true, if it was only her. But she *wasn't* only Nyx here. That was the entire point.

She exhaled, dropping the barrier that kept her apart from Kaliaris and immersing herself in the Station. In a being far older even than Jevryn. On the other side of the library door, Griff struggled through his own bond with the Station.

Kaliaris' senses roared through Nyx, and she was *everything*. Not the patch of floor that held Jevryn, but the entire floor. Not only the floor and the walls, but the room and the building. The earth beneath and around it. She shivered with a violent delight and the whole of everything—of this *world*—that she encompassed shivered with her.

She vaulted Jevryn out of the floor and tossed him into the air. Dozens of vines grew from the walls and floor and ceiling in a blink, twining around him, wrenching that awful sword from his hands and flinging it at her feet. The vines had crawled over nearly every inch of his body, holding him suspended in a nightmare web, when her mind cleared enough to realize he wasn't fighting her anymore.

No, the son of a bitch was *laughing*. It startled her enough that she forgot to focus on the door, and Griff burst in right as Jevryn said, "Very good." Nyx had a feeling the bastard would have slow-clapped had his hands been free.

Griff—large, fur and feathers gone black—took in Nyx, then the sword at her feet, then Jevryn encased in vines and once again laughing to himself. "What in the name of the skies is happening here?" Griff demanded.

It was a valid question, and Nyx wasn't certain she knew the answer anymore. She avoided a response by crouching to examine

Jevryn's sword. It didn't look any different from any other weapon she'd seen, and yet…there was something about it.

"Nyx," Griff began, "do not touch—"

But she already had, the hilt in her right hand, the flat of the blade resting against the palm of her left. A flare of power swept through the sword, felt like it swept through *her*. It was darkness and violence, but it was also calmness and peace. An empty expanse that was both promise and inevitability.

She looked up. "What kind of magic is in this thing?"

"Jevryn?" Griff's voice came out sharp and on edge.

Feeling whatever it was that fueled the weapon, she supposed she could understand why Griff would be nervous about her holding it. She was practically giddy on the feeling. It was disturbing.

"What kind of magic, indeed." It was such a Jevryn answer she had to stop herself from rolling her eyes.

"Fine, don't tell me," she said. "But don't cut off anything else in my Station with it." She placed the sword back on the floor, relieved to have it out of her hands. And yet her fingers itched, half-wanting to curl around the hilt again.

No, thank you. I already have one magical weapon to get me into trouble, I don't need a second.

Nyx decided her best course of action was to act like she had the upper hand, even if she doubted she truly did. "You can go meet with Councilor Loclyn," she told Jevryn. "Find out what you can about the Kyvren conflict. But you are coming back *here* before you go *there*, and you are taking me with you when you do."

She retracted the vines without warning. Jevryn dropped six feet to the ground, landing with obnoxious grace.

"To ensure your cooperation," she continued, "I'm keeping Kaden."

"You're keeping…Kaden," he repeated slowly.

"He's your right hand these days, isn't he? If you've kept him around this long, I imagine he must be terribly useful to you. So you can have him back when you return with information." It wasn't the real reason she wanted him, of course. The real reason was that, no matter how much she'd told herself it wasn't her problem, she couldn't shake the memory of how *empty* Kaden had looked earlier.

Whatever Jevryn had him doing, it was clearly taking a toll on him. Maybe a break, even a short one, would do him some good. Tobi had been asking about him again. If anyone could bring some life back into Kaden, it was the kid.

Jevryn looked like he was about to argue—proving that either Nyx had hit a little closer to home than she'd realized about Kaden's usefulness, or Jevryn was simply a contrary bastard—when Griff said, "This seems reasonable."

Jevryn shot him a sideways glance.

"You will gather the necessary information and return here," Griff continued. "And then"—his attention swiveled to Nyx—"we will *discuss* the possibility of your also going to Kyvren."

Her stare connected with Jevryn's. "Fine," they agreed at almost the same time. *Ugh.* She could do without them saying anything in tandem ever again.

"Jevryn, I would speak with you a moment. Nyx, there is an issue involving Liya and shadow that I believe could do with your personal attention."

Nyx frowned and searched through Kaliaris, until she found Liya and Valedan locked in their room, and the rest of the Station's inhabitants glued to the hallway outside of it. Nyx started to ask Griff for an explanation, but he had a severe look in his eyes that made her decide she didn't want to be in the middle of whatever discussion was about to occur.

She left her father to Griff's tender mercies and went to find out why everyone was in the damn hallway.

19

Since Griff had mentioned there was an issue involving Liya, rather than talking to the others in front of the woman's room, Nyx settled for the expedient of dragging them through the Station and into the cafe. The relief that flashed across Seth's face when he saw her pretty much told her how Griff must have reacted when she and Jevryn had started fighting.

"You okay?" Seth asked her softly. She'd instinctively pulled him closest to her when she'd drawn them all into the room.

"Yeah, I just..." She shook her head. "I'll tell you about it later." Addressing the room at large, she asked, "What happened?"

A few minutes of everyone except Kaden excitedly talking over each other later, she had the whole story. Once she had it, she looked at Morgen. "Did you feel anything different when your shadow was"—what was the appropriate word for this?—"possessed?"

Morgen, never one to give an unreasoned answer, thought about it a few moments before shaking his head. "No. I wish I could say I did, but even when I grabbed it after Kaden pinned it, nothing *I* felt changed."

She nodded. She wasn't surprised. People didn't feel their own shadows. They were nothing more than a result of blocked light, which really begged the question of how they could be possessed and struck with knives.

Nyx turned to Kaden. "How did you know the shadow wasn't right?"

He shrugged. "It didn't smell right."

She frowned. "It had a scent?" She waved her hand before he could answer. "Never mind, of course it did. Liya's, right?"

Kaden gave her a look she didn't know how to interpret, and nodded. He certainly hadn't grown any more loquacious in his time away.

"How long was it here?"

He studied her again. "You don't know?"

The reminder that Kaliaris was oblivious to this particular problem irritated her. Along with sight, Kaliaris lacked scent as well. It had never seemed like a necessary sense before. "No. Do you know when it appeared or not?"

"A few seconds before Seth entered the cafe."

"And what were you talking about while it was here?" Given all the information Liya had had to threaten Rothbert with, Nyx had a feeling however she connected to shadows, she could hear through them.

Her friends all shared a glance, and no one answered her.

Nyx crossed her arms. "I kind of need to know, and if you don't tell me, Griff will."

It was Evra, surprisingly, who answered. "Morgen was complaining that he is not privy to every detail of your personal life." Evra said it so deadpan that it took all of Nyx's accumulated experience with the Amazon to recognize the snark behind the words.

Then they sank in and a sliver of unease fluttered through Nyx. "Did you happen to mention Jevryn by name during this conversation?"

Three shared, guilty looks confirmed as much.

"That's…never been a problem in the Station before," Morgen said. There was a question in his words, but she was fighting too much of a rising panic to answer it.

"Was anything else mentioned?"

Jevryn's voice rose in her mind, calmly reciting the number of descendants the other councilors had once had. His eyes, cold and unyielding as he'd asked, *Do you know how many of those descendants remains alive today? One. And she is standing before me now.*

"Only a mention of your irritation with the councilor and that it was of a personal nature," Evra said smoothly.

That wasn't too much, was it? No one was going to string together her parentage out of something so miniscule. Not if even Morgen, who knew a lot more than that, hadn't put it to—

Morgen's eyes went wide, flying to Nyx. "No."

"Do *not* say what you are thinking out loud." Even if she was relatively certain none of the present shadows were listening, both because if Liya's shadow had screamed, Nyx suspected getting stabbed had hurt her, and because if Kaden had noticed the abnormality in shadow the first time, he likely would have noticed if it had returned. Since he was once again impersonating a piece of furniture, she was guessing he didn't sense anything.

Morgen raised his hand. "Can we discuss it later?"

She blew out a breath. "Sure. Later." A long while and a couple of drinks later, hopefully. "If Jevryn comes out here, do *not* tell him about this." If Jevryn thought there was even a chance the secret of their connection had gotten out beyond the people in this room, she didn't trust that he wouldn't decide to contain it in the most final way possible. Because if word of it got out and someone decided to kill her, that death would take Griff and the Station with her.

Kaden was the only one who didn't immediately agree.

She pinned him with a stare. "Can you at least not tell him until he gets back?" She didn't understand where his obedience, his seemingly genuine loyalty, to Jevryn came from. She understood why he'd first gone with Jevryn, after Amentia Furor. He'd been at loose ends, and Jevryn had promised a better life for him and his sister and Morgen. One where they presumably weren't fugitives forever. But that alone didn't warrant true loyalty to Nyx's mind, especially when Jevryn had basically gotten Kaden into this mess to begin with.

"Gets back?" Kaden echoed.

Which was when she realized she had forgotten to fill them all in on a few key details. "Right. Jevryn is going to find out some information for me. I don't know how long it will take him to find it, but I don't trust him to do what I want without leverage." She looked at Kaden. "You're my leverage."

He stared at her.

"Hostage," she clarified. "You're my hostage. He gets you back when he brings me information and agrees to take me where I want to go."

If Jevryn had looked confused by Nyx's taking of Kaden as a hostage, Kaden himself looked…well, livid might be an understatement. "Can I talk to you in private?" he ground out.

When they were alone—in the meditation room, since Jevryn and Griff were still taking up the library—Kaden bit out, "What are you doing?"

That was honestly a great question. However, when backed into a corner, act like you know what you're doing. "I have to believe you're familiar with how a hostage situation works."

He spoke slowly, enunciating each word. "I don't have time for this."

Nyx raised her eyebrows. "You work for Jevryn. If he says you have time, you do, and he didn't put up much of a fight."

"Then you undo it."

"No." Maybe she would have, if it had just been about sticking it to Jevryn. But she remembered how shocked Morgen had looked when Kaden walked in, and she kind of thought Kaden owed him an explanation.

"*Nyx,*" he growled.

She threw up her hands. "It's a few days at most, you can deal with it. Your old room is where you left it and, in case you've forgotten, your best friend is where you left him, too. There's also an eight-year-old who turns nine in a few days who would be over the moon if you came to his party. He sent you an invitation, but you never answered it." He opened his mouth, but she didn't let him argue. "You look like shit, Kaden. Take the fucking vacation."

He had the kind of look on his face when she left that, if he'd been a different man, would have meant he was about to put his fist through the wall. But Kaden Moor didn't do uncontrolled explosions. He *did* stand right where she'd left him, though, as if he really wanted to violently explode but was pointedly choosing not to.

Nyx made her way to Liya's room, stopping to pick up three things—well, two things and one person—on the way: a first aid kit, a certain dagger she hadn't had cause to use since the Shadow Market, and Seth. She held the second out to the third.

Seth raised his hands. "Nyxi darling, I'm not sure what I've done to make you think I'm untrustworthy, but I don't need to be stabbed so the magic dagger can tell you whether I'm lying or not."

She rolled her eyes. "Veritas isn't for you, it's for Liya. A nice, invisible you is going to get her blood on the dagger and then tell me if she's lying or not. If it turns black she's lying, if it turns blue she's telling the truth."

They went up to Liya's room, Nyx visible, Seth not so much. She knocked out of politeness, even if she didn't quite feel like being polite. The door opened, revealing Valedan, who looked about as happy as everyone else in the Station right now.

Nyx held up the first aid kid and said, "Don't look at me like that. She's the one who went shadow-hopping in my Station. I can hardly be held responsible if someone noticed and decided to do something about it."

He relented, stepping aside to let her enter, then closing the door and watching as she carried the first aid kit to the bed. Liya was propped up on about half a dozen pillows, holding a folded towel against her shoulder.

"Let's see it," Nyx said.

"I'm fine," Liya answered. "The shadow always takes more damage than I do."

"I'm a Guardian. No one's going to be dying of infection on my watch."

Liya relented and let Nyx peel the towel off her shoulder. Both her eyes and Valedan's tracked the movement of the towel. It didn't surprise Nyx that people from a planet with something called a blood throne would be concerned with the movement of an item that had blood from one of them on it. And they were right to be. But unfortunately for them, they didn't see when Seth swiped the towel, the real thing replaced with illusion.

Nyx cleaned the wound which, as Liya had promised, wasn't as deep as Nyx would have expected. Then she stood and backed a few steps from the bed, until she felt Seth's hand at her back.

"I'm glad you weren't seriously injured," she said, "but what the hell were you doing spying on my friends?" Nyx was angry, and she didn't bother trying to hide the fact. "When you came here, I *knew* you were running from something that could likely cause me prob-lems. I gave you a place to stay anyway, and I didn't push you for answers. I only pried when Valedan showed up, and even then I kept it to public records and only looked far enough to ensure you weren't putting anyone else here in danger. I respected your privacy, but you haven't done the same for me."

Liya winced.

"Do not talk to her like that," Valedan warned.

"It's okay, Vale. She's right." To Nyx, Liya said, "I'm sorry."

Nyx wasn't entirely sure that sorry cut it right now. It hadn't been until the poker night that she'd suspected Liya's affinity for shadows was slightly more than just an affinity, and it wasn't until her display with the guards that she'd been certain. Now she was kicking herself for not realizing just how dangerous that talent could be. She'd been distracted—by the Harvester, by the drama of Liya's situation, by knowing she would have to contact Jevryn—and hadn't put together that Liya might be able to do more with shadows than simply move them around. That she might be able to see and hear through them, and from multiple rooms away to boot.

"Have you spied on us before?"

"No."

Seth tapped once on Nyx's back, indicating Veritas had read that answer for truth in Liya's blood.

"Not before today," Liya said earnestly. "I swear it. When I came here, Kalvar said I could trust you, and I did. I haven't used the shadows against anyone here. I mean, I did cheat at the poker game, but that was just a bit of fun. I never did anything more until today. I only wanted to make certain Rothbert hadn't snuck back into the Station—"

Nyx wanted to snap that it was impossible to sneak into the Station, except Liya had just proved otherwise.

"—but then I heard Councilor A-Morridahn's name and I was curious. I tried to get into the library, but I couldn't."

That was…interesting. Had it been something Jevryn had done that kept Liya out, or was it possible for the Station to repel Liya's abilities? The Station's responses were hyper-keyed to Nyx's emotions, and when Jevryn was around her focus tended to narrow to a tunnel vision. It wasn't beyond the realm of possibility that she'd locked the room down thoroughly enough to keep Liya out. She just had no idea *how* she would have done it.

"So I decided to wait in the cafe and see if I could learn anything. Or to see if Councilor A-Morridahn actually came out," Liya finished in a rush, her expression earnest.

Nyx narrowed her eyes. The confession felt real—the slight edge of guilt, the almost innocence of it—but this, not being a simple yes or no, wasn't something Veritas could distinguish for her. There was also something in the words and Liya's manner that was clearly trying to prompt Nyx to answer Liya's unasked questions. Such as was Councilor A-Morridahn truly here and, if so, why?

It wasn't magic—nothing like Valedan's charm or Morgen's influence—only artfully directed human guile, made all the more potent because Nyx felt certain the emotions behind it were genuine. That the Liya who had just begun to open up around Nyx and her friends, the Liya who'd helped Kalvar study for months, was a real side of Liya. But now that Valedan had returned, she was sliding neatly back into the Liya she was more accustomed to being —one Nyx was certain was very good at ferreting out information and using it to her—and Valedan's—advantage.

Nyx considered her next question. Liya had truthfully answered that she hadn't spied on any of them before, but there was wiggle room in the definition of "spying". "Have you ever made a shadow take a canine form and either follow, or simply remain near, me or the Station?"

Liya frowned. "No."

Seth tapped her once, and she could feel the curiosity in his touch. Nyx let out a breath. The black dog wasn't Liya's. And judging by Seth's curiosity, it wasn't his either. Not that she'd ever really thought it was. But it begged the question of if it even existed at all.

Nyx cleared her throat, which was Seth's cue to return the real bloody towel to the place the illusion currently occupied. She met Valedan's gaze and held it for a moment, then Liya's. "If either of you spy on anyone in my Station again, you will no longer be welcome here, and you can find another way back to Alzherra, because I won't be providing it. Am I clear?" Before Valedan's arrival, Nyx would never have thrown Liya out because she would have had nowhere else to go. She had Valedan now, and her life more or less sorted out, and Nyx highly doubted the Blood Prince of Alzherra couldn't find a way to get them home without Earth's Station. Not when portal stones seemed to be the universe's least kept secret.

Liya nodded. "I understand. I *am* sorry."

Nyx sighed. "I know." She got as far as the door before Liya's curiosity overcame her better sense.

"*Is* Councilor A-Morridahn truly here?"

"Why do you care?"

Nyx thought Liya's eyes would fall out of her head, they widened so much. "Jevryn A-Morridahn is hardly *ever* seen. The other councilors are at least approachable, if you consider that it takes a pristine claim to royalty or power and navigating through a galaxy's worth of obstacles to gain even the possibility of an audience with one 'approachable'. But it can be done.

"No one, and I mean *no one*, outside Councilor Jevryn A-Morridahn's direct oversight has seen him in centuries. Do not get me wrong, most of the planets under his purview—Alzherra included —prefer it that way, as he rarely interferes or brings down sanctions, but it does beg the question of what he is doing on *Earth* of all places, talking to you."

Nyx didn't answer. Mostly because she was trying to think of *how* to answer, but Liya seemed to take it as an invitation to continue.

"I would say he was here for Morgen, except Morgen doesn't seem to be worried that he's a wanted fugitive and a councilor is on-planet, and unless I am very much mistaken, that was Kaden Moor downstairs. Who appears to be working for Councilor A-Morridahn."

Nyx could have kicked herself. About eight times over now, but at least Liya's inquiry proved she'd been telling the truth about not spying before today. She clearly didn't know Jevryn had been here during Nyx's memory issues, or that Maruca had. And it wasn't as if Nyx didn't know, before now, that Liya must have realized who Morgen was. Liya knew where Kalvar came from. She suspected Kalvar had explained Morgen's presence by saying he helped him escape Arkadia, and since Morgen hadn't been worried about it, Nyx hadn't been either.

Nyx had never worried about having Liya here, because it was easy to keep her—and anyone else—from learning anything they shouldn't. That lack of concern was feeling a lot like hubris now and she was scrambling to compensate for it. Liya was just curious, but that curiosity was dangerous. Especially when Nyx suspected it stemmed from the fact that she was currently desperate to win her way back into the Alzherran royal family's good graces. If the Blood Matron liked clever people, who was more clever than someone who had information on the—apparently—most reclusive member of the All Council?

But cleverness, in this case, was a short road to disaster. Nyx couldn't send them back to Alzherra, where they might decide to talk about the Earth Guardian who liked to yell at Jevryn, and who got away with doing so. Not to mention, if Riven Gare Ru worked *only* for the Alzherran royal family, she was going to need Valedan if she was going to have any hope of Riven talking to her.

But by far the worst thing roiling in her gut was the certainty that Valedan and Liya were risks Jevryn would not want to take. She had no doubt he would use them for the expedience of ensuring Riven's cooperation. She just wasn't certain what he would do with them after.

"If we could only speak with him," Liya was saying, "I'm certain that—"

"You're certain that *what*?" Nyx hardly recognized her own voice, harsh and cool. She sounded...older, she realized. She sounded more like Jevryn. "What do you imagine you have to say to him that he would care to hear? He's over nine-hundred years old for stars' sake. He concerns himself with very little and trust me when I say that what he *does* concern himself with, you don't want to be in the way of."

Because he'll view you as nothing. An obstacle, or a tool. Or both. He'll use you for the latter and he'll rid himself of you when you become the former.

But Liya was still young enough to not care. "It has to do with the object Riven's ancestor made, right? That's why he's here? He's the person you contacted to ask about Kyvren."

Nyx ran through her options. They were too curious and too motivated for their own good, and wouldn't let it go. They thought they wanted to meet Jevryn? Fine. "*If* Councilor A-Morridahn decides he needs to speak with you, he will. Until then, you are both on your best behavior. Do not discuss his presence here with anyone. That includes your guards and Rothbert. Because I can assure you of one thing: Councilor A-Morridahn dislikes it when something he has taken an interest in has an obvious security breach."

That, at least, had the gratifying effect of giving them pause.

20

Nyx left Liya's room. Once they rounded the bend in the hallway, Seth reappeared. He raised an eyebrow at her and she shook her head. No questions yet. She took him up to their room, blacked out the windows, and killed the lights, plunging them into absolute darkness.

"Why Nyxi," he purred in her ear, "I had no idea that stabbing, subterfuge, and threats put you in the mood for clandestine assignations."

"'Clandestine assignations' is redundant, and you can't see it but I'm rolling my eyes."

"It may be redundant, but it sounds cooler than 'assignations' by itself. Am I to take it, given this lovely darkness, that you have no idea how to recognize an infected shadow?"

"I was thinking of them as possessed, but infected shadow has a nice ring to it."

"So that's a *no*, then, Nyxi darling?"

"It's a *no*." His resultant lack of answer had a weighty air to it, and she smiled. "On a scale of one to ten, how pissed off are you that someone else figured out how to trick the Station's senses before you did?"

"A thirteen. She wasn't even *trying* to trick its senses. She doesn't know they exist."

She reached out and gently petted his hair. "There, there, it will be alright." She could feel the heat of his expression and burst out laughing. "You should see your face right now."

"*You* can't even see my face right now."

"No, but I can imagine it, and it's hilarious."

"I'm glad you find my suffering amusing."

"I have to find something amusing. Otherwise I'm left with the reality of the royal spies whose shadow movements I can't track, and the fact that I just took my ex-boyfriend hostage to get my father to do what I want."

"Sure, and I've got some ocean-front property for sale in Earth Between."

"I beg your pardon?"

"You took him hostage because you feel sorry for him."

She wished she could see his expression, because she couldn't tell by the tone of his voice what he was thinking. "And how do you feel about that?"

"Well, he is going to bring down the cheery Station atmosphere with all the silent brooding and glowering, but I think you really succeeded in pissing him off with the whole hostage thing, so I'm going to choose to enjoy his irritation."

"You're a veritable saint," she said dryly.

"I know. It's a burden being this perfect, but I try not to make others feel inferior."

"If you keep this up, I'm going to strain my eyes from how hard they're rolling."

"Would you rather talk about Jevryn? Because I'm dying to know why Griff tore out of Liya's room like he thought you were going to die."

Nyx tried to play it off easy. "Griff just doesn't like it when we argue."

"Uh-huh. Was the nature of the argument verbal or physical?"

"Technically physical."

"Define 'technically'."

"You know how the councilors have some control over the Stations? It was kind of a contest of wills over that control."

"Why?"

Nyx held her arms out, despite the fact he couldn't see it. "I don't know. He was irritated, I was irritated, we decided to express the irritation. It was therapeutic. Griff panicked a little when I picked up Jevryn's sword. Admittedly, the thing has some weird-ass magic powering it, but nothing bad happened. And I got what I wanted, so…" She trailed off. When Seth didn't pick up the thread of conversation, she prodded, "What are you thinking?"

"Nothing you'll like."

"Such as?"

"Please don't punch me in the stomach."

"Will you just spit it out?"

"You and Jevryn are…very similar in some ways." She punched him—lightly—on the shoulder. He caught her wrist and spun her so her back was to his chest, trapping her against him.

"Next time, remind me to make it a blanket no-punching-in-general request." He rubbed his cheek against hers. "I didn't mean it as a bad thing. I just mean that the two of you are probably going to keep clashing due to the similarity."

"And what exactly is that similarity?" she ground out.

"You're both…prickly."

"Prickly?"

"Mmm, like a cactus."

"I know what the word means."

"Like a cholla cactus," he continued. "Get too close and the spines literally jump out to embed themselves in you. Try not to let him cut you too much."

"You do realize you're the one who mouthed off to him first, right?"

She felt his shoulders rise and fall against her as he shrugged. "That's my job. You're supposed to let me mouth off to him so you don't have to."

"If I let you mouth off to him, you'll provoke him into murder, and then I'll have to spend my life locked in a feud with him to avenge your death."

"Well, as long as you're avenging me, I suppose it's fine."

She elbowed him in the stomach. Honestly, if she didn't, he'd be disappointed. He grunted and squeezed her tighter. "Now that we've established I'll avenge your wrongful death, can you let me go? I need to go talk to Kaliaris and find out if there's anything I can do to block Liya's shadows, and I need you to go let everyone know that, for the time being, it's better to be safe than sorry on the private conversations."

"I think you're getting a little ahead of yourself," Seth said. "There's this one teensy thing you've neglected to mention."

She frowned. She couldn't think of anything...

"You asked Liya about black shadow dogs?"

Oh. That. "It's probably nothing. I've never really seen it. But I keep catching flashes out of the corner of my eye sometimes."

"When is it ever nothing?" Seth protested. "And why didn't you tell me?"

"Honestly? Because I'm not sure it's actually there, and whenever you think I won't notice, you keep looking at me like I'm a fragile flower whose mind is about to splinter apart at any given moment. I didn't really want to tell you I might be seeing things."

"If you think you might be seeing things," Seth said, his voice tight, "after your mind kind of did splinter apart and get put back together, you should tell someone. Like your concerned boyfriend."

Why? So he could *be concerned*? She was already aware the thing might not be real. "Well, now you know."

He sighed and knocked his forehead on her shoulder. She patted his head, but refrained from saying *there, there* again.

"If you see it again, tell me."

She answered his sigh with one of her own. "Fine."

***

Seth left to talk to Morgen, Evra, and Kalvar, and Nyx left for the Station's Heart. Kaliaris let her in without a fuss, carefully floating her to the floor of the vine-filled enclosure.

"How did Liya's shadows go unnoticed? And was it me or Jevryn who kept her out of the library?"

<Greetings to you, too, Nyx Fortuna. My day has been lovely, thank you for inquiring.>

Nyx blinked. Of all the times to develop a sense of humor, Kaliaris chose *now*? "Hi, Kaliaris, how was your day? Was it at all impacted by the fact something can sneak around your premises without you noticing?"

A whisper of air rustled through Kaliaris' vines like a sigh. <Sight is not a sense I possess, unless I am looking through yours or Griff's eyes, when you allow it. I cannot *see* shadow. Perhaps outside I could feel it, were the day warm enough, as a shadow is a type of shade and provides some measure of cooler air, but that is not the case indoors. And until your Kaden pinned one with a dagger, I had never before known a shadow capable of making sound.

<So that, Nyx Fortuna, is how she snuck around unnoticed. As for how she was kept from the library, that is more complicated. But the simplest explanation is that the room was enclosed in a ward of death magic. Liya's magic, like most magics, is based in life and thus unable to cross such a boundary.>

Nyx frowned. "I didn't feel that boundary." Shouldn't she have felt it if Jevryn had created a death wall in her Station?

<Perhaps you should have Jevryn explain the mechanics of it to you. Is that not what fathers are supposed to do? Explain things?>

Damn, K, way to cut straight to the heart. "He's not a father, he's an unwilling DNA contributor. About his death magic—are you capable of containing it?"

Kaliaris hesitated before answering. She had the distinct sense, through their bond, that they were considering quibbling with her about something she'd said. Maybe they'd taken offense to her description of Jevryn as a "DNA contributor", though she couldn't fathom why they should be concerned with it.

In the end, though, Kaliaris only said, <No. Jevryn's magic cannot be contained because life cannot contain death. Leastways, it *ought* not be able to.> Kaliaris' vines gave a rippling shudder. <The Salyrians were a truly frightening species. The planet that gave birth to them was... Well, let us say that even in this undeath I and my kind find ourselves in, Lethe-Alihana is counted strange even amongst us.>

Lethe-Alihana. The name settled into Nyx, like a piece of herself she hadn't realized she was looking for. "Jevryn's planet—they're one of you? One of the Stations?" She didn't know why she hadn't put it together before. She'd known his homeworld was gone, had been sad knowing she would never have a chance to set foot on the world where half her heritage came from, so it should have clicked for her that the planet's soul, having been Harvested, still existed somewhere. She tried very hard not to dwell on why it filled her with longing—on why she would want to visit there—just as she had refused to dwell on why she hadn't been the slightest bit interested in finding out where her mother had been born.

<They are…not accessible in the manner most of us are.>

"Meaning?"

<Meaning that, as Altiran belonged to Koral, Lethe-Alihana belongs to Jevryn A-Morridahn. Forgive me. I failed to consider that you might have some emotional attachment to them.>

That Kaliaris had apologized at all spoke to the influence she and Griff had had on them over the past few months. It was a shocking enough occurrence, coming on the heels of their almost-joke in greeting, that Nyx decided to overlook the fact they'd basically called the Salyrian half of her heritage an affront to nature. Naturally, having felt like an oddball her entire life, she would discover one of her homeworlds was thought strange.

"It's fine," she told Kaliaris. "It doesn't matter." She certainly wasn't going to tell Jevryn she'd like to meet the soul of the planet he'd grown up on. She wondered if Lethe-Alihana found it comforting to have one of their people around, or if they resented Jevryn for their current condition. Kaliaris' hatred for the Council had only been tempered by Nyx's promise to try to free them from their current existence.

"So Jevryn's magic can't be contained inside the Station, and you can't recognize when Liya's possessing shadows." Nyx didn't know if possession was an accurate term for what Liya was doing, but she'd been too angry at her to bother asking about the ins and outs of how her magic worked. "Is there another way to prevent her shadows from flitting around unseen?" She wanted to believe Liya's promise that she wouldn't use the shadows to spy within the Station again. But Nyx was a lot less trusting than she used to be.

<You could ask Jevryn about death magic.>

Nyx snorted. "Pass. Any other ideas?"

<You could ask Jevryn for another set of binding bracelets.>

"Any ideas that don't involve me asking Jevryn for favors?" Or putting magical restraints on a friend, even if she was currently angry with said friend.

Kaliaris' vines rippled in a sigh again, as if Nyx was ruining all their fun. <You recently had a conversation with your Seth in total darkness. I presume this is because you understand that shadows

require light to form. For while shadows are a type of darkness, darkness itself is not a shadow.>

"My best option is to have every important conversation in total darkness?"

<That, or have your Kaden present. He seems quite adept at sensing the abnormal shadows.>

Her choices were her not-quite-father, plunging herself into complete darkness, or her ex-boyfriend. "Guess it's a good thing I'm not afraid of the dark," she muttered. She started to leave, then stopped, glancing over at the clear glass through which she could see Laiveran. He sat on a soft, faded brown couch, flipping through a deck of cards, Fangs curled on his lap.

Lately, whenever she came down here, she felt uncomfortably like a zoo attendee observing an animal in its habitat. He didn't know she was here—the glass was soundproof and one-way, allowing her to see in, while from the inside it simply looked like the interior room of what she suspected had once been Laiveran's home. Fangs' steady company had calmed Laiveran's confused outbursts, but Nyx still didn't quite know what to *do* with him.

And yet when she came here, she always felt obligated to interact with him. She walked to the door set into the glass wall.

<You do not need to speak with him,> Kaliaris said. <He doesn't understand, and he is not in distress. Regrettably.>

"I know." But Nyx wasn't entirely convinced. She knocked, watched Laiveran's head come up, watched him place the deck of cards down and scratch behind Fangs' ears as he asked her, "Who could that be, sweet girl?"

For the last few months, it was always some version of this when she knocked. A mild surprise, but lack of concern. And when Laiveran opened the door, he wore his usual expression, the one that said he thought he'd seen her somewhere before, but couldn't quite place where. Then his expression cleared, as it always did, and he said, "Oh, you must be Nyaera's friend, from work. You'll have to forgive me, I can't remember your name."

"It's Nyx," she answered, as she had the first time, letting his mind place her into a category it could understand. She accepted his usual smiling invitation to come inside, sat in the same chair by the door that she always chose, and listened to him fill the air with unimportant chatter as he went about making tea. It was the same experience every time, with hardly any variation, and she didn't trust it.

When Laiveran had first come here, she'd treated him a bit like someone with Alzheimer's. She'd known that wasn't what he had, but she had been able to manage him with few blowups by thinking of him that way. But recently, there had been no blowups. No sudden fits of rage, no moments of mistaking Nyx for his dead wife. If she asked him about Nyaera, he would smile and laugh, and say his wife was putting extra hours in on one of her projects. He never would say which project. If Nyx asked about the Harvester, or anything related to it, he would frown and say that he'd never heard of such a thing, and had she perhaps confused him with someone else?

From the outside, it was easy to believe he'd lapsed into a point in time in his mind—one when he'd inhabited the house Kaliaris had replicated for him—and was living an unspecified day over and over again. He never faltered. When she asked Kaliaris what Laiveran did when she was gone, he inevitably gave her a dry recitation that involved sleeping, eating, calisthenics, reading, and cards. Or some variation thereof.

Never once had Kaliaris noticed Laiveran doing anything out of the ordinary. Never once had he attempted to hurt Nyx or escape. And yet…

Laiveran put a filled teapot on a tray with cups and saucers, carried it over to the small table between the couch and Nyx's chair. "So," he said, after pouring tea and handing her one of the cups, "what brings you by?"

Nyx had given a variety of answers to this question in the past. Vague-sounding reasonings she imagined a barely known acquaintance might give. He always accepted them in stride. She'd found she could hold a pointless conversation with him for over an hour, a multitude of words spoken and yet nothing ever truly said. But she could never shake the feeling that there was more beneath Laiveran's easy placidity.

Maybe it was that suspicion, the one she couldn't quite shake, that had her drawing the Harvester from beneath her shirt in answer to Laiveran's question. She thinned the Hiding on it, allowing him to notice it. To see it. To feel it. "I came to ask you about this, actually."

Beyond the walls of the room, Kaliaris hissed. Whether because they disliked being faced with the thing that had destroyed them and trapped their soul, or because they thought Nyx's showing it to Laiveran was a move far beyond foolish, she couldn't say.

Laiveran looked at the Harvester, his expression one of mild interest that anyone might show at someone presenting an item to them for inspection. But there was a tenseness around his eyes, an echo of that hunger she'd seen when he'd taken her to the prison on Lehine. He swallowed slowly. "And what is this?" he asked, his voice as mild as the look in his eyes.

"You don't know?" Nyx asked innocently. "I thought you'd recognize it."

Outside the room, Kaliaris' vines gave a pulse of concern. She could practically hear him demand to know what she thought she was doing. That would have been difficult to answer, as she didn't quite know. She just knew that she'd gone months without getting a single reaction from Laiveran that she thought was genuine, and she was willing to push the envelope a bit, so to speak.

Laiveran shook his head. "I'm afraid I don't."

"But Nyaera told me you were familiar with this type of magic," Nyx said. He flinched at his wife's name. A minuscule movement, but it was there. "That you could identify it. You haven't even looked at it."

He shrugged. The movement was stiff. "It does not look like anything with which I am familiar. I'm sorry if you were led to believe otherwise." He stood, picking up the tea tray. "I am afraid I have an early start in the morning, if you don't mind?"

"Of course." She tucked the Harvester behind her shirt and exited the room. On the other side, she looked through the one-way glass. Laiveran carried the tea tray to the kitchen, setting about the business of clearing away the cups and saucers as if nothing was wrong. But his mouth was a tight line and his hands, when they gripped the cups and saucers, kept tightening to the point his knuckles whitened.

She didn't know what kind of game Laiveran was playing—if he simply didn't want her questioning him about the Harvester all the time, trying to get him to give away its secrets, or if he was attempting to lull her into a false sense of security with an eye towards escape—but she did know one thing: he knew exactly what the Harvester was. He knew exactly who *she* was. And he was pretending, every day he woke up here, that he didn't know where he was or why.

When she returned to the Station proper and found Jevryn had already left, she told herself that it was just as well. She wasn't in the mood to talk to him again anyway.

21

Seth couldn't believe what he was about to do, and that was saying something. He had, after all, done a fair number of arguably stupid things in his life. But standing in front of Kaden Moor's closed door, Seth decided this might rank near the top of that list of stupid things.

Ah, well. No reason to start making smart decisions at this point in his life. He raised his fist and knocked. A few seconds later the door opened—Seth hadn't been certain it would—revealing a glowering Kaden. The man was *always* glowering. It was a miracle he didn't strain his facial muscles. That expression shifted, for the briefest of seconds before Kaden covered it, into relief.

And if Kaden was relieved to see Seth, that meant he'd expected Nyx or Morgen. The two people who were, presumably, the reason he hadn't left his room since he'd been taken hostage the previous afternoon. For a moment they simply stared at each other, and then Seth flashed him a grin. "You aren't going to invite me in?"

A muscle clenched in Kaden's jaw, but he stepped to the side and held out his arm in invitation. Still a man of few words, Seth noted, strolling into the room. It was utilitarian in the extreme. Considering the Station attempted to give its inhabitants whatever would make them most comfortable, some might find the room unexpected, but Seth wasn't surprised that minimalism was Kaden Moor's happy place.

Kaden struck him as the kind of person who preferred everything to be straightforward, black-and-white. A lot of Enforcers did. They had to, because most people weren't good at being told *be here, do this, eat that, wear this* every day of their lives. Seth was still surprised Morgen had lasted as an Enforcer as long as he had, and suspected it was only because Kaden and Maruca had formed his unit, and they'd moved from regular duty to special assignment fairly early on in their careers.

Kaden, on the other hand… Well, Seth also wasn't surprised Kaden was still working for Jevryn, despite the fact it was clearly sucking the soul out of him. Guy hadn't had a lot of soul to begin with, and the extra removal was telling.

"You should consider sprucing up the place. Maybe a nice painting, over here." Seth framed the wall across from the bed with his hands. "It practically begs for an ocean panorama."

Another brief flash of of emotion crossed Kaden's face and his eyes narrowed, like he was trying to discern if Seth was making a pointed dig. Maybe the guy had a problem with oceans that Seth didn't know about.

"Or a lovely forest. Deep dark cave. Gaping maw of the abyss? Let me know when I'm getting close to what you find peaceful and relaxing."

Kaden folded his arms across his chest. "I didn't realize you'd taken up interior design in your spare time."

"And here I thought you had no sense of humor."

"What do you want, Seth?"

That was a complex question with a simple answer: Seth wanted the people he cared about to be happy. Right now, Morgen—though he would never say it—was unhappy because the guy who might as well be his brother, who had been no-contact for the last six months, had reappeared without warning and failed to give him the time of day. Nyx was unhappy because she was good at taking responsibility for things that weren't her problem, and she likely felt responsible for Kaden's having taken himself off to do whatever he'd done that put the current dead look in his eyes.

"I want a truce. I know I'm intimidating, but you don't have to hide in here on account of little old me." Seth jerked his thumb toward the door. "I can be on my best behavior."

Kaden lifted his eyebrows. Seth shrugged. Yes, he was needling him, but it was needling with a purpose. Unfortunately, while Kaden looked like the stereotypical male easily bullied into taking action by having his bravery questioned, there was a little more going on underneath the hood.

"Your best friend is too proud to admit it, but he's upset that you've hardly spoken to him."

Kaden took a few moments to respond. "Is he my best friend? Or is he yours now too?"

Yours now too. From Kaden's perspective, it probably looked like Seth had slipped neatly into his life. Seth had his best friend, his ex-girlfriend, and the Station he'd lived in for a brief time.

Seth understood that feeling—like you were slowly losing everything. He'd been feeling it for months, every time he looked at Nyx and she wasn't really there, because she was too hyperfocused on solving a problem. The difference was, he hadn't let go. He hadn't walked away. He'd done that once and learned his lesson. Kaden still didn't seem to have figured that one out.

"Friendship isn't a limited resource, but it is a two-way street. Try fixing some of your bridges or you aren't going to have any left."

He headed for the door.

"How many bridges are you suggesting I repair?"

Seth paused. "Primarily? The oldest one. But if you wanted to fix the other one, Nyx would be your friend if you let her."

"And if I don't want her to be?"

Seth wasn't going to shed any tears over the fact. Even if what Kaden meant was that he didn't want to be around Nyx because friendship wasn't what he wanted from her. They both knew he wasn't getting anything else. "Then I'd tell you that she's busy with Arrivals until noon, and the rest of us will be in the gym."

Seth could tell, by the way Kaden's jaw *didn't* tighten, that he had him. He left, to give Kaden time to come to terms with it, stopping on the way to the gym to drag a protesting Kalvar away from his books.

"I left the mercenary life for a reason," the kid complained as they headed over to the mat-covered section of the floor, where Morgen, Evra, Liya, and Valedan were already stretching. Apparently, having her secrets outed made Liya less shy rather than more.

"Physical activity is good for the brain," Morgen told Kalvar. Evra nodded in enthusiastic agreement.

"What they mean," Seth said, "is less bitching, more stretching."

Kalvar rolled his eyes and plopped onto the mats with a groan. Five minutes later, Kaden joined them.

22

Nyx spent the first three days after Kaden's arrival trying and failing to find much pertinent information on Kyvren. If she was going to go there, she wanted to be prepared. But where she could find entire libraries of books on other planets, subjects ranging from things as macro as their environments and ecosystems and social structures, to things as micro as a feud between two families in a specific time period, Kyvren was nothing more than a handful of paragraphs in various encyclopedia entries.

Those paragraphs covered the basics, identifying Kyvren as an export planet, occupied by the Dwarven race, known for its ore supplies. The Meerkin were hardly more than a footnote, named only as "prior inhabitants of a vicious nature", which set Nyx's teeth on edge. The planet had one habitable continent boasting two mountain ranges on opposing sides. The northern half was dominated by thick forest that gradually transitioned to grasslands on the southern half.

She did find a reference to a single scientific article on the planet's "scourge" and, after tweaking her search of the Archives multiple times, managed to track it down. The "scourge" turned out to be none other than the fire rains Vorex had spoken of. When he'd told his story to Nyx, she'd been envisioning literal fire falling from the sky. Once she'd read the article, she determined that hearing "fire rains" had to have been a result of her translator spell doing a poor job.

Rather than flaming raindrops, the fire rains were actually a very basic life-form. Her translator had likely gotten "fire" as a mistranslation of the life-form's color—red—and "rains" as a poor translation of its means of reproduction—via spores that were shot high into the air and then rained down. Called *unda* by the Meerkin, the description in the article put Nyx in mind of nothing so much as quarter-sized amoebas. They were almost liquid in appearance and could cover vast quantities of grounds at high speed via a mechanism similar to pseudopods.

During most of Kyvren's annual cycle, the unda combined in large colonies in deep rock basins formed by the planet's chitin ore, where they appeared like a single organism. During this phase they were dormant unless disturbed, and Nyx deduced these must be the "fire pools" Vorex had spoken of. Individual unda could not survive long if separated from the larger colony, and during the unda's non-dormant phase, the colonies traveled in waves across the land.

That non-dormant phase was during the planet's spring. As temperatures warmed, the unda entered a high-energy state and traveled from the pools in streams, seeking any life-form—plant or animal—that produced magic. They then fed off that magic, resulting in the death of the organism that had born it. Once the unda had ingested a sufficient amount of magic they reproduced, jetting spores into the air, which then rained down seeking magic of their own. If they found it, they grew into the adult stage and formed colonies of their own. If not, they died off shortly thereafter.

The armor the Meerkin made from the chitin ore was the only effective known defense against the unda. They ate any magical defenses, including wards and protective spells. The armor worked because, as the unda made their homes in the ore basins during their dormant cycle, contact with it made them slip back into their dormant state.

Nyx finished reading the article, which concluded with the suggestion that the planet be labeled as restricted access with extensive decontamination procedures required for any person or object leaving the planet, to "prevent the spread of a life-form that would no doubt flourish invasively on every planet in the known universe."

The article naturally sent her looking for a few pieces of information that would be critical if they were going to be traveling to Kyvren. Such as, was the inhabitable continent of Kyvren currently in the spring season? How long were the days and were the unda active at night? How were the visiting humans going to survive on the planet if it did happen to be spring on Kyvren?

Naturally, she couldn't find any of the answers, even with Griff helping her search the Archives. It simply wasn't publicly available knowledge. The Dwarves had been dropped on Kyvren centuries ago, the Meerkin ousted, and it had been a largely shuttered planet ever since.

By the time Tobi's birthday party rolled around, Nyx was frustrated by the lack of available information, and starting to get anxious awaiting Jevryn's return. She hadn't imagined it would take him very long to find out what they needed to know, but she was starting to think she'd been overly optimistic.

She hadn't even done anything useful by keeping Kaden here. He avoided her like the plague, and from what she could tell via occasional check-ins through the Station, his time off didn't seem to be doing anything to improve his mental state.

He went through the motions, spending most of his time with Morgen, though some of that time surprisingly included Seth in their number. She didn't even think any fists were thrown between them outside of sparring matches in the gym. She wondered if part of that was because Kaden was still very much a walking automaton. Whatever was wrong with him, it wasn't going to be fixed by a few days off. A fact made more obvious when she went to the cafe to leave for Tobi's party, and Kaden wasn't there.

She glanced over the assembled group—Morgen, Evra, Kalvar, and Seth—before settling on Morgen. He hesitated before saying, "He's not coming."

It reminded her of the time they'd been gathered to go out to Dead Earth and Kaden hadn't been there. Only this time, she didn't think he was going to come strolling in late, claiming he'd lost track of time.

He wasn't coming? The hell he wasn't. She'd told Tobi he would be there, and she wasn't going to ruin a kid's birthday by showing up without his favorite person. "Wait here, I'll get him."

She ran up the stairs, down the hall to Kaden's room, and

knocked. No answer. Knocked again. No answer. She pushed the door open. He sat on the edge of his bed, feet flat on the floor, elbows resting on his thighs, gaze on his clasped hands.

"We're going to be late."

He shrugged. "Then you should leave."

"I told Tobi you'd be there. He's going to be disappointed."

The first hint of emotion she'd seen since he'd arrived flashed in his eyes. Annoyance or anger, she wasn't sure which, but at least it was something. "And whose fault will that be?"

"Yours, if you don't get your ass downstairs."

His teeth clenched, a muscle ticking along his jaw. But he stood up, walked to the door. Paused at her side, so he had to turn his head when he spoke. "Don't make any more promises on my behalf. And Nyx? The next time you think I look like I need a vacation, remind yourself it is none of your damn business. I'm not one of your strays."

He walked away and she let him without giving a response, because what was she supposed to say to that? That she'd cared about him once and she didn't have a switch she could flip to make herself not? That she found it easier to care now that he wasn't a part of her life anymore?

Both were true, but neither changed the fact that he was right. It was none of her damn business. She went downstairs, where everyone except Seth had already headed out the door.

He flashed her his trademark grin. "You have such a way with people, Nyxi darling. He's in a great mood."

She started to snap something back, but then the fight fell out of her. She didn't have anything in her at the moment.

"That bad, huh?" He slipped his arm around her waist as they walked out. "What happened?"

She blew out a breath. "I was reminded that his wellbeing is none of my concern and told to mind my own damn business."

Seth laughed. "You never mind your own business." He dodged the elbow she attempted to jab into his stomach, slid his arm around her again.

"It doesn't bother you?" she asked.

He shrugged. "It's not bad that you care. Anyone can tell the guy's not right. But I don't think it's anything you can fix."

"Maybe not, but—" She froze as a flash of black to her left

caught her eye. This time, she didn't see a glimpse of a dog disappearing among the trees. This time, bright blue eyes burned like pools of fire in a face that wasn't quite canine. It stood on all fours, a massive beast of solid muscle with shoulders the height of her own. If she stood in front of it, those flame-blue eyes would be even with hers.

It was difficult to pinpoint the way—aside from the size—the creature wasn't *quite* dog-like. It's face bore most of the similarities —long muzzle, whiskers, but a slightly wider face than most dog breeds. The ears, though sharp and pointed, were too short and oddly shaped. It's body was barrel-shaped and stocky, yet for all that it looked nimble. A thin ridge traced the length of its spine. As if the creature noticed her looking, that ridge snapped up, revealing a line of spikes that continued down the long tail. Its lips split in a macabre grin, revealing rows of sharp fangs.

None of that, though, was what caught her attention most. No, it was the way the black dog didn't seem to be fully corporeal. The sleek black of its hide felt half-shadow, which was why she had wondered if it was Liya's. It *looked* as if its paws touched the ground, and yet there was something in its stance that made it appear more as if it hovered just above it. And there was something about the blue of its eyes that nagged at her.

Softly, she asked Seth, "Do you see it?"

"Oh, I see it."

Well, at least she wasn't hallucinating. "What is it?"

"No idea. But I don't think it wants to make friends."

It begged the question, "What do you think it does want?"

Seth didn't answer. Voices sounded down the path. The beast's head snapped in that direction and then it was gone, loping away in complete silence over ground strewn with fallen, brittle leaves. It ducked behind a large tree and didn't reemerge.

Seth took a step forward, but Nyx grabbed his arm. "There's no point, it's gone."

But, this being the first time he'd seen the dog, he naturally had to go check for himself. He came back, a pinched expression on his face. "It's gone."

She heroically restrained herself from saying *I told you so* just as the voices they'd heard crested the hill just down the path, and Morgen and Evra emerged.

"We came to see what was taking so long," Evra informed them. "Why are you standing in the middle of the road?"

Nyx shrugged. "It's a nice road?" she offered. Surely, heading to a kid's ninth birthday party wasn't the time to bring up spectral dogs.

Seth, apparently, thought it was the perfect time. "Do either of you know what this is?" He summoned a life-size illusion of the dog in less than a second.

Morgen shook his head. Evra's eyebrows drew together in a frown and she walked around the illusion, studying it. "No," she said finally. "It bears some similarity to the greshas on Scythia, but only in size and general form. Greshas do not have the ridge spikes, or these here at the elbow joint," she said, pointing out the inch-long spikes on the backs of the front elbow joints that Nyx had missed, but Seth obviously hadn't. "You saw this here?"

Nyx nodded.

"What was it doing?"

Well, there was no help for it now. "Best guess? Following me."

Evra folded her arms across her chest. "You do not seem unsettled. I take it this is not the first time you have seen the creature?"

"It's the first time I've gotten a good look at it and been certain it's not just a figment of my imagination."

Evra pursed her lips. "Have you considered—"

"No."

"You do not even know what I was going to say."

Nyx knew. "You were going to suggest I tell our most recent visitor about it," she said, choosing her words carefully in case any prying ears were nearby.

"He does possess a depth of knowledge the rest of us do not. He might be able to identify it."

He might also be able to use it as the perfect excuse to say she shouldn't go to Kyvren. *You are being stalked by a spectral dog? How odd. Certainly not the time for you to be flitting off to other planets.*

"I don't want him to know. We don't have that kind of relationship."

Morgen raised his hand. "Can I ask what kind of relationship you do have? Might it, by chance, be familial? Paternal, even?"

How did she get herself into these things? Nyx turned and knocked her forehead against Seth's collarbone.

"I'll take that as a *yes*. Dare I ask how this occurred?"

"Not in any good way. And if it's all right with you, I'd really *really* like to not talk about it. I just want to go to Tobi's birthday party before we're unforgivably late, and pretend to be normal."

Morgen's expression softened. "Of course. I'm sorry, little Guardian."

Evra held up her hand. "There is the matter of the beast, before we blithely carry on."

"I've never seen it inside the Station," Nyx said. "And this is the first time it's confronted me instead of running off. And it *did* run off when it heard you guys coming. I don't think it will be a problem when we come back, and I'll figure out what it is now that we've gotten a decent look at it. Good enough?"

The look on Evra's face said she didn't quite think so, but she didn't argue. Nyx put the dog out of her mind as they completed the walk to the Warlock's. They found Kaden and Kalvar waiting for them outside the shop and they all went in together, then out the back door into the courtyard behind it.

The chaos of children was in full swing. They ran, they screamed, they exuded an abundance of energy. Tobi spotted Kaden and his eyes lit up so much it was a wonder they didn't spark and catch fire. He ran over and threw his arms around his former prison planet guardian.

Nyx was starkly reminded, in that moment, of the scar that ran the length of Kaden's torso. The one caused by an injury that should have killed him, and would have if the boy now hugging him fiercely didn't have access to a power far greater than it seemed his little frame should be able to channel. There was a bond there—they'd each saved the other one that day—but Tobi was too young to think of it in those terms. He just knew that his hero—the person who had protected and sheltered him during the worst time of his life—was here.

For a moment, Kaden just stood there, and Nyx thought that disconnect between his emotions and the rest of himself was going to be too much to overcome. It broke her heart, just a little bit. Because when they'd come back from Arkadia, Nyx had been too new as a Guardian to block out the Station's senses, and she'd woken up every night when Kaden's nightmares had driven him to check each of the kids' rooms, to reassure himself that nothing had happened to them. That Kaden wasn't here right now. This Kaden was nothing but empty stillness. Then the hard shell around him shattered and he leaned down, hugging Tobi back.

Seth's eyes tracked the pair as Tobi dragged Kaden over to the badminton game he'd made Diana and the Warlock get him after playing it at the Station's Neighborhood Barbecue Day.

"Tell me about the whole prison planet thing again," Seth said. "I'm still having trouble picturing Kaden fucking Moor being Surrogate Father of the Year to a bunch of wayward children."

Nyx didn't oblige him—thinking about it made her think about Lana and Fari, who hadn't made it out, and thinking about them still hurt too much. She elbowed him in the stomach instead.

He grunted. "For fuck's sake woman, what was that for? I didn't even say anything bad about him."

Nyx shook her head, unable to hold back a smile. "When the first word out of our kid's mouth is 'fuck' I'm blaming you."

"You know damn well you cuss more than I do. Besides, I've recently been informed I have years to rein in my swearing habits before I have to worry about passing them on." He sounded just a little bit wistful, and she had the feeling if it were up to him, a few years would be more like a few months.

Nyx was more conflicted about the matter. All of this—the families, the community—still felt like something she was very much on the outside of, no matter how hard she'd worked to become a part of it. People in Earth Between knew her—she'd taken pains to get to know all of the business owners, to visit the town regularly and make connections—and she was relatively certain that people liked her. But she could also tell that she was still a Guardian to them more than she was Nyx, and so long as she was, she would never quite fit into the fold the same way everyone else did.

She knew what it was like to grow up on the outside of a world you could never belong to. If she had kids, she didn't want them to grow up feeling that too. She wanted them to have the effortless inclusion every other child here did. And she wanted to be able to mingle with the adults as easily as Evra and Morgen were talking with Diana and the Warlock, and the four of them with another couple.

And it stabbed her in the heart a little to know that Seth could go mingle among them as readily as anyone else, but that when she joined the group the dynamic would change. Only a little—the slightest edge of guarding to people's words, a decrease in their easiness—but she would feel it. Across the courtyard, the Warlock's gaze met hers. Something—regret, hesitation, Nyx wasn't sure—flickered in the other woman's eyes, and for a moment it looked like she would break from the group to come talk to her. Then Diana said something and the Warlock turned back, laughing, Nyx forgotten.

Seth wrapped his arms around her and tugged her back against him, his chin coming to rest on her head. "They'll get over the Guardian bit in time," he said softly. "You do belong here, Nyxi."

A smile tugged at the corner of her lips. He always knew exactly what she was thinking. "Didn't anyone ever tell you it's rude to read minds?"

He pretended to take the question seriously. "I think a pretty girl might have mentioned it once."

She shook her head, still smiling, her melancholy fading in the light of the one person who always, always understood her. "Come on." She stepped out of his arms and took his hand. "Let's go be social."

<h1 style="text-align:center">23</h1>

The party wound down late in the afternoon, culminating in an uneventful walk back to the Station despite—or perhaps because of—the vigilance with which she, Seth, Evra, and Morgen kept an eye out for the spectral dog. By the time they got home, Kalvar was giving all of them the side-eye but, being Kalvar, he didn't actually say anything.

Nyx's tension had just eased when she stepped onto the Station grounds and her anxiety immediately returned. Immersed once more in Kaliaris' senses she *felt* their visitor, a thundercloud of concentrated power shut up behind the library doors, and her stomach sank. She chose to not say anything as they went inside, waiting until the others had drifted off, until only Seth waited with her, because Seth could always catch the smallest of shifts in her mood.

He nodded at the library. "What do I get if I correctly guess who's behind Door Number One?"

"To come with me." After what had happened last time, she'd decided maybe being alone with Jevryn wasn't the brightest idea. "Please don't piss him off, I'd rather I didn't have to lock you in the basement again for your own good."

"You know," he teased, "when you say it like that I start to wonder if I'm allowing myself to be handled in ways that are unhealthy for me."

She rolled her eyes. "Since death is more unhealthy than temporary lockup, I don't feel bad."

"I don't know, I may have to rethink our eventual marriage so long as we're in the Station. There's a huge power imbalance here I can't compensate for. I'm financially dependent on you, you control my housing, and now you're controlling where I go in the house."

"*So* funny," she said dryly, "but I know you." She stepped closer, her hands on his waist, and whispered in his ear. "I'm willing to bet you have at least six bank accounts under six different identities and can leave me whenever you feel like it."

He turned his head, nipping her ear. "Good thing I don't feel like it, then. What do you say we horrify Jevryn by making him wait, while we go upstairs and—"

The library door creaked open and Griff cleared his throat. Loudly.

Seth sighed. "You know, delightful as it is being surrounded by friends and family, I'm beginning to understand why people say you shouldn't live with them."

Nyx stepped back, taking his hand. "Come on."

The first thing she noticed was that Jevryn was sitting. She rarely ever saw him sit. She suspected this was because he took great joy in looming, and it was difficult to loom while seated. Also, because his spine appeared to be a steel bar incapable of curving, and it could not be comfortable to sit for long periods of time so inflexibly. His cool gray eyes flicked to Seth, a measure of irritation surfacing in them.

Seth flashed him a grin. If it was petty to take joy in having a boyfriend Jevryn disapproved of, then Nyx was petty.

"The Station access to Kyvren has been shut down," Jevryn began without preamble. "It would appear that someone informed the Meerkin of how to coerce the previous Guardian into giving up their post"—he sent a pointed look at Nyx, who shrugged—"though it was several weeks after their return before they managed to do so."

That explained how Riven had gotten on-planet. Still, none of this was news Nyx couldn't have already guessed at. "You're just now finding all this out?"

Jevryn sighed. "You are under the illusion that because we are called a Council, the other members and I operate under amicable conditions, wherein information is freely shared. Allow me to dispel that illusion. We share nothing that we must not. We were all aware of the Meerkin's recent escape from Arkadia because that planet is under full joint control.

"But Kyvren itself falls to Councilor Loclyn. She claims to have shut down Station access to contain the Meerkin, and that the planet was not deemed of enough interest for anyone to look deeper into the matter until now."

Not deemed of enough interest. A memory of terror shot through her, of Koral's fingers grazing her temples. "So when Kiev called it one of your most valuable planetary assets, he was, what? Using that as an excuse for Koral to break into my head?"

"Yes. And no. It was *once* quite a valuable asset. The ore the Dwarves mine there is integral to the creation of Enforcer armor. That armor was an edge desperately needed in the early years of the connected universe, but we have far more of it now than could ever be needed."

A hot ball of rage spun in her gut. *Far more of it than could ever be needed.* While the Meerkin had *died* for lack of it. No way in hell was she letting him go to Kyvren without her. Maybe he hadn't been directly responsible the first time around, but if his calm recitation was any indication, he didn't care enough to do anything to help the Meerkin now.

She managed to sound halfway civil when she asked, "Did you find out anything else?"

"Only that Councilor Loclyn intends to let the situation sort itself out. She is confident it will resolve itself in an...acceptable manner."

Meaning she thought the Meerkin would die.

"The Dwarven race was never prone to wanderlust and they do not reproduce quickly. Over ninety-nine percent of their number are on Kyvren. Those who are not have relatively little contact with the main body of their race. There are few to notice if the Kyvren population goes silent."

"And there's no one else on Kyvren? That's it—the Dwarves and the Meerkin?" The little bit of information she'd found on Kyvren said as much, but she wanted it confirmed.

"It is an export planet, Nyx, with little else to offer. There are far better places in the universe to be, and frequent travel would only increase the risk of one of their particularly dangerous basic life-forms migrating elsewhere in the universe."

Okay. That would make things simpler, at least, if there weren't any outside forces to contend with. "When do we leave?"

His mouth twisted in a grimace. "Have I any hope of convincing you to remain here?"

Seth snorted. Nyx ignored him and said, "No."

Jevryn made a noncommittal sound in his throat. "Arradin? What is your opinion?"

Nyx looked between them. She recognized the tone of voice Jevryn had used, the way he was looking at Griff now. She crossed her arms. "Hey, I'm not twelve, and this isn't a field trip. I don't need joint permission to go."

Jevryn's face took on a pinched expression. He rattled off an irritated statement to Griff in a language Nyx didn't understand. One that her personal translator spell—and the ones soaked into the Station and the Between—didn't either. Griff's head tilted to one side as he concentrated. After a few moments, he replied in the same language Jevryn had used, stumbling a bit over the words.

It must be Jevryn's language, Nyx realized—*her* language—and Griff was rusty from not having spoken it in a few hundred years. The cadence of it tugged at her, made her long to know how the syllables would taste on her own tongue. For a while, she simply listened to it—to them. The exchange was an oddly intimate one to witness, despite—or perhaps more so because of—the fact she couldn't understand the words they spoke.

Jevryn and Griff fit back together like magnetized puzzle pieces, discussing things in the same manner they must have done a thousand times before. Jevryn rattled off strings of clipped words while Griff's responses were calm, faintly amused, and interspersed with a liberal dosing of sighs. She watched them and she saw herself and Seth in their body language, their ease. She wished, in that moment, that time really could be spun backwards. That Griff could have the life he should have had, with the man he loved, and they could have grown old together and died within the natural span of their lives. She would never have been born, in that scenario, but she wouldn't exactly be alive to be bothered by the fact.

All of the sudden a smile—an *actual* smile—tugged at the corners of Jevryn's lips before he spoke. Whatever Griff said in response made that mirth die instantly. The conversation took on a somber tone, and Nyx let them continue because she could have listened to that language for hours, uncaring that she couldn't understand a single word. That, and because she assumed they were talking about her, and it was best to just let them get it over with.

But then Jevryn's eyes turned blue and a whip of short, sharp hurt cracked through her. She had puzzled out on her own, from what Seth had told her, that blue meant sorrow. Jevryn wasn't talking about *her*. He didn't possess enough emotion where she was concerned to shift his eye color. Which meant he was standing here, taking up her time, ignoring her while conversing in a language that should have been her birthright but she couldn't understand, and she wasn't even the subject of discussion.

Hot irritation replaced hurt. Maybe she'd given up expecting Jevryn to care anything about her, but he could at least have the decency to not talk about something completely unrelated to her *while she was in the room.*

She snapped her fingers. "*Hey.* I happen to be right here, and it's rude to talk in front of people when they don't understand what you're saying."

Griff turned to her, an apologetic look on his face. "I am sorry, Nyx. It was not my intention."

"I know it wasn't *yours.*" Jevryn was the one who'd started the conversation.

Griff gave Jevryn an encouraging look and the councilor turned to her. His expression was, if possible, even more pinched than it had been before. "I…apologize as well."

It was the most pained, stilted apology Nyx had ever heard. She was going to have to tell Griff to stop trying to get Jevryn to be polite to her. He obviously didn't care. He'd all but told her he didn't care. And Griff trying to get him to act like he did was doomed to end in failure. Not to mention it was awkward.

Yet, somehow, the hopeful look on Griff's face made her grit out, "Don't worry about it."

And maybe that forced nicety was worth it, because Jevryn didn't give her any further difficulty, only said, "Kyvren, then. Who else will you be bringing with you?"

Seth raised his hand. He'd been remarkably well-behaved this entire time, and she was reminded that he was a lot less impulsive than he acted. He might pretend he had no impulse control, but he wouldn't have survived her mother—and years in the Shadow Market—if he *actually* had none. He enjoyed acting like a chronic teenager because it made other people underestimate him. Though she was guessing, by the way Jevryn was looking at Seth, that the act hadn't fooled the councilor in the room.

Not for the first time, Nyx wondered what had passed between Seth and Jevryn while she'd been unconscious after her mother had fixed her memories. That *something* had happened, she was certain. But she'd never brought herself to ask. Given how much Seth disliked Jevryn on her behalf—which, yeah, kind of made Nyx go all gooey inside—she was fairly certain it was nothing that could be put in a positive, or even a neutral, category.

"Hawthorne," Jevryn said in a tone dry enough to desiccate a cactus. "I did expect your presence was a given. Drahl and al'Daemon as well, I take it?"

"Probably," Nyx hedged. "And…possibly two others."

Jevryn's brow furrowed. "Kaden's sister remains with their foster mother, and I was under the impression the Tiagren boy was to attend school soon."

"Maruca's not invited, and yes, Kalvar is testing soon."

"Then who else remains?"

Nyx worried her bottom lip between her teeth. There was a fine line with Jevryn—what was safe to tell him and what wasn't. But Liya and Valedan didn't know Nyx was his daughter, only that she was on speaking terms with him, so they weren't in danger from knowing things they shouldn't. And since she was going to need them if she wanted Riven to talk to her…

"The heir to the Blood Throne of Alzherra and his fiancée?" she offered.

Jevryn looked like he was debating the merits of strangling her. She tried not to remind herself that he'd likely been debating those merits since the day she'd been born.

"Are they here?" he asked, voice coated in a fine layer of frost.

"Yes."

"Are they aware that I am here?"

She decided there was no advantage in lying, at this point. "They know you were here before. I don't think they know you're here right now."

His eyes fluttered briefly closed. "Bring them to me."

Nyx thought that was the worst possible thing that could happen to them. It was going to make Liya and Valedan's day.

The heir to the Blood Throne and his Lady of Shadows were, as Nyx had anticipated, extraordinarily pleased to be summoned by Councilor A-Morridahn. They entered the library looking far more self-assured than Nyx ever would have at their age. Then again, Elena Fortuna had done absolutely everything possible to ensure Nyx *had* no sense of self-worth, so maybe that wasn't much of a competition.

Liya and Valedan gave identical bows—it didn't surprise Nyx that both genders in a matriarchal culture would give the same type of deferential greeting—then straightened in tandem.

Valedan spoke as they rose. "Councilor A-Morridahn, it is an honor to meet you."

Nyx restrained a snort, but it was a near thing.

That muscle at the corner of Jevryn's eye twitched, as if he'd sensed the urge from her. "I understand you are familiar with the metalworker who made the Guardian's bo staff."

"I am."

"And that she asked you questions pertaining to a similar item."

"Yes."

"You believe these items to have been made by the Gare Ru family that has long been sworn to your own."

"Yes, Councilor. Riven has told me many stories from her family line. Given their aptitude for magical metallurgy, and the stories she has told me of her ancestor, I am fairly certain that the works are from them."

Jevryn's hand had long been resting on the hilt of his sword, as if the weapon were a convenient countertop. His fingers now drummed idly along the leather-wrapped hilt, and Nyx didn't think she was overreacting by suspecting he was debating whether or not to draw it. She edged closer to them, in case intervention should become necessary.

Jevryn noticed and his fingers stilled. "And you have agreed to approach Riven on the Guardian's behalf."

Nyx hadn't thought it was possible to feel any more distant from Jevryn. To feel like he cared any *less* about her. But hearing the dispassionate way he talked about her as "the Guardian" proved her wrong.

Jevryn waited for Valedan's nod before asking, "Why?"

Valedan frowned. "I beg your pardon?"

"Why agree to broker this meeting? From what the Guardian tells me, your family is quite protective of their pet metalworkers, and I find myself curious to understand your willingness to intercede on her behalf."

"If I may be candid, Councilor A-Morridahn, I find myself in the unfortunate position of having disappointed both of my mothers. The first can be won over with apologies and expensive imported spices. The second one is both my tutor in strategy and the rightful possessor of the Blood Throne. She will require something more substantial in apology. Such as, perhaps, the return of her favorite metalworker."

Jevryn arched one eyebrow. "As well as a connection to the councilor who oversees her planet?"

Valedan gave a demure half-bow. "I would never be so bold as to presume a connection between us, Councilor."

Jevryn's fingers twitched slightly, like he longed to clench them around his sword hilt. Valedan *could* be a bit much. "Do you have anything currently in your possession that belongs to, or was made by, Riven?"

"I have these." Valedan flicked the sword earring dangling from his left earlobe, the design a complement to the shield hanging from his right. "She made them for me."

Jevryn held out his hand expectantly. When Valedan hesitated, he said, "They will be returned to you later this evening, in their original condition."

Valedan unclipped the earrings and dropped them into Jevryn's palm. "Does this mean you will allow us to travel with you to Kyvren?"

"Perhaps." Jevryn dismissed the two with a flick of his wrist, and they went with the kind of grace and acceptance Nyx knew she herself would never be capable of mustering.

When they were gone, she crossed her arms and said, "Well?"

"I require time for preparations. I also require accommodations here. You may inform those who will be coming with you to be prepared to leave within the week. And Nyx? We are going to Kyvren to speak with, and possibly retrieve, Riven Gare Ru. You may speak with the Meerkin, should conditions allow such an interaction, but you are not to interfere in what is occurring there. Should I determine any such intervention is required, *I* will handle the matter. Am I clear?"

"Perfectly." She had no intention of following the instructions, but what Jevryn A-Morridahn didn't know now could explode his head later.

"Good."

She refrained from responding with *great* and instead asked, "What should I be preparing for?"

"To remain by my side, follow my orders, and not attempt to intervene in happenings far beyond your control and understanding."

She blinked. Griff looked pained, and Seth was very obviously restraining laughter.

"While I'm sure those instructions soothe your ego," she bit out, "they don't prepare me for conditions on the planet. They don't tell me what to pack or what to expect."

"You will be provided with appropriate clothing and gear prior to departure. Expect some difficulty as we attempt to retrieve a single person from a war zone without a specific known location for them. If you require instruction beyond that, I might suggest a full night of restful sleep before departure."

Nyx decided it was a miracle actual flames didn't burst from her ears. He'd done it again—that thing where he all but told her he thought she was an idiot. She couldn't believe all those childhood fantasies she'd had about working hard to impress her father had been for *this* man.

He continued on, either not noticing, or choosing to ignore, her reaction. "Now, if you would fetch Kaden, I require my Tracker returned to me."

Oh, he required *his* Tracker returned? That irritated her, too. But she left to get Kaden. Mostly because the sooner she did so, the sooner she didn't have to stand around being condescended to.

Griff's sigh, as she and Seth left, practically filled the room.

Two hours later, a still-fuming Nyx reflected that her father had managed the impossible: he'd driven her to voluntary cardio.

"'Go for a run', Evra said," she muttered as she jogged along the perimeter path. "'It'll clear your head', she said." Nyx couldn't say it was having the promised effect. Or maybe it was just that she wasn't getting less angry about anything. And when she passed that damn wall closing off Seth's garden, her irritation over not knowing what was behind it hit a fever pitch.

The need to know burrowed into her and refused to let go, worming deeper and deeper as she went back inside, showered, and dressed. When Seth walked in he didn't make it two feet inside the door before she stabbed a finger at him and demanded, "What's behind the stupid wall?"

He grinned at her, closing the door. "It's killing you, isn't it? Not knowing?"

She didn't share his amusement. "It's been *five months*. If it's a garden, what the hell are you growing in it?" It was winter for stars' sake, not that that *really* mattered in the Station, which could shift the climate in a particular area to fit any whim.

He stalked toward her, cocky grin still on his face. "You're telling me you haven't peeked? Not even a little, not once?"

She ground her teeth together. "I've been trying to be good."

He reached her, slipping his arms around her waist. "You were never a good girl. Definitely more of a brat."

She brought her knee up but he'd been expecting it and he blocked, twisted, swept her leg out. She crashed to the bed, him on top of her.

"See what I mean? Brat."

"Seth," she said, her voice deceptively mild. "I'm going to kill you."

"No, you won't. You like me too much." He brushed his nose against hers. "It's your birthday present."

She blinked, her instinctual retort dying on her lips. "What?"

"What's on the other side of the wall. It's your birthday present.

It took me a long time to get it just right, but I finally have it. So you're going to have to hold out a few more days, I'm afraid."

She stilled. A few more days?

"You forgot your own birthday, didn't you?"

"I..." She trailed off. She *had* forgotten. It had never meant anything good to her in Dead Earth. It had just been a date stamped on her driver's license. The date she'd woken up in an apartment, alone, with no idea who she was.

"Hey, what's wrong?" His thumbs swiped across her face, brushing away the tears leaking from her eyes.

"I haven't had a birthday since you left." Not a celebration, anyway. That first birthday, a year into her isolation, had passed her by unnoticed, drowned in a sea of monotony and misery. And then she'd met Kaden, and she hadn't wanted to explain that she'd been abandoned *on* her birthday. And he'd never even asked when it was. So many things he'd never asked that she'd been grateful for at the time—grateful that she didn't have to try to explain. Now she realized that lack of interest for the glaring warning sign it had been.

When he'd left... She hadn't had much in her to hope, after that. She'd tried, one year—she couldn't remember which one now— bought a small cake and a bottle of champagne and watched her favorite movies all night. And she'd cried all night, because she was never possessed of a positive enough persuasion to turn a sad situation into a happy one. All buying the cake had done was remind her that she had no one to share it with. She hadn't made the mistake of trying again any other year, had done her best to let the day pass her by unnoticed.

She'd gotten pretty good at it. Good enough that now she hadn't even realized the date was approaching.

"I know," Seth said softly. He kissed the corner of one eye, then the other. Then her forehead. Her nose. Her lips. "I'm sorry. It's why I wanted this one to be perfect. I know it won't be. Nothing ever is. But I wanted to make something good enough that the bad ones can't block it out. And I want to do the same thing next year, and the year after that, and every year after. I want to make you happy, Nyxi."

She smiled through the tears still leaking into her hairline. "You do. You always have."

A hint of laughter returned to his eyes. "Even when I call you a brat?"

He always had to push his luck. "Shut up and kiss me."

He was smart enough to do just that.

24

Seth was gone when Nyx woke the next morning. Given she'd slept in until seven-thirty, she wasn't terribly surprised. He'd left a note on his pillow that said *Earth Between. Back soon.* He'd time-stamped it for oh-seven-hundred in the upper right corner, so she would know what time he'd left.

She dragged herself out of bed and was arrested on her way to the bathroom by another note, one that had been pushed under the door. She retrieved it, unfolding the thick cream paper to find Jevryn's handwriting.

Since we are to travel, I wish to see how your adeptness with portal magic has progressed. Meet me by Temerex's enclosure at nine. There is no need to bring portal magic of your own—I will be providing you with carefully measured quantities, in order to determine your efficiency.

Nyx ran her fingers up her left forearm, feeling the row of bracelets there, each one filled with portal magic. She never took them off. She slept, exercised, ate, and showered with them on, unwilling to be without the safety they provided, even within the walls of the Station. Even if they'd landed her halfway across the universe when her memory had been skipping, because *that*, thank the stars, was a situation that couldn't repeat itself. She kept them all Hidden, because she had no desire to risk them being stolen because they looked expensive, or—if she was truly unlucky—recognized for what they were.

She found it more than passingly amusing that Jevryn thought she was actually following the instructions he'd given her so many months ago not to use the magic he'd given her unless she had to. Not that she had any intention of letting him find out. She was more than happy to use the portal magic he provided while hers went untouched and undetected.

If she rankled at his arrogant assumption that she would both answer his summons and do as he bid, well, she chose to ignore it on account of his being the only person who could actually teach her how to use her magic. It would have been nice if he'd shown up sometime before they intended to actually leave the planet to impart some of that hands-on instruction, but she wasn't surprised. Not when she suspected she knew exactly where his decision to invite her to train this morning had come from.

Given that suspicion, once she'd showered and eaten breakfast, she made her way up to Griff's room. He bid her to enter at the first knock, and so she did. She rarely ever came into Griff's space—having spent so long as the Station's Avatar, most of that without much autonomy of his own, she'd had the sense that he treasured his privacy, and so she rarely invaded it—and she was struct once again by how beautiful it was.

Here the Station appeared to play fast and loose with the laws of physics, as Griff's room was far higher than any point of the building appeared from the outside. The walls and floor were a rich, warm brown stone, covered in rugs and tapestries that softened the space and dampened any echo of sound. It wasn't square or round or rectangular, but something in between, as if it were a natural room etched from a cliff by time and nature. The far wall, on the side of the room opposite the door, wasn't a wall at all. That side of the room was completely open to the world beyond, void of any barrier that might trap a person within. Beyond it, the ground waited hundreds of feet below.

No doubt it was a comforting view to a person accustomed to having wings, but it was one that made Nyx just the tiniest bit ill if she stood too close to the edge. Griff was stretched out before that edge now, one talon dangling carelessly over it, the other holding a book open on the stone floor before him. He appeared to have just started it and, if the expression on his face was any indication, found it riveting.

He finally looked up, and she could feel a smile from him, even if his eagle's face couldn't actually make one. "Good morning."

"Morning. Good book?"

"I do hope so. I have been waiting to read the concluding volume to this series for approximately nine centuries, so I suppose there is much to live up to."

She blinked. "You remember the plot to a book series you read nine centuries ago?"

He chuckled. "I remember liking them enough to decide to reread them." He nodded to a bookshelf, where a row of books bore spines with covers similar to the one held in his talon. "And Jevryn brought the concluding volume with him."

She hesitated, almost didn't ask, but then did. "So you and Jevryn *are* talking." She wasn't entirely certain how she felt about that. Though it was, ultimately, none of her business. It simply felt like everyone who had a right to bear the councilor a grudge was finding a way to look past it.

Kaden was in his current predicament as wanted fugitive because Jevryn had sent him away with the Harvester years ago, and yet he had no problem being glued to the man's side. Temerex had decided to permanently look past his abandonment of her, if the way she'd followed him when the councilor had gone outside last night was any indication. Now Griff was reading a book Jevryn had given to him, and having conversations with him, many of which were undoubtedly about her.

What was it about Jevryn A-Morridahn that inevitably made people forget the horrible things he'd done and soften toward him? Was she doomed to the same fate?

Griff must have sensed the turmoil in her question, because he placed the book aside and sat up, giving her his full attention. "Not, I think, in the way you mean. Though I cannot deny there is an allure in being known as what I once was, in having someone remember the pieces of me that I no longer have the freedom to be. But I chose to open communication with him for a very specific purpose. He is not unaware of that fact."

She could well guess what that purpose was: her. "Did you ask him to give me magic lessons?"

"Untrained magic is dangerous, both to you and to others. As I am bound not to speak of your particular magic's uses, the responsibility for that tutelage lies with him."

So, yes, he'd asked Jevryn to give her magic lessons. "Look, I'll take what he can teach me, because I need it and there's no one else to do it, but as for everything else? You can just stop. I know you loved him once—maybe you still do." He started to speak but she rushed on, needing to get it all out. "And I know he loves you, but he doesn't love *me* and he's never going to. And honestly? It hurts more, you trying to make him act like he cares. I appreciate you wanting to help but just…let him be whatever he is. It's easier for me that way."

"Nyx—" he started.

"Please don't say anything," she begged. "Please don't try to make me feel better, or tell me that he just doesn't know how to deal with me, because I *know*, okay?"

Griff wanted to argue with her. She saw it in his face. But he relented. "If that is what you need from me, then I will not."

"Thank you."

"But you will be leaving with him in a few days, and I will not be there as a buffer. I know you do not wish to, but I think it would be wise for the two of you to have a discussion before you depart. Don't respond now," he said, forestalling the protest that leapt to her lips. "Only consider it. All right?"

"All right," she relented, solely to make him happy. When he held out his left foreleg in invitation, she stepped in and hugged him. She hadn't realized how much she'd needed a hug until that moment.

"Everything will be fine," he told her. "You will see."

She squeezed him a little tighter and then released. "I'd better go." Jevryn seemed like the kind of person who thought you were late unless you were fifteen minutes early.

She wended her way down the stairs, out the back door to where he waited by Temerex's enclosure. Sulkily, Nyx determined the mare had definitely forgiven Jevryn. She was lipping at his hand while he scratched behind her ear, a happy look in her reptilian eyes.

Jevryn's head lifted as Nyx approached, surprise evident on his face. "You came. And you are early."

"Is my punctuality an issue?"

"No." The word was slow, drawn out.

She didn't pause, didn't wait for him to tell her what to do or where to go. If they were going to practice with portal magic, they would have to leave the Station's grounds, so she picked the boundary nearest to Tem's stall and walked toward it. When Temerex nickered after her she felt guilty for not pausing to say *hello*. But pausing would have meant time around Jevryn that wasn't directly related to training. She'd rather get the training out of the way so she could get away from him.

She crossed off the Station grounds, felt that peculiar draining away as she became just Nyx once more, mortal and no longer capable of subduing everything around her with a thought. She felt naked and vulnerable, as if this state—being only herself—was the unnatural one. She decided she needed to make a point of going into Earth Between more often.

"Well?" she asked when Jevryn joined her. "Am I to recite lines of theory I read in books, or are we jumping straight to you handing me a thimble of magic and seeing how far I can get with it?"

He merely studied her in answer, his face inscrutable. It went on long enough that she grew uncomfortable.

"What?" she snapped. Because it was so much easier to snap at him. It was a relief to be angry with him. Far better than being the woman who had begged for his attention upon finding out who he was.

"I was attempting to determine the answer to a question," he said. "Unfortunately, I believe I have discovered it."

A hot lick of shame flared through her. He'd discovered what? That she was every bit as disappointing and unyielding as he'd suspected? And why should that bother her, when she was being as prickly as possible on purpose?

Because you're being difficult because you want him to say that it doesn't matter. That he's changed his mind and he wants to be your father. Because you want to be your worst self and have him love you anyway.

Stupid. She was still that stupid, forgotten child inside who wanted to be wanted. Her eyes burned, frustration rather than sadness, and she opened her eyes wide, forcing the tears back.

"Are we going to get on with this, or—" She cut off when she caught motion behind and to the side of him. Kaden walked toward them. After she'd sent him to Jevryn yesterday, he'd left the Station and hadn't returned. Nyx didn't know where Jevryn had sent him, and she honestly hadn't expected him back.

Now here he was. But he wasn't precisely returning to the Station, was he? No, Kaden was walking straight for them, a bag slung over one shoulder, another gripped in his hand.

"What are you doing here?" she asked when he reached them.

He opened his mouth, as if to answer, but never got the chance. Jevryn's hands shot out, one clamping on her wrist, the other on Kaden's.

"I must apologize," the councilor said. She had the distinct impression it was actually Kaden he was apologizing to.

Nyx felt the buzz of magic from the bracelets lining his forearms beneath his robe and understood what he was going to do a split second before he actually did it. Terror and anger and pure defiance spilled through her, and in that split second, she called on the portal magic from her own bracelets.

It whipped out, clashing against Jevryn's. She wielded on instinct, uncertain what exactly she was *doing* with the magic she held. She felt the intent behind his own, the way it should be pulling them through space and time to some other place. But hers was there alongside it, fighting not to be taken, fighting to claw her way out of his magic's grip.

No wonder he'd been so careful in his note to tell her not to bring magic of her own. He'd wanted to make sure that when he did *this*, she had nothing to stop him with.

"Let go," he ground out.

She felt the swell of his power, cresting against hers like a tidal wave, and shoved back against it. "You first."

"You obstinate child, I am attempting to be gracious in giving you what you asked for."

Before she could bite out that she hadn't asked to be forcibly taken off-planet without warning, without her friends, movement caught her eye. Seth was running toward them. Jevryn noticed him at the same time, his lips thinning, and she realized he'd been being gentle with her—or toying with her—up to now, because suddenly the intensity increased. His power whipped around her, targeting the places where her own had latched on, tearing at her footholds with the savageness of hurricane winds.

She buckled beneath the onslaught, slowly giving way to the immense chasm of his ability. Winning. He was winning.

Seth reached them just as she felt that rift between worlds open. He reached for them, his hand clamping on Jevryn's, trying to pull it free of her.

But the portal was reaching its zenith, and the magic—it wasn't around Seth. Not all of him. Jevryn didn't open portals the way she did, with visible doorways that could be stepped through. He wrapped his magic around people and pulled them through to where he wanted them. It usually happened in the blink of an eye, and the only reason she could see it this time was because her resistance was slowing him down.

But she *could* see it. Could see that only Seth's hand, where it clamped hers and Jevryn's, and a portion of his foot were caught in the swirling vortex of Jevryn's magic. If that portal fully took hold, transporting her across galaxies, when it snapped shut it would cleave those parts of Seth within the sphere of influence from those parts of him without.

She panicked, shoving against Jevryn with everything she had. If she could just break free of him... But she couldn't. She had no idea what she was doing. She was reacting on instinct, lashing out like a cat trapped in a cage. What she was doing felt similar to what Jevryn had done on Amentia Furor, when he'd pulled on her ability to hold Laiveran in place—but it wasn't exactly the same.

And she knew it wouldn't be enough when Jevryn's magic stopped trying to rip itself out of her grip and simply folded around hers, growing over it like a cocoon. Once it closed, once it encompassed hers fully, the game would be up.

Desperate, she threw her magic around Seth, so when that cocoon closed, it closed around him as well. Then the ground dropped out beneath her. The world disappeared and reappeared a blink later, the winter-dead Station grass replaced by Kyvren's lush grasslands.

"Nyx." Jevryn's voice was a dead, cold sort of calm. "You must let go."

"I can't." Something was wrong. She felt it, the way her magic surged out of her, then surged back, a tide coming in and out, dragging Jevryn's to-and-fro with it, but she had no control. The tide was growing stronger, faster, more erratic. As if the two magics—hers and Jevryn's—had melded, were twisted together, and she couldn't untangle them. Jevryn's hands were still clamped on hers and Kaden's arms, unable to let go while their magic was all mixed up.

But Seth—Seth wasn't trapped in that same loop. "Get away," she told him. "Now."

"Not happening, Nyxi."

Jevryn ignored everything but her. "Call it back."

But she couldn't. The pulses of hers—and Jevryn's—magic quickened, building to some horrible crescendo, and she knew that when it reached it, nothing good would come to anyone caught in its radius.

And Seth wouldn't let go. Not voluntarily. She did the only thing she could. She took one step to her left, drew her leg up and delivered a solid kick to Seth's midsection, putting everything she had into it. He stumbled back, eyes wide, sliding out of the reach of hers and Jevryn's entangled magics a second before they detonated.

She was flung back, as if the explosion was a physical one, her arm wrenched from Jevryn's grip, and the world disappeared again. When it reappeared, the surrounding grasslands told her she was at least still on Kyvren.

She was also utterly alone.

25

Seth stood in the space where Nyx had disappeared—where they'd *all* disappeared—and cursed. Lengthily and with great inventiveness. What the hell had Jevryn been *doing*?

Seth had gathered, by the looks on both Kaden's and Nyx's faces, that neither of them had been prepared to go anywhere. Nyx had been pissed. Kaden had looked like he'd finally summoned enough emotion to also be pissed. Seth didn't think it was a coincidence that Kaden had gone just out of sight of the Station, portaled out with a portal stone and then returned, presumably via another, in possession of two bags that were likely the provisions and supplies for this trip, but he *did* think Jevryn had, perhaps, failed to mention when they would be leaving for that trip.

And yes, Seth had been following Kaden, because they might have come to an understanding of sorts, but he still didn't entirely trust him. Which he was glad of, because if he hadn't he would be sitting at home, wondering where Nyx was with no way to get to her. Kyvren was one of the few places the Shadow Market didn't actually have access to. And he was pretty certain he was on Kyvren, because where else would Jevryn have taken them?

Seth pulled a rock from his pocket. He perpetually kept half-a-dozen or so on hand out of old habit, and he crushed it between his fingers now, just to see if it would work. Magic caught and the window to Earth yawned opened, not far from the Station's boundaries. He exhaled. He could get them home if he needed to. The only problem was, there was no *them.* Nyx was gone.

He watched the portal slowly close as the magic fizzled out. Something had gone wrong with the portal magic Nyx and Jevryn had used. Seth had no idea *what,* but he'd felt it swinging wildly between them, as if they were both trying to direct it and it couldn't decide which of them to listen to.

Then the stubborn woman had kicked him out of the line of fire, and in the time it took him to regain his feet and dash back, they were gone. How the fuck was he supposed to find her now?

The obvious answer was that he wasn't. His only portal option was home—which he wasn't going to use without Nyx—and he couldn't magically track anyone. The group that had just disappeared could do both, which meant *they* were going to find *him.* Jevryn, at least, should be able to portal back to this exact location, and Nyx would make him do it. There was just the question of *when* they would be able to. Given what he'd felt in the magic between Nyx and Jevryn, Seth had a feeling it might be a while.

That meant he needed to stay in this general area for ease of being found, and find a place to hole up. The only problems were: (a) the general area was boring as fuck, (b) it had no shelter, and (c) he'd never been good at staying idle. Seth considered the situation. Jevryn wouldn't have brought them to the middle of nowhere. He would have brought them close to a settlement. Given that the land on three sides of Seth was open, empty grasslands as far as the eye could see, the only reasonable location for that settlement was on the fourth side. The one with a nice, large mountain range a couple miles in the distance.

The peaks, bare of vegetation, were towering monstrosities of dark gray rock that loomed over the surrounding landscape. They didn't look particularly inviting, and it begged the question of whether they housed Meerkin or Dwarves. Either way, Seth decided he might as well, while waiting for rescue, make headway in a useful direction.

He began walking toward the base of the largest mountain and, though it pained him to do so, he didn't mask his trail, so Kaden would be able to follow it. He pulled his own magic around him as he went, becoming invisible to the naked eye. If the mountain housed Meerkin, he could discard illusion and start making friends.

If it housed Dwarves, he could sneak around their lair and hopefully find something useful.

Because he knew Nyx. She might not have wanted to come to Kyvren right this moment, without Morgen and Evra, but now that she was here and that number tattooed on her hand had dropped another digit, she wouldn't leave until she accomplished her purpose. The sooner he helped the purpose along, the sooner they went home.

He liked home. He selfishly didn't want home to get fucked up by a bunch of centuries-old people who, near as he could tell, sucked at cleaning up their own messes. So he would just start early on the cleaning up bit, and once Nyx found him they could skip to the going home part.

The sun beat down on him mercilessly as he walked. He was not fond of unmitigated sunshine, and he was going to be very disappointed if he reached the mountain only to discover that no one lived there after all. By the time he was within a hundred feet of the base he still hadn't seen a single soul. Given that this was a planet locked in a civil war, if people lived here, he would expect to see at least a few sentries. He didn't.

He reached the rock face and, after walking along it several hundred feet in both directions from his starting point, finally found the entrance. It was little more than a gash in the rock, and if he hadn't seen a faint red glowing beyond it, he would never have called it an entrance.

He hesitated for only a moment. He might tease Nyx that she could never resist a mystery, but they were cut from the same cloth. Slipping through the opening, he found himself in an arched tunnel. A few feet ahead the walls were clear, like glass, and behind them was a glowing mass of red.

He wrapped the illusion of his invisibility more tightly around him and stepped forward. For a moment, nothing happened. Then the red mass began to move, and as it moved, sounds clanged out like an apocalyptic choir, discordant and chaotic, like they wanted to be too many things at once. Behind him, he heard the rough scrape of stone as the entrance sealed shut.

Well, if it looks like a trap, it probably is.

He heard the approach of footsteps and had a split-second to decide what to do. Whatever this tunnel was made from, it had clearly alerted the mountain's inhabitants that they had a visitor. He couldn't get back out, and if the people coming were smart, they would comb the tunnel until they found him, illusion magic or not. He could probably still avoid them if he *wanted to,* but...he might learn more if he just, say, let himself be captured. Or, rather, *appeared* to let himself be captured. He let his illusion go.

Four people—four Dwarves—marched into the tunnel. Seth gathered his magic carefully. There was an art to getting abducted as an Illusionist. If he just stepped back and let the facsimile of himself handle the work, he risked getting caught out. Yes, his illusions were tactile and could stand up to some roughhousing—hell, Bryn Morrigan had once tortured an illusion of him for two days and never figured it out, even knowing what he was—but it was difficult when it was more than one person his illusion needed to respond to, and there would likely be walking involved.

No, he was better off letting them apprehend the *real* him, then making the swap whenever they arrived at their destination. Unfortunately, he never got the chance. They took one look at him and the Dwarf nearest the tunnel wall swung a massive hammer at it.

The glass didn't crack, didn't release what Seth was pretty sure were the unda Nyx had told him about. Instead, an awful sound tore through the tunnel, burrowing into his ear drums, worming its way into his skull and echoing there, over and over and over, until the only relief from it was for his mind to shut down.

When he woke he was in a cell in a narrow room lined with other cells. He was alone. The ever-present set of throwing stars he kept on him at all times were missing. More importantly, so were his portal stones.

26

Nyx sat on her shins, hands splayed out to either side of her in the thick grass, trying to breathe through the pain ratcheting through her body. It felt like an electric current was pulsing in her veins and wouldn't stop. The reverberations from the explosion of her and Jevryn's magic racked her, and she didn't know how long she sat there, immobile, waiting for them to subside.

It became clear, after some time had passed, that they weren't going to. The pulses did lessen in intensity and grow farther apart, but she still felt like she was being intermittently shocked with a cattle prod as she forced herself to her feet. Hesitantly, she reached for the portal magic in her bracelets. Pain seared the mental fingers she reached for it with and she jerked back. The pulsing aftershocks rippling through her body increased again in speed and intensity and she bent double, breathing deeply again for another minute until they lessened.

Once she could straighten, she glared at the portal magic bracelets. Whatever she'd done when she'd attempted to stop Jevryn—however their magic had become entangled and then wrenched apart—the aftershocks were hell, and trying to use portal magic would make them worse. She wasn't going anywhere her own two feet couldn't take her any time soon, and that was a problem.

Because Jevryn was gone. Kaden was gone. *Seth* was gone. She hoped, desperately, that she'd managed to kick him clear of the blast zone. That he was wherever they had first landed on the planet. Both because that meant she might have a chance of finding him, if he remained there, and because she hoped it was near the Meerkin, since Jevryn likely would have portaled them near territory that would at least be friendly to Nyx. That Seth could charm the fur off a Meerkin in under five seconds, she didn't doubt. If he was with them, he would be fine.

She *needed* him to be fine, wished with vicious self-irritation that she hadn't removed the Hiding she'd once placed over his heart. But after what Jevryn had told her—that she'd inadvertently made Seth into an anchor for her portal magic and that, under the wrong circumstances, she could drain that anchor and kill him out of sheer inexperience or ineptitude, she'd opted to remove the Hiding.

She wasn't planning to forget all of her memories and portal to him by instinct again, but she hadn't wanted to take any chances, so she'd removed the possibility that it could happen. Now she had no idea where he was. *If* he still was.

She refused to go down the black well of those thoughts and spun in a slow circle. Grasslands. Nothing but tall grasslands in every direction. The blades of grass were tall, up to her thighs in some places, the stalks thick and—when she touched her finger to one—sharp. The fact that she was in grasslands and not forest told her that she was somewhere on the southern half of the continent, which told her…nothing.

She didn't know which areas of the continent the Dwarves or Meerkin made their homes in. She didn't know how close it was to nightfall, because she had no idea how long the day-night cycle on this planet was, though she forced herself to note the time on her watch—zero-nine-twenty-seven—so that when the sun *did* inevitably set, she would know how much time had passed.

She noticed, with a kind of detached calm, that it was warm here. Considering the article on the unda had mentioned that they were active as things warmed in the spring, this didn't fill her with confidence.

"Maybe this is their version of winter," she muttered to herself, "and spring is blisteringly hot. Who knows, it could happen."

She couldn't do anything about the seasons. What she could do was make a decision, and that decision was either to stay or to go.

She had no idea how far apart this last portal had flung her from Jevryn and Kaden. From Seth, she was guessing it was pretty damn far, because she'd caught a glimpse of mountains when they'd first arrived, and she didn't see a single mountain in sight at present.

She had no chance in hell of finding Jevryn or Kaden through anything other than dumb luck. She couldn't currently portal and had no idea how long it would be until she could. While she could stand here and hope intelligent life found her, and that that intelligent life was Meerkin rather than Dwarven, she didn't like the odds. Also, given her scant information on the planet, she had no idea what kind of natural predators it might boast. Knowing her luck, she would sit still for five minutes and get eaten by the Kyvrenian version of a bear. Or bitten by something nice and slithery and poisonous. Really, the possibilities were endless.

No, walking had the potential to yield better results. If she found running water, following it might lead her to civilization. And if it didn't, at least she would have found water. Not that she had anything to purify it with. If she made it back to Earth after yet another interstellar trip gone sideways, she was going to turn into one of those extreme preppers who went everywhere wearing cargo pants, the pockets stuffed with water purification tablets and protein bars, a piece of flint strapped somewhere on her person, and a collapsible water bowl dangling from her belt loop by way of a carabiner. Just in case.

At least she had Constance. And now that she knew what her bo staff really was, that meant she basically had any weapon she might need at her disposal. It was something. She also had the mercury boots, which had become her daily footwear out of the apparently not-so-paranoid fear that she might end up in a situation just like this one. So if she needed to run away really fast, that was an option.

She picked a direction—roughly north, by the position of the sun —and started walking. Every now and then, the grass was broken up by a large bush, or a lone small tree. Every now and then clusters of large, dark gray rocks would break the landscape, the formations ranging in size from a car to a small house, but aside from that the terrain varied little. She wished it would, because traipsing through thigh-high grass was mind-bogglingly tedious, sweat-inducing, and resulted in no small amount of thin cuts to the bare skin of her hands and forearms.

Three hours passed with no sign of water or intelligent life. She was thirsty. So, so thirsty. The temperature wasn't overly warm—if she had to guess, she'd say around seventy-five Fahrenheit—but there was no shelter from the sun, and the exercise was reminding her that she had done what she usually did in the mornings: drank coffee, not water. If only she'd known her father was going to yank her off-planet, she would have hydrated properly.

The one bright side was that she thought she might be able to portal at some point in the near future. The electricity-like zings pulsing through her body were, while still frequent enough to make her feel like her neck muscles might permanently seize up, growing further apart. She didn't know how long it would take for them to subside entirely, but at least the question of *will they subside* was no longer a constant worry in her gut.

Ahead of her rose what appeared to be the one lone hill in the otherwise flat landscape. She had been steadily making her way toward it ever since she'd caught sight of it. The landmass was tall enough that she hoped the vantage point would give her a better idea of what direction to continue going. She hit the base and began the ascent, sending a mental *thanks* across the universe to Evra for making her build a cross country course with extremely varied terrain, much of which was hilly.

Nyx wished her best friend was here now. If Evra al'Daemon had said *we will make for the hill to survey our surroundings*, Nyx would have felt one-hundred percent certain that reaching the hill would yield a positive result. Since going to the hill was Nyx's decision, it felt more like she was playacting a competent person. When her memories had been Hidden, that leftover sense she'd had of what to do in various situations—how to fight, how to move, how to think—had felt natural. It had felt like something she could rely on, a skill that she had believed in because it had been so ingrained in her that she'd kept it even when she couldn't keep hold of who she was.

Now that she *knew* who she was, all of that training felt like the child's play it was. Not that it hadn't been accurate, or useful—it had been and was—but it was also something Viktor had taught her not because he believed in her, or loved her and wanted to take care of her, but because Elena Fortuna had wanted her and Seth and Viktor kept busy and out of her hair. Nyx's survival training had been limited predominantly to exercises in the—admittedly vast—woods surrounding their cabin, with only occasional excursions to Dead Earth. She'd been taught how to survive in one very specific environment: Earth. Specifically, one geographical region of Earth. And she'd always known there wasn't any real danger, because her mother wanted her kept alive, so no matter what happened, Viktor would keep her breathing.

This wasn't Earth, Viktor wasn't here to look for her, and the potential danger was very real. Real enough that it went from potential danger to actual danger once she reached the hill's summit. Because there, on the other side, were streams of red unda snaking toward the base. And when she glanced back the way she'd come, thick veins of red spiderwebbed through the tall grasses there as well.

When had it cropped up? Had it been following her the entire time, and she simply hadn't noticed because she'd been focused on reaching the hill, and there hadn't been any sounds to cause her to look back?

Here and there the unda were mounded, writhing in masses that seemed to bubble. She watched as one of those mounds dripped down to rejoin the flow, leaving the withered husk of one of the landscape's sparse bushes in its wake. Clearly, the bushes had something of magic in them where the grass did not.

She spun in a circle, scanning the surrounding area. In terms of terrain and landmarks, it was all but identical as far as her eyes could see. In terms of the creeping unda that would rip the magic from her body if they caught up to her, there were only two clear paths—to her left or to her right. Ahead and behind, all that red moved unerringly toward her, as if it sensed a particularly high-reward food target. And unless she was much mistaken, it was speeding up.

Her gaze swiveled between the two clear directions. Left or right? Did it even matter? Then the ground began to rumble. A sound like thunder built, and movement to the right caught her eye. She squinted past the cloud of dust in the distance and saw—oh shit. That rumbling and thunder was a herd of several hundred *somethings*, likely hooved and definitely panicked, galloping straight for her, pursued by another undulating mass of red.

She whispered *los*, activating the mercury boots to their lowest setting, and *ran*. Her gaze was on the ground in front of her. The training she'd been doing with the mercury boots at the Station had proved that the first danger in using them was tripping over her own feet, or stumbling over an unexpected rock or bit of uneven ground. She focused on noting potential hazards, all the while the rumbling of the earth intensified. The constant thunder of fleeing creatures grew louder, telling Nyx they were gaining on her despite the aid of her boots.

Fleeing panicked human didn't have shit on fleeing panicked herd animals, a fact that was apparently as true on this planet as it was on Earth. Already her muscles screamed and her lungs burned. The boots' ability to amplify her movements didn't magically grant her better lung capacity or stamina. She'd determined they were best used for a short-term emergency burst of speed, or for when she needed to jump really, really high.

It was a very short matter of time before she either ran out of endurance, or got tired and sloppy and tripped. She needed a temporary safe space, one that took her out of the path of the oncoming herd without taking her *into* the path of the unda. The unda that were rapidly closing in on her. The first problem, at least, could be solved by the presence of a tall tree, but this accursed place *had* no tall trees. It did have a rock formation jutting from the ground a few hundred feet ahead.

Nyx put everything she had into running, her quadriceps muscles screaming as she flew forward. The herd was almost upon her and she didn't need to look back to know that. She could *feel* it, so much energy and momentum gaining on her.

She was fifty feet from the rock formation, the sense that she was about to be swallowed by running bodies and trampled beneath hooves imminent. Thirty feet and her legs and lungs threatened to give out. Fifteen feet and she was *almost* there.

Ten feet. Five.

A heavy shoulder clipped her back, sending her sprawling. She had just enough presence of mind to get out the *exa* command to her boots before she slammed into the side of the rock. The impact knocked the breath from her lungs. She sucked in harsh gasps of air and forced herself upright, pressing her back to the rock.

The herd of animals, as large as bisons but sheathed in white fur and with horns more like a gazelle's, streamed around the rock in an unending wave. The crush of bodies was near enough that one too-close brush, one animal being knocked aside by another, and she would be crushed against the rock or knocked beneath the hooves of the panicked animals.

Nyx examined the rock formation as well as she could without moving. Rectangular at the base, it had no convenient overhang to hunker beneath, being widest at the bottom and becoming ever more narrow as it went up. Still, it *went up*. She needed to climb. To climb, she needed to be facing the rock.

Her heart pounded out an erratic beat in her chest at the prospect of turning around. The ordinarily simple movement felt impossible. The herd ran so close by she could easily be hit. If she did get turned around, she wouldn't be able to see them.

And if you stay here, you're going to get consumed by magic-eating alien amoebas.

Okay, that one did it. She turned. Her hip brushed a furred rump and the animal kicked out at the unexpected touch. Its hoof grazed her thigh but didn't hit head on. It would bruise, but right now adrenaline dulled the impact.

Nyx looked above her, found handholds and toeholds, and climbed. Once her feet cleared the height of the stampede she paused for a moment, resting her forehead against the rock and taking a deep, shaky breath. Her cheek stung and blood trickled down her face, a parting gift from that first shove against the rock. Adrenaline made her light and heady, and she started climbing again before the lightness could turn to shakiness.

The rock formation wasn't very high—about twelve feet, she guessed—and she reached the top quickly. It was a small space, barely four feet across but flat, and she collapsed onto it gratefully. With her eyes closed and her forehead kissing the chalky surface, the thunder and rumble of the passing herd was almost soothing.

She lifted her head as the last of the animals ran by. The unda had converged into a single force, streaming across the ground like rushing water. As she watched, the distance between the unda and the back of the herd diminished. And though it was the nature of this place, and nature was rarely kind, she closed her eyes when the first animal went down, swallowed by a red wave. When she looked again, it was to find a new problem. Her little island was surrounded by a sea of red—and that red was crawling upward.

Shit. Shit, shit, shit. She'd known the unda fed off life that contained or produced magic, but she hadn't known if they could *sense* it. But of course they could, because what life-form didn't have a method of locating its food source? The unda crept up the sides of the rock, moving slower than the mass taking down the tail end of the fleeing herd, as if the unda weren't certain if she was worth the diversion.

She felt like a horror film heroine who had fled upstairs and locked herself in the one windowless room. She'd temporarily escaped a gruesome end, but that end knew right where to find her, and she had nowhere left to go.

Movement caught her eye and she jerked her gaze left. There, impossibly, was a figure cutting through the lake of red. Black armor sheathed their body from neck to toe, and a cloak—yes, an actual cloak—streamed behind them as they ran, its hood pulled over their head, obscuring the face. Not that it mattered. The cloak might be a new addition, but she'd seen that armor just this morning, and she knew that run, knew the swift, determined, economical strides.

Kaden Moor closed the distance between them, racing to reach her before the unda did. He clearly wasn't worried about the red sea he ran through, and it was then that she remembered what Jevryn had said, what the Council had *used* the ore mined on Kyvren for: to make Enforcer armor. The same type of armor the Meerkin had used the ore for to protect themselves and their young from the planet's fire rains.

Kaden wasn't worried about the unda because he didn't need to be. He was completely covered in armor made from the ore mined from this planet. He was immune. And though the knowledge of how that armor had come to be in the Council's—and therefore his—possession infuriated her, it was also the only reason she might, possibly, survive.

Emphasis on *might.* The creeping mass of red was five inches from the top of the rock. They kept pausing every now and then, as if unsure if she was up there. The urge to Hide herself was strong, but if they could sense magic use, all Hiding herself would do was confirm that she was there to be eaten.

She gauged the distance between her and Kaden. He was in a dead run, maybe a hundred feet off. By the time the unda finally spilled over onto her plateau of former safety, Kaden had closed half that remaining distance. When he skidded to a halt at the base of the rock, she stood in the dead center of the flat top, a mere six-inch radius of clear space around her feet.

"Jump!" he barked.

She had about one second to think of all the ways this could go horribly wrong. The distance between her and the ground wasn't so much that it was *impossible* for Kaden to catch her, but if she hit him badly he'd either drop her or she'd knock him over. In both those scenarios, *he* would be fine, but she would be touching ground and potentially eaten alive.

No choice. She took what little clear space was available to her, gathered herself, and jumped.

27

Nyx hit that brief, weightless moment at the apex of a jump, and then she was falling. Below, Kaden adjusted his position to compensate for the trajectory of her fall. She crashed into him, arms landing on his shoulders, legs clamping around his waist, breaking her fall and holding herself up as his arms locked around her. He grunted at the impact, took two stumbling steps back and then caught his balance.

When it was clear he wasn't going to fall over, she dropped her forehead to her arm, sucking in a deep breath while she watched the rushing river of red pass by below, streaming around Kaden's boots. Her mouth, refusing as always to filter itself, popped off. "I don't think I've ever properly expressed how grateful I am for your freakishly large muscles."

He made a noise. It took her a moment to identify it because it was such an un-Kaden-like sound.

"Did hell freeze over?" she asked. "Because I would swear you just laughed."

He gave a short grunt in response. There. That was more like the Kaden she knew. She kept her mouth shut after that, waiting while the wave of unda continued around them and trying not to feel awkward about the necessity of being wrapped around him. Given that he'd been pretty pissed at her the last time she'd spoken to him, she doubted he was any more thrilled about the current situation than she was.

Adults, she reminded herself. *Life-saving necessity. Totally doesn't have to be awkward.*

After what felt like hours, but frequent glances at her watch assured her was only minutes, the last of the unda moved past them, leaving blessedly uncontaminated ground in their wake. They were moving slower now, the colony waiting as some of their number stayed mounded over fallen bodies, feeding.

Nyx didn't *hear* slurping sounds, but the frenzied movement of those mounds made her feel like she should. She didn't like to think of how easily that could be her right now. If Seth was somewhere out in all of this, without armor, if he wasn't safe with the Meerkin... She pushed the thought out of her head. Worrying about him wasn't going to help her find him.

"Is it safe to get down?" she asked. Silently, she added, *Please know the answer to that question.* If his knowledge base was as limited as hers, she might be fucked unless they found the Meerkin quickly.

"Yes."

The unda hadn't moved out of sight yet, but she supposed Kaden could just pick her up again if they came back. She unlocked her legs and dropped. Her feet found purchase, and Kaden released her and stepped away. Now that she could see in a direction that wasn't what's-on-the-other-side-of-Kaden's-shoulder, she spotted a second black-clad figure in the distance. Their hood wasn't up, revealing the long black hair and rigid posture that made it all too easy to identify Jevryn A-Morridahn. And all too easy to see no one else was with him.

She asked anyway. "Is Seth with you?"

Kaden's expression was difficult to read beneath the deep over-hang of the cloak's hood, but he didn't hesitate before shaking his head. "According to Jevryn, you knocked him clear of the portal. Unless he's left on his own, he should be at the original portal desti-nation. I imagine the Meerkin have found him by now."

Relief was an instantaneous drop in her stomach. Had Jevryn volunteered this information, or had Kaden actually cared enough to ask? Given that he was still speaking in a wooden monotone, she doubted "cared" was the correct descriptor. More likely he'd thought about it through a practical lens and determined she wouldn't go anywhere without the information.

She dusted her hands on her jeans. "Great. Let's get Jevryn and he can portal us to Seth."

Kaden did hesitate this time, but she didn't have the opportunity to contemplate it because the sound of an explosion jerked her gaze back to where the unda were concentrated in large mounds over what had once been animals. One of those mounds had ejected puffs of red high into the air, the released spores spreading like the cloud of ash from a volcanic eruption. The next mound did the same. Then the next, and the next, and the next.

"Get down." Kaden jerked at the ties holding his cloak. She knelt with him as he whipped it over their heads and settled it over them like a tent. It was heavy like a weighted blanket, and thankfully large, the material draping on the ground around them.

She reached for a piece of the pooled fabric, flipping it over to inspect the external side. Small hammered scales of Kyvren's ore were sewn onto the outside like sequins. The only thing that saved it from looking like a mermaid cloak was the black color and the fact the scales had a matte finish rather than a shiny one.

She took in the cloak, with its deep hood to protect from the spores, then took in his armor. "Did you know Jevryn was going to pull this stunt?"

Kaden met her angry gaze, his own eyes still dead and tired. "Would you believe me if I said no?"

"If it was the truth, yes."

"I didn't know. Jevryn told me to meet the two of you outside the Station with your armor so you could acclimate to it without the Station's interference. Maybe I should have suspected, but honestly, I quit asking questions six months ago."

"Why?"

"Because he answers them."

She…didn't have anything to say to that. Or maybe she did, but he'd already made it quite clear that he wasn't going to be humoring her curiosity with regards to his personal life. So questions like *why are you still working for him?* and *can I interest you in a rant about why Jevryn is a bad person to put your faith in?* were off the table.

Silence stretched between them, and if there was anything more awkward than huddling in a makeshift tent with your face two inches from your ex while you waited for the outside world to be navigable again, she didn't know what it was.

Speaking of… "Please tell me you know of a way other than trial-and-error to tell when it's safe to come out from beneath the cloak?"

"I imagine Jevryn will let us know."

"And how is Jevryn going to know it's safe if he's also huddling underneath a cloak?"

"We're only under the cloak because of you. Jevryn has these." He tugged first at a piece of cloth hanging around his neck that could be pulled up over the mouth and nose. Then he found the cloak's hood and pulled a piece of fabric from the inside of it. She could see how, when the hood was on, the piece would hang down in front of the face like a veil. Both it and the neck-cloth were bedazzled with tiny chitin-ore scales, sewn in with enough spacing to allow them to be breathed and seen through.

"How does the armor work?" she asked. "And why doesn't he just use the insulating atmospheric spells the Council made when they first discovered the universe?"

"I asked him the same question. The problem with the insulating spells is that they are magic, and the unda eat magic. Including protective spells. Wearing one is like lighting a signal beacon to any unda within a ten-mile radius. The spell would protect you for a short time, but unless you have an endless supply of magic to keep powering it—which would only draw more and more of them to you—eventually they'll eat through it. It's the same with other magic use. You can use it even if they're in the area, but they'll start eating it the second it leaves your fingertips. Short-burst spells are best."

"Can Jevryn's death magic kill them?"

"Yes, but he says using enough to kill them in quantity would only draw more of them, and there isn't any point when we have the armor."

Nyx tugged at the cloak covering them. "How does it work?"

"The chitin-ore masks magical signatures, making the wearer appear as magically-inert life or landscape. But while the unda can and do crawl over inert things, because the unda makes its home in the natural ore basins, they avoid it during the feeding season.

"The basins are where they go when they're in their dormant state, so they won't voluntarily come into contact with it while hunting. The spores have some small ability to navigate in the air and will avoid landing on it if possible, but if they do make contact they can be brushed off the armor easily enough, as they won't cling to it."

They lapsed into another silence. The air was growing warmer and increasingly humid as they continued to breathe in the small, confined space. It reminded her uncomfortably of that time she and Kaden had fogged up the car windows in a parking lot one night like they were teenagers out past curfew. And no, that wasn't yet another awkward thought in the awkwardness that was this moment.

Thank the stars it was too dark beneath the cloak's cover for him to read her memories in her face. She hit the light-up dial on her watch, navigated to the stopwatch screen and pressed the start button. Might as well know how long it took for the spores to stop falling, in case the information should prove useful later.

Whenever crouching quietly got to be a bit too much—read, whenever having absolutely nothing to interrupt the portal magic spasms still pulsing through her got to be too much—she checked to see how much time had elapsed. After four checks and twenty-one minutes, forty-two seconds, Kaden shifted slightly. She wanted it to be a my-knees-are-tired-from-being-bent-this-long shift, but she had a feeling it was more of an I'm-about-to-break-the-silence shift.

"How have you been?" He asked it softly, and in the darkness of the small enclosed space it felt like far too intimate a question. He'd said it so quietly, so tentatively, that she almost ignored it. If she didn't answer, if she pretended he hadn't asked, he probably wouldn't push it.

How had she been? It was the kind of question that was nine kinds of loaded when asked by him and in that manner, and who knew what answer he was looking for, or what question he was really asking. How had she been in a general sense? How had she been since her memories had been given back to her? How had she been since he'd brought her mother to the Station? How had she been since she'd broken his Link to her?

She didn't know how to answer the question. Because it was a complicated answer, and it wasn't his business anymore, and she suddenly understood exactly why he'd been so pissed at her for forcing him into "vacation".

Her voice was overly bright when she said, "Good. Great. How have you been?"

"Good," he answered dryly. "Great."

Apparently, when trapped in a dark space with nothing better to do, everyone became a comedian. And while she *was* grateful Kaden had found her before she was eaten alive by magic-eating blobs, she would really like for this little moment to be over.

Wait a minute. Her brain did a quick rewind and focused on the fact that he'd found her on a foreign planet when he should have had no idea where she was.

"Kaden," she said slowly, "how exactly did you find me?"

"Not the way you're worried about." Did she detect a faint note of bitterness in his voice? When she didn't respond, letting the weight of her skepticism fill the space, he said, "A Link is a one-time magic, Nyx. Once it's broken, it can't be made again. Ever, to anyone."

The tenseness that had crept into her shoulders eased. "Then how?"

"You have all your memories back and Viktor Hawthorne was a Tracker. You don't know?"

She laughed. "This may shock you, but Viktor didn't exactly want us to know how his magic worked. Seth and I's favorite pastime was running away and seeing how long we could stay gone. Considering Viktor was the one who had to drag us back to purgatory each time, giving away his trade secrets wasn't in his best interests. I *did* think he had to have a trail to follow." Seeing as how she'd been blasted across the planet by malfunctioning portal magic, and skipping through a portal didn't leave a trail, she considered herself understandably confused.

"A trail is the quickest method, and the only one guaranteed to return a result without luck, but it isn't the only way. If a Tracker knows the scent marker for the person they're looking for, they can scan an area for that marker. Think of it as a pulse of magic that spreads out in all directions from the Tracker. How far that pulse travels depends on the strength of the Tracker's magic. If the marker they're looking for is within range, it pings back. Depending on the ability of the Tracker, their magic may be able to identify markers similar to the one they're actively searching for." He paused for a moment. "That's how I found you when I went looking for your mother. Jevryn gave me Elena's scent marker, and I picked yours up instead. It was similar enough I knew you were closely related."

Knew she was Hidden, was what he didn't say. She had the oddest feeling he was on the verge of apologizing—why else bring it up?—and considering he'd never once said *sorry* when she'd needed him to, she wasn't much interested in being on the receiving end of it right now. She cleared her throat. "And if the marker you're looking for isn't within the range of your magic?"

He let out a breath that was almost a sigh, which was once again about twenty times more expression than he ordinarily showed. But he answered the question. "Then I move to the outer edge of the searched area and try again. When we were separated here, Jevryn was close enough that I found him on my first try. You took several more, and it's fortunate I got the right direction on the second search. The smartest course is generally moving outward in a block pattern—if you pick a straight line and keep going, your quarry could simply be getting farther and farther away from you in the opposite direction.

"It's why if you're trying to find a person in a large geographical area without a trail to follow, you want a team of Trackers on the job."

Made sense. But... "Why do I get the feeling you aren't telling me that solely to educate me on the fascinating ways of the modern Hound?"

"Because I'm not. I'm trying to explain why finding Seth isn't going to be as easy as you want it to be."

Nyx frowned. "We shouldn't need to find him if he's back with the Meerkin. Jevryn can take us there." He'd portaled them to that precise location the first time, he could do it again.

"About that. There's—"

Jevryn's clear, sharp voice rang out. "The rains have passed, for now."

It wasn't until that moment—hearing his voice—that Nyx remembered how very, viscerally pissed off at him she was. What the hell had he been thinking, surprise portaling her here? Griff was going to murder him and she was going to enjoy watching.

She and Kaden patted at the inside walls of their "tent" to knock any spores off the outside, then carefully flipped it over their heads. The sudden influx of bright sunshine made her squint. Once her eyes adjusted, she and Kaden did a mutual inspection to make sure none of the spores had gotten on them, and then he gave his cloak a final shaking out and put it back on.

Nyx eyed the ground around them, littered with spores except for the small oval of space the cloak had covered. "Is that safe for me to walk on?"

He shook his head. "Not yet. Wait here."

"Not like I have much choice," she muttered as he jogged off. She couldn't help but wonder why Jevryn was still so far away, and wasn't making a move to come closer. Had he finally developed good sense and realized she would be pissed at him and he didn't want to deal with her? Kaden reached him and was handed two items: a black bag—one of the ones he'd been carrying when he'd come to meet them outside the Station—and something smaller that she couldn't make out.

They spoke for a minute, then Kaden jogged back. He handed her the smaller item, which turned out to be a canteen. *Thank the stars.* She uncapped it and drank half the water before it occurred to her to stop and ask, "How much water do we have?"

Kaden just looked at her.

"This is it?"

He nodded.

"As in, this is the only water ration *I* have, or this is the only water ration we *all* have?"

Another blank stare.

"Great." She thrust the canteen at him. "You could have told me that before I drank half of it."

He pushed it back at her. "You need it."

"And you don't?"

He shrugged. He was impossible. Honestly, she didn't know why she bothered talking to him at all. At any rate, if Jevryn could find her a sandwich on Amentia Furor, he ought to be able to get them more water. Still, she only drank another mouthful before declaring herself no longer thirsty.

Kaden took the canteen and handed her the bag. "Get changed." He faced away, giving her privacy, at which point Jevryn did the same, far away though he was.

She unzipped the bag. One set of chitin-ore armor, one chitin-ore cloak with veil and mask, one pair of chitin-ore boots. Given that she was wide out in the open, shucking out of her clothes felt weird. Just because she couldn't *see* anyone didn't mean there wasn't sapient life on this planet seeing her. Then again, any sapient life on this planet probably wasn't interested in the naked human body outside of purely scientific interests, so what did it matter?

She changed quickly. The armor fit her so well that Griff had to have given Jevryn her measurements for it after the councilor had first agreed to take her to Kyvren. It fit more like regular clothing than what she envisioned when she thought the word *armor*, but having seen the damage it could prevent when a flying dinosaur had latched talons into Seth's armor and he'd barely been scratched, she didn't doubt its efficacy. She tried and failed not to feel dirty for putting it on, knowing how it had been obtained. Stolen goods from a stolen planet, taken from a people who had been deemed disposable simply because they were inconvenient.

She couldn't undo it. But she could try to make someone fix it.

She finished dressing but paused before putting on the new footwear, staring at her mercury boots instead. She hadn't gone a day without wearing them since she'd gotten them. They had saved her life once already today. She didn't want to lose them.

But they weren't capable of repelling the unda. She sucked it up, put on the new shoes, and packed the mercury boots into the bag along with her discarded clothing. She clipped Constance onto the armor's tactical belt, strapped the bag with her old gear onto her back, and threw the cloak over all of it. And no, wearing a cloak didn't make her feel like she was cosplaying. Not at all. It would have been fun if it wasn't real.

"You can turn around now."

Kaden did.

Nyx eyed the ground. "It's safe for me to walk over this now?"

He nodded.

"Good." Her gaze shot to Jevryn and fury boiled up in her. "Because I think I'm going to kill him."

She took off at a dead sprint. Judging by the way Kaden yelled and lunged after her, he was worried she was *actually* going to kill the councilor. She wasn't. Well, she was relatively certain she *couldn't,* anyway. She was just so *angry.*

Anger made her fast—faster, at least, than Kaden who was running after her. Long-term there was probably no question that he could outlast her in a chase, but short-term all that muscle slowed him down.

Jevryn, no doubt hearing the sound of rapidly approaching footsteps, turned to face them. His eyes widened. "Nyx, stop," he ordered.

Yeah, she didn't think so.

Jevryn's eyes shifted over her shoulder. "Kaden." The short, clipped name was just as much of an order as the command he'd given her to stop had been.

Unlike Nyx, Kaden obeyed. She heard a grunt of effort and then a hard, heavy weight slammed into her back. He had tackled her. Actually *tackled* her. They went down, skidding another few feet toward Jevryn—at which point all that magic spasming over her body activated. The world exploded.

This time, when she came out the other side of the portal magic blast, Kaden was still holding onto her. He took the brunt of the impact as they slammed into the trunk of a tree, bark scratching against the side of his face.

When she pushed away he let her go. She gained her feet, twigs crunching beneath her boots as she did. They were in forest now. *Deep* forest. That portal blast had been large enough to move them from the southern half of the continent clean through to the north. However far she'd been from Seth before, she was farther now.

"What just happened?" she asked.

"Resonant interference," Kaden said, picking himself off the ground.

She stared at him. A line of sweat ran down the side of his face, mixed with the dirt from their impromptu landing and a thin trickle of blood from a shallow scrape. His expression was as unreadable as ever. When she hardened her stare, all it did was elicit a shrug in response.

"Resonant interference?" she echoed.

"That's what Jevryn called it."

Okay then. "What does it mean?"

"Practically? The two of you get too close to each other and—" He bumped his fists together, let his hands fly open as he dragged them apart in the universal gesture of something going *boom*.

"And theoretically?"

Kaden shrugged again. "He spared me the details. I was supposed to keep you from getting too close to him."

"Great job," she muttered.

"I didn't expect you to attack him the moment you had the option." He studied her. "Why are you so angry with him?"

"Aside from the fact that he basically abducted me?" No answer, just that steady silent gaze. "You wouldn't understand."

He crossed his arms. "Try me."

She shook her head. She had no idea what Kaden would think if she told him what Jevryn's relationship to her was. "Can you find him? How far away are we?"

Kaden didn't push it. Instead he crouched, hand splayed across the forest floor, and a pulse of magic moved in an outward circle from him. She felt it wash by, like ripples in a lake, and then go still. A moment later, he stood.

"He's two miles that way." He pointed and started walking. She fell in beside him.

"How big is your range, exactly?"

He gave her a look.

"What? Is it inappropriate to ask about the size of a Tracker's range?"

He turned his focus straight ahead.

"Do you guys keep little black books so whenever you run into other Tracker friends you can compare notes? Sadie's range is bigger than John's but not as big as Jack's?"

His voice was perfectly monotone as he said, "The less you talk, the more lung capacity you have for walking." But she would swear there was a faint tick at the side of his mouth. As if he was trying really, really hard not to smile.

What would you know? Apparently all it took to get Kaden Moor to *almost* show emotion was a dangerous planet and really bad innuendo.

28

J evryn was waiting for them. He sat with his back against a tree, his long legs stretched out in front of him, his eyes closed. Someone else might have made the mistake of thinking he was asleep. To Nyx, it looked like he was praying to a divine entity for patience. Which was the moment she realized she didn't even know enough about her own father to know if he believed in divine entities.

Probably not. He was a touch too arrogant to pray to anyone but himself. Oh, now there was a thought—maybe he was praying to *himself* for patience.

She took the unexpected opportunity, as she stopped a foot or so shy of the distance that had sent them hurtling away from each other last time, to study him. He was so still he looked more like a statue than a man. She couldn't even see his breathing from this far away.

Studying him now, he looked tired, despite a face that came nowhere close to reflecting his true age. His skin was still unlined, at least while no expression marred it, and she found herself once again unsettled by how close he looked in age to her. He looked slightly older than Kiev, as if he'd spent more time outside of the Nexuses' influences than his twin, but he still looked more like Nyx's older brother than her father.

She knew she'd been staring too long when she realized Kaden was watching her, watching Jevryn. The councilor finally deigned to open his eyes, not a hint of surprise at seeing them. He'd undoubtedly heard them walk up.

"Have you made up your mind?" he asked.

"About what?" She didn't know how she knew he was talking to her and not to Kaden.

"Whether to keep the necessary distance between us or to foolishly waste our time being forcefully separated again. Though I must warn you, should you choose the latter, it comes with risk." He drew back the sleeve of his cloak, revealing the row of bracelets along his forearm. Half of them were empty. "Resonant interference depletes portal magic at an absurdly high rate. We can only manage so many repeat performances before I no longer have the requisite amount to return us home."

She took a careful step back. "What *is* this? What did I do?"

"Two mages should never attempt to use portal magic with competing objectives within the same sphere of influence. The magics become confused. As it is a naturally occurring magic that answers to those with the proper ability to wield it, as opposed to an inborn magic that can answer only to the one who produces it, portal magic will attempt to do whatever a nearby mage asks of it. My will would have been sufficient to prevent such an occurrence, had you had no magic of your own on you. However, as you did and attempted to use it, the two merged.

"I began to take us from Earth, but you—" He broke off, brow furrowing. "What *were* you thinking of? Not remaining on Earth, or the blast would have attempted to return you there."

She gritted her teeth. "I just wanted to get away from you."

"Ah. Naturally. As I said, the magic becomes confused with competing commands. I wanted to bring us here, and you wanted to be as far from me as possible. The magic attempted to do both and became entangled. Therefore it executed my command first, and yours second. It will take some time for it to untangle itself and respond to new commands.

"Currently, the nature of the entanglement means that you and I must be within a certain proximity for the magic to activate. But when it *does* activate, it attempts to carry out both commands again. As we are already on Kyvren, which was my intent, it sends us apart, which was yours."

"So you can't portal us to the original landing point? To Seth?"

"Unfortunately, no."

She let that sink in. Somehow, when she'd noticed her own problems with portal magic, she hadn't really believed it would be affecting Jevryn too. He seemed so untouchable. "And there's no way to make this stop?"

"Time eventually makes all things cease."

Great. He was feeling philosophical. "How much time?"

"A day, at least. Perhaps more. The stronger the wills involved, the longer the interference lingers, and we have already proved you to be quite stubborn."

She wanted to snap something about apples and how they didn't fall far from the trees that grew them, but Kaden was here. "You didn't think about that before deciding to portal me without my consent?"

"No, as you were not supposed to be carrying any portal magic with you, and I did not detect that you were." He paused. "I still do not."

"I'm a *Hidden*, you immortal ass, and weird shit keeps happening to me. So I Hid the portal magic."

"I see."

That was all he had to say? "Are you going to explain why you thought this was a good idea?"

"No."

The simple refusal sent her blood pressure skyrocketing. She turned abruptly and walked ten feet off, her hands curled into fists. The deep black that veined her hands and arms when the chaos thorns kicked her emotions into high gear was spreading beneath her skin as she tried and failed to get a grip on herself. It was as if her ability to regulate had gone entirely out the window. Some combination of the past few months of anxiety, the revelations that had come before them, and the general amount of upheaval that had come before that.

She was *tired*. So tired, and very thirsty, and pissed off, and she couldn't get to Seth, and Jevryn was still *Jevryn*.

She turned on her heel and stomped back to the invisible line of perfect distance separating her from her father. "If you ever get the bright idea to *surprise me* again, don't. I don't care why you thought this was necessary, but here's a suggestion—the next time you want to do something this stupid, ask me first."

He remained perfectly calm. "If I had told you that you needed to leave your friends behind, that the only person I had any intention of taking to Kyvren was you, would you have agreed?"

"That depends on *why* you believed it necessary."

"And that is why I did not ask."

Of course. Because he hadn't had—and apparently still didn't have—any intention of explaining things to her. Or of taking what she wanted into account. "How far are we from the original portal point?"

He arched one annoyingly perfect eyebrow. "I haven't the faintest idea." Whatever the look on her face was, it apparently prompted him to explain further. "Resonant interference leaves no room for control, especially when your original intent was so vague. When we are close enough for the magic to activate, it pushes the two of us apart. It doesn't specify *where* or *how far*.

"This has now occurred twice. The only thing I can tell you with any certainty is that we are on the correct continent. It is, however, a rather large one. We could be ten miles from the original portal location, or several hundred."

She looked between Jevryn and Kaden, and the reality of the situation finally sank in. She was lost. In an alien wilderness. With her ex-boyfriend and her deadbeat dad. Perfect.

"We have two options," Jevryn continued. "One, wait for the resonant interference to dissipate and then portal to the original location. As I have explained, this could take anywhere from one to several days. Two, Kaden may search for Riven's scent marker, in the hopes that we find the proper direction."

No wonder Jevryn had wanted Valedan to give the scent marker to Kaden before they'd left. He'd never planned on taking the young royal with them. Still, Nyx had a slight correction to make to option two. "Seth's."

"I beg your pardon?"

"Kaden may search for *Seth's* marker. At the moment, I don't give a damn where Riven is. We find Seth. *Then* we look for Riven."

"If that is what you wish." He stood, the movement stiff. "As you have proven yourself inept at maintaining proper distance, the two of you may lead and I shall follow."

"Sure," she said breezily. "Let's go."

Kaden's eyes, fixed on her, narrowed as she all but skipped away. He was right to be suspicious, though her reasons weren't all that nefarious. After they'd been walking for a few minutes she turned, quickly, in time to see Jevryn before he, too, halted.

"Are you limping?" she asked the councilor. And did it bother her, the teensiest bit, that he might be hurt?

"Has anyone ever complimented you on the astuteness of your observations?"

Any momentary compassion she might have felt evaporated. "You know, for a guy who's like nine-hundred years old, you don't act very much like—" She cut off before the words "a father" could leave her mouth.

"Much like...?" he prompted.

She shook her head. "The point is, I didn't think you were capable of the same bodily injuries as we mere mortals."

Even from this far away, she could see the faintest hint of lavender tinge his gray eyes. She wanted to ask him what the color meant. She wanted to know if her own eyes had ever looked like that. Why hers didn't seem to change as often as his.

"I am as capable of sustaining injury as the next individual. I am, as you said, an immortal ass—not an invincible one." He made a go-on motion with his hand.

She turned and resumed walking. Mostly because, having proved himself *not* invincible, she had been struck by the over-whelming urge to strangle him. She could just make him lose consciousness for a minute or two. It would be very therapeutic, and he'd still live to get them off this planet.

She was so lost in joyful fantasies of a temporarily unconscious Jevryn that it took her a moment to notice that Kaden kept glancing at her out of the corner of his eye.

"What?" she finally snapped.

"He's different with you."

She couldn't stop the little leap her heart made, the brief moment of hope that, in some small way, she *meant* something to her father. "How so?"

"Just...different." Kaden shrugged. "More human."

She vehemently quashed the nascent hope inside her. "He's just hoping to use me to get to Griff." Though at this point, that justification was becoming a little tired. A little less believable. If he'd wanted to use her to get to Griff after she'd found out who he was, it would have been simple: all he would have had to do was pretend to love her. Hell, pretend to *like* her.

"I don't think it's that."

"Then what *do* you think it is?"

Kaden was silent for long enough she thought he wouldn't answer. Or that he was going to say something hilariously off the mark. He did neither. "He notices you. You've only been around him a handful of times, so I'm not sure you realize how unusual that is. He doesn't *see* people. At best, he finds the necessity of interacting with them irritating."

"Pretty sure I irritate him beyond all measure."

"When people irritate him, he dismisses them. I think he can only put up with me because I keep my mouth shut unless we're discussing things he finds important. Half the time, he forgets I'm there."

She stopped walking when he did. This was officially the chattiest Kaden had been since she'd brought him back from Arkadia. Naturally, it was only because he was trying to solve a problem.

"He doesn't try to get away from you," he said. Spoken more like a question than a statement.

She didn't say anything. Kaden hadn't been there when Jevryn had been doing nothing *but* getting away from her as fast as possible, and she'd been begging him to stay.

"When you wrote, he dropped everything. He called me back from—" He shook his head. "He didn't think or plan or do anything he usually does before he makes a decision. He just went."

Nyx could see why all of that might seem compelling to Kaden, but it equaled nothing to her. So she existed in Jevryn's mental space. Was she supposed to feel honored by that scrap of a difference between how he viewed her and everyone else, when the end result was still something less than care and a universe less than love?

"What's your point?"

His eyes searched hers. "I guess I'm wondering if you found that answer you were looking for."

He'd figured it out, then. Just like Morgen had. She was going to have to do a better job of hiding her feelings, or everyone in the universe was going to know Jevryn was her father simply because she mouthed off to him.

"Is there an issue?" Jevryn called. It must have been killing him to have to maintain physical distance between them, something Nyx shouldn't have found nearly as satisfying as she did.

"No issue." Kaden crouched, fingers splaying against the earth, magic rippling from him. Seconds ticked by. Then he stood, shook his head, and chose a different direction to lead them in.

Nyx followed, trying and failing not to let worry eat at her. Because no matter how many times she told herself that it was fine, that Seth was safe with the Meerkin, a little voice in her mind wouldn't stop whispering, "But what if he's not?"

29

Nyx spent the next four hours hiking, and alternating between daydreaming about water and daydreaming about food, neither of which they had. As luck would have it, when that first explosion of portal magic had knocked them all to separate places, the second bag Kaden had been carrying—the one that had apparently contained such useful necessities as food, water, and medical supplies—had been lost. Since neither she nor Jevryn could use portal magic, they couldn't make a window into somewhere else and retrieve replacements, either.

They'd had the one water canteen only because it had been strapped to Kaden's person, and it was now empty. Which was a feat in and of itself, because apparently they were all martyrs, as she'd never been engaged in such a long round of no-you-take-it arguments in her life. They'd ended up splitting it, and she would wager it hadn't been enough to do any of them much good. The funny thing about water? It wasn't something you thought about a lot until you didn't have it.

She was thinking about it now. Her lips were dry and starting to crack, and she was getting that slightly heat-dazed, muzzy feeling she used to get in Tempe, before she'd realized that, in the desert in summer, one should not step a foot outside without a gallon of water in tow. The armor must have been spelled to within an inch of its making, because she didn't sweat nearly as much as she should have in it, and that was probably the only reason she didn't feel worse.

As it was, she blamed the heat daze for the fact it took her longer than it should have to realize the sun was beginning to set. She had tuned out of almost everything except putting one foot in front of the other, and waiting here and there while Kaden did his Tracker thing. He had yet to pick up anything of interest, and working through a Tracker's grid pattern, it turned out, could be extremely tedious.

The only positive development so far was that the magic twinges rolling through her body like clockwork had gradually slowed their frequency and intensity. It felt less like being shocked, now, and more like a spasm that rippled to encompass every muscle. And she wasn't so out of it that she hadn't noticed that, as the time between the spasms had lengthened, Jevryn had drifted gradually closer to her to no ill effect.

Was there some kind of distance formula involved with resonant interference? Something like the number of magic twinges multiplied by the time elapsed between them, divided by the intensity expressed as a decimal? And how exactly would that convert to feet? There was a reason she'd never been particularly dedicated to math as a subject of study.

She didn't know if there was a mathematical formula and Jevryn was doing the calculations in his head, or if he was simply pushing his luck, but the space between them had gradually shrunk to a disappointing eight feet. On the bright side, this meant they had to be closer to regaining the ability to portal, and therefore closer to getting back to Seth. And food, and water.

The sun began to set when it was only four in the afternoon, by Nyx's watch. Either Kyvren had less than twenty-four hours in one of its days, or it had really long nights. They didn't so much find shelter for the night as they found an area to put their backs to and thus narrow down the directions that needed to be guarded. A few miles back they'd run into a ridge that ran through the forest, and the vertical drop from there to where they stood below provided a decent enough place to rest.

They broke camp just as the sun melted below the horizon, though Nyx only called it that because sleeping outside at night on a foreign planet sounded mildly more civilized when she thought of it as "breaking camp". Realistically, they had no camp to make. It turned out that if you had no food, no water, no tent, and no gear, settling in for the night was as simple as putting your back to the nearest supportive surface. In this case, that supportive surface was the sheer earthen face from the ridgeline above.

Kaden chose a spot to Nyx's right, a few feet away. Jevryn chose one to her left, a conservative twelve feet from her, and eased down, careful of the leg he'd been limping on all day. She still didn't see any blood and he'd never complained, so hopefully it wasn't serious. She told herself her concern was purely for the fact that if it *was* serious, it would slow them down, and not because she was worried about him.

She didn't have the emotional capacity to worry about him. Not when the sun was setting and Seth was out there, alone. At least, shitty as her circumstances were, she had Jevryn and Kaden. What if Seth hadn't found the Meerkin? Or what if he had and they, understandably distrusting of bipedal races at present, had left him to his own resources? What if the unda had come and he'd had no protection, no safe place to be?

She pressed the heel of her left palm into her stomach, pushing against the anxiety as if it were a physical thing she could quash. She would know, wouldn't she? Even without her Hiding around his heart, she would know if the space in the universe that was uniquely Seth-shaped was suddenly empty. Right?

She pushed harder against the emptiness in her gut and closed her eyes as the last bit of sun disappeared beneath the horizon and true night fell. She had never liked sleeping alone out of doors. It had always sounded romantic in books—sleeping beneath the stars, the fresh air on your face and the soft sounds of night birds and the chirping of crickets filling the air—but whenever Viktor had made her sleep outside overnight, she'd always felt too exposed. A room had walls and she could feel the space between them, could know the finite area in which something else could inhabit the space with her. A room had doors or windows that would have to be opened for someone else to come into that space. Outside, there were no boundaries to keep someone away, no turning of a door handle to signal the arrival of an intruder, no sheets to burrow under to feel cocooned and safe.

Outside, there was just emptiness. The vast, unyielding

expanse of so much world around her, knowing that anything could be in it and feeling alone and small for the knowledge. She wrapped her cloak around her, pulling it tight, but she shivered as the temperature plummeted with surprising swiftness. Despite the fact that on Earth she wouldn't be going to bed for several hours yet, she was exhausted and longed for sleep. But she couldn't bring herself to close her eyes. The absolute darkness curling around her should have made closing her eyes feel like less of a risk—if she couldn't see anything anyway, what was the danger? —but it didn't.

If Jevryn or Kaden were having any similar issues falling asleep, they didn't voice them. She shivered more, harder, and finally drifted off to the sounds of unknown insects filling the night. The sound was a little bit like crickets. It wasn't soothing.

Nyx woke significantly warmer than she'd been when she'd fallen asleep, and it took her a moment to realize it was because another cloak had been draped over her in addition to her own. It smelled ever-so-faintly of sandalwood, and she opened her eyes, looking for its owner.

Night still held the world fully in its grip, but the stars were a little brighter now, and she made out Jevryn to her left. She couldn't see his eyes to verify, but she thought he was awake. Finding Kaden took a little longer, as he wasn't where he'd been, to her right. It wasn't until she stood and looked up, backing a few feet away from where she'd been resting, that she caught his outline atop the ridge.

Of course he was keeping watch. And of course he hadn't bothered to tell anyone, to let them shoulder part of that burden.

Then again, maybe Jevryn expected him to do everything.

She tossed Kaden's cloak over her shoulder and climbed, joining him at the top. He didn't so much as glance in her direction as she approached. When she handed him his cloak, he took it wordlessly, fastening it on. She stood with him as time ticked by, the silence between them carrying that slightly different quality that night gave things. When she inhaled, about to break it, he shook his head, lifted his hand, and pointed.

She followed in the indicated direction. After much squinting, she finally saw it. Glowing eyes in the darkness. Big, golden, and feline.

Meerkin?

He obviously saw the question in her face, because he nodded. She frowned. If this was a Meerkin, then why was Kaden taking so many pains to be quiet? While they were technically looking for Seth, the Meerkin were on the eventual need-to-find list too.

Nyx indicated the two of them, then pointed at the Meerkin eyes. He shook his head. No, he did not think they should go out there. But why? If it was only the one Meerkin—but then she noticed a second pair of eyes glowing in the night. Then a third, and a fourth, and a fifth. Those eyes were fanned out around them, forming a careful perimeter of their location, and she would wager there were more Meerkin she couldn't see.

They weren't moving. Only watching. Somehow, that made it a little more eerie.

Kaden turned his head, his whispered words so soft she barely caught them, despite the fact his lips were a fraction of a centimeter away from touching her ear. "You should go back to sleep. I don't think they'll move until morning."

Sure. Like she could just drift off knowing they were surrounded. If it was that easy, he could do it.

Oh, yes, now that was good. It was her turn to whisper in his ear. "I'll take over the watch. You're the one who hasn't slept."

He clearly didn't feel that was a suggestion worth dignifying with a response. But he didn't tell *her* to go back to sleep again either. They passed the remainder of the night without speaking a single word more between them. When the sun rose, they joined Jevryn on the ground below, and the Meerkin approached.

30

Nineteen Meerkin closed in on them in an ever-tightening circle. They'd moved away from the ridge so she and Jevryn could avoid being pushed too close together as four Meerkin streamed down it with lithe grace, but she was still down to a mere five feet separating her from him. The magic twinges hitting her body had calmed overnight to one every fifteen minutes or so, but they were still there, meaning the resonant interference was still very much an issue. If the Meerkin kept pressing them in, they were going to have a problem.

Then again, now that the Meerkin had drawn near, she realized they had another problem entirely. The Meerkin she had met on Arkadia had had their armor fused to them. When they'd passed through chaos pockets on the way to the prison planet, chaos had fundamentally altered them, melding the armor with their bodies on the cellular level, until it became a part of their genetic makeup. The children born to them on Arkadia had been born with armor instead of fur.

The Meerkin surrounding them did not have armor for fur— they were *wearing* armor. She remembered Vorex telling her that when the first of them had hit the chaos pockets on the ley lines, those Meerkin who had been able to turn back had done so. He hadn't known if any of them had managed to return to Kyvren and survive.

Clearly, they had, because Nyx was staring at their descendants. And judging by their hostile expressions, the laser-focus of their stares, they did not recognize her as their "kin who is not of our kin". And why would they? Vorex wasn't expecting her. She'd counted on being recognized by the Arkadian Meerkin. Instead, she had Meerkin born on Kyvren, and given the way their gazes swiveled to Jevryn and growls broke out in their throats, Nyx's little group wasn't going to be given the benefit of the doubt.

One of the Meerkin stepped forward. She was neither the largest nor smallest of the group, but it was clear, by the way the others deferred to her, that she was in charge. "Councilor A-Morridahn." The voice was severe, ruthless, and utterly cold. "Did your disfigurement so bother you that you took time away from murdering my kin to have your scar removed?"

Nyx's blood chilled. The Meerkin thought Jevryn was Kiev. And Kiev was involved in this conflict. Her gaze snapped to Jevryn's, but his face was as inscrutable as ever.

Nyx took a half-step forward. "He's not Kiev A-Morridahn." She said only that, a short, to-the-point statement so simple it couldn't be mistaken, so quick she could get it out before anyone cut her off.

The Meerkin who had spoken swiveled her head, fixating on Nyx. "And who would you be, that you dare to speak?"

She swallowed and truly, deeply hoped that Vorex was still alive, that he had been in contact with this particular group of Meerkin, that he had told the story of how they had escaped Arkadia. That he had said her name. "Nyx Fortuna. I met your Elder, Vorex, on Arkadia."

A ripple went through the Meerkin, murmurs of "Kin who is not of our kin" and "She travels with the golden-haired one, like he said."

An angry flick of the leader's tail silenced the murmurs. "What proof can you offer, she who claims to be Nyx Fortuna?"

Nyx tilted her head, removing the Hiding from the chaos thorns in her cheek as she did. They drew too much attention in the Station, so she'd taken to Hiding them. "These."

A fresh wave of murmurs, and the leader must have sensed a losing battle against people who *wanted* to believe, because she didn't question Nyx's identity further, though it looked as if she wanted to. "Then I must express disappointment, Nyx Fortuna, to find you in the willing company of our greatest enemy. Did you help my kind once only to betray us now?"

"He's *not* Kiev."

An angry swish of her tail. "Your kind are not so indistinguishable to us that we cannot identify this one. You seek to deceive us."

"He's *Jevryn* A-Morridahn. Kiev's twin brother."

The fur on the Meerkin's forehead wrinkled in a frown, and she turned her head to converse quietly with the Meerkin next to her. When she turned back, she only said one word. "Twin?"

Surely the Meerkin had twins? Though they were rare in most other Earth animals, same as humans, they did occur. Not that she had any idea if cats were capable of having identical twins, though surely they were? *Please, please let this be a translation issue.* "Two siblings born at the same time who look identical."

The Meerkin leader stared at her. "No two beings are identical."

"Not forever, typically," Nyx allowed. "As people grow, even two who started out identical will develop differences. One more musculature, perhaps. Differences in weight, in how they choose to present themselves. Differences in the scars they carry," she said pointedly. "I gave Kiev A-Morridahn the scar on his face. I have no love for him. But this is not him. I would not bring someone here to harm you."

Silence reigned, until Jevryn broke it. "You must be intelligent enough to understand that, were I my brother, you would already be dead." His tone very clearly said they could all *still* be dead soon.

Jevryn A-Morridahn, everyone. A paragon of diplomatic sensitivity. She was guessing he hadn't been allowed to do much of the initial talking whenever the first universe-wide explorers found new planets.

"What he meant—"

"We understand quite well what he meant. But Kiev or Jevryn, it matters little. He is a councilor, either way. And you, who we would have welcomed under other circumstances, are not welcome here at his side."

That hurt more than Nyx expected it to. She opened her mouth to defend herself, to explain to them that they didn't understand, that there were nuances and shades of gray, but she stopped herself before the words came out. Yes, there were nuances. Yes, the world existed in shades of gray. No, it was not her place to explain to them, as if they were naive, which of those nuances should be palatable to them, which gray areas they should be willing to swallow down.

She had come here for Riven, yes, but she had mostly come because she wanted to help the Meerkin. If she had to leave without Riven, she could accept that. If the Meerkin didn't want her help, in the only form she had to give it, then she needed to accept that, too.

"I understand. I won't lie that I came here with a purpose, and that he"—she nodded at Jevryn—"was the way that I could get here. So I took it. One of my friends is missing here. I won't leave without him, but I give you my word that once we find him, if you want us to go, we will.

"But I will say that he *can* help you, if you let him."

"Nyx," Jevryn warned.

She didn't care. He'd told her not to interfere in what was happening on this planet, true. She'd never agreed not to. "When your planet was stolen from you, he wasn't a part of the decision. He's culpable by neglect. I understand if that is still too much culpability for you to accept his help. But since he is capable of rectifying the sins of his past, I think he should."

The leader made a trilling sound in her throat that could have been a noise of consideration or dismissal. "I hear much of what *you* believe and what *you* would do. I find it telling he himself has said nothing of a similar nature." She turned her focus on Jevryn. "So tell me, Councilor A-Morridahn, whom the kin who is not of my kin claims is not so very bad a man, what is your purpose here?"

"A selfish one. I seek one of the Dwarves called recently to this planet."

"And her claims that you can help us? What of those? Does she have the power to promise your aid to us?"

"No."

Nyx's heart sank. It had been a gamble, promising that he would help. Hoping that if she did, he would follow through on it.

"However, if you help me find the Dwarf known as Riven Gare Ru and acquire them, alive, then I will render to you what aid I am capable of."

"And what are you capable of?"

"Neutralizing the sizable advantage that is Kiev."

"Am I expected to believe you would kill your own brother for us?"

"No. That I will not do, even should you ask it. But I will remove him from the equation. And"—here Jevryn paused, as if he couldn't believe the words he was about to speak—"once Kiev is dealt with, I will help you broker a peace."

The Meerkin leader's tail flicked irritably at the word "peace", as if it left a foul taste in her mouth. "This is…something to consider. I do not trust you, Jevryn A-Morridahn, so I suppose it is fortunate for you that the decision on this matter does not lie with me. You will travel with us to meet our Elder. Vorex will decide your fate."

Something tight in Nyx's chest eased at this confirmation that Vorex was alive. That he had survived so many years in exile to return to his home. It was something she held onto as they marched off, the Meerkin remaining around them in what one could charitably call a protective circle or uncharitably call a guard detail.

She wanted to ask how long it would take to reach Vorex. She wanted to ask if the Meerkin knew if Seth was safe. But the leader had stalked off without ever giving them so much as her name and, somehow, looking to the nearest Meerkin and saying *hey, you there, can I ask you ten-billion questions?* didn't seem like a particularly winning strategy.

So she walked in silence, Jevryn four feet to her left, Kaden significantly closer than that at her back. He was either drilling a hole through the back of her neck with his gaze, or he was very convinced he needed to be Right There in case something unpredictable happened. She couldn't decide if it would be more or less creepy if he tried to talk to her from that vantage, but she would never know, as Kaden Moor was not known for his conversational skills, and this moment proved no exception.

But, as it turned out, one of the Meerkin *was*. On the smaller side, with rust-colored fur and prominent ear tufts, he'd been steadily making his way closer to Nyx over the last half-hour, trading places with other Meerkin in the group. Nyx suspected this was out of a hope that the Meerkin leader wouldn't notice, while Kaden—if the way he kept inching closer to her was any indication —seemed to think it meant the Meerkin was harboring nefarious intent.

When Kaden got within a foot of her she stopped abruptly, and the only reason he didn't run smack into her was because he had great reaction time. She looked over her shoulder, mouthed *back off,* and walked directly over to fall in step next to the Meerkin who was clearly trying to approach her.

"Hi. I'm Nyx." Not that this Meerkin didn't already know that, but introducing herself only seemed polite.

"I am called Jori." Jori's whiskers trembled with what—if the bounce in his step was any indication—was barely restrained excitement.

There were a lot of questions Nyx wanted to ask, but the most pressing one came out first. "I apologize if this is a rude conversation starter, but you don't happen to have any water, do you?" She didn't know how long it would take to get to wherever Vorex was. Her throat was dry, her eyes were dry, her skin was dry, and with the sun climbing higher in the sky, water was pretty much the only thing her body had any interest in focusing on.

"Oh, of course!" The Meerkin armor had small clips where items could be attached, and Jori detached a small canteen from his and handed it to Nyx. Comprised of the same material as the Meerkin armor, the container was thin and slender, almost more like a large flask than a proper canteen.

Nyx would guess it held twenty ounces, max, and she hesitated. "I don't want to take all of your water." Earth's feline species could be very water efficient, but that didn't necessarily mean the Meerkin were.

"There is a stream we'll stop at midday. I'll be fine until then and if not, I can borrow from the others. Oh, speaking of others!" Jori looked at Kaden and Jevryn before darting away, apparently no longer concerned with having his actions noticed by the leader of their party. Likely because, soon after reaching Nyx's side, the leader had swiveled her head around, given Jori a pointed I'm-watching-you look, and then returned her attention to what was before her.

Nyx watched as Jori talked to a couple other Meerkin and then returned, one canteen in hand. "For the golden-haired one. No one was, ah, inspired to share water with the one who looks like Kiev."

Right. Nyx held the new canteen out behind her and Kaden took it. She pulled the stopper from hers and drank half of it, forcing herself to drink at a reasonable speed so she didn't slosh half of it out of her mouth, as usually happened when she was very thirsty and drank too quickly. Stopping was difficult. The whole canteen wouldn't have taken the edge off her thirst, and half was doing even less. But she'd been promised a stream in half a day. Judging by the time the sun had set last night, and that night itself had lasted only six hours, she didn't think she was in for more than four hours of travel before they reached the stream, so…

She put the stopper back in the canteen and asked Jori, "Seeing as how this one is yours, will *you* be offended if I share it with Jevryn?"

"Is he…really not like Kiev?"

She took time to consider her answer. "I think he's a fundamentally selfish person," she said honestly. "But I don't think he's an intentionally cruel one. And he doesn't revel in death." When he'd killed Koral and the Kumir, he hadn't taken any *joy* in it. Though, admittedly, the ruthless efficiency with which he'd done it simply because he'd viewed it as necessary was arguably scarier than if he'd done it because he liked killing people.

Jori nodded. "If you wish to share, I have no objections."

"Thank you." She tossed the canteen at Jevryn without bothering to call to him. Given the few feet of distance that separated them, she would guess he'd heard everything. He caught the canteen with one hand, staring down at it a moment before unstoppering it with a resigned look. He took two swallows, sealed it, and tossed it back to her without a word.

She wasn't clear whether the message was that Jevryn thought himself too important to need more than a smidgen of her charity, or if he was trying to be nice and leave the rest of the water for her. And speaking to him to find out was not a good option. Uncivil words would come out of her mouth, and she didn't think exchanging barbs with Jevryn in front of the Meerkin would present a very united front.

She considered the remainder of the water. She really wanted to drink it all. Instead, she offered the flask back to Jori, who shook his head. "You keep it."

She slid the pack with her old clothes off and stowed the canteen in it before putting it back on, thanking Jori again.

"It is no trouble." Jori's excitement still hadn't died, and its source became apparent when he said, "I can't believe I'm actually meeting you. Vorex is my quite distant uncle. I was without family when he returned and he has been so kind. And *you* were the one to bring him home."

Jori had hero worship in his eyes, and Nyx felt uncomfortable. "You know I didn't really do anything, right? I was just in the right place at the right time."

Jori shook his head emphatically. "I have heard the story many times. You believed Uncle Vorex's words, believed the truth of my people over the lies you had been told. You gave our lost kin the path home."

Nyx considered explaining that she hadn't grown up on a steady diet of Council propaganda, and so believing the truth when it was staring her in the face hadn't been that difficult. But she had a feeling Jori would only argue with her again, so all she said was, "Anyone who talked to Vorex for more than five seconds would know he was telling the truth. Any decent person would have done the same thing in my place."

Jori's face fell. "If that is true, I cannot claim to have met many decent people outside my own kind."

"Are things..." Nyx hesitated, not sure how to ask what she wanted to, especially when Jori seemed so young. But then, if he was old enough to be out on this patrol, he had to be *old enough*. "Vorex told me a brief overview of what happened when the Dwarves first came here. But I don't know how things have been since."

They walked along in silence for a bit, and Nyx kind of wanted to kick herself for taking the sunshine out of Jori's face. But eventually he answered. "I grew up being told this planet belonged to us, though it never felt like it did. The Elders would tell us stories that their Elders had told them, about how once we were the only sapient species on Kyvren. About how once our one clan was many, and though we occasionally had disagreements with each other, we did not know the meaning of war.

"They said that we understood this land and how to survive on it, and we came from it and so it was ours. But it never *felt* like ours to me. Before Vorex came, our people were split into two factions. Those who lived in the territory the Dwarves allowed us to occupy, and those who rebelled and lived outside of it in small groups, unwilling to accept that the Dwarves had any right to tell us where we could and could not be. These groups sought to take back our planet.

"I was born into one of the dens under Dwarven oversight. My parents believed the rebels were dangerous, and if we wanted to have any chance at a stable life, we should remain within the safety of our allowed territory.

"Even from a young age, it didn't feel quite right to me. My parents would be sent out to the fire pools for weeks at a time, retrieving ore for the Dwarves, and return home exhausted. But my own life was still fairly sheltered, and did not seem so terrible to me. I suppose I was too young to understand what I didn't have.

"My greatest difficulty was remaining within the safety of the den when the spring rains came. It is a not uncommon trial. Meerkin children are curious to a fault, and restless. It does not matter how much you explain the dangers of the rains to cubs, we all attempt to sneak out at some point. If we are very clever, we succeed."

Out of the corner of her eye, Nyx noticed the leader of the group dropping back to within hearing range of their conversation. If Jori noticed, he either wasn't worried, or had decided he didn't care.

"Around the time I had completed thirty circuits of the Anigar, I thought myself very clever."

Nyx furiously tried to remember the conversion Morgen had done on Meerkin age, and thought this would have made Jori roughly eleven in his story. She still had no idea what "circuits of the Anigar" referred to, but she was now relatively certain it wasn't revolutions of Kyvren around its sun.

"I had made a friend from a neighboring den," Jori was saying, "and I very much wanted to see her again. So I did. And while we were outside the safety of the dens, the rains came." A ridge of fur stood up along Jori's neck. "I survived, obviously, and so did she, but it was at no small risk to the Elders who recovered us. That was the first time I truly understood the anger the rebels harbor toward the Dwarves.

"You see, my parents and the other adults worked gathering ore, but they were not allowed to keep it. Each den was left with only a few sets of ancient armor. Armor that only fit a few, and those few therefore responsible for hunting for an entire den during the rains. I never went hungry—the Elders took great pains to hide the scarcity of food during those times, and as children we were always provided for—but the adults often went without. And when things were bad enough, the adults who had no armor would go out to hunt, despite the danger. That is how my parents died, when I had attained only forty-two Anigarian circuits."

Nyx furiously calculated. He'd been…fifteen?

"You might say it radicalized me. All my life, my parents had told me that remaining under Dwarven rule, not invoking their ire, was what kept us safe. That we needed to remain small and unseen, to not create trouble so the Dwarves would have no cause to take action against us. That when our territory was reduced in my twenty-third circuit, and then again in my thirty-seventh, all because the Dwarves are incapable of *not* extending their reach, that it was *necessary*."

Jori's body trembled with anger as he walked. The Meerkin leader fell in on Jori's other side, and the younger Meerkin continued. "My parents did everything they were supposed to. They complied, unfailingly, and they died anyway. Died *because* of it. So I ran away to join the rebels. Where I met Vidrin"—Jori nodded at the leader of their group—"who made it clear I had a lot to learn. So I did. And what I learned was that we had no hope of reclaiming the planet given the Dwarves' numbers and their stranglehold on our resources. At that point, we sought only freedom, not control, because that was all we thought we could have. We stole armor and we stole ore to make armor, so we could live freely in the wilder lands the Dwarves are not so adept at surviving.

"Though I was surprised to find we had some allies among Dwarvenkind. Perhaps more surprised to find the rebels accepted them. As much vitriol as Vidrin harbors—"

Vidrin made an amused yowl noise in her throat and dropped back to walk in step with Jori.

"—you'd think she would have no room in her heart for anyone save we Meerkin, but it is actions that matter to her. And there are Dwarves who have risked much in order to aid us with ore acquisition. Even so, we did not have the numbers to *do* anything until Vorex and the others returned."

Jori quit speaking. He seemed to take comfort from Vidrin's presence at his side, and they walked in silence for several minutes before Nyx finally asked, "What happened when Vorex came home?"

"We had hope." It was Vidrin who answered. "Our seers had predicted his eventual return, though I admit, given the age it would make him, there were many of us who believed them mistaken. But so he came. He attempted to negotiate with the Dwarves. Given how many Meerkin returned with him, they agreed to a meeting. I assure you that Vorex's terms were kinder than any those of us who have been on-planet would have devised. But we let him persuade us to offer them because we wanted an end to bloodshed and fear. We wanted freedom."

"What were the terms?"

"We would neither force the Dwarves to leave nor force them to remain."

When Nyx had last talked to Vorex, he had been adamant that the Dwarves wouldn't be allowed to stay on Kyvren. She wondered what had happened, in the short time after his arrival, to change his mind.

"Our terms were that the Dwarves could remain on Kyvren, so long as they acknowledged that all lands were ours by right. All ore stockpiles were to be returned to us, with Meerkin having first claim upon dens and future deposits, with the promise that no Dwarven-kind would be left unprovided for in resources or protective gear. It was more than they ever did for us, and we would have upheld our promises.

"They could remain, so long as they respected our laws and our ways. Or they could have one circuit of the Anigar to put their affairs in order and make a life somewhere else." Vidrin's claws shot out, digging into the earth as she walked. "I thought we had a chance. As Jori said, we are not without Dwarven allies, and they spoke passionately on our behalf."

"But the Dwarves didn't agree?"

"They never even considered it. History is oft rewritten, especially when it is unkind, and it takes precious few generations for truth to be erased. Most of the Dwarves believe that we are vicious creatures. Their histories claim we lured them here with promises of collaboration and a new home after they sucked their old planet dry, and that once they were here we attempted to turn them into slaves. To hear them tell it, we sent them out to gather ore for us, not telling them of the risks of the unda, and they died in droves under our merciless treatment."

Vidrin gave a short, low growl. "Vorex tells us it is true they lost many—almost half—of their numbers upon arrival, because their egos were too large to believe they could need protecting from 'some pretty red mist'. Only once they kept dying did they finally listen to our advice and let us teach them how to survive here. They thanked us for it by clawing us in the gut while we slept, and yet they have the gall to paint *us* as the monsters.

"It was apparent, by how very little time their leaders spent deliberating on the offer, that they had no intention of agreeing to anything we asked. That, and the fact that all the while we were negotiating, they were surrounding us, their chosen meeting place just outside their stronghold of Eravendrin. But we were no fools, either, and our own warriors were hidden nearby.

"The battle that day was long and bloody, and neither side can be said to have profited from it. The Dwarves who allied with us who did not die that day were exiled. It was a poor choice on the Dwarves' part, as the exiles' information proved invaluable to us in launching counteroffensives. We were reclaiming ground, and control. We were doing it carefully, so as not to cause undue loss of life, and eventually, we would have fully reclaimed our home. And then Kiev A-Morridahn arrived."

That darkness that lived deep inside Nyx, the one she worked so hard to hide, the one Seth had always been instrumental in keeping at bay, woke and stretched little tendrils out at mention of Kiev. She'd thought she hated him before—after what he'd done to Griff, to Lana and Fari, to her, to Temerex. Then she'd learned he was her uncle and that, somehow, had given her enmity new depth.

Now he was *here.* She didn't need Vidrin to explain further in order to guess what had happened once he'd arrived. Not when Jevryn's earlier words had confirmed his brother possessed the same magic he did.

"How bad was it?"

"His first attack wiped out several of our units in their entirety. We were unprepared. The Dwarves tend not to be gifted with magic adapted for combat. They are, by and large, craftsmen, and it is to their craft that their magic bends. It gives them formidable weaponry, but it has made us not fear large scale magical attacks outside of that weaponry.

"So while we do have the ability to produce magical shields, we had worked those shields to be effective against physical attack. They did nothing to protect from the darkness Kiev cast upon us that day. And if we have since rewoven our shields to defend against him, he is powerful. Shielders such as myself provide us mostly with the time and safety to run when he chooses to take the field of battle.

"It has brought our efforts at reclamation to a standstill, as we are only capable of effective offenses when we have word that he is not on planet. When he is, the Dwarves' remaining city of Eraven-drin becomes practically unassailable."

"Why is he here?" Nyx asked. Why did he suddenly care about this planet? It had gone nine centuries being all but ignored by the Council so long as the Dwarves shipped out the ore they mined. Jevryn had declared it worthless in terms of further resources, and though the rest of the Council knew the Meerkin had returned, they weren't involving themselves in the matter. She would say it was Jevryn's involvement that had brought Kiev here, except Kiev had made his appearance *before* Jevryn.

"That," Vidrin said, "would be a question for the one you have brought with you."

The only problem with that? She was relatively certain Jevryn didn't know.

"You mentioned one of your friends has gone missing here?"

Hope was a rapid intake of breath. "Yes. Have you found another human? Male, light brown skin and black hair?"

Vidrin shook her head. "You are the only humans our patrol has found. It is possible he was found by another, but we will not know until we arrive back at the central den, tomorrow afternoon."

That made a sinking feeling spread through Nyx's gut. If they were arriving at the central den the next day, then Seth wasn't there. She hadn't caught much more than a glimpse of the place they'd first portaled to, but she was certain it had been grasslands, not forest. Her knowledge of how biomes shifted was admittedly limited, but she doubted the odds were very good that they could go from dense, lush forest to grasslands in a mere day of walking.

"Is the central den in the forest?" she asked.

Vidrin nodded. "At the base of Vorex Mountain." Nyx must have looked as curious as she felt because Vidrin laughed and said, "Yes, it is named after him. Those who turned around on the ley lines all those centuries ago and returned to Kyvren renamed the mountains in honor of our lost Elders, of which only he remains. He was terribly embarrassed upon learning it."

Nyx's lips twitched. She could see Vorex being embarrassed by living in a place that bore his name. Her momentary mirth fled as the Meerkin leader returned to the head of the group, and Nyx was left with only the near certainty that Seth would not be waiting for her when they reached the den, and the knowledge that she had to go there anyway, because she had no better choice.

Her gaze shifted sideways to Jevryn. She didn't like that she was now having to calculate, again, if he'd lied to her. She was certain he wouldn't view it as lying. She had never specifically asked him where he'd taken them when they arrived. She'd just asked if he could portal them to their original landing point. Kaden was the one who'd said that Seth should be safe with the Meerkin.

Nyx stopped walking until he caught up with her.

He took one look at her face and a resigned expression crossed his. "What?"

"Where did Jevryn first portal us? What was the plan when we arrived?"

"I don't know exactly." The hard stare she gave him prompted a bit lengthier explanation from him. "We didn't discuss the finer planning, as I didn't think we were leaving for several days. He obtained coordinates for the location of a Meerkin den. As far as I know, that's where he took us."

She wished she could tell if he was lying, the way she could always tell when Seth was. But she'd never known, with Kaden. Not when she'd been with him in Dead Earth—*obviously* not then—and not after he'd come back from Arkadia. Which was funny, because if one of them was going to be a better liar, it should have been the trickster Illusionist, not the duty-bound straight-laced Hound. Except it really had nothing to do with how good either of them was at lying. Seth was, in point of fact, an excellent liar. But she knew him, and that knowledge was so deeply ingrained in her that she could see past his bullshit where other people couldn't. She didn't know Kaden like that. She didn't think *anyone* knew Kaden like that.

"Why?" he asked.

"Because I've recently been informed we're reaching the Meerkin's central den tomorrow."

Understanding lit his eyes. "I see."

"So, since *I* can't walk up to Jevryn and quietly ask him where the fuck he planned to take us, I need you to do it. Please emphasize that if I even *think* he's lying to me, I will walk right up to him and let resonant interference fling us apart."

She would not do any such thing. She had a very healthy desire to return to Earth unharmed, with Seth, two things that would be difficult if all of her and Jevryn's portal magic became depleted. But he didn't need to know that, and his opinion of her was low enough that he would probably believe she'd do it if provoked.

Kaden, proving there was some wisdom somewhere in all of his silence, didn't argue at being designated as her and Jevryn's go-between. He simply went to the councilor's side. Nyx watched Jevryn's reaction as they talked, but the most emotion he showed was a tightening of his mouth that made her certain he was angry, though perhaps not at her, for once.

"Well?" she asked when Kaden returned.

"As far as he knows, the coordinates he obtained were for a Meerkin den. Given Kiev's previously unknown involvement in this planet, he admits the information 'might be unreliable'."

Nyx closed her eyes.

"I'm supposed to instruct you to 'not jump to unreasoned conclusions and panic'."

A flare of anger was a pulse from the chaos thorns in her cheek, a flash of black veining in her hands, there and then gone. She wished she wasn't having so much difficulty keeping control of that anger all the sudden, but she hardly thought it was an "unreasoned conclusion" to suspect that Seth might not be somewhere safe and sound after all.

She took in a deep breath, deeper, let it out. Seth, she reminded herself, was smart. He was also an Illusionist. If he needed to hide in an open field in bright sunshine, he was more than capable of doing so. He carried portal stones around like some Dead Earthers carried loose change, so in a worst-case scenario, he could just go home.

"Fine," she ground out. "Jevryn can have the benefit of the doubt for now."

They reached the stream Jori had promised mid-day, and it had that kind of crystal clarity most Dead Earth streams had lost long ago. That didn't mean it was safe to drink, of course—the clean appearance of water didn't speak to the bacteria or microorganisms that might be blissfully hidden to the naked eye—but the purification spell on Kaden's canteen resolved any possible issues on that front.

After drinking more water than was probably wise, given the amount of walking left to do, the only thing that could have made Nyx happier on a physical level would have been food. She hadn't eaten in almost twenty-four hours, and she was starving.

Unfortunately for the hungry humans in the group, the Meerkin were quite comfortable going most of the day between meals, and so did not travel with emergency rations. When Nyx had asked Jori what they did if something prevented them from returning to their base, he had responded, with an air of bewilderment, that they hunted.

By the time they reached the Meerkin's shelter—what they referred to as a temporary den—dug into the hard-packed dirt along the forest's long-running ridgeline, she was more than happy to accept the ration of dried meat allotted to her for dinner. She would also have been happy to accept the fresh berries the Meerkin had, but Jevryn had pulled a small box from his cloak pocket, placed one into it, and then informed her the berries would not agree with her biology.

When the evening meal, such as it was, was finished, the Meerkin wasted no time in settling in for the night. Nyx, Kaden, and Jevryn were given a small area at the very back of the den, in a natural nook. Likely so that if one of them tried to go somewhere in the middle of the night, they would have to walk past all of the Meerkin to do it.

The small space allotted to them presented a challenge, given the dangers of resonant interference, but the twinges had slowed further over the course of the day, and Jevryn had allowed the necessary distance between them to shrink to two feet. They still couldn't risk shifting too close to each other in the night, which meant Jevryn took the right side of the nook, Nyx took the left, and Kaden got the space in the middle. The only thing more awkward than being lost with your ex-boyfriend and your deadbeat dad in an alien wilderness? Going to sleep in a nook in a cave with your ex-boyfriend serving as the physical buffer between you and your deadbeat dad.

How the hell do I get myself into these things?

If Nyx could answer that question, she probably wouldn't be here. She rolled onto her side, facing the wall of the nook, and pressed her palm against the tattoo on her chest that was a twin to the one on Seth's.

He was okay. He *had* to be okay. Because if he wasn't, if Seth was gone… She shut that thought down, hard. She was not going to go down the mental road of preparing for the worst to come. She was not going to imagine him dead so she could try to process her grief in advance so it wouldn't hit so hard.

Because he wasn't dead. He was fine. Seth was a survivor. He'd done years of surviving away from her side. The fact she couldn't see him, feel him, hear him, didn't mean that he was gone. It just meant they were apart. And soon they wouldn't be. Soon, they would reach Vorex, clear up any misunderstandings between Jevryn and the Meerkin, and either Vorex would know where Seth was, maybe with another Meerkin den, or the resonant interference would be gone and Jevryn could take her to him.

She clung to that belief as she listened to Kaden and Jevryn breathe, both of them doing so with such rhythmic perfection that they had to be faking sleep. But it was soothing, in its own way, a bit of white noise to drown out the foreign space, and exhaustion soon tugged her into darkness.

31

Unlike Seth, Kaden Moor was not a man who accidentally cuddled in his sleep. This was fortunate. He did, however, seem to have an unconscious need to be on alert at all times, even while sleeping, which meant she woke up to his back pressed against hers as if they were buddy fighting in combat. He'd given her the difficult work of defending him from the wall, and he had the task of fending off Jevryn.

She didn't move, because the den was quiet around her, and no light yet spilled in to indicate the dawn was coming. She looked at her watch. The time on it wouldn't correlate to any sunrise on this planet unless it was sheer coincidence, and as she'd forgotten to check it before she went to sleep, it wouldn't even tell her how *long* she'd been asleep. But the glow of the watch face was still comforting, somehow, and the time and date let her place where everyone should be in the Station, what they would be doing right now.

"What time is it?" Kaden asked softly.

He'd woken silently, in that way he could go from asleep to alert without the slightest shift of his body to give it away, without even an alteration in the rhythm of his breathing. She wondered how she'd never noticed that, when they'd been together. She supposed she *had* noticed it on some level—how quiet he could be, how even his unconscious body seemed bent to his will, as if he gave it commands before he fell asleep and it didn't dare deviate from them

—but she hadn't known anything about where it came from because she hadn't really known anything about *him*. Hadn't known that that level of control had to have come from some place deeply unhealthy. That it was either an ability born from a need to control himself and his surroundings down to the level of absurdity, or it was an ability drilled into him through training. She still didn't know which it was. If forced to guess, she'd say both.

He had never talked about his parents, but from what Maruca had told Nyx on Nethrayne, she'd bet that while the trauma of their disappearance had left Maruca with a need to fill the role of protector, it had left Kaden with a need to control himself. That he viewed himself as the one thing he could determine the outcome of, and he did so ruthlessly.

She let the glow of the watch dial fade. "Does it matter?" she asked, just as softly, so as not to wake Jevryn or the still-sleeping Meerkin. "The time's irrelevant here."

A moment passed in the darkness. "It always made you feel better, before. Knowing."

It had. Because before Kaden had come along, when she hadn't known herself and no one else could remember her, the passage of time had had a tendency to blur together. She had marked her hours by the ticking of the hands on the watch face, her days by the digital display that could be counted on, without fail, to inform her of the month and the date and the day of the week.

She hadn't known it, then, but her fixation with time had started long before her isolation in Dead Earth. It had started in the isolation of her youth. With a sports watch far too big for her child's wrist, procured for her by a boy with a grin and a penchant for shoplifting, who had always been trying to make her smile.

She was still wearing that watch, right now. And he was still always trying to make her smile. And she missed him.

Please, please *be okay, Seth.*

"He'll be alright."

She'd been quiet too long. "I know."

"Hawthorne is…oddly resourceful." Kaden's voice held a note of what sounded like grudging respect.

"Careful," she teased. "I might start thinking you don't hate him."

Another lapse into silence before he said, "I don't."

She gave a soft snort. "Sure." That's why, after they'd come back from Amentia Furor, the two of them had been well on their way to beating the shit out of each other before she'd intervened.

"I don't," he repeated. "I can't hate someone who makes you that happy." And then he was gone, wending his way expertly through the darkness of the den, and she was reminded that the entire time he'd been at the Station this go-round, there hadn't been a single scuffle between the two of them. She'd chalked it up to Kaden's emotional deadness. She hadn't considered that maybe the two of them had actually been getting along, whatever that looked like.

A rustle of robes was Jevryn sitting up. He muttered something in that non-translated language—the one he'd spoken with Griff that landed on her ears like chimes, the one she wanted to ask him to teach her—that made her think he'd been awake for most, if not all, of her brief conversation with Kaden.

"It's polite to let people know you're awake when you're in a communal sleeping situation," she snapped.

"Forgive me. It seemed as if you and Kaden were having a moment. Interrupting felt rude."

Having a moment? Gee, thanks, Dad. There went the "D" word again. She really had to stop thinking it in her head, even sarcastically, or it was going to slip off her tongue when she least wanted it to.

Around them, the den was coming awake. Soft lights glowed from somewhere above, and the rustle of fur and clink of armor filled the space. A twinge went through her—a magical, not an emotional one—and stopped her from needing to ask if the resonant interference had dissipated. Warily, she eyed the distance between herself and Jevryn. She couldn't afford to be flung across Kyvren again.

"It is nearly passed," he informed her.

Easy to read, thy name is Nyx.

"Triggering an incident at this point would require physical touch," he continued, "so it shouldn't be an issue." Translation? He wasn't lining up to give her fatherly pats on the shoulder any time soon.

Just stop thinking of him as your father, she begged herself. But that was like telling someone not to picture a glittery pink unicorn. As soon as you tried *not* to picture it, your mental landscape was full of nothing but prancing, glittery pink unicorns. Especially if you had always wanted a glittery pink unicorn.

Nyx had always wanted a father.

You have one, she reminded herself. *You have Griff. Is he not enough for you?*

He was. Of course he was. And yet she wanted…*something* from Jevryn. Why did the mere inheritance of genetic material have this pull on her? She was partially built from her mother's DNA too, and stars knew she wasn't running around seeking Elena Fortuna's presence or approval.

Was it because Elena had proved herself so thoroughly awful, had hurt Nyx badly enough, that that rift could never be mended? Did Nyx simply need to let Jevryn cut her a sufficient number of times so that her response to him became avoidance rather than want?

"Is something the matter?" he asked.

She let herself look into his eyes, into those silver-gray irises that were the mirror of her own. She let herself note those features of his that she too possessed. She let it cut, she let it hurt, and she absorbed it into herself. Then she turned away from him.

In the den's busy morning preparations, she spotted Kaden sitting with Jori. So she turned back to Jevryn, because there *was* something the matter, actually, and maybe she shouldn't care, but she did.

"You're killing him," she said softly. Jevryn's brow furrowed in confusion, so she clarified: "Kaden. I don't know what you have him doing, but it isn't good for him. Maybe you've had centuries to see the worst the universe has to offer, but he hasn't. Consider letting him go."

She got up and went to join Jori and Kaden. When he noticed her, the Meerkin's head lifted in that manner she was beginning to think of as a Meerkin smile, his ears perked and whiskers pointed forward. "Good morning."

"Good morning. May I join you?"

"Please."

She settled next to Jori and across from Kaden, receiving a breakfast ration of dried meat that she finally asked the origin of.

"Adika," he replied. When he added a descriptor at her request, she recognized 'adika' as the animals that had nearly trampled her as they ran from the unda. She felt like there was something sad about that—about knowing that the adika who had lived through the unda's pursuit might yet become the prey of something else. She knew it shouldn't bother her. It was the circle of life. Cats were predators. Herd animals were prey.

But it *did* bother her today. Maybe it was only that the animals that arguably harmed nothing were the ones destined to be picked off by those whose nature and biology demanded it. Then again, she thought sourly, maybe she would learn there were sapient plants and the adika were just as guilty of harm as everyone else. Maybe there truly was no ethical consumption. Hadn't she read something about trees talking to each other through root networks, and plants being able to recognize people who'd pruned—and therefore harmed—them? Maybe existence was nothing *but* harm. Endless, repetitive cycles of harm.

You're in a chipper fucking mood this morning, she thought bitterly. *Would you like to opine next on whether the air is sentient and the mere act of breathing is a cruelty?*

It was a good thing neither Kaden nor Jori were disposed to further conversation, because she truly had no idea what would have come out of her mouth if they were. As it was, she had an abundance of time to contemplate the fairness of existence as they finished breakfast, after which the Meerkin packed the den and they set out once more across the expanse of forest.

Now that she wasn't lost or afraid of imminent death by unda, Nyx could appreciate that it was a beautiful planet. Well, the forested half was, anyway. She'd never been much for open plains of emptiness. They lacked a certain mystery. Forests, on the other hand, were the very embodiment of mystery, and today she could appreciate it.

It was funny how a person's perception of their situation affected how they viewed the world around them. If going for a hike through the woods, a person was likely to view those woods as peaceful and serene, as an oasis of nature in a growing desert of civilization. A place where one could attempt to find that ancient core within themselves that connected man to the world on a more fundamental level. If a person was lost in those same woods, the forest became a place of danger, an unknowable labyrinth that housed predators and boasted very little in the way of safety. In both scenarios, they were the same woods. The only difference was the person in them.

A shadow fell over her, and suddenly Jevryn was walking at her side. They were in the middle of the Meerkin unit, though that unit was so spread out that the two of them had more than enough privacy to have a quiet conversation without being overheard. A conversation Jevryn apparently intended to have. "You appear contemplative this morning, *na'tria*."

She wondered if he threw that last word in there in an attempt to get her to ask what it meant. If he wanted to ensure she at least responded to the question or if, having spoken his native tongue so recently with Griff, it was simply more on his mind.

Either way, she ignored it. "I've been kidnapped by my father, my boyfriend is missing on a planet that could kill him without the proper protective equipment he doesn't have, my ex-boyfriend might be headed towards irreparable damage to his mental health, I'm really, *really* hungry"—dried meat only took a girl so far—"and existence may be an endless cycle of harm. So yeah, I guess I'm 'contemplating' all of that."

Jevryn clasped his hands behind his back. "I am not sure which of those points I should respond to first."

"It's not a pop quiz."

He frowned. "Pop quiz?"

"An unexpected test."

"Ah. Life frequently feels like an unexpected test. No matter how long you live, something always manages to surprise you."

"Is that your way of telling me I shouldn't be upset that you kidnapped me and my boyfriend is missing?"

Behind Jevryn's back, his hands twitched. She wondered how long it would take her to drive him to pinching the bridge of his nose. If Seth was here, they would already be betting on it. She could just hear him say *I bet it's the next words out of your mouth.*

"I...apologize for Seth. It was never my intention to put him in any danger. I underestimated the connection between you."

Nyx blinked. Had he *actually* just apologized to her? It wasn't a very good apology, but it was a one-eighty from his usual approach of blaming *her* for everything that went wrong. Maybe there was a chance that—

No. She shut that train of thought down hard. "So you're sorry about Seth, but not about the kidnapping?"

Jevryn unclasped his hands, pinching the bridge of his nose with the left.

And that round of betting goes to imaginary Seth.

He clasped his hands once more behind his back. "Are you always this difficult?"

"No. Usually, when people kidnap me, I'm much, much more difficult."

Jevryn sighed. "Abduction was never my intention."

She could quibble with that but decided it was pointless. "Then what was?"

He shook his head. "I do not believe this is the time or place for that discussion."

They walked a few more paces, until she realized he wasn't going to say anything more. "So you're *not* going to tell me?"

"No."

"Fantastic. If you aren't going to answer that question, what are you here for?"

His gaze went to Kaden, who walked twenty or so feet ahead of them. Jevryn slowed his pace and Nyx matched, until the distance between them and Kaden had increased to the point that her and Jevryn being overheard was impossible.

"With regards to Kaden—whatever else you may think of me, I do not force service from anyone. He remains in my employ because he wishes to."

Jevryn might not force cooperation, but he certainly coerced it. "Have you forgotten that I was there when you made him your offer? Come work for him if he and Maruca want to have a future that doesn't involve running from the Council?"

"That was neither a coercion nor a threat. Given the nature of the offense for which he and the others were convicted, along with the fact that I was likewise implicated as a potential co-conspirator, there is precious little I can do to sway the Council's opinions on restoring the Moor's good names. Only proving that Alistair was behind the Harvester's initial theft can do that.

"I offered him the chance to be involved. After certain events transpired, I suggested he might wish to reconsider that involvement. He requested to stay and, after careful consideration, I allowed it."

"Why?"

"He is very good at what he does, he takes orders well, and he doesn't talk overmuch."

"I mean, why did he ask to keep working for you?"

Something in the set of Jevryn's mouth told her he hadn't simply misinterpreted her initial *why* but rather deliberately answered the wrong one. "That is a complicated answer. Or perhaps it is a simple one. So often, the one masquerades as the other. Regardless, his reasons are not mine to give away. If the answer is so important to you, ask him for it."

"Do you think he'll give it to me?"

"I very much doubt it."

Great.

They walked in silence, until it grew awkward and he said, "Well. I only wished to clarify the nature of his employment, so you were not laboring under mistaken assumptions."

He moved away. She should let him go, shouldn't ask the question burning on the tip of her tongue, but she was herself, so she couldn't. "Wait." He turned back. "Why would you care if I had the wrong idea?"

"Because despite telling you that I am a terrible man, it would seem I do not want you to think me one, after all."

Nyx pondered those words. For the next three hours and forty-three minutes, as they made their way to the central den, she pondered them. But she still didn't know what to make of them.

32

The central den lay at the base of Vorex Mountain. Before it, the Meerkin had cleared the trees from a semicircle of space—maybe a thousand feet at the radius—and layered half of the deforested ground in crushed ore. The face of the mountain that met the cleared area was coated in ore in a matching semicircle, the same way someone might put a rock facade on the exterior of a home. Put together, the area looked as if someone had taken a full circle and folded it at a ninety-degree angle, leaving half on the ground, half on the mountain face.

Nyx supposed it was an easy way to unda-proof the housing. She spotted other areas higher up the mountain, without the same ease of access as this one, that were also covered in ore. Smaller entrances, she presumed, though she couldn't see the way in on them any more than she could see it here, at what she assumed was the primary entrance. Only once they reached the mountain face, and the three Meerkin ahead of her leapt up and disappeared did she see it—an overhang of rock that curved down slightly, hiding a narrow horizontal gap.

The Meerkin, being agile quadrupeds, had no difficulty leaping up and through the gap in a single, graceful motion, like a cat jumping onto a bookshelf. The humans were not so fortunate. Nyx dipped under the overhang and looked up. The gap was several feet above her, but the ore coating the space below it provided convenient handholds, and she found it easy enough to climb. At the top she rocked a bit, swung and hooked her left knee onto the ledge, and shimmied through on her stomach.

Nyx was relieved to find that, once through the entrance gap, the space opened up in both width and height. Light came from above, small spheres that hummed with magic and washed the walls in pale, soft white. Jori had waited for her to make it through, and she in turn waited for Kaden and Jevryn before they set off down the tunnel.

Her gaze was immediately drawn to the walls as they walked. The smooth stone was covered, from the space where it met the floor on each side all the way up to the curved ceiling where the light spheres nestled, in paintings. The caliber of the talent varied, from what had to be children's' stick figure drawings on up to scenes that looked like the work of a master artist.

Jori caught her looking. "The cubs were inspired this season. I do not believe they left a single surface unadorned."

"The Elders don't mind?" she asked. When Jori's furred brow furrowed, she elaborated. "That they've drawn on your primary entrance pathway?"

"I do not understand the question. Why would they mind?"

It was Nyx's turn to frown. How was she supposed to explain this when the Meerkin didn't seem to have a clue? "On Earth, if a child were to draw on the walls of the home, their parents would most likely be upset."

"Why?"

"Because the house is supposed to look nice."

"What is nicer than children expressing their joy? What is nicer than seeing how they see the world? When the Meerkin were many clans instead of one, how much art adorned a clan's primary entrance—how many different young paws could be found in the making—was an indication of the clan's strength and future. We cherish our young. To suggest their voices should be hidden away would mean we do not believe they are worthy of notice. Forgive my saying so, if I misunderstand, but it sounds as if your Earthlings do not value their young enough."

"I think most Earthlings love their children." At least, she *hoped* that was the case. "But our society—or at least, the one in the region where I grew up—puts a lot of emphasis on appearances. If someone's child is too messy or not well-behaved, it's viewed as a failure in parenting."

Jori gave her a look that was nothing short of horror. "Am I to take it your cubs are expected to behave like small adults?"

Nyx was doing a terrible job of explaining this. And she didn't even know if what she was saying was truly representative, or only representative of *her* life. "Not *all* the time, but in many ways...yes?"

Jori shook his head. "Cubs are *cubs*. As they grow they must learn to behave as adults, but to grow into that adulthood without bitterness they must be allowed to experience the full range of their youth. Perhaps your Earthlings should reconsider this practice."

He said this last bit as if he fully expected Nyx had both the authority to speak to all of American society on behalf of its children, and as if society would collectively adjust its behavior if the correct conclusions were drawn. Which pretty much told her that in his world, if a Meerkin brought a matter they considered of vital social importance to the rest of their clan, the other Meerkin would consider it in earnest.

Violent race, my ass, she thought.

They passed out of the entrance tunnel and into a small antechamber, where Vidrin ordered them to wait. They waited, under the watchful eye of a handful of the Meerkin they had arrived with, while the remainder followed their leader.

A few minutes later, Vidrin returned and bid them to follow. The tunnel she led them through was short, opening into a large, cavernous room that immediately put Nyx in mind of a meeting hall. Even knowing the odds of Seth being there were next to nothing, she scanned the room, hoping. But it was easy enough to see that his perpetually smirking face wasn't among the Meerkin crowd.

Worry clawed at her and she shoved it back. She had to clear up the matter of Jevryn with the Meerkin—and the Dwarves that were mixed among them—before she could help Seth. She was surprised by the number of Dwarves here, even given what Jori had told her about those who had defected.

There was a shuffling in the center of the room as Meerkin parted to reveal the unmistakable form of Vorex. Her heart lifted as she saw him, lying on a bed of white adika furs. He rose to his paws, moving stiffly with old age. "Kin who is not of my kin. It is unexpected to see you, though the surprise is not an unpleasant one."

She gave him a genuine smile, one she couldn't have kept at bay if she'd tried. "It's good to see you too."

He beckoned her forward. "Come, come. Though we know each other little, we weathered too much together, in too short a time, for us to stand on ceremony now."

She didn't need much more of an invitation than that. She ran forward and, since it certainly *seemed* as if he was offering hugs, accepted one. It was a one-armed affair on the Meerkin's part, his massive paw spanning the width of her upper back as she squeezed him in return.

"I'm glad you're safe," she whispered into the chitin-armor skin of his neck.

"The sentiment is one I return." He patted her back and let her go. "But perhaps you could tell us why you are here now, and why you come in the company you do. Even if it is not the company I am told was first suspected." He hid his anger much better than Vidrin had, but it was clear that he wasn't any more thrilled than the other Meerkin had been to find Nyx with Jevryn.

She considered her words—if there was a best way to say them, a way that would sound polished and meaningful—but in the end, she did what she always did. She just told him. "We came here looking for someone—a Dwarf whose family has lived elsewhere for generations, but whom I think was called back here soon after you returned. But that was mostly an excuse, on my part. I wanted to know how you were, and if there's anything I can do to help."

Vorex's face was inscrutable. "I see. And it is with the intention of helping us that you have brought Councilor A-Morridahn with you?"

She started to protest that *he'd* actually brought *her*, but decided it wouldn't help her case any if it sounded like she had no control over his actions. Not that she did, but...

"He was the only way I could get here," she said truthfully. She really wished they could have this conversation in private, even while she understood perfectly well why they were having it in public. The Meerkin didn't appear to keep secrets from each other. "I won't lie to you—in a general sense, I don't trust him. But I trust that when he gives his word, he will keep it. And..." She hesitated, but there was no point in dancing around reality. "If he wanted to come here and hurt you, he could do that without me, and there would be nothing I could do to stop him."

A low grumble of discontent rippled through the crowd.

"If it helps at all, he really does hate his brother," she added. "The specifics aren't mine to relate, but they are soap-opera worthy."

Kaden glanced at her out of the corner of his eye. Yes, yes, she *knew* she was babbling. She risked her own glance at Jevryn to find his posture its usual rigid perfection, though his mouth was creased in a more severe line than usual. She couldn't tell if he was pissed off, or trying not to laugh.

Vorex appeared to be trying to maintain the dignity his station required, but after a few moments of careful deliberation, what he asked was: "What is a wash song? And what makes events that incur hatred worthy of it?"

Of course "soap opera" hadn't translated. "It's—you know what? Never mind." Somehow, she didn't think trying to explain soap operas to a species that had no idea what television was would be a productive use of her time. Also, she very much wanted to watch one, all of the sudden. As soon as she got home, she would. Screw the Harvester, screw Jevryn and her obnoxiously evil uncle, she was going to go home and make a giant bowl of popcorn and marathon twelve seasons of whatever show had twelve seasons, with Seth. He would pretend to hate it for all of two episodes before ultimately becoming more invested in the outcome than she was, and she would love every minute of it.

They would be doing couples' shit. And she would be present with him and she wouldn't worry about the rest of the world and she would live a little. But to do all of that she needed to *find him* so she could take him home. Accomplishing that task involved not fucking this conversation up by making references that didn't translate across societal boundaries.

"The point is, while Jevryn has made it clear he won't kill his brother on behalf of anyone here, he *is* willing to contain him."

It wasn't Vorex who answered, but another, battle-scarred Meerkin near the back of the room. "Do you think us incapable of handling this threat ourselves?"

You don't ask questions with easy answers, do you? "I don't know your capabilities, so I can't honestly answer that. I do know *his*"—she nodded at Jevryn—"and they are formidable. I imagine Kiev's are comparable."

"We do not require his assistance," another Meerkin said, rising from a sitting position to her full height. "This is *our* battle. This is *our* land. We will not be beholden for our deliverance to one of the same individuals who stole our birthright from us in the first place."

Nyx understood their thinking. She didn't even disagree with it, exactly. "You're right. The fight for your home is yours. Which is exactly why I would say that Kiev shouldn't be a part of it. He is Jevryn's problem—not yours. Kiev has no right to be here. So the offer to remove him is there, if you want to take it, with no obligation and no debt for its doing. I leave that choice in your hands."

Vorex once more took the reins of the conversation, his attention turned to Jevryn. "The kin who is not of our kin has much to say on your behalf, yet you seem to have no words of your own."

Jevryn gave a barely perceptible shrug. "She is possessed of the youthful tendency to speak earnestly and at length. I find myself, in my old age, possessed of a tendency towards observation and silence."

"Perhaps you could do us the courtesy of breaking that silence." Vorex's tone carried a certain undercurrent of leashed impatience Nyx was all too familiar with. She felt it herself every time she spoke to Jevryn.

The councilor, apparently being in a benevolent mood, acquiesced to Vorex's request. "Kiev is, as she says, my responsibility. His continued existence is an unfortunate necessity, but I am quite willing to remove him from the equation with nothing bartered for it."

"I see." Vorex settled onto his stomach, his paws out before him in a classic sphinx pose. Nyx wondered if his joints were aching. His age was more evident now than it had been before, and wondering how much time he had left was a swift ache in her heart. "I may believe that you would remove Kiev, but what will come of us after? When the blood and the dust have both settled, am I to believe your Council will allow us to live in peace, when so much history lies between us?"

"What the Council as a whole might or might not do if given command of your situation is irrelevant. Each councilor has sole purview over various planets in the ley line system, and I have bartered and threatened my way into control of this one. I will not fight a war for you, even should you wish it, but I *can* guarantee that should you win that war, you will be left in peace."

Nyx stared at Jevryn. The entire time he'd been gone, after she'd given him her initial suspicions about Riven, he'd been gaining jurisdictional control of Kyvren? Why? Or…had he already told her why, in his own way?

…despite telling you that I am a terrible man, it would seem I do not want you to think me one, after all.

Vorex's whiskers twitched. "I must reiterate a disbelief that you will simply let us be. A man who, by his own account, prefers to wait and observe is not one to go to such lengths without reason."

A moment of silence passed, as if Jevryn was weighing whether he truly needed to respond. Finally, he said, "It has become apparent to me that you and your people are deeply beloved by Nyx. She is invested in the outcome of your situation and I believe that, should I refuse to aid you, she will foolishly attempt to do so on her own. I would find it irritating if she were to come to harm."

Vorex took this in, studying Jevryn before saying, "Would you approach me, Councilor A-Morridahn?"

Murmurings of objection stole through the room, but Vorex silenced them with a decisive flick of his tail. Jevryn condescended to do as requested. Once he had reached Vorex, the Meerkin leader raised up, putting his face to Jevryn's and…sniffing? Yes, he was definitely sniffing, as if he was taking in Jevryn's scent.

He then lowered himself back down with a groan. "Very well, then. I will accept this explanation. However, the Meerkin must discuss this matter on our own before we make a decision. Jori will show you to private quarters, where you may recover from your journey."

Nyx stepped forward as Jevryn stepped back. "I'm sorry, but there is an urgent matter I have to ask you about. We came here with someone else—another human named Seth. Do you know if he's here with you? Or in another Meerkin den? He would have arrived yesterday."

Vorex shook his head. "I have received no reports of such a nature. There are some dens far enough out that we might not have received word yet. Do you know where you initially arrived?"

Nyx turned to Jevryn. His brow furrowed in concentration, and only when he drew a thin stream of portal magic did she realize she hadn't felt a single resonant interference twinge all morning. The magic hummed and circled around him, drawing a nervous rumble from the room's inhabitants. One particularly nervous—or, depending on how charitable one was feeling, particularly enterprising—individual hurled a spear at him. Both the metal spear tip and the wood of the shaft blackened and turned to fine ash in less than a second before they came within six inches of Jevryn's face. He didn't even bestir himself enough to look in the direction it had come from.

The hum of magic around him died. "We arrived approximately seven-hundred miles in that direction." He pointed.

Murmurings stole through the room.

"What?" Nyx asked. But she had a feeling she already knew *what.*

A feeling that was confirmed when Vorex said, "That is the location of the Dwarven stronghold of Eravendrin."

That bad feeling Nyx had swelled, crested, crashed. "We have to go."

"Nyx," Jevryn began, but the look she gave him cut him off. She wasn't hearing *Nyx* right now. She wasn't going to stand in this room and listen to him say *Nyx, we must be cautious* or *Nyx, we must think this through.*

She needed to go. And however much it might make her feel better to tell Jevryn that this was all his fault and he needed to fix it, that if he hadn't taken her without warning Seth wouldn't be in this situation, that if he didn't do what she wanted him to now neither she nor Griff would have anything to do with him again, she didn't know if any of those things would work on him. He could be prickly, and if she got his hackles up, he might refuse on principle.

But there was one approach that, given the oddness of their earlier conversation, she thought *might* work. She met his gaze, needing him to look into her eyes and see his own. Hoping that, buried somewhere deep inside him, that similarity *meant* something to him. She put all of the supplication she was capable of into a single word. *"Please."*

If he said *no...* Even though his returned ability to use portal magic meant she now could too, she couldn't get to where Seth was on her own. Even if Jevryn was willing to give her the portal coordinates, she didn't know how to use them. She'd read about them but she only understood how they worked on a theoretical level. If he refused to take her, there was very little she could do about it save ask the Meerkin for directions to Eravendrin and set out on foot.

Jevryn's lips parted, then closed, his gaze flicking to Vorex before coming back to rest on her. "At the risk of sounding uncaring, you are in the middle of something at this moment."

She remembered to breathe. That wasn't a *no*. She turned to Vorex. He would understand. She had no doubt of it. "My friend was left outside Eravendrin."

Vorex bowed his head. "Then you must help them, even as I must urge you toward caution. Eravendrin is vast, and I cannot send any of my people with you, as we have made no decision with regards to your...companion, and it is our way to take time in the deliberation of important matters."

"I understand."

"I can, however, offer you what knowledge we possess." He motioned a nearby Meerkin to him, and after a whispered exchange the Meerkin loped off, returning a few moments later with a scroll, offering it to Nyx.

Vorex said, "This cannot leave our den, but you may study it, before you depart."

She unrolled it, revealing a map of Eravendrin. Kaden and Jevryn crowded her, each of them looking over a different shoulder. On the paper, the lines of Eravendrin stretched beneath the surface of Kyvren like roots, twisting and splintering, as if they were trying to reach the very core of the planet. She found the scale in the upper right corner of the map and wondered if her translator spell had bungled the distance translation. Because if it was right, while Eravendrin might only cover a single horizontal square mile, it stretched *several* miles down.

To Vorex, Kaden said, "Is there somewhere we might discuss this in private?"

"Of course."

"I can take them, Grand Uncle," Jori offered.

Vorex nodded and swiveled his head toward the back of the room. "Beren, if you would go as well? I am certain they will have questions you are best suited to answer. We will delay our debate in any official capacity until you return."

A Dwarf rose from the back. Given the number of Earth's other myths and mythical creatures that she'd found real-universe connections to, Nyx wasn't all that surprised to find the Dwarven race met with most of her preconceived notions on their appearances. Beren was short and stocky, with the heavily developed arms and shoulders that made sense for a people who spent most of their time mining, metalsmithing, and—if popular wisdom held true— swinging war hammers. There was something slightly neater in his appearance than she'd expected, perhaps in the almost glossy shine of his russet beard, and he had a surprisingly gentle air about him.

He nodded at them in greeting, following with the rest of them as Jori led them out another tunnel and through a circular opening into a small room. Once they were in, Jori turned back to the opening, tracing a rune that was scratched into the stone wall. The opening turned an opaque gray, and all sounds from the other side cut off.

Curiosity got the better of Nyx and she came up to Jori's side. "What is it?"

It took him a moment to understand she was talking about the results of his rune-tracing. "The boundary spell?"

She nodded.

"A basic visual and auditory inhibitor. Do your own versions look different?"

"We don't have them." When Jori's eyes widened she added, "I mean, I'm sure someone else in the universe does, but my planet, at least, doesn't."

"How do you have any privacy?"

"Doors."

By the look on his face, *doors* was not a word that translated. "What are 'doors'?" He repeated the word carefully, as if it were unforgivably foreign.

"It's like, if you took a solid piece of stone or wood that fit exactly in this space"—she indicated the bounds of the opening— "and attached it to the wall so you could swing it open or closed." She mimed the action.

"That sounds...interesting." He said *interesting* the way most people said *baffling.*

"Nyx?" Jevryn said mildly, redirecting her attention.

Right. She slipped her pack off, grateful to not be wearing it after so much walking, and set it at the foot of the room's low table. At least, she assumed the foot-high slab of stone set in the middle of the room was a table. Then she carefully unrolled the scroll Vorex had given her. She once again found herself sandwiched between Kaden and Jevryn, each one holding a side of the scroll to keep it flat. Apparently, the only people who had the decency to give her any personal space were Jori and Beren, both of whom had settled on the other side of the table, and neither of whom felt compelled to say anything.

In fact, now that she'd quit asking about doors, no one was talking, and Nyx was pretty sure she knew why. "I know what you're going to say," she told Kaden. He lifted one eyebrow, so she obliged him, miming his deep voice. "It's too complex. Seth could be anywhere inside, if he even *is* inside. Infiltrating a city of this magnitude would require months of research." She switched back to her normal speaking voice. "I know all of that, but I don't care."

Beren cleared his throat. "Eravendrin is Eravendrin for a reason. The name has no direct translation but means, roughly, 'that which cannot be escaped', and the layout is designed to make movement within the city slow. If your friend is within, they will have taken him to the prison at the heart of the city. It is unlikely you could enter Eravendrin without being caught, and far less likely that you would get out."

"Even with him?" She pointed at Jevryn. "I'm not one to suggest people should abuse their authority, but can't he just order them to let us through? He *is* technically in charge." If he couldn't wield that authority, why had he gone to the trouble of gaining jurisdiction over Kyvren?

Beren shook his head. "My people never had much interaction with the Council. So long as we provided the ore shipments they required, we were left alone, and that was how we liked it. When the Meerkin returned, we were informed the ore shipments were no longer necessary, and the planetary dispute was our problem.

"I was already here with the Meerkin by the time Kiev arrived. Before he came, the Meerkin's complete reclamation of the planet was inevitable. My people knew this. It is the only thing that would have enticed them to accept Kiev's offer of aid. They have no respect for the Council itself, and they will not be eager to let another councilor into the city, even if he claims control of this planet."

Nyx looked at Jevryn. "Can't you just, I don't know, *make* them let you in?"

Jevryn smiled. It was a very broad smile, full of teeth. "Of course. Ordinarily, should a Councilor experience difficulty in routine oversight, the matter can be resolved with an adequate number of Enforcers. That is not an option for us, due to both time constraints and the sensitive nature of our purpose here.

"That leaves us with me. I am sure that, were I to kill a few hundred of them, they could be made to see reason. Am I to understand this is the method of approach you wish to take?"

He...was not joking. He absolutely knew she would never say yes, but he wasn't joking about his willingness to do it. "No," she said flatly.

"We don't even know if Seth is inside the city," Kaden said.

The man had a valid point. Seth was Seth, after all. Clever enough not to get caught, bold enough to walk right into the city if the urge struck him. Nyx stared at the map. "Beren, are there guards posted aboveground?"

"Not as such. There are warning systems in place at the outer perimeter of the city. They will pick up any movement aboveground that crosses the threshold."

"And at the entrances?"

"The mountain has...other measures."

She would worry about what that meant in a moment. For now, she spun to Kaden. "What's your range?" He gave her that same blank look he'd given her the first time she'd asked. *Seriously?* She jabbed her finger on the map, picking a place inside the perimeter, but away from the entrances, in case any Dwarves happened to be coming or going. "If Jevryn brings us here, is that close enough for you to tell if Seth's inside the city?" He hesitated and she lost her patience. "Who exactly do you think I am going to sell this information to if you give it to me?"

He shook his head. "It's not that."

"Then *what*?"

It was Jevryn who answered. "A Tracker's range aboveground is easily quantified. Belowground, most have a fraction of their ordinary range, if any, and their precision suffers. He is attempting to decide if he wants me to know the extent of his capabilities in that regard. Which means they are either quite impressive, or quite unimpressive. I have my theories on which, of course."

"Isn't it in his personnel file? Do the Enforcers not keep records on that kind of information?"

"Of course. His file listed his subterranean abilities as negligible and unreliable, which I believe to be—what is that Earth phrase? Ah, yes—utter horse shit."

Kaden ground his teeth. "If he's in the city, I'll know."

"From the vantage point she chose?" Jevryn asked.

"Yes."

"Anywhere in the city?" Jevryn asked lightly.

"Yes," Kaden answered, now sounding as if the word caused him actual pain.

Jevryn's eyebrows crept up. "Interesting. Let us test it."

A spark of portal magic lit the air, and Jevryn and Kaden vanished. Had the former still been here, Nyx could have cheerfully committed patricide. *So* considerate of him to leave her behind.

Across the room, Jori looked more fascinated than disturbed by the impromptu departure. Beren, however, was looking a little green around the beard, so to speak. "He is as his brother is, then."

"In some ways," Nyx allowed. And hopefully not in too many more.

"How did you become acquainted with him?" Beren asked.

"It's...kind of complicated. But mostly I know someone who knows him." Not wanting to be asked anything else about Jevryn, she turned the conversation to more practical matters. "What can you tell me about Eravendrin?"

Shadows fell over Beren's face. "It is a city like no other."

"I'm sorry," Nyx said softly. "It was your home."

He shifted. "It was, yes. But the ground it is carved into was never truly my people's. It is...difficult to reconcile my childhood love of the place I was raised with the truth of how it came to be."

Nyx's curiosity got the better of her. "How did your people come to live on Kyvren? I mean, I understand the Council brought you here, but why? Where is your own planet?"

"Our own planet is uninhabitable, now."

"What happened?"

"We have many stories of it, passed down through the generations. The most prominent one tells of the beginning of the end. Dwarves mine, you see. It is in our blood, it is what we do. And we mined deep into the heart of our birth planet until, eventually, we woke something that was meant to remain buried beneath the earth, and it became our destruction."

Nyx couldn't help herself. "Are you telling me that your people —that the Dwarves—*dug too deep?*"

The intensity of her question seemed to take Beren off guard. "In essence, yes."

"What did you find?"

Beren shook his head. "Our ancestors refused to write it down or speak its name. The histories passed down say only that it killed three-quarters of our people before the Council offered us refuge on Kyvren. You might have thought we would be grateful for the rescue, but gratitude has never been a virtue of my kind.

"Neither"—he gave her a pointed look—"has leniency been among those virtues. Do not go to Eravendrin, Nyx Fortuna. It will not be kind to you."

She shook her head. "If Seth's there, I have to go. So you might as well tell me—there must be *some* way to sneak into the city, right?"

"If there is, I am unaware of it. All entrances into Eravendrin lead to the Hall of Revelation, and no one who possesses magic can cross it without announcing their presence to the entire city."

"What if someone had a way of hiding their presence?" she asked.

"If the mechanism behind that means was magical, then this someone would still be found out. Each of our master smiths is capable of novelty in creation. One such smith created the Hall of Revelation. It is a clear tunnel wall, inside which are trapped a mass of the unda. They are held at bay within its grasp, but they seek magic. If one with magic enters the hall, they will attempt to reach them. They will fail, but their movements will strike the keys of the great organ of Eravendrin, and play the song of your magic for all to hear."

"That's...an interesting choice."

"Indeed. Givlan the Smith was, unfortunately for my people, a great lover of music. I grew up with the frequent sounds ringing through the city, so it never bothered me, but I was told it was quite unpopular after the initial installment." Beren turned somber. "Do not attempt to steal your way inside the city. It will not end well."

"Is it not possible to get out of the Hall of Revelation before we're found?" Hiding them in the Hall itself would be too draining on her magic, when the Hall was announcing to everyone in the city that they were there, but if she could get *out* of the Hall and Hide them…

Beren shook his head. "I have never seen anyone do so. The exit seals if the Hall recognizes a new magical signature, and it can be struck to play a note which drives most interlopers into the embrace of unconsciousness."

Nyx rubbed at her right temple, where the vein had decided to throb. She couldn't sneak inside by magical means, the Dwarves were completely comfortable stonewalling a councilor, and short of letting Jevryn kill large swaths of them, there wasn't much he could do about that fact. The only non-Dwarf who could walk into that place without issue was Kiev, and he certainly wasn't going to help them.

An idea stirred in her brain just as Jevryn and Kaden walked back in. The fact they were walking in proved that Jevryn did indeed have *some* limitations—while portaling out of buildings wasn't an issue, portaling *in* to buildings was dangerous unless one was intimately familiar with the space.

She kept staring at the doorway, hoping, but Seth didn't walk in behind them.

"He's within the city," Kaden said, and her remaining flicker of hope died.

It's a good thing, she told herself, *it means he's alive.* Hounds couldn't Track a dead body. That was, after all, how Seth had finally hoodwinked Viktor's magic—by creating the illusion of death, an illusion to negate every living trait he and she had. It had worked where even her Hidings couldn't, because Elena Fortuna had had a hook in Nyx's magic, a parental override of a magical variety that always formed Viktor as an exception to her workings.

"Do you have a headache?" Jevryn asked. He was frowning at her.

She realized she was still rubbing at her temple and dropped her hand. "I'm fine," she lied. "If Seth's in the city, then that's where we're going."

"I believe we previously agreed that going inside Eravendrin would necessitate a bloodbath," Jevryn said. "Have you reconsidered that approach?"

"No. But I think I have a way around it." Because that idea that had started forming when Jevryn and Kaden returned had now coalesced into a plan. She wasn't certain it was a *good* plan, but it was the only one she had.

33

Nyx explained what she needed from Jori. He did not, to his credit, laugh at her. He simply left, returning twenty minutes later with a Meerkin child in tow. She was unbearably cute, with glossy black fur and bright green eyes, the tops of her shoulders only just reaching Nyx's knees. She wore what looked like nothing so much as a double-sided apron with dozens of pockets, all of them bursting with the tools of a painter's trade. The kit looked like it weighed as much as the Meerkin did.

"Nyx," Jori said, "this is Myrla, our brightest artist. Myrla, this is Nyx Fortuna, the kin who is not of our kin."

Myrla's whiskers trembled. "I'm so excited to meet you. Did you really like my paintings?"

"I did," Nyx said honestly. "And I'm grateful you're willing to help us."

Myrla drew herself up, chest puffing out. "I have a condition."

She looked so serious that Nyx had to work not to smile. "Name it."

"The condition is for *him*." She turned to Jevryn. "I was told you don't break your word once you give it. Is that true?"

Jevryn inclined his head.

"Then I want your word that you won't bring anyone else to our planet. And that if anyone else tries, you'll stop them."

Jevryn, confronted with sixty pounds of determined Meerkin

child bristling with paints and brushes, appeared to be having diffi-culty knowing if he was supposed to take her seriously. Nyx narrowed her eyes at him, and he straightened.

"If I need to bring others here to assist with the current conflict, would that be acceptable?"

Myrla mulled this over. "If Vorex agrees to it, then yes."

"Very well, then. You have my word that it shall be so."

"Good. Then let's make you look like your brother." She hopped onto the low table and walked over to Jevryn. "Sit, please."

Jevryn lowered himself to the floor, crossing his legs, and took on what Nyx considered his mostly neutral yet long-suffering expression. Myrla inspected his face, then began pulling out vials of paint that she carefully lined up on the table next to her. "Where does the scar run?"

"Here to here." Jevryn dragged his finger from just above his left eyebrow diagonally down.

"Did it damage the eye?"

"Regrettably, no. Only the back of the eyelid."

Myrla made a considering noise. Then, looking mildly embar-rassed, she said, "I haven't seen the scar. I haven't actually seen any scars on bare skin. We have fur to cover such things. It would help if I could see one. Do any of you have one? Preferably one similar in size to the one I need to recreate?"

Nyx had one on her calf from that fun time she'd been bitten by a mermaid, but it was a tangled mess and wouldn't look anything like what Myrla needed to paint. She could think of one rather prominent scar Kaden had down the front of his torso, but consid-ering the wound it had resulted from would have been fatal if not for Tobi's intervention, it also wasn't a similar reference point. As for Jevryn, she had this odd feeling that if he had scars—and surely he must, after nine centuries of living dangerously—he would not be willing to bare them.

"I believe this one is close." Beren shrugged out of his shirt, displaying a long scar that ran along his right forearm.

"It's the correct size," Kaden said, "but the age is wrong. Kiev's is newer, so the skin around it is less healed."

Nyx frowned. Since when was Kaden so familiar with the current condition of Kiev's face?

"I see," Myrla said. "I have never done this particular kind of work before. It may take me several attempts to produce a passable result. Please be patient with me."

Over the next two hours, Nyx watched as Jevryn's face was painted, then scrubbed clean, then painted again. Over, and over. Beren left, once it became apparent he was no longer needed, taking the scroll with the map of Eravendrin with him. As Nyx waited and watched, there was a point where she was afraid this wasn't going to work. The scar was taking on the right shape and looking more realistic with each pass—due in no small part to frequent direction from Kaden—but it wasn't blending into Jevryn's face. It looked like a painted-on scar, not an actual part of his body.

She might have been asking too much, hoping that a member of a species that didn't even have bare skin, much less wear makeup on it, could create a special-effects-level scar that could pass close scrutiny. But there had been something in the vivid realism of Myrla's tunnel paintings, in the minute attention to detail, that had made Nyx think she could do it.

Myrla put the finishing touch on her latest attempt and looked to Kaden. "Is this right? Ignore that it doesn't blend yet."

Nyx let out a breath. Blending came later, apparently.

Kaden inspected the scar, gaze running critically over it, before nodding.

"Wonderful," Myrla set her brush down, flexing her paw.

"Do you need a break?" Nyx asked. She had asked twice already, but Myrla had refused, as she did now.

"No, it's okay, I'm used to painting for hours, and it's better if I finish before it sets. Besides, Councilor A-Morridahn is being such a good subject."

Councilor A-Morridahn had been sitting completely immobile with his eyes closed for nearly all of the last two hours. Nyx would bet, by the way the muscle beneath his left eye twitched, that he had never, in all his long life, been referred to as a "good subject".

"Is there anything else I should take into account?" Myrla asked.

Nyx thought back to the one and only time she had seen Jevryn and Kiev together. Remembered thinking he had looked a little older than his twin.

"If you could make him look slightly younger?"

Myrla frowned. "He does not look terribly old now."

"No, but if you could just…smooth things, I guess? When he

smiles, he gets the slightest wrinkles at the corners of his eyes. I'm guessing Kiev doesn't."

Myrla's failure to answer immediately was pretty much a guarantee that there wasn't much she knew to do about that.

Jevryn's lips barely moved as he said, "Fear not, *na'tria*," he said, using that word she didn't know again, "I assure you I am in no danger of smiling any time in the near future."

Myrla giggled. "You're quite funny, Councilor A-Morridahn."

Nyx and Kaden shared a look. Jevryn was many things. "Funny" was nowhere on the list.

Myrla selected a new brush, dipping it into the mixture she'd created to match the color of Jevryn's skin. Nyx knew it wasn't actually paint in the sense that they made on Earth, or it wouldn't still be pliant once it dried on Jevryn's face, but she kind of kept expecting him to look like he was wearing a mask at any moment.

Carefully, the Meerkin began blending the color at the edges of the scar above Jevryn's eyebrow. "*Na'tria* is a pretty name," she told Nyx. "Do you have several?"

She stiffened. "It's not one of my names."

"Oh, I'm sorry. It didn't translate, so I assumed."

Myrla's brush had moved on to Jevryn's eyelid before he said, "It is a nickname, of sorts."

"What does it mean?"

"As there is no simple translation, I fear the explanation would take more eloquence than I am capable of." In other words, he had no intention of telling them.

Eloquence, Nyx thought. *Sure. It probably amounts to something along the lines of "irremovable thorn in my side".* Or who knew? Maybe his language was flexible enough that the sentiment of "child I didn't want who's been adopted by the ex-boyfriend I'm still in love with so now I have to be nice to her" could be condensed into a nifty little word that rolled right off the tongue.

"There," Myrla said a few minutes later. "Will this do?"

Myrla looked to Kaden for confirmation, no doubt because he'd been the one offering specific feedback throughout the process, but it was telling that Jevryn did as well.

"It's very good," Kaden told her.

Nyx had to agree. Because when she looked at Jevryn, she saw Kiev looking back. If she looked hard enough, she could see the false hand in the making, but only because she *knew* what to look for.

She blew out a breath. This would work. This *had* to work. She tore her gaze away from the disturbing sight that was Jevryn's makeover and smiled at Myrla. "Thank you so much. You've put a lot of work into your craft, and I hope you only get to make beautiful things from now on."

"But this *is* a beautiful thing," Myrla said. "It will help you rescue your friend. Nothing can be more beautiful than that."

Aliens, Nyx thought. *Even the young ones are damnably well-spoken.* She helped Myrla pack her supplies back into her pockets and watched her go, more determined than ever that nothing bad could happen to these people.

"Better not to let the ink dry too long, so to speak," Jevryn said. He stood and a series of cracks went through his body, some small proof of his mortality. "We should be on our way."

Nyx grabbed her pack and slung it onto her shoulders. Unexpectedly, Jori bumped his face into Nyx's stomach. "I wish you a safe journey. I hope no harm comes to you."

She smiled at him. "Thank you. We'll be careful."

"Will you?" Jevryn sounded skeptical. "I should be delighted, were you to show caution. I believe it would be a first."

Jori stepped back, and Jevryn's magic wrapped around Nyx.

34

Nyx was still annoyed by how smoothly Jevryn could portal them. Whereas her portals opened like physical doorways that had to be stepped through, when magic answered his call it curled lovingly around them like mist, depositing them in his chosen new location with little fuss.

He has had nine centuries of practice, give or take, she reminded herself, as the world came back into focus.

Nyx blinked, turned in a slow circle, then fixated on Jevryn, her eyes narrowing. "This is not the outer perimeter of Eravendrin." No, this was the inside of a building. Specifically, it was the inside of a library. One that appeared to be hollowed out of a single piece of shiny black rock, the floors flowing seamlessly to the walls, where rows and rows of books nestled into recessed shelves. There was also an enormous tree growing in the center of the room. Its trunk was wide enough that even if the three of them linked hands they couldn't encompass it, and its branches fanned wide above them, like a mesquite tree's.

"Once again, I find myself compelled to comment on the astuteness of your observational powers," he said dryly.

Nyx jerked her gaze from the tree. Her irritation peaked and the filter fell off her mouth. "Stars, you are *such* an asshole."

His face took on a pained expression that couldn't be… Yes, yes it was. Mister I Am in No Danger of Smiling Any Time in the Near

Future was fighting to keep from doing precisely that. He'd needled her on purpose, knowing she would mouth off to him and—judging by the fact that he looked down, ostensibly to flick invisible dust off the cuff of his sleeve—he didn't want her to realize as much.

"Where are we?" she demanded. They obviously weren't on Kyvren anymore. Portaling to the inside of a building, her portal magic books liked to remind her, was dangerous and should only be done when one was intimately familiar with a space.

"Home," he said simply.

That was when she realized the token he'd given her, the one hanging on her necklace next to the Harvester and his ring, the one tied to an anchor he'd told her would take her to his home, felt... settled. She'd never realized it had felt *un*settled until presented with the difference.

"We can't be home," she protested. "We are supposed to be outside Eravendrin. We don't have time for this."

Jevryn sighed. "If it had taken Myrla another half-hour, or a full one, or three or four, to finish her work you would have waited without complaint. Therefore, your notion of the time we do or do not have appears to be entirely based upon what you deem a necessary delay. I am deeming *this* a necessary delay. It will not take more than an hour."

He left. He did so by walking to the nearest wall and portaling, presumably to whatever was on the other side of that wall. Because, she realized as she took a closer look at her surroundings, the room had no doors, no windows, no exits of any kind.

How did a portal witch ensure his guests didn't go snooping around in his house? He stuck them in a room that could only be exited by portaling out of it. Another portal witch could leave the house—to somewhere they were familiar with—but trying to portal anywhere else *within* the house would be a messy form of suicide. Yes, it was possible to portal oneself two or three or four feet in a chosen direction without knowing what lay at that chosen destination. So, presuming the walls were not thicker than that, a witch could theoretically jump to the other side of them.

The problem would concern what lay on the other side. Bad, painful, life-ending things happened when one attempted to portal into a space already occupied by something else. Griff's book on portal magic had contained a lengthy chapter dedicated to this risk, complete with detailed drawings that rendered these potential outcomes in grotesque detail. Presumably to deter the reader from attempting such a thing despite the warnings.

Even if Nyx had been willing to take the risk, she couldn't. Near as she could tell, in order to do it, one would have to be able to portal like Jevryn did, by wrapping the magic around oneself. Nyx needed the doorways her magic formed. She could open them to places in her line-of-sight, she could open them to random places on planets connected to the portal map, but if she tried to envision an unknown space three feet from her, it didn't work. The doorway simply didn't take form.

Griff was right, she thought irritably, shrugging out of her pack and dropping it to the floor. She needed an instructor, and the only candidate for the job had just blinked out of the room. She glanced at Kaden who appeared, as usual, unbothered and unreadable. "Have you been here before?"

"Not to this room."

But he'd been in the house, then. "Do the other rooms lack doors as well?"

"There are some connected suites, but aside from that, yes. And before you ask, no, I didn't know he was taking us here."

She hadn't actually been going to ask, this time. She'd already figured out that, while Jevryn might value Kaden as an employee, that didn't mean he felt the need to share plans with him or otherwise inform him of menial details—such as his intention to take them to a completely different planet rather than simply across the planet they'd been on—in advance.

Galactic distances are not a big deal to Jevryn, she reminded herself. To him, popping into his house for an hour was probably akin to exiting the highway for a gas station break on a roadtrip—it was a short diversion and then they would be back on course. She just wanted to know what he'd come here *for.*

She also wanted to snoop. This room belonged to her father. So even if the fact he'd left her in it meant there likely wasn't anything of a hidden or secret nature to find, she still wanted to look. Because it was his. Because, in an alternate timeline of events, she might have grown up here.

For one ludicrous moment, she pictured it—a tiny version of

herself on the woven rug before the fireplace, toys messily spread around her. Griff and Jevryn both there, and—

No. Her hands clenched into fists and when she looked down, they were veined in black. She shook them out. This wasn't the time to be nostalgic for some past that could never have been. In any world where Griff and Jevryn were her two loving parents, she would never have been born. She would never have met Seth. So there was no point in daydreaming about it, in getting angry over it. She just needed to hold it together until Jevryn came back, and to do that, she needed a distraction.

Fortunately, she had one ready. He was watching her silently from across the room, broken-glass green eyes as inscrutable as ever.

"I couldn't help but notice you seemed surprisingly well-informed on Kiev's appearance," she said. He'd corrected details so minuscule she doubted anyone in Kiev's inner circle—if he had one —would even have noticed.

Kaden didn't deign to grace her with so much as a shrug, presumably because she hadn't asked him a question.

"You work for Jevryn," she said, stating the obvious. "So the only way you know Kiev that well is if Jevryn has been working with him. If that's happening, it's information I need to have. I can't risk that—"

"Jevryn isn't working with Kiev."

"Then why do you—*oh.*" The answer hit her all at once. Kaden's familiarity with Kiev. That thousand-yard stare he'd come back to the Station with. "He's had you working for Kiev? Undercover or something?"

Kaden shrugged. Stars, getting answers from him was like pulling teeth. Well, not really. Teeth actually came out if you pulled hard enough. "Why would he do that? And why would Kiev trust you? He has to know who you are." Put that way, it really didn't make any sense. Maybe she had jumped to the wrong conclusion.

She didn't expect an answer and was more than a little shocked when he gave one. "Kiev doesn't trust me. He knows I worked closely under Jevryn before the Harvester went missing, and he suspects I'm working for him now. He's not doing anything about me for the same reason Jevryn sent me to him— they're both hoping to get something about the other one out of me."

Holy shit. That wasn't just dumb, it was catastrophically dumb. "Why would you agree to that? How long have you been doing it?"

He exhaled heavily, as if he knew she wasn't going to let it go and he might as well answer. "Half a year, give or take."

That would have been almost right after he'd brought her mother to the Station. But that would mean... "Have you been to Kyvren before?" Her voice was hard. "Did Kiev bring you there? Did you know what he was doing?"

"No. I didn't know he was involved with Kyvren at all. Like I told you, he doesn't trust me. I'm not privy to most of what he does, and he frequently disappears for days at a time. It would appear I know one place he's been going to, now."

"Why are you speaking in the present tense like you still work for him?"

He gave her that look she'd become all too familiar with any time they'd had a serious conversation after he'd come back from Arkadia. The one that said she was being naive and the answer was obvious.

"You're going back," she said flatly. "Why?"

"Being here now doesn't change why I went then."

"And why was that?" she bit out. "For Jevryn? Why are you even still working for him? The man is—"

"Your father?" he challenged.

She snapped rigid. It wasn't that he hadn't made it obvious earlier that he'd guessed, it was that it still sucker punched her every time she heard it out loud. More so now, because they stood in Jevryn's home. "Genetically speaking," she ground out. "What's it to you?"

He shrugged again. "Solves the riddle of why he kept finding reasons to ask about you when I first came to work for him."

She opened her mouth—and shut it. He'd nearly gotten her. Classic Kaden Moor. Don't want to answer questions about yourself? Deflect. Dangle something someone else wants into the conversation, until they've forgotten what they wanted out of you in the first place. Well, she wasn't going to let him derail her by tempting her to ask questions about Jevryn. Not when she was trying very hard to ignore her familial connections, at present.

But it was also obvious this conversation was going nowhere. Still, she gave it one last try. "Whatever you're doing for Kiev—it isn't good for you. And if quitting that means quitting Jevryn, then I think you should."

She wasn't prepared for the anger that flashed in his eyes. He crossed the room. The movement was quick but unhurried, until he loomed over her, hardly any space between them. His expression was harsh, and so was his voice. "Where am I going to go, Nyx? What exactly do I have to go back to?"

There was a bleakness in his tone that made her suddenly uncertain. "Kaden..."

"The Enforcers were my *life*, and that's gone. I don't have a home to go to. My adoptive mother doesn't need the trouble, my sister's having an identity crisis, my best friend is too busy playing house to remember anyone whose name isn't *Evra* exists, and you — " He bit off whatever he'd been about to say, shook his head and started over. "You think what I'm doing isn't good for me? I don't really give a damn."

She flinched, and his voice softened. "I'm glad you're happy, Nyx. Honestly, I am. You deserve to be. So go be happy and forget about me. Stop taking me hostage and wanting me to interact with people and be something I'm not. Stop trying to *fix me*."

Her first reaction was denial. She wasn't trying to fix him... was she?

"Is there a problem?" Jevryn's voice stole across the room like creeping ice. He'd portaled in so silently she hadn't heard him arrive.

For a few seconds longer, she held Kaden's gaze. Maybe she *was* trying to fix things. Not him, exactly, but his position in life. Maybe it was some bizarre form of leaver's guilt—which would be a hell of a thing, considering he was technically the one who'd left —that made her feel responsible for where he was right now. Morgen *was* at the Station because of Evra, and they were both at the Station for Nyx. And Jevryn was her father. What if he had asked Kaden to work for him because he'd known Kaden had a history with her?

It didn't make any of it her fault. She knew that. She couldn't control Jevryn's actions any more than she could control being related to him. Morgen had made his own choices. He'd gone into the Enforcers for Kaden and Maruca, but it had never really been what he wanted. Now he was making the life he did want, and it wasn't as if he didn't have room for Kaden in it, if Kaden wanted to show up.

As for Nyx herself…even if Seth hadn't been in the picture, even if she'd decided to try again with Kaden, she could never have been enough. Kaden Moor had a hole inside him. She didn't know where it stemmed from, but she realized now she could never have filled it. Only he could do that. Except he wasn't trying. He was hollowing himself out deeper and deeper instead, and that…that was his choice.

So, yes, she was trying to fix it. And she needed to stop. "No, there's no problem."

She stepped back and looked at Jevryn. She blinked, then squeezed her eyes shut for a full second and looked again, but she was still seeing the same thing. Jevryn was holding a large silver serving platter, atop which were three cups, three plates bearing sandwiches, and a very large glass pitcher of water.

"You brought us here for lunch?" she asked incredulously.

"Among other things. You did inform me you were in a state of extreme hunger, we have all suffered from inadequate nutrition up to this point, and you liked the sandwich before."

She scrutinized one of the plate's contents. It did appear to be the same type of sandwich he'd made for her on Amentia Furor. He'd brought her here because she'd liked his food? What in the name of the stars was going on? Was this Jevryn trying to be nurturing? And if so, why the hell was he bothering with it now?

"Unless you are not in the mood for sandwiches?" Did he sound…uncertain? "I could prepare you something else."

"This is fine," she managed. She would have said it even if she hadn't meant it, because she was suddenly worried if she rejected this offering he would go make a seven-course meal, and she didn't want to delay their return to Kyvren any longer than it had already been delayed.

She was anxious to get to Eravendrin and find Seth. But since Jevryn hadn't seemed to be particularly moved by being reminded that someone's life was on the line, the quickest method to getting to her goal appeared to be sitting down and eating lunch. Or, she supposed, standing and eating lunch, as Jevryn had carried the tray to what she'd mistaken for a tall, wide circular display table, but which was apparently a dining table.

She took her place around it while Jevryn distributed plates and cups, placed the water pitcher in the center of the table, and vanished the serving platter. He hadn't actually vanished it, of course, he'd portaled it, but it was such a smooth transition that it felt as if the platter simply disappeared. If she hadn't been a portal witch, she wouldn't have even caught the flicker of power that accomplished the feat.

How could he *do* that? If she wanted to portal an object to another location, she'd have to open a visible rip in the fabric of reality and toss the object through. The only time she'd seen Jevryn work with a visible doorway was when he'd buffered the one she'd already opened on Nethrayne.

"You are capable of doing the same," Jevryn said, obviously noting that her gaze was still fixed on the empty space where the platter had been. "It is only a matter of precision. Given enough practice, it will come naturally."

"Practice," she said flatly. "Sure. How am I going to do that, exactly? I have a limited supply of portal magic and very little knowledge of what I'm doing. And since Griff, at least, cares whether or not I suffocate on a planet that has insufficient oxygen, I've promised not to gain experience via the trial-and-error method."

She picked up her sandwich and bit into it. Flavor exploded on her tongue. Stars-fucking-damn it, why did he have to make such good sandwiches? She'd blamed her appreciation of the previous one on how hungry she'd been at the time. While she was also hungry now, she thought she could say—this being her second time having the sandwich—that it was objectively good.

She closed her eyes, savoring it as she chewed. There was something in it that was...not quite spicy and not quite pickled, but a similar flavor that packed a punch of something extra. And whatever the sauce was made from? Divine.

She'd eaten almost all of it before Kaden said, "You actually like these?"

Her gaze snapped up. If the amusement in his eyes was any indication, her enjoyment of the meal had been written all over her face. Apparently, she'd been forgiven for trying to fix him. "You don't?"

"The taste is…unusual," Kaden said diplomatically. "I guess I don't have the requisite tastebuds to appreciate the flavor."

Nyx didn't know if he meant it literally, but it hit her that way—that she liked something Jevryn liked. That she might like it because she'd inherited his tastebuds and that predisposed her *to* like it. That maybe the ingredients were ones from his home planet. Had seeds from Lethe-Alihana's gardens survived? It was possible. She could see Griff vegetable gardening, for some reason, and if he had, Jevryn would never have let what he'd grown die.

Which made her wonder: "Did Griff ever live here?"

Kaden and Jevryn stared at her. Likely because there was no logical leap in the conversation from food appreciation to Griff's potential residence here, save the connections that existed in her mind.

"No," Jevryn answered eventually. "This place came…after."

"Is it a Station?"

"No. Not in the way you are imagining."

"But it's a Nexus, right?" Kaliaris had told her the soul of Lethe-Alihana belonged to Jevryn. Was she…was she standing within the remnants of her home planet?

"In a manner of speaking," he replied.

What the hell did that mean? She started to ask, but Jevryn spoke first. "Returning to the matter of portaling—you asked how you are to learn. I could teach you."

The abrupt shift in subject matter—and the offer—knocked her off balance. "What?"

"You are in need of practice. Arradin would like it to be without risk to you. I can provide that."

Irritation sparked. She was still just a little bit miffed that Griff had asked Jevryn to teach her, despite her asking him not to. "It might have escaped your notice, but you'd have to actually spend time around me if you plan to teach me anything."

"That can be arranged."

"Oh, can it?" She dropped the remainder of her sandwich onto the plate and dusted her hands of crumbs. "Six months of forgetting I existed and suddenly you can arrange to be my private tutor? Did you finally find the one paternal bone in your body or did Griff just give you puppy eyes back at the Station and tell you to be nice to me?"

"Kaden, I must ask you to leave." Jevryn lifted his hand, obviously intent on portaling Kaden away.

"He already knows," Nyx protested.

"Then he can grant me a moment alone with my *daughter*," Jevryn said shortly. Magic sparked and Kaden—and his sandwich—disappeared.

Nyx glared at Jevryn. "Do you do that to him all the time? Pop him in and out of places he can't leave on his own? You can't just play with people like they're dolls in a dollhouse. Also, please do not refer to me as your daughter."

"You take an uncommon interest in Kaden's plight in life. I took it to understand you were quite devoted to the Hawthorne boy, or am I mistaken? As for your accusations, I do not play with people, but I do not coddle them either. And I will refer to you as my daughter if it suits me, because that is what you are."

Rage—the slow, simmering kind that had been building over time but kept on the back burner—boiled up. Her fingers itched, the veins turning black beneath the skin, creeping up the backs of her hands to her wrists. She managed to keep her voice calm, but it was lower than her normal speaking voice. "Unlike you, I am capable of caring about the welfare of people that I am not currently romantically pining after. I suggest you look up the opposite of coddling, because what you're doing here is about a million miles past that. As for what you call me, fine. Call me your daughter if you want. We both know you only do it when you want to irritate me."

He gave her an appraising look. "Is that what you believe?"

"Considering this is only the second time you've used the word and the first was when we were physically fighting? Yeah, seems reasonable."

He closed his eyes and steepled his fingers, touching them to his lips. If she were an artist, she would have an entire collection of paintings of Jevryn titled *The Ancient God Seeks Patience* and this one would be the focal piece.

When he lowered his hands and looked at her, his eyes had shifted from silver to amber. "I do not know how to be your father—"

"You've made that abundantly clear."

"—but I can, perhaps, be a mentor of sorts."

She waited, but he said nothing else. "Why?"

He hesitated. Long enough that it made her distrust the truth of his words. "It is apparent to me that we will likely find ourselves in situations such as this, where we must work together, more and more often. To do that, we must become accustomed to one another. As things stand, we…clash."

That was putting it mildly.

"Training you in portal magic use will hopefully alleviate that. In addition, you also have a right to understand the Salyrian half of your heritage. Perhaps more so than I realized."

Trust Jevryn to need time to understand why a person would want to know where they came from. He seemed to stand so entirely outside whatever mold had created him that she wondered he hadn't shattered it the moment he was born.

He waited for her answer as she weighed which one to give him. This wasn't what she wanted—this acknowledgment of her existence in terms of obligation and functional practicality, no trace of emotion involved. It was precisely why she hadn't wanted Griff to ask him to help her. Because she thought Jevryn would do pretty much anything Griff asked, and she needed something more. Viktor had taught her almost everything she knew out of an unquestioning devotion to the will of the woman he'd loved, and it had been a hollow, empty sort of care. She didn't want another person going through the motions for her at the behest of someone else.

She needed more. She deserved more. So she shook her head. "Portal magic won't be an issue for me much longer." She lifted her hand, the tattooed three having twisted into a two. "I know enough to return to my anchor if I'm lost. Beyond that, there's really no need. As for working together, we could manage that well enough if you would simply treat me like someone who deserves to be informed of the things you intend to do before you do them. You can tell Griff you made the offer and I declined it."

"Not everything I do in life, *na'tria*, is because of Arradin. Though I can see, from your perspective, how it might appear so." He paced a few steps from the table, then returned. "I did not handle your learning of our relationship to each other in an admirable manner. I was unsettled at the time, though it is no excuse.

"Yet you are too old for me to present myself to you as something that I am not. A parent should be patient and understanding and kind. I am none of those things. But I do not wish any harm to come to you.

"And I wish you to understand those parts of yourself that have come from me. Salyrians are not—were not—an easy people. There are facets of our nature I believed you had simply not inherited, though recent evidence would lead me to believe you are instead exceptionally adept at repressing them. Knowledge—of this, of portal magic—and protection is what I can offer you."

His words seemed to linger in the silence that followed. What he offered wasn't Griff's unconditional love. But it wasn't Elena Fortuna's disdain, either. Nor was it Viktor's robotic help, as she'd feared. It was…something. But was it enough?

"You think we can learn to work together?" she asked.

"That is the goal, yes."

"You do understand that working *together* doesn't mean that I shut up and do whatever you tell me to like Kaden does, right?"

"It has become abundantly clear that you would never behave in such a manner, even if I desired it. Which, you should know, I do not."

His facial expressions whenever she stepped out of line begged to differ, but she wasn't going to quibble with him on the matter. "It also means you have to take what is important to me into consideration."

"That can be arranged."

"Then prove it. I assume part of the reason you came back here was for portal magic?"

"Yes."

It had been an obvious reason, once she'd calmed down enough about the delay to think it through. The resonant interference had drained so much of what he'd carried with him, and he didn't strike her as the type to make do with a lack of resources if he didn't have to. "Then I need you to take a letter to Griff."

He pondered it. "I could send it for you, via companion journal."

Of course he'd given Griff one, as he'd given her one. "No. I don't want you to read it, or his response." The companion journals were only keyed to their owners. She couldn't write the message—

the pages wouldn't take the ink by her hand—she would have to dictate it to Jevryn for him to write, and his knowing the contents would defeat the entire purpose. Even if that weren't the case, there was no guarantee Griff was sitting by his journal, and she needed a response before she moved forward. She needed to know something, just one little thing, before she told Jevryn *yes* or *no*.

"Very well. You do not wish to come with me?"

She tapped her numerical tattoo. "If I go back and leave again, this two becomes a one."

"I see. I admit some surprise that you are not asking me to bring your friends from the Station, when I return."

She wanted them here, but... "It's too many people to take into Eravendrin, if we have to enter the city." Her friends weren't any better at being told to stay behind than she was. If they came to Kyvren now, there would be no talking them out of coming with her to get Seth. "Will you go back for them once we've gotten Seth?"

"If that is your desire."

"Okay. Then I need some paper."

She half-expected him to portal that in, too, but instead he walked to a small desk, withdrew a sheaf of paper and something that bore a striking resemblance to a fountain pen, and brought them to her. She placed the paper onto the table, put her body between it and Jevryn, and wrote:

Griff,

What does "na'tria" mean in Jevryn's language? Sorry if that isn't the right spelling, I'm guessing. Is it bad? Please don't mention to him that I asked.

P.S. Sorry, that was rude. I'm okay. Generally pissed off, but okay. Seth is...Seth got separated and there were some complications, but we're going to get him back. I promise. Jevryn can explain everything, since it is entirely his fault. I'm sorry if I worried you. Also, I'm sorry Jevryn looks like Kiev right now.

—Nyx

She did a trifold on the paper, as if she was going to place it into an envelope, though of course she didn't have one of those. She debated Hiding the writing on the paper from Jevryn alone, but she wouldn't be able to Hide Griff's response. Besides, this was a test of sorts.

She handed it to Jevryn. "Don't take too long."

"Very well." He vanished.

35

Left alone, Nyx gave into the desire to explore. She approached the tree in the center of the room first. Its bark was soft, almost velvet to the touch, and so deep a brown it was nearly black. The dark green leaves of the canopy dripped long, curling indigo flowers, and if she could have reached one, she would have picked it. From there she investigated the contents of the desk drawer from which Jevryn had procured her paper and pen, but it disappointingly held nothing else.

For the most part the room was tastefully, though minimally, decorated. Books were the only thing it held in abundance, and this she didn't mind. Even if she couldn't read them and wished she could. The books a person chose to surround themselves with said much about them, but these titles wouldn't translate. She picked a few up at random and was flipping through what appeared to be a tome on botany—she'd just found a likeness of the very tree in the center of the room—when Jevryn returned, a severe expression on his face.

"How did it go?" she asked.

The severity of his expression intensified, and he wordlessly returned her letter. She decided not to push it and unfolded the paper. Griff had scrawled his response beneath her own correspondence.

Nyx,

I am grateful you are safe, but I will always worry over you and Seth—that is my privilege and my duty. I can only imagine how you must be feeling right now, and wish I could be there with you.

As for what you have asked, the term does not have a direct equivalent in your language. It is a philosophical idea, of sorts, rather than a specific thing. In essence, a na'tria refers to something that comes into one's life and alters it in some fundamental way.

It can be an event, an object—even an epiphany. In rare cases, a person. It is something one views as having irrevocably changed the course of their life. It can be positive, negative, or merely neutral, depending on what it is or how it is viewed by the person who claims it. I would suggest recalling the precise sentence in which it was used, if possible, in order to determine if the connotation is positive or negative.

Please return soon. Kaliaris is grumpy without you.

—Griff

She smiled. It had taken time, but Kaliaris had finally come around to her. It was a nice feeling, being liked by her Station. As for the other thing… She reread the description of *na'tria*.

In rare cases, a person.

There was no doubt Jevryn was using it to refer to her. She'd assumed, when he'd first started saying it, that the term was derogatory in some way. Not because his inflection had indicated any such thing, but because he was bothering to call her anything at all. She would never have guessed he viewed *her* as something that had irrevocably changed the course of his life.

How had she changed it? By the way she'd been conceived, which would give it a negative connotation? By the fact she'd brought him back into contact with Griff, so it could be positive? But neither of those things were truly about her, and it was her—not his past trauma or his present day hope—that he was calling *na'tria*.

She hadn't wanted to be meaningless to him. This was evidence that she wasn't. That had to be worth something, didn't it? She folded the letter into quarters and tucked it into the interior pocket of her cloak.

"Okay," she told him. "Portal magic. Learning my heritage. I can work with you on those. But there needs to be a schedule. You can't just stop by the Station unannounced whenever you want. Griff and I deserve to know ahead of time."

He dipped his head in acknowledgment.

"And stop treating me like I'm stupid. The condescension is grating."

"I have never thought you stupid. Merely impulsive. Any other conditions?"

"Yes," she decided. "I need another sandwich. To go."

His brow furrowed. "'To go'?"

"You know"—she mimed wrapping something—"packed so as to be easily transported and taken with me."

Jevryn apparently decided—wisely, in Nyx's opinion—that in the grand scheme of things, a sandwich was a small price to pay. He vanished, reappearing five minutes later with a small wrapped item, and Kaden. He handed the former to her. "Your sandwich. To go."

Kaden gave her an odd look that she ignored.

"Thank you." She retrieved her pack and placed the sandwich inside, on top of her regular clothes, before resettling the bag onto her shoulders. "Can we go now?" There was an insistent itch beneath her skin, a background anxiety returning to the forefront, demanding to find Seth before something went terribly wrong.

He's fine. The man can, to all intents and purposes, turn himself invisible.

Jevryn strode to the center of the room, stopping a few feet from the tree's trunk. "Come here."

She wanted to demand *why*, but he'd done everything she'd asked him to without arguing, so she went to stand next to him. He swept his left hand out before him in a circular motion, palm facing down. The floor around the tree split, revealing a one-foot-wide ring of glowing blue magic.

She stared at the black stone floor, finally recognizing it for what it was. "Your home is built from thalacite? On top of a portal magic well?" And whatever he'd said about this place not being a Station, it had certainly just responded to him as if it was.

"Not a well, no. A vast reservoir, yes. Bring forth the planetary map."

She wiped her palms on her thighs. It felt strange to do this with an audience. Jevryn was one thing, but Kaden was kind of just *there* in the background. He might be used to being forgotten in a room, but she wasn't used to tuning out people as if they weren't there. But Jevryn was giving her an expectant look so, drawing on the multitude of magic now at her disposal, Nyx summoned the map. If she also took the time to refill her bracelets, well, who could blame her?

She'd forgotten how heady it felt, being surrounded by so much magic. So much energy, so much *potential*. She would have thought it would be easier this time—resisting the urgent need to use that magic, to *go*. But it wasn't. If anything, it was worse this time. Maybe it was her need to find Seth that was making the magic feel as if it pulsed in her veins like adrenaline demanding an outlet.

The map sprang up around her, stunning in its expanse. Glowing silver dots swam in the space, clustered together in little galaxies, filling the room from wall to wall.

The sheer magnitude of it took her breath away. "I couldn't see this far on Lehine," she whispered. She'd had access to as much magic then as she did now. While her efficiency had certainly improved since then, and she'd been practicing with the map, she still wouldn't have expected to see *this* much more.

"Portal magic comes in a variety of grades," Jevryn explained. "The well on Lehine is of a mid-grade quality. *This* reservoir contains the purest magic that can still be found."

"Does that explain the…" She trailed off, not quite sure how to put it.

"Euphoria? Yes. You are showing remarkable restraint, considering your lack of exposure."

"I do operate a ley line frequently." Though they weren't portal magic in the same sense this was, they were still portals. And Kaliaris' had called to her so strongly the first time she'd seen it, she would have dived straight into it had the Station's previous Guardian not restrained her.

"That is a type of exposure, I suppose," Jevryn conceded. "Look at the map. Find Kyvren."

She looked at the plethora of points, feeling more hopelessly lost than ever, now there were so many more of them. "I don't know how. I've been trying to understand how to label the planets for months. But I don't know these galaxies. I have no idea where in the universe we are."

"Ah. You have been attempting to navigate this as you would a land map or a star chart, then?" His voice held only the simple question, not the condescension she'd told him she could use less of, so it didn't irk her as it otherwise might have.

"What other way is there?"

"Memory, of a sort. The map shows you where you can go, yes. But once you have portaled to a planet—or used portal magic on it—the map holds a memory of that use. It is a familiarity that should call to you when the map is active, so long as you possess enough magic to reach those planets with which you are familiar."

She chewed on that for a moment. "So the map is different for each portal witch? We each have to blaze our own trail?"

"Yes."

"Isn't that kind of inefficient?" Wasn't the useful thing about a map supposed to be that a few people did the hard work of striking out into the unknown, and everyone else benefitted from their hard work?

"If you are thinking of it like a traditional map, yes. But as the portaling ability is inherited, and the magic is similar between those of the same bloodline, it is possible to learn to detect the trail of those genetically related to you. Think of it as a magical signature, as it were.

"You can learn to look at this map and see where I have been. Once you are familiar with that, you may learn to tell how recently I have been to a location. It is theorized that the reason behind this is that members of a family, under ordinary circumstances and in most cultures, do communicate with each other. Among that communication would be an understanding of which planets that bear someone's signature are actually safe to go to. Whereas, should you be able to pick up the signature of *any* portal witch, you might think a planet safe for bearing that signature, when it might well be the case they died there, or otherwise barely escaped it. Does that make sense?"

"I think so." If a random portal witch happened upon the trail Nyx had left on the underwater planet, where she'd nearly frozen to death and been bitten by a mermaid to boot, or the one she'd left on the oxygen deficient planet, they might choose to go there, thinking it safe. If only Jevryn could detect her signature, he could simply ask her if the planet was safe, should he wish to go.

The implications of that hit her all at once, drawing her gaze from the map to Jevryn. "You knew. You knew Kiev was on Kyvren before we went."

"Yes—and no. I had never sought out that planet before and had no reason to suspect he would have cause to do so, either. I recognized his signature once I began to move us, at which point you had begun making your objections known. Our magic became entangled, and there was no stopping our travel." He lifted a hand, palm out, forestalling her next words, and proving she was predictable when he said, "Yes, I could have told you he had been there after our arrival. But you were quite angry with me, and I will admit I saw no benefit to doing so when it was clear to me he was not currently on the planet."

She let it go. "How did you know he wasn't on planet? Can we sense other portal witches?" She couldn't say she'd ever felt Jevryn. Not in the way she could now feel Elena Fortuna and Serenity Kormadin in the Hidden network, if she focused on them. She'd never known he was on Earth when he'd portaled there—not until he stepped over the Station's boundary and she felt his arrival through Kaliaris' senses.

"Sense, no. That would be deeply unfortunate for our privacy. However, for those we are related to, whose magical signatures we can feel? For them, it is possible to tell whether their last portal to a planet was to it or from it. Kiev's last portal on Kyvren was a departure. It still is, if you are wondering. He has not returned."

She knew she should move on—attempt to locate Kyvren and return to it—but there were so many things she still didn't understand. Things that didn't make sense and she needed them to. "I understand the familial markers on the planets, so to speak, but is that the only way to read the map? How is it useful? When you started doing this, no one in your family had been anywhere. There weren't any safety markers. What good is seeing all this"—she indicated the wealth of dots surrounding them—"if I can't know they're safe unless you tell me they are? How does that let me know where Earth is and how to get to it? Why is it a map if nothing's labeled?"

Jevryn smiled faintly. "I told you that you are *thinking* of it as a map. I did not say it was one. What you see around you—the dots representative of the planets, laid out in correlation to each other—is not seen by every portal witch. Most of them, yes. But in the early years of exploration, I did encounter a few with the requisite strength of ability who yet never manifested this. When I attempted to determine why, I came to the conclusion it was because they had no concept of a map in the first place. Often they were people who had never before left the place of their birth, and that place was small enough that navigating it was a feat easily achieved by memory alone, or verbal directions that were given, not in miles and an equivalent of your cardinal directions, but in landmarks."

She frowned, thinking that through to its logical implications. "Most of us project maps because our upbringings taught us to use maps to navigate?"

"This was Arradin's belief, yes. I have never managed to ideate a better one."

"So the people who don't use maps," she said slowly, "what do they see?"

"Very little for a very short period, in my experience."

Nyx stared at him blankly.

He clarified: "They jump to the first place the magic pulls them, unseeing and unprepared, and they die quickly."

Nyx put her hand over her face, covering her eyes.

"Are you well?" Jevryn asked.

"No. I think you just tried to make a joke."

"'Trying' implies I have failed."

She let her hand fall away. "It was about death."

"I deal in death, *na'tria*." There went that word again. Was it supposed to be affectionate, or was it a constant reminder to himself that she had upended his life? "Have you no sayings on Earth about art imitating what the artist knows?"

"You are not an artist." She pointed a finger at him. "Death is not an art."

Kaden cleared his throat and Nyx startled. She had kind of forgotten he was in the room. "You were going to locate Kyvren?" he supplied helpfully.

Right. She returned her focus to the task at hand.

Familiarity. That was what Jevryn had said. That she would feel it for those planets she'd been to. But familiarity was just a concept, wasn't it? She saw Seth and he was familiar to her because she had decades of memories made with him. Because she saw him and drew on those memories and thought: *home*. Except... She'd felt the familiarity of him even when she *couldn't* remember him. She'd known there was something about him that was innately *hers* even when she hadn't been able to explain why.

She closed her eyes, gathered curled wisps of portal magic to her and then sent them out in a swift pulse, a ring of magic that traveled out from her in all directions. Something pinged, calling back to her and she turned, walking through the sea of planets until she found one near the back of the room that felt entirely right. It called to her, and she felt herself—her life—wrapped up in it. There was something peaceful about it, the sense that if she went there, everything would be right again.

She reached out, but the dots weren't solid. She couldn't grasp one and pull it to her, could only curve her hand around it, lovingly. She looked at her Jevryn. "Earth?"

He nodded. "Look again. Farther."

Reluctantly, she took her focus from Earth, putting the planet at her back and sending another wave of magic out. Once again, Earth tugged strongly at her. But she'd been prepared for it this time, and tuned it out as best as she could, until she felt a new tug, drawing her deeper into the map.

She stopped before another planet, but though it felt familiar, it didn't feel like Kyvren. It felt like wonder and confusion, hope and anger, fear and discovery. Like the finding of something lost. All things she'd felt deeply, at one point or another, during her time on one specific planet.

"The Shadow Market?"

"Yes."

She hadn't opened a portal from that planet, but she had used the small bit of portal magic she'd stolen from the Keeper of Shadows' well to bolster the portal Seth had opened to Earth with a stone. She'd held that gateway open longer than the stone's magic alone would have allowed, much in the same way Jevryn had held and expanded the portal Nyx had opened from Nethrayne.

As if thinking of it drew her there—or perhaps it was thinking of her and Jevryn's magic working in concert that did so—she found herself standing before another planet. It was desperation and pain.

"Nethrayne." She reached out, swiping her fingers through the dot—and shuddered. It wasn't her own magic, nor the cool, controlled steadiness she instantly identified as Jevryn's, that made her do so. It was another signature, so similar to Jevryn's and yet so opposite—a burning heat and the potential for unpredictability.

Hello, Uncle. No sooner had the thought swept through her than another followed on its heels—the realization that his signature felt fresher than her own, that he had been to Nethrayne *after* her. That when he had gone there, he would have felt not only Jevryn's signature, but hers as well.

Her eyes met Jevryn's. "He knows about me."

"He knows there is a new witch in our line, yes. A signature is not so specific that he can deduce your precise relation to us, nor can he pluck your identity out of thin air."

She folded her arms across her chest. "You said all the councilors' descendants were dead. Provided he doesn't have reason to believe he has his own illegitimate child wandering around the universe, I can't imagine it will be that difficult for him to deduce I'm yours. Not when—" *Shit.* Panic raked sharp claws across her chest. "He can follow my trail. To Earth, to Amentia Furor—*everywhere.*"

Jevryn raised his hand, as if the very movement could forestall the breakdown she would dearly love to have. "Almost everywhere. Regarding Amentia Furor, at least, he is not yet informed. You left no signature when you traveled from Lehine through to Amentia Furor. It is my suspicion you instinctively Hid it, though I could not say why you did so then, and not after."

Nyx could. She had been terrified on Lehine. She'd been abducted, locked in a cell by a mass murderer who wanted an object she held, and in the midst of all that she'd uncovered the net of her mother's Hiding. That much fear, that much trauma? She would have Hidden herself on instinct and not even realized she was doing it. Now that she had the entirety of her memories, she knew she'd done it often enough growing up. It was the very reason Jevryn had given for why he'd left her to be raised by her mother—that Hidden children required Hidden parents, because a Hidden child would Hide on instinct before they understood how their power worked, and they might become lost and never find their way out. With her memories regained, she had to concede that one small point to him: she had needed Elena Fortuna, whether she'd wanted her or not.

"Kiev will not come to Earth," Jevryn continued. "He is not allowed there unless I accompany him. Within the Station, you are safe."

Was she, though? An image of the spectral dog flashed in her mind's eye. The way she'd felt as if it was watching her. The way it never came onto the Station grounds. "All he has to do to remove me from Earth is to tell the other councilors about me."

"Which he also will not do. A lesson on your culture, *na'tria*—family matters are never shared with those who are *not* family. He would no more speak of your existence than he would tell the rest of the Council that it was I who destroyed Koral."

That was all well and good, except for the part where she was pretty sure Kiev was a psychopath. Jevryn had very specifically said she was safe at the Station—not if she left it. Which meant he didn't think her genetic relationship to Kiev would protect her from him. In all likelihood, given how he appeared to delight in tormenting Jevryn, if Nyx's uncle thought she could be used against him in any way, he would do everything within his power to acquire her.

She chewed on her lower lip as she shifted her focus from Nethrayne to the next planet that felt similar. The next one that bore all three of their combined signatures. "You're certain he isn't on Kyvren now?"

"You tell me. Untangle his signature from ours."

That part wasn't difficult. She'd been itching to do it since she'd felt Kiev's mark, not wanting to be associated with him.

"Good. Now, focus on the magic attached to his signature. In what direction was it moving? Toward the planet, or away from it? Examine your own signature first, and see if you cannot make the correlation there, to gain a feel for the use."

She tried, but it felt as it had when she'd been trying to manipulate the map back on Earth—she just didn't understand what she was doing, and she grudgingly admitted as much.

"May I?" Jevryn asked.

She wasn't sure what he was asking permission for, but she nodded. He lifted his left hand and a spiral of magic answered his call, working alongside hers to overlay the map she viewed with one of his own. At first, she didn't feel anything different. But then his magic drew her focus to his own signature, drawing her not to simply view it, but to inhabit it.

It was like the difference between standing on a cliff, watching a river hundreds of feet below, and standing beside the river, then wading into it. Standing on the cliff, it might not be apparent which way the water was flowing, but ankle-deep in it, the direction of the current would become immediately apparent.

She could feel that in the signature—the direction, like a soft current, flowing away from Kyvren. Now that she'd been shown the way, she slipped from Jevryn's signature to Kiev's, taking comfort in the off-world-flowing current she felt there, as well.

"Gone," she said with relief. "He's still gone."

"Good. That will suffice, for now. One ought not overdo a first lesson. Are you ready to leave?"

She wished that answer was a resounding *yes*, but it wasn't. "Mostly. Look, I know this was my idea, but do we have a plan past you impersonating your brother?"

"Should we require more of a plan than that, you will find we are in a situation dire enough that prior thought would not prove useful. But it does bring up another matter—namely that I know how Kiev thinks and acts, and you do not. As you and Kaden will be presumed as two of Kiev's trusted guard, it would therefore be unwise for you to speak at all, even if asked a direct question. You will not know how to act as one of Kiev's. Will that be a problem for you?"

"No one is going to think it odd if I refuse to speak?"

"No." It was Kaden who answered, and the flat tone of his voice didn't lead her to ask further questions.

"Okay. No talking. Not a problem."

"Good," Jevryn said. "And Nyx? I may have to do things you will find distasteful. Try not to react."

He motioned for Kaden to step forward and join them. Since Nyx had already seen Jevryn portal both people and things from the other side of the room, she wondered if having Kaden physically join them was symbolic, or if it served a more practical function. If he portaled multiple people, did they all arrive the same distance apart from each other as they'd been when his magic took hold of them?

It was the kind of question that an hour ago would have frustrated her to no end. Now, she realized she could just ask it. And if

Jevryn had meant what he'd said, then he would give her the answer.

She would, she decided. Once they were out of Eravendrin, once she had Seth back and he was safe, she would ask. It felt...not precisely *hopeful*, but...steadying? Like she finally had one of those tethers in the world that having parents was supposed to give you— that appeal to a greater store of lived experiences, the knowledge that if she needed help she had someone to ask.

Kaden stepped up next to them and Jevryn's magic washed over her, the dark yet oddly soothing interior of his home fading, replaced shortly thereafter with the hard-stalked grass of Kyvren and the looming shadow of Eravendrin.

36

Jevryn had brought them to what she thought was their original landing point on the planet, several miles from the base of the mountain. She wondered why he hadn't portaled them directly to the entrance. When she asked as much, he said, "I have not been to the base of the mountain. Could you remember a place well enough, having only seen it from afar, to replicate it in your mind's eye in sufficient detail to portal there from memory?"

Good point.

He took her silence for the *no* that it was. "Always remember that experience with the use of magic does not grant one abilities of the mind outside of it. It is no great difficulty to portal *here* and use of line-of-sight to portal *there*. Arrogance and complacency is how a portal witch dies." Having dispensed this wisdom, his magic curled around them once more, and Nyx found herself mere feet from the vertical slash in the mountain that was the pathway into Eravendrin.

Jevryn's demeanor shifted the moment they arrived, a tangible difference Nyx could feel in the space between them. When she thought of him, the first descriptors that came to mind were cool and aloof. He always struck her as icily calm, utterly in control. That ice had now shifted to the unpredictability of heat, the calm control replaced with an air of brazen power and the indifference of the man who possessed it.

No sooner had they appeared than he strode for the city's entrance, sparing neither glance nor comment for her or Kaden, as if their following promptly was a given. Kaden had started walking immediately when Jevryn did, but Nyx had to trot to catch up, falling in next to Kaden just as they passed inside the mountain.

She saw the telltale red gleam of the unda as they approached, but she still wasn't fully prepared for the Hall of Revelation. Unda surrounded them, stretching from the ground on either side of them to meet at the apex of the tunnel, trapped behind a clear wall like fish in an aquarium. As Jevryn walked through, they hurled themselves at the glass. With each impact, a sound like a striking gong clanged through the mountain, deep and resonant and ancient.

Kaden followed and the sound produced by the unda's attempts to reach him changed, no longer bone-deep and fathomless, but a steady, unshakeable bass. A note that could be held in perpetuity forever and never change. Or perhaps it *could* alter over time, but it would do it so gradually that the difference would be difficult to notice.

Then Nyx walked in. The unda stilled. For one moment, silence reigned, and then the unda, rather than hurling themselves at the wall, swam along it instead, slipping against the surface as if trying to entice, rather than attack, her. The resultant sound was sweet but haunting, a melodious susurration filling the hall.

Beren had told her the sounds from the hall filtered through all levels of Eravendrin, like a church organ spreading through a chapel. That they had become accustomed to the sounds. She wondered if the ones the hall made for her now sounded to the inhabitants of Eravendrin like they did to her—like the sweet ripple of a wind chime paired with the soft whisper of a slow-moving creek. She wondered if everyone who walked through this hall felt comforted by the audible reflection of themselves, as she strangely did, or if it became tedious to hear it, day after day.

She heard a different sound from the far end of the hall, another striking gong, albeit one that sounded like a poor imitation of the one the hall had made for Jevryn. A Dwarf approached, a war hammer held in his right hand. He did not run but his stride bespoke haste. The full beard that claimed his face nearly up to his cheekbones made it difficult to discern his expression, but his entire body projected a concern he tried but failed to hide.

He stopped just before Jevryn and struck the handle of the war hammer to the ground, bowing over it in greeting. "Councilor A-Morridahn."

Jevryn spared him a brief glance, hardly more than a flicker of his attention. He walked past the Dwarf, as if he knew precisely where he was headed and couldn't be bothered with interruptions. Judging by the way the Dwarf began practically jogging to keep up with Jevryn's long stride, but didn't seem surprised, this was normal behavior for Kiev.

"We were not expecting your return quite so soon, my lord."

My lord? Really?

Jevryn continued walking as if he hadn't been spoken to.

"I apologize, but I must speak with you a moment." The words sounded unnatural coming out in the Dwarf's gruff voice, as if apologizing and requesting were both foreign to him, and he had only learned them due to necessity.

Jevryn halted. He was a tall man by human standards, and appeared even more so looking down his nose at the Dwarf, his expression one of obvious irritation. "I cannot seem to be bothered to recall your name, at present."

A flush of red stained the Dwarf's cheeks, high up where his beard didn't cover. Nyx thought it was anger, rather than embarrassment. "I am called Dagnar."

"I said that I could not be bothered to recall it," Jevryn said, "not that I wished you to fill the gaps in my memory."

That flush in Dagnar's cheeks deepened.

"However, since you have taken it upon yourself to do so, what is it that you find so pressing you must bother me with it now, *Dagnar?*" He said the Dwarf's name as if his knowledge of it was now a threat.

Dagnar's jaw clenched. He unhinged it and managed something close to civility. "We were not expecting your return."

"Yes, I did hear you the first time and found it unworthy of note. However, since you insist upon bringing it to my attention, I now find myself *fascinated* to hear why that would be a problem for you."

Dagnar shifted. "We...have not yet made progress with Riven."

Nyx had to work not to visibly react. Maybe she was ignorant and Riven was a wildly popular Dwarven name, but she doubted it. Doubted that, even if it was popular, the Riven to whom Dagnar referred wasn't the very one she had come here to find. Not when Kiev was involved. And given that Kiev *was* involved, there could only be one reason for it. That he knew—or suspected—Riven's family's involvement in the Harvester's creation. She had wondered what would bring Kiev to this planet, what would cause him to offer his aid to the Dwarves. She had her answer.

Jevryn made a *tsking* sound. "How disappointing."

Ropy tendrils of black curled off his wrists, taking the form of phantom snakes. Nyx had never before seen his magic manifest in a visible way. She had felt it—the way it filled a space, the way the breadth of it stole the air from a room—but even when he expended it in quantity, as he had that day on Nethrayne, when he had killed so many with so little effort, she hadn't *seen* it. She could only assume, therefore, that this visible manifestation was one of Kiev's hallmarks. No sooner had she thought it than the spectral dog rose again in her mind's eye.

Jevryn's snakes undulated toward Dagnar. The Dwarf paled, but he didn't step back, as if he knew that doing so was dangerous.

"Since you are incapable of delivering results," Jevryn said calmly, "I will have to obtain them myself. Take me to Riven."

Dagnar's hesitation was underlit with anger. "We had an agreement, my lord. That we would get the answers you seek, but you would have no direct contact with Riven. That was why my people agreed to your proposal."

"Did I *specifically* agree to have no contact with her?" Jevryn asked silkily, his voice almost soothing. "I highly doubt I would have been so remiss in the finer details of our arrangement."

The phantom snakes hissed, and Dagnar's voice took on a note of panic. "If we had the two weeks you promised us—" He cut off as one of the snakes opened its mouth. Its tongue flicked out, licking across Dagnar's cheek. Where it touched, the dark brown of his beard bleached white. The strands fell to the floor, the newly revealed skin turning black.

"Necrosis of the skin is such a nasty thing," Jevryn told Dagnar calmly. "It spreads quickly enough when left to its own devices, but even more so when my mood is foul." The patch of black skin grew larger.

Nyx tried to keep her expression neutral but knew she must have failed when Kaden's fingers brushed lightly against her wrist.

Only when she looked at him did she realize how wide her eyes had gone, how she felt like all the blood had drained from her face. He gave the slightest shake of his head.

She swallowed and forced herself to watch the unfolding events. She couldn't slip into the bored indifference Kaden showed, as if he'd seen this a dozen times before—as she realized he probably had—but she set her mouth in a firm line and clasped her hands behind her back so they wouldn't tremble.

"I can continue," Jevryn said. The strip of necrotic skin had grew. On Dagnar's other side, a second phantom snake opened its mouth, tongue flicking out but not quite touching his face. "If I do, your healers will need to carve out half your face to keep you alive. Or"—here he paused for effect—"you can make the intelligent choice."

I may have to do things you will find distasteful, Jevryn had told her. But this—this went several leagues beyond *distasteful*. And yet she stood there and she kept her mouth shut and she watched it happen. Because she had said that she would, because it had already been done and couldn't be *undone*, but it didn't feel right. Felt worse because she had asked Jevryn to play this role, not truly understanding what she had asked of him. And because maybe, if she was a little bit stronger, she would think of something to say to make it stop.

She wished she could see everything in black-and-white so she didn't have to care in this moment. The Dwarves had stolen the Meerkin's home, so they were bad, and she therefore didn't have to care about what was happening. But life wasn't black-and-white. She might be on the opposite side of this battle, but she wasn't naive enough to think that meant everyone remaining within this city deserved every terrible thing that came their way. It didn't mean she thought what Jevryn was doing was okay even if she knew—even if she *hoped*—that he was only doing it because it was what Kiev would do in this circumstance.

The necrotic patch grew larger. The second snake moved closer. And Nyx couldn't do it anymore. She stepped forward—

"Fine," Dagnar spat. "I'll take you to her."

Jevryn's lips split in a way that made her finally understand the meaning of *psychotic smile*. "A wise choice. And here"—he lifted his hand—"you see I can be generous."

The snake's tongue licked once more across Dagnar's cheek. But this time, where it touched the sick black of necrosis vanished. The skin was still *dead*, Dagnar's beard still gone. Jevryn hadn't reversed the damage, but he had removed the magic of death from it, leaving damage that looked more natural.

Dagnar's eyes sparked with defiance, but he leashed it and led them out of the Hall of Revelation. Jevryn's phantom snakes coiled back into him, and she tried to catch his eye. But he refused to look at her as they followed Dagnar deeper into Eravendrin.

37

Nyx thought of herself as a person with a fairly decent internal compass. She loved puzzles and mazes, and remembering her way through the twists and turns of large buildings had never been a problem for her. Fifteen minutes inside Eravendrin, though, and she understood why Beren had said it meant "that which cannot be escaped".

The city was a labyrinth of caverns and tunnels, and she became hopelessly lost quicker than she preferred to admit. Several times a tunnel would end abruptly at a sheer drop, only for a large flat rock to rise up at the edge to ferry them through the darkness. And it *was* dark. Where the Meerkin's den had been filled with light, Eravendrin was a place of gloom broken intermittently by flickering torchlight.

Nyx had only the certainty that overall they were twisting, down and down, as if they descended a corkscrew that was drilled into the depths of the earth. She decided, as the weight of the mountain above pressed down on her, that she was not made for underground survival. Despite the vast openness of the caverns they passed through, the impressive scope of the city, she couldn't shake the feeling that she was trapped. It was the lack of windows, the damp of the air. The knowledge that, already, she didn't know how to get *out*.

The Shadow Keep had been similar, so deep underground, though that place had felt ordinary in a way this one did not. Because the Keep had been filled with people who had been organized in a way Nyx understood. People doing their jobs with a sort of mundanity that had made it all feel familiar.

And while she had no doubt that somewhere within Eravendrin Dwarvenkind was doing the same, she was not in that part of the city. The halls here were empty, as if this heart they strode through had been abandoned. As if it was kept empty so that, should someone escape the prison it led to, they would find themselves in an empty tomb. Guards, if posted, would always point to a way out. If one could follow a trail of people, they could eventually find their way to *somewhere*. But in their absence, the labyrinth became even more unnavigable.

But more than the added confusion, the sheer desolation would suck the hope out of a person. The stopwatch Nyx had started when Dagnar first began leading them now showed forty minutes. Forty minutes could feel like an eternity when you were alone. Add in the sheer number of directional choices a person would have to make as they attempted to find their way out, coupled with the eerie silence, and it would drive anyone mad in far shorter a timespan than one would otherwise think possible.

And as they moved deeper, she couldn't shake the feeling that each time they chose a tunnel, the one they had just left *shifted*. Logically, she didn't think any magic could move hewn tunnels without causing the collapse of the earth around them. It made her think perhaps it was only the doors that shifted, blocking previous exits and revealing new entrances, and it was either the design of the place or the magic of it that made one feel as if the pathways themselves changed.

She tugged on the thinnest sliver of portal magic, just enough so, reaching through it, she could feel the solidity of her anchor on Earth and be reassured by the certainty that she could return there, even from this place. She would not become trapped or lost or crushed beneath the weight of so much rock. Jevryn gave her a sharp look, and only once she let the thread of magic slip back into its bracelet did he return his focus to the path ahead of them.

Dagnar turned a corner and led them into a corridor lined with cells. Nyx's heart thundered in her chest. The air had grown warm, stiflingly so, and sweat trickled down her spine, settling in the hollow of her back and plastering her shirt to her skin. She let the others precede her and scanned the cells as they walked. But this area was nearly as empty as the walk down had been. Either Eravendrin didn't find much need to imprison people—which seemed unlikely, given the complexity of the route they'd taken—or its decision makers had placed Riven in a little used area.

Considering what Dagnar had said about the agreement they'd struck with Kiev, it didn't sound as if they were keen on having an outsider interrogate one of their own. She wondered if they had put Riven here, in this otherwise uninhabited place, because they had known Kiev would eventually insist on seeing her, and they didn't want witnesses when that time came. If that was the case, what were the odds Seth would be in this section, too? And if he wasn't, how was she going to find him in this place?

It ate at her that she couldn't just ask, that she had to remain silent, because Jevryn wasn't asking either. What if he didn't? What if, now that he was being handed access to Riven—the only reason *he* had come here in the first place—he lost sight of the promises he'd made to her? What if he forgot all about Seth?

If he did… Well, it was no matter to her. Now that she was inside Eravendrin, she could Hide and remain within it. She could Hide Kaden, too, whether he liked it or not. Jevryn couldn't portal them out if he couldn't find them. Kaden would track Seth, and maybe she didn't have an anchor point on this planet, but she did have one to Jevryn's home. She could return there, refill her stores of portal magic, and either attempt the jump back to Kyvren on her own, or choose the smarter route of pulling Arradin's book from the shelf, as Jevryn had told her to do when he'd given her the anchor to his home in the first place, and wait for him to show up to take them back.

Plan in place, her anxiety settled. Ahead, Dagnar halted.

At this stop, Jevryn said, "I cannot help but notice that I do not see Riven." His tone heavily implied that he hoped Dagnar hadn't been foolish enough to mislead them.

"No, my lord. But there is…another matter. You wanted to be alerted of anything unusual, and this was quite unusual. A man—of the Human base—walked into the Hall of Revelation. Upon his capture, he refused to speak anything of substance"—here Dagnar grimaced—"except for one thing. He asked if we knew a Riven Gare Ru."

Jevryn's expression turned lethal. "Where is this individual now?"

"Isolated, as Riven is. Would you like to see him after you speak with Riven?"

"No."

No? What the hell did he mean *no*? Nyx inhaled sharply, about to break the no-talking rule, because *fuck him* if he wouldn't take her to Seth, and—

"I will see him now."

Nyx's righteous indignation died, and as Dagnar led them down another hallway it was everything she could do not to demand he move faster. They moved to another section of cells and this one— she could make out a form in this one, in the third cell down on the left, a shock of familiar black hair against the stone.

"Unlock it," Jevryn ordered.

Dagnar hesitated, but in the end, he did.

"I require privacy," Jevryn said. This time, when Dagnar balked Jevryn's gaze narrowed, turning flame-hot. His emphatic *now* was all anger and heat, so unlike the icy calm it would have been if he wasn't playacting his twin.

Dagnar left, closing the corridor door behind him. The second it shut, Nyx rushed to the cell. A body lay on the ground inside, back to the door, but she could still see half his face—bruised, bloodied, his eyes closed. He was curled protectively around his stomach, and he was still. So, so still.

Sick heat flushed her stomach. She rushed inside and knelt next to Seth, hand trembling as she brushed his hair back from his fore- head. His skin was barely warm beneath her fingertips and he didn't react. Didn't wake. He always woke up. The slightest touch, the slightest sound. Especially from her.

It's not him. Her gut said it with certainty, had *been* saying it since the moment she saw him, but her brain didn't quite believe it. He felt so real beneath her fingers.

Not him, her gut insisted. The only problem was, if this was an illusion, she didn't feel him elsewhere in the room.

"Is he—" Kaden cut off when her head snapped up. She looked past him, over his shoulder. She hadn't heard or seen the door open at the end of the corridor. To all appearances, it was closed and had been since Dagnar had exited.

She stared straight at the empty space in front of it and ground out, "You fucking asshole." Then she ran, past Kaden and Jevryn, past the empty cells, barreling into an invisible Seth. It was half a hug, half a tackle, and he dropped his illusion as she knocked him to the ground.

His back hit the stone floor and he grunted. "For fuck's sake, I think you broke a rib."

"You are such a prick," she snapped.

"Me? What did I do?"

"That."

He followed her pointed finger to the cell. "I didn't make a half-dead illusion of myself with the aim of distressing *you*, Nyxi darling. It was for the benefit of the masses."

"What masses?"

He shrugged. "They send a guy through every couple of hours. Besides, I thought you always know when it's not me."

"I do. I did. That's not the point."

In his most patient, cautious voice, he said, "Dare I ask what *is* the point?"

How was she supposed to explain? The way her heart had nearly stopped in that first moment, before she'd gotten close enough for her senses to tell her that it wasn't him. The way she'd been afraid that her gut telling her it wasn't him had only been her desperate need to *believe* that it wasn't.

The way that, real or not, seeing him like that—bloody and broken and unmoving—had hurt. How it had twisted her insides into knots and made her regret every second of the last few months she'd spent locked up in anxiety instead of living.

"The point," she said slowly, "is that I didn't like it. The point is that you scared me."

His lips quirked up. "Were you worried about me?" He sounded entirely too pleased by the notion. "You know I'm hard to kill. I'm too difficult to find."

"*I'm* going to kill you if you ever make me see you like that again."

"Well, out of everyone, you do have the best chance of success."

"I'm being serious," she said. He opened his mouth and she cut him off. "If you make a why-so-serious joke right now, your murder will become imminent."

He cupped her face with one hand. "(A) so much violence, once again directed at me. (B) there isn't a single other person I know who understands *Joker* references."

"(C)" came Jevryn A-Morridahn's voice, "we must be moving on."

Seth's gaze flicked to Jevryn, then back to Nyx, his eyes wide. His expression was a mixture of irritation and wonder, like he remembered he was pissed at Jevryn on her behalf, but something more pressing was getting in the way of his anger. "Did he just try to be amusing?"

That *would* distract Seth. "'Try' being the operative word," Nyx confirmed.

Seth's voice dropped to a whisper only perceptible by her. "He's trying to work his way up to dad jokes? Also, I'm impressed you didn't murder him."

She sighed. "It was touch-and-go there for a bit. Also, you don't have to whisper, Kaden figured it out."

Seth rolled his eyes. "Of course he did. What else did I miss?"

"A lot. I'll fill you in when we're not surrounded by the crushing weight of a mountain." She stood, offering him a hand. "At which point you can also explain how you got locked up in Eravendrin despite your mastery over illusion."

He took her hand and hauled himself up, grinning as he said, "After carefully considering my options, I got caught on purpose."

Of course he had. "Why?"

"Thought I might learn something interesting."

Nyx restrained those "violent tendencies" Seth was always harping on her about. "And did you?"

"After busting out my rusty lock picking skills, yes. Your uncle's here, but then"—his gaze flicked to Jevryn—"considering Dad's cosplaying him, I'm guessing you knew that already."

Jevryn's face, upon hearing Seth, of all people, refer to him as "Dad", remained impressively impassive. However, if impassivity could convey that it would prefer to be expressing hostility, Jevryn managed it.

"Yeah," Nyx said sourly, "we know he's here. Seems he made a deal with the Dwarves—his help in exchange for them getting Riven here." She frowned. "Though I don't know why, exactly. He doesn't have the Harvester so he can't need to know how it works."

"He doesn't. Riven's in the cell row next to mine. Kiev's trying to find out how the Harvester was built. I can't say for certain, but I'm pretty sure he's hoping she can build him a new one."

Nyx didn't reach for the Harvester, but she felt it, pulsing faintly against her chest, a flash of warmth like it always gave whenever it was mentioned. "She just told you that?"

He shrugged. "Not in so many words. I slipped into the adjacent cell while she was asleep, played up the fellow prisoner angle, asked her what she was in for. She said she had a great-great-something grandfather who made something he shouldn't have, and she was paying for refusing to do the same. I used my exceptional powers of deduction to infer she meant the Harvester."

Cold seeped into her bones, and she looked at Jevryn. "Why would Kiev want another Harvester?" Yes, the obvious answer was that it was a powerful object, and powerful people liked to be in control of powerful objects, but she doubted Kiev wanted the Harvester—or a replica of it—just so he could put it in a glass display case and never use it. Nor was it like a nuclear bomb where having one meant, in theory, that anyone else who had one would refrain from using it against you to avoid you doing the same to them.

"I do not know."

"Can you hazard a guess?" The Harvester literally ate worlds. Her one misguided experience in using it had shown her that, while it *could* be used on a smaller scale, if one kept using it, they wouldn't manage to stay small-scale for long. Its hunger was endless, and it longed to swallow everything around it. So unless using a second Harvester while someone was trying to destroy you with the original would prevent said destruction, she couldn't reasonably think that Kiev wanted it for protective reasons. Which didn't leave any *good* reasons for him to want one.

"I can," Jevryn said. "But I will not do so here. We can discuss this when our time is not so limited."

She opened her mouth to protest, remembered they were supposed to be trying to get along and that he hadn't told her *no,* only *later*, and instead said, "Then let's get Riven and get out of here."

Seth frowned and pressed the palm of his hand to her forehead. She shoved it away. "I don't have a fever just because I didn't argue with him."

"The very fact you know exactly why I checked for one tells me you wanted to argue, but didn't. Why?"

"Maybe I'm growing as a person."

He snorted. "Yeah, okay." But he let it go, because he was Seth and he knew how to pick up the don't-push-me-on-it-now vibes she was throwing out.

"Make yourself useful," Jevryn told him, "and disappear again."

Seth studied him for a moment. "I don't know what's going on here, but what I told you after her mother fixed her memories still stands." Then he vanished.

Nyx would have demanded to know what Seth was talking about, except Jevryn portaled from one end of the room to the other in the blink of an eye and opened the door, once again making Dagnar privy to their words.

"Take us to Riven's cell," Jevryn demanded. In the face of his clipped words, the Dwarf clearly decided silent compliance was in his best interest.

They entered another corridor of cells, Jevryn and Kaden in the lead, Nyx and Seth following. This space was nearly identical to one they'd found Seth in, all the way down to the fact that this one also housed precisely one prisoner. Riven Gare Ru sat in the corner of her cell, knees pulled up to her chest, elbows resting atop them. Her face was bruised and as they walked in, she opened her eyes. They landed on Jevryn and turned bright with fury.

Riven said something, but Nyx couldn't hear it. Her ears had filled with a rush like a roaring river, drowning out sound. She turned back toward the door they'd entered through, but her body was sluggish, the movement taking all of her effort. A heavy, oppressive weight settled onto her chest, as if gravity had intensified. She felt tethered to the ground in a way she never had before, as if she'd previously had wings and they had been torn from her back, leaving her stranded.

Three things happened in rapid succession. Jevryn, who had

walked deeper into the room than Nyx, Kaden, or Seth, spun to look at the door. Dagnar, standing in that doorway, dropped to the ground as if he was a puppet whose strings had been cut, his eyes lifeless. Revealed in the space where he'd been, Kiev A-Morridahn stepped over Dagnar's body, a smile stretching across his face.

38

Upon seeing Kiev, Nyx understood where that feeling in her chest—that sense of being stuck—came from. Just as Jevryn had once used his and her combined portaling abilities to prevent Laiveran from leaving Amentia Furor, Kiev was now using his own to do the same thing to her. She couldn't portal. And just as she'd found it difficult to physically move when locked in that previous battle for competing dominance, her limbs now refused to obey her.

Kaden and Seth both lunged for Kiev. Phantom serpents spilled off his arms. They encircled Kaden, halting him in his tracks, but Kiev couldn't *see* Seth. Nyx didn't know what would happen if Seth touched her uncle, but if it was that easy to kill Kiev A-Morridahn, he wouldn't still be alive.

Her eyes and her mouth, at least, still obeyed her. She looked to where she knew Seth was and screamed, "Seth, stop!"

Kiev followed her gaze. More serpents spilled onto the floor, racing for that space, and Seth did the only thing he could—he turned visible before the serpents touched him by accident. The phantom snakes stopped just shy of him, surrounding his feet in a tight circle.

Kiev laughed. "The Illusionist, how delightful." To Nyx, he said, "I should have realized you wouldn't have gone anywhere without him. The two of you are so codependent."

Nyx's blood chilled. She didn't have to guess any longer if that resemblance she'd seen between the phantom snakes and the spectral dog was only in her head. Her uncle had been spying on her.

Her heart tripped in her chest. The snakes were too close to Seth —closer to him than they were to Kaden.

Kiev looked past Nyx to his brother, practically beaming satisfaction. "Jevryn. It is such a delight to find you finally taking an interest in things that matter again. Imagine my surprise when Loclyn told me you had traded oversight of Aldiba for oversight of Kyvren, of all places.

"And I had to ask myself, what would my recluse of a brother want with a useless planet? Unless, of course, it was the very thing *I* wanted from it as well. You haven't played games with me in centuries. It has me feeling quite nostalgic."

"I am not playing games with you." Jevryn walked toward them as if in slow motion. Under different circumstances, she would have found it comical, but given that it meant he was likewise affected by Kiev's pull on dominance—if not as fully as she was—she couldn't find anything funny about it now.

Kiev's grinned widened. "Of course we are playing games. What do you call *him*?" Kiev indicated Kaden. "I've been wondering what you were doing with him for months. I must admit, he is *very* good. The things I've had him do have made worse men snap." Again, Kiev addressed Nyx, almost as an aside. "I do apologize for returning him to you in such poor mental condition. It really couldn't be helped."

Nyx's stomach turned. She didn't know what to say, but he didn't seem to want a response. She felt like she was in a circus and Kiev was the ringmaster, putting on a show and expecting her to play her part, but she didn't know what the act was.

Kiev tapped his finger thoughtfully against his lips, still looking at her. "I cannot believe Jevryn was so generous as to bring you here, right to me. Earth's Guardian, far from the safety of her Station. A budding little portal witch who likes to go traipsing about the universe, leaving her footprints all over it and thinking no one notices."

He leaned in closer to her, as if relaying a secret. "*I* noticed. Do you want to know why? It is because you feel so very much like *family*." He shot a mock-pitying glance at Jevryn, whose slow-motion walking had almost brought him within arms' reach of Nyx.

Kiev straightened, returning his attention to Jevryn. "I am dying to know how poor, lost Arradin is handling this development. He was insufferable that last time you brought him home to see mother, what with his constant talk of either adopting or going to see the surrogates. If I recall correctly, that was the night you put your fist through the tranquility room's wall, and he finally understood that you were never going to give him the one thing he truly wanted: a happy little brood of children.

"And now you've gone and made a bastard with someone else." He made a *tsking* sound. "I must admit, it came as quite a shock. I had not thought you even moderately inclined toward feminine company. But it is no matter." He clapped his hands together. "What is important is that she is here now. Shall we discover what she is made of? What do you think, brother? Have you managed to breed a *true* A-Morridahn?"

A torrent of black smoke shot from Kiev, straight at her. She struggled but the crushing weight wouldn't let her go, no matter how she battered against it. Death arrowed for her—and then Jevryn lurched in front of her. He opened his mouth, jaw distending in a way human jaws were not meant to, and swallowed Kiev's magic. He gagged immediately, but his mouth clamped shut, holding Kiev's magic.

Slowly, so slowly, his hand reached for hers. His skin was shot through with black veining, his body shaking, as if the magic he'd ingested was trying to batter its way free of him. He dropped to one knee, and it was that—her fear at seeing Jevryn, whom she couldn't help but view as invincible, falter—that gave her the strength to move. Not much, but enough to take the hand he was reaching toward her. Because she'd understood, with that movement, what he meant to do.

Skin touched skin. An acid burn licked through her veins, that same feeling that had gone through her on Amentia Furor when he'd drawn on her ability to portal. He drew on it now in huge gulps and she let it go willingly, desperate to believe that if she gave him enough, if she gave him everything she had, he could get them out of this.

Magic rose, shuddering and violent, not at all the smooth flawless transition that typically defined Jevryn's portaling. The ground shook. The walls shook. A slab of stone split from the ceiling, falling towards Kiev. Before she could see if it hit, the interior of Eravendrin melted. For a split second, they were in limbo—a frightening, chaotic limbo unlike anything she'd experienced in previous portals —and then they were crashing violently onto the ground just outside of the Meerkin's central den. Crushed stone and dust rained down, chunks of rock pelting her, bruising and drawing blood.

When the debris stopped falling she looked for Seth, found him next to Kaden and Riven. It was seeing Riven that made her understand where the debris had come from. Jevryn hadn't just portaled *her*—he'd portaled her cell and half of another. If the cuts and welling bruises on all of them were any indication, he'd taken pieces of the ceiling with them as well.

Taking in Kiev's magic—stepping in front of the attack that had been meant for *her*—had weakened him, and this was all he'd had the control for. He was on his knees, his back still to her, his hand lightly clasped in hers. He'd stopped drawing on her ability, the acid scream of that theft gone. He convulsed, falling forward onto all fours.

She scrambled around to face him. All of his veins were raised and black beneath his skin, like hers became when the chaos thorns heightened her anger. His irises were gone, eyes wholly black from lid to lid. He convulsed again, like his body was trying to expel what he'd ingested, but his lips, black as if painted, were pressed into a determined line.

"Jevryn?" she asked, her voice higher than normal. "What do I do?"

He didn't answer. His left hand clutched at his chest, and she didn't know if he could even see her through the pure black of his eyes. Another spasm tore through him and she gripped his shoulders, trying to hold him still, hoping it would help. All it did was let him find the inner strength to knock her hands away.

He got out two words, barely intelligible through his clenched jaw. "Do not—" A stain of black seeped through his teeth and he broke off, swallowing as the veins on his forehead bulged.

"What do I do?" she asked again. "Tell me how to help."

A harsh, gurgling sound came from his throat and he collapsed.

No. No, no, no. She rolled him onto his back and felt his neck for a pulse. Nothing. He was base Human, so she should find a pulse there, shouldn't she?

His eyes stared unseeing at the sky, black tears trickling out the sides. He looked dead, but he *couldn't* be dead. He was Jevryn A-Morridahn. He was a death magic user, so even though it looked like he'd *eaten* other death magic, that shouldn't kill him, right?

"Now would be a really great time for you to have told me *anything* about us." Like how his magic worked, or if Salyrian biology differed from other humans in any significant way. What the fuck to do if he ever decided to *eat* death magic.

In the absence of specified knowledge, she only had the basics to work with. She pressed the heel of her hand to where his heart should be and felt nothing. No steady, reassuring thump. Interlacing her hands, she placed them over his chest and started compressions.

One minute ticked by on her watch. Two. Three. "Come on, you arrogant bastard, *wake up.*"

Chest compressions had to be strong to be effective. It was why, if they had to be done for any length of time, you were supposed to trade off with someone else regularly. But she couldn't hand the task off. Not to Seth who'd arrived next to her, not to Kaden now crouching across from her at Jevryn's other side. But it didn't matter, because she didn't grow tired. Not when the same black that lined Jevryn's veins had now streaked up her hands and arms, a black she'd always thought came from the chaos thorns, because that was the first time it had ever happened to her. Black that always lent her a strength she'd also attributed to chaos.

Now, with her heritage known, she wasn't so sure. Not with Jevryn's earlier words resurfacing in her mind: *There are facets of our nature I believed you had simply not inherited, though recent evidence would lead me to believe you are instead exceptionally adept at repressing them.*

She couldn't think about those words right this moment because Jevryn wasn't waking up and he *had to.* Eventually, her arms did start to ache, the steady numbers on her watch providing proof she'd been at this for twenty minutes. Seth placed his hand gently on her upper back. She had a feeling this wasn't the first time he'd tried to get her attention.

"I'm sorry, Nyxi, but I think—"

"No." She pressed violently down on Jevryn's chest. "Wake up, do you hear me? Just wake the fuck up." He wasn't gone, he couldn't be gone. He hadn't told her anything about where she came from, like he'd finally promised he would. He'd barely begun to teach her about portaling. She hadn't had time to decide how she felt about any of it, how she felt about *him*. She hadn't had time to find out if maybe, someday, there was a chance he could still come to love her.

Tears stung her eyes, rolled off her cheeks onto his chest. She squeezed her eyes shut. "Jevryn?" Nothing. Her voice, barely more than a hoarse whisper: "Dad? Please, *please* wake up."

Silence reigned. She kept her eyes closed and finally stopped trying to resuscitate him. Her hands were limp and heavy on his chest. In the back of her mind, a small voice that sounded a lot like her own was chanting *not happening. This isn't happening.*

Pain welled in her chest and it felt like something woke inside her. Something she'd glimpsed before but never really connected with. It curled through her arms, down her hands, dripped off her fingertips.

A few seconds later, a rough touch brushed against the outer edge of her palm. Her eyes flew open. Jevryn's hand was covering hers. His usually smooth voice rasped out, "Not. Dead. Yet, *na'tria.*"

The black receded from his sclera, pooling in his irises. Beneath her hands, she felt the *thump thump thump* of his heart.

Alive. He was alive.

Relief and confusion and anger flooded her. She jerked her hands free, leapt to her feet, and ran. Past the the Meerkin and Dwarves who'd gathered at their crash landing, and into the welcome coolness of the den.

39

S eth did not call after Nyx, but only because they were surrounded by over a dozen of the Meerkin and this was already more of a scene than she was going to be comfortable with once she processed what had happened. He looked at Jevryn, who had attained a semi-vertical position and mostly looked normal again, if you ignored the fact his pupils couldn't be distinguished from his irises.

"You good?" Seth asked. "You aren't going to keel over dead if I leave?"

"That was never a danger," Jevryn said icily.

"Great." He clapped his future father-in-law on the shoulder and ignored the way Jevryn almost collapsed beneath the slight weight. "I'm gonna go get Nyx. You and Kaden can get Riven out of the cell you thought it was necessary to bring with us."

Jevryn scanned the area, until his gaze came to rest on Riven's cell. He gave an exhale that was somewhere between a dragon's breath and a snarl, and since Seth wasn't entirely certain what the cause of that frustrated noise was, he hesitated about leaving.

"I've got this," Kaden told him.

Deciding Kaden had a lot more practice decoding Jevryn than he did, Seth nodded. He jogged into the den, using the entrance Nyx had disappeared through. His hopes of a wide-open communal space, where Nyx would be easy to find, were dashed the second he clambered up through the unique entrance. He stood in a tunnel, illuminated with pale lights. It was inviting and open, with children's paintings covering the stone walls. He made his way down the path and came upon a subadult Meerkin making another addition to the artwork.

She lay flat on her belly, the tools of her trade splayed around her, brush held in her opposable-thumb-bearing paw as she added a careful brush stroke to her work. The painting showed what could only be Nyx and Kaden standing in a small room as a Meerkin who looked suspiciously like the current artist painted Jevryn's face.

"Do you like it?" the Meerkin asked.

"I do." He crouched next to the artist, studying the painting. "I particularly like how well you captured the glowering expressions Jevryn and Kaden always have."

"They are quite stoic," she said gravely. "I thought perhaps all human males behaved so, but you appear less serious."

Seth flashed her his trademark dashing grin, the one that had always translated across species lines. "I can think of no greater insult than to be taken seriously." He lowered his voice in a conspiratorial whisper. "I'm the fun one."

She giggled, leaving his trademark grin with a one-hundred percent inter-species success rate. "Are you Nyx's friend? The one she was so worried about?"

"That's me. Seth Hawthorne."

"I am called Myrla. I painted the scar on Jevryn's face, so he could look like his brother. Was it effective?"

"*Highly* effective. I stand before you as living proof."

"You aren't simply saying that to make me feel better? I saw Nyx run by a moment ago. She was upset, and neither Jevryn nor Kaden were with her."

"They're still outside. We ran into some complications, but they didn't have anything to do with your stellar artwork. I do think Nyx could use a friend right now, though. Do you know where I can find her?"

"I heard Jori send her down to the reflection pools. It's a nice quiet place to be alone."

Seth verified that he wasn't violating any of the dwelling's rules by following Nyx, obtained directions, and went to the reflection pools. The first room was a large cavern with an equally large pool in the center. A few Meerkin lounged at the edges, staring into the water or dozing lightly. Nyx wasn't among them.

Obeying the only rule he'd been given—don't talk at the reflection pools unless you and your conversational partner are alone—he skirted the edge of the water until he came to the first of two tunnel openings. He walked through it. Myrla had said the smaller pools were on a serpentine loop, so it didn't matter which opening he went through—he'd get through everything eventually.

He passed through several smaller rooms that were all empty, but when he saw a slight opening just off the main loop, a little area that was almost hidden, he knew he'd find her there. He squeezed through the opening, which was hardly more than a split in the rock, grateful he wasn't claustrophobic.

Nyx sat by the edge of the pool, knees drawn up, arms slung over them as she stared into the water. He dropped next to her and bumped his shoulder into hers. "Penny for your thoughts?"

She snorted. "You know I don't sell mine for less than a quarter."

He fished in his pocket, pulled out a quarter and offered it to her. She stared at the coin before taking it and rolling it between her fingers. "It's real."

"I would never try to buy your thoughts with illusory money."

"Why in all the stars would you have an actual quarter in your pocket? It's not like you can buy anything with it outside of Dead Earth."

He shrugged. "It's a habit. Started when I was a kid. Never left the house without one, in case we decided to sneak out of the valley."

She looked at the quarter, then at him. "The bubblegum machine?"

He nodded. The closest city that could be reached from the valley they'd grown up in had had a grocery store with one of those bubblegum vending machines, the ones with the red base and the clear plastic spheres filled with brightly colored bubblegum balls.

Nyx's endearing but problematic insistence on adhering to a moral code that didn't allow for theft had meant the bubblegum was one of the few things he could get her when they were kids that she would actually take. One, because he could afford it, and two, because giving her the quarter and letting her slide it into the slot and turn the handle meant he could prove he hadn't shoplifted it.

She'd only asked once where the quarters came from. He'd said Viktor, which hadn't entirely been a lie, though he might have implied they had been given to him rather than the actuality of his stealing them.

"I don't think I've had bubblegum since I was fourteen."

She'd been fifteen, actually, the last time they'd stopped by that machine. There had been a family in front of them—two mothers and their daughter—and it was as if watching them had clicked something into place inside her mind. He never was sure if the something was that *that* was what a happy family was supposed to look like and, having been confronted with it, the experience had been soured for her, or if she'd suddenly realized that she was, by Dead Earth's unwritten social rules, too old to get genuinely excited over twenty-five-cent gum.

Either way, he'd watched a spark in her die that day, and he would have given anything to give it back to her. By that point, always having a quarter in his pocket had been a habit, and he'd never quit it. She was, currently, holding the same quarter he'd put in his pocket the morning he'd left her in that apartment in Tempe. The same quarter that had, against all odds, stayed with him all the years they'd been apart.

He closed her fingers around it. "I paid up. I believe that means I'm owed thoughts."

"One thought," she countered, slipping the quarter into her pocket.

He spread his hands in defeat. "I'll take what I can get."

"I can't lose you."

He frowned—that wasn't what he'd been expecting—and reached out to brush a strand of hair from her face. It had the intended effect of making her look at him. "I'm not going anywhere. I told you, I'm in this with you. Nothing that's happened here has scared me, Nyxi."

"Yeah, well, it's scared me. I thought… I didn't know where you were. And since *I* almost died within a few hours of arriving on this planet, I—"

"You *what?*" His fingers tensed, tangling in her hair, but she didn't seem to notice. "You were supposed to be safe with Jevryn and Kaden."

He listened with more patience than he felt while she filled in the gaps of what had happened to her after they'd separated, and he took back everything he'd just said about not being scared. He hadn't worried about her because it had never occurred to him that she could be separated from Jevryn. The councilor might be an arrogant asshole, but he was a well-traveled, very powerful arrogant asshole who also happened to be Nyx's father. Seth didn't trust Jevryn with her emotional wellbeing, but he had trusted that Jevryn wouldn't let her come to any physical harm.

She finished her recap of events, bringing it back to the present. "With what just happened to Jevryn, I..." She trailed off. "Maybe it was naive, but I didn't really think he *could* die. He's been alive for nine-hundred years so it's safe to say he's pretty good at *not* dying. But if even he can come that close to death, given what he is, what chance do the rest of us caught up in this mess have?"

Seth used the hand still tangled in her hair to tug her closer. "I'm not going to die, Nyxi." He loved her too much to leave her.

"You can't promise something like that."

"Watch me." He closed his mouth over hers, not gentle, but taunting. Pushing. Because she liked to be pushed, because she liked to fight, and he knew he'd drawn her out of that dark place she'd gone to when she climbed onto his lap and sank her teeth into his bottom lip.

A throat cleared. Loudly. Nyx dropped her forehead onto his shoulder like she was beating her head against a desk, which gave Seth an unobstructed view of Kaden standing in the narrow entryway. There was a look in the ex-Enforcer's eyes—a desperate longing Seth understood all too well—that made Seth hold her just a little bit tighter.

"Vorex is asking to see you both." Kaden's gaze lingered on Nyx for a second longer. "And the unda are active again in the area. I would advise against going out." He stepped back, leaving as silently as he'd arrived.

"He's gone," Seth told Nyx. "You can stop using my collarbone as a surface for self-flagellation."

She lifted her head. "Why do these things happen to me?"

"You're a wanton hussy, throwing yourself at me in public?" he offered, immediately blocking the elbow she aimed at his midsection.

"*You* kissed *me*, jackass."

"Yes, but if you had a shred of moral fiber you'd have said, 'No, Seth, not by the reflecting pools'."

"Where's *your* moral fiber?"

"I never said I had any. I embrace my inner wanton hussy."

"You're insufferable."

He grinned. "Don't be so sweet, you'll spoil me." His stomach chose that moment to rumble, loudly and insistently. The Dwarves of Eravendrin had subscribed to the belief that prisoners should be fed only basic fare, and sparingly at that.

"Spoiling you," Nyx said, "would be having the foresight to bring you a sandwich because I knew you'd be starving."

He leaned closer. "Nyxi, darling, please tell me you are in possession of a sandwich meant just for me."

She tugged her bag over, withdrew a sandwich, and presented it to him.

"Marry me," he demanded.

She rolled her eyes. "You're a couple years early."

She wasn't taking him seriously. She hadn't the first time he'd asked her to marry him, either, and now that he was ahead of the time restrictions she'd placed on when he was allowed to ask again, she'd decided he still wasn't serious. He considered convincing her of how very wrong she was, but this didn't feel like the place or the time. She'd been through a lot since arriving on Kyvren. She was worried about the Meerkin, and her uncle had just tried to kill her, resulting in the near-death of her father.

Yeah, not the best time. He was impulsive and impatient, but he had been sure about this for years. He could wait. She hadn't run away screaming when he'd suggested they have a couple kids at some point, so eventual odds were in his favor.

Given that, he let her brush him off, let her think he was joking. "I'm just practicing before the actual big moment." He took the sandwich. "Where did you find this? Neither the Meerkin nor the Dwarves strike me as sandwich people."

"I had Jevryn make it for you."

Seth paused, food halfway to his mouth. "Is it poisoned?"

She smacked him on the shoulder. "No, it is not poisoned. I told him I wanted one to go, so he made me one. I didn't say it was for you."

Well, that was a relief. He bit into it. He was hungry enough that it could have been the most disgusting thing he'd ever had and he still would have happily eaten it. But horrible it most certainly was not. He couldn't put his finger on the flavor profile, and truly he was too hungry to slow down to try to figure it out, but there was one thing he could say about his future father-in-law: he made a damn fine sandwich.

He finished and found Nyx staring at him intently. "Yes?"

"Did you like it?"

This seemed like a much more intense question than whether or not he had enjoyed a meal. He wiped his fingers on his jeans and said, cautiously, "I did."

She blew out a breath. "Oh, good. Kaden doesn't like them and I was worried I only liked them because Jevryn does and we have abnormal tastebuds for things no one else will be able to appreciate. I don't think I'm ready to find out how similar we are or are not."

Nyx had spent their entire childhood wanting a father. She'd wanted it so badly—been so convinced that her father was out there, looking for her—that she'd half-convinced Seth that some day this theoretical man would show up and rescue them from their misery. There had been an entire year when she was nine where she'd written her father a letter every week, recapping the non-events of their lives, certain that when her father came for her, he would want to know all of the mundane details about the time he'd missed with her. She hadn't wanted to forget them, so she'd written them down.

If Elena hadn't found those letters and laughed so hard that Nyx burned them all, Seth would go back to that godforsaken valley and retrieve them, just so he could throw them in Jevryn's face. Then he would explain, in excruciating detail, how the man didn't deserve Nyx as a daughter but, since he had her, he needed to fucking try harder. Agreeing to teach her about her magic and her heritage because they needed to work together—and because she "had a right to know"—didn't come within a country mile of trying hard enough. And if Seth did suspect there was more to it than that—that Jevryn did actually care about her but wasn't quite ready to admit it to himself—that didn't count for much until the man actually showed it.

"You don't owe him anything, Nyxi. Take what he can teach you, if you're comfortable with it, but he hasn't earned anything else."

She bit her bottom lip, rolling it between her teeth. "He took me to get you," she pointed out. "He swallowed a magical death bomb for me."

"Those are both on him. If he hadn't tried to basically kidnap you here, none of that would have happened in the first place. What was his rationale for that, anyway?"

"He never would say, but I've been thinking about it, and I think getting to where we are now *was* the point. When we were alone on Amentia Furor, he taught me a little about portal magic. It wasn't exactly father-daughter cozy, but it's probably the closest approximation of it he can imagine. I think maybe he was trying to recapture that. To see if we could find some common ground without the distraction of other people."

"So he kidnapped you?" Seth pressed. She was thawing, it was obvious, and he wished she would keep a little more ice between her and Jevryn.

"I didn't say it was a *good* thing to do, but I think maybe it's the best he *can* do." She paused before continuing on. "Evra said something to Morgen once. About needing to recognize when we want more from people than they can give. I don't think Jevryn can give very much."

Yep, she was thawing. It wasn't that Seth didn't want her to have a relationship with Jevryn, it was that he didn't want her to get hurt any more than she already had been. And he knew her. She was not, in this regard, with this one thing she had wanted for so long, capable of downgrading her expectations. "His not being capable of giving much doesn't mean you have to accept his scraps."

"I know that," she said defensively. "You think I'm not still mad at him? I am. I haven't developed unrealistic expectations. I don't think he's suddenly going to hug me and tell me he's so sorry for not being there my whole life and also now he loves me. But I did just watch him almost die, to save *me*, and I think I need to see if there's anything more to that. I'm not going to beg for his attention, but...I'll let him try. I'll see how much he's *willing* to try. And if it's not very much, then I'll learn what I need to from him and that will be the end of it."

Seth didn't believe her for a second. When she cared about people, she was all in. But she was also a lot tougher than people gave her credit for. Sometimes more so than even he gave her credit for. "All right. I'll put ruining your father's life on the back burner, then."

She rolled her eyes. "Thanks."

"You are *so* welcome." He grinned. "Now that we cleared that up, want to make out until your ex comes back to find out why we haven't gone to meet Vorex?"

She shoved him hard on the shoulder. "No, jackass."

"You're still saying the sweetest things to me." He stood and pulled her up with him. Walking out of the reflection pools with her, bickering in silent glances the way only they could, he felt happier than he had in a long, long while. Because she was finally here with him, fully present, in a way she hadn't been these last few months.

They reached the primary level of the den and a branching of paths where she tugged him left. "Come on, Vorex is this way. You'll like him. I think—"

A boom shook the den, stone dust raining around them.

Nyx's eyes went wide. "What was—"

Another boom, and another. He heard a crash, like an area of the den had collapsed, and then Meerkin were streaming through the tunnels. They were either wearing armor or putting armor on as they ran, maintaining awkward three-legged gaits while they buckled one-pawed.

Nyx jumped into the fray, running as if she was a part of the pack. Seth dove in with her. The Meerkin made a bubble of space around them, accommodating their bipedal gaits that stuck out awkwardly in the sea of quadrupeds.

"What's going on?" Nyx asked the Meerkin to her left. He wondered if she knew them, or if she was just asking the nearest person.

"Attack," the Meerkin answered. He didn't elaborate, and Nyx didn't ask him to. She did increase her speed. Seth kept close on her heels, so much so that when she stopped abruptly at the den's exit, he ran into her back.

She pulled him to the side, out of the flow of Meerkin rushing to defend their home.

"You can't go," she told him. "You heard Kaden, the unda are active and you don't have armor."

Stars damn it. "You're not going out there alone."

"Look around us." Meerkin streamed by them. "I'm not alone."

"I don't like this."

"I know."

He didn't want her to go. He knew she *had* to go. She cared about the Meerkin and she was here, so she would never let them fight without her. And knowing she was related to Kiev, knowing this attack was likely retaliation for their taking Riven? No, she would never stay within the safety of the den.

He curled his hand around the nape of her neck, drew her close and pressed his mouth to hers. "Fucking be careful."

"I will." She pressed another quick, hard kiss to his lips and then she was gone, slipping out the entrance with the last of the Meerkin.

Seth dropped onto his stomach and shimmied out of the entrance, remaining beneath the overhang. It was all covered in crushed ore. No unda were coming here. If any of them started shooting spores, he was a brief climb away from total safety.

He watched Nyx in the crush of bodies, saw as she unclipped Constance, the weapon lengthening into her usual bo staff, albeit with the addition of two blades, one at each end. She didn't need to use it, however. By the way she ducked around people and they didn't react, he could tell she'd Hidden herself from everyone but him.

Dwarves poured from an impossibly wide-stretching portal at the tree line. He didn't see Kiev—hopefully Jevryn had dropped half a ton of ceiling on the guy and the best he could do at the moment was open this portal for others to work through—so in lieu of that most prominent of threats, Seth assessed. Nyx had asked him not to leave the den, and he wouldn't go farther than this. Given what she'd told him about the unda, that was suicide without armor, and he had no intention of dying. But that didn't mean he couldn't help.

He pondered the nature of that help. Small-scale illusions wouldn't be beneficial right now. Not when he wasn't out there to follow misdirection with a very real cut from his blades. But he could go big. Something big enough that they couldn't help but believe what they were seeing.

Belief always helped an illusion. At its most fundamental level, crafting an illusion meant convincing someone that what they were seeing was real. Making that first image, that first feeling, believable enough that it took root in their mind and flourished. The more an

Illusionist believed in what they were creating, the more real it was, and the more likely that others would lend their belief to it.

Looking at the scene before him—Dwarves and Meerkin in battle—he knew exactly what illusion to craft. He held an image of it in his mind, one he'd seen on screen several times, and gathered his magic into a column of will.

40

Nyx ran through the clashing Dwarves and Meerkin. As an individual fighter in this skirmish, she wouldn't be particularly useful, which was why her goal was the portal at the tree line. It stretched in a wide rectangle as far as her eye could see, constantly spewing out a fresh line of Dwarves to add to the battle. Numbers, Nyx quickly realized, the Dwarves would need.

The Meerkin may not have learned warfare before the Dwarves came to their planet, but they were born predators, and they had adapted. Quick and agile, they dodged strikes from hammers and axes with preternatural grace. Their signature move seemed to be scaling their opponent's back, ripping off their helmet, and biting through the neck. They did it quickly, efficiently, and with great success.

No wonder the Dwarves had made a deal with Kiev. If they were unwilling to surrender, they desperately needed the advantage he could give them. But there was no flow of death magic coming through the portal now. Had Jevryn managed to significantly injure his brother?

She wanted to see, she wanted to *know*. Both that, and how he was managing a portal this large for a sustained period of time. No matter how efficient he was, this had to require a mind-boggling amount of portal magic. And Jevryn had said there wasn't a well on this planet. So how was Kiev doing it?

Hidden, she wove through the fighters, past the point where the chitin ore protected the ground, until she reached the portal. She ran along its length, searching. But as she ran, the unda, drawn by the massive magical expenditure that was Kiev's portal, streamed in. They fell upon its edges, feasting, and still it did not falter.

Nyx did. Because the unda were drawn to her too, crawling up her boots, drinking down the Hidden magic that coated her. It was like the difference between blood dripping out of a paper cut and geysering out of a severed artery. She let the Hiding go. Instantly, the unda that had crawled over her feet and ankles stilled. Now that the protective coat of her Hiding was gone, they contacted the chitin-ore armor and sloughed off, only reawakening once they fell back into the pool of other unda.

A deep, powerful roar split the air, instantly stilling the battle-field. A great shadow fell across the land. Nyx looked up. Overhead, a black dragon spread its colossal wings against the sky. The effect was instantaneous. Faced with a creature of immense size that none of the planet's inhabitants had ever seen before, everyone scattered. The Meerkin streaked for the safety of the den, the Dwarves for the escape of the still-open portal.

Nyx, barely five feet from that portal, fought not to be swept up in the tide of fleeing Dwarves. There was no moving *away*, there was only dodging when she could, digging in her heels when she couldn't. As it was, she was knocked to her knees twice, barely managing to gain her feet both times before she was trampled underfoot. Another Dwarf clipped her shoulder, spinning her back to face the portal. Another knocked into her back, sending her sprawling, a booted foot landing just to the right of her face.

Darkness fell over Nyx and suddenly everyone was scattering *away* from her, as if she were the epicenter of a blast. The black dragon landed behind her with a snapping of jaws and the illusion of earth sent flying by its impact. Two massive claws landed to either side of her, the dragon's chest at her back, as if she was its master and it had come to protect her. Above her its jaw unhinged, a roar issuing from its mouth along with billows of flame.

Nyx shoved to her feet as the last of the Dwarves fled back through the portal. In their absence, as the portal began to collapse from the edges, she finally spotted Kiev. He stood next to the spectral dog, his hand on its shoulder, his irises a demonic shade of red.

His face was littered with scrapes and bruises, his lip split. He saw her and smiled, a harsh baring of teeth.

Fear surged through her. But he didn't send another jet of death magic at her. He didn't attempt to drag her through the portal as it continued to shrink. Instead, he pulled a metal canister from his robes and tossed it at her. As it landed, she half expected it to explode.

Kiev's hand slipped from the spectral dog's shoulder. He said something to the creature. Then he turned his back on her, walking away. The dog bounded through the portal and it closed behind him.

Death padded toward Nyx on silent paws, baring its teeth in a snarl. The dog showed no fear of the dragon at her back. Either because it was only a construct with no individual mind to be fooled by illusion, or because it *knew* the dragon was only an illusion. Whichever it was, the dragon could no longer help her, and keeping it here, when the unda clambered over it, had to be sucking Seth dry for no purpose. He clearly came to the same conclusion because he let it go, scales and claws blinking out of existence.

She could hear him, yelling at her from so far away, from that patch of ore-covered ground. Could see, in her peripheral vision, someone running toward her, though she couldn't make out who without taking her eyes off the dog. And she definitely couldn't take her eyes off the dog.

Shall we discover if you managed to breed a true *A-Morridahn?*

Kiev could only be referring to one thing—did she possess the same death magic that ran in his and Jevryn's veins? Could she survive an attack by that magic, as Jevryn had? Being possessed fully of all her memories, she could say with confidence that the first thing she'd killed larger than a mosquito was the Kumir on Beaureguard's grounds. And she'd done that with a sword, not magic.

If she had inherited her father's talent, she hadn't the slightest clue how to access it, much less use it. And surrounded by unda, it would do her little good at the moment.

Magic. The construct was magic—had to be—but it wasn't wearing armor and yet the unda weren't swarming it. Why not? She remembered that feeling she'd had when she'd seen it with Seth, the feeling that it wasn't entirely corporeal. As if it wasn't fully here.

The construct tilted its head, as if waiting for her to bolt. It might not actually be a flesh-and-blood predator, but it was designed off the basis of one—and it was, presumably, here to hunt *her*. If she turned and ran, it would chase her.

She had never wished so strongly as in that moment that she could portal the way Jevryn did, could pluck herself from this space without needing to step through a doorway. If she opened one next to her, would she have time to jump through it before the construct attacked? How much magic would it cost her, with the unda present? If she stood here without moving, would it do nothing more than stand here and watch her? If it didn't, if it touched her, would she die?

She took a slow, careful step back. The dog moved with her, one paw advancing as if matching her steps. The running figure in her peripheral vision came close enough for her to identify: Kaden. Raising her voice without yelling, as if the black dog was truly nothing more than a wild animal she was trying not to frighten, she called, "Stop. It's made of death magic. You can't touch it."

She didn't know if it would kill him on contact, or just whatever part of him it touched. Either way, she didn't want to find out, and she breathed a sigh of relief when he listened to her and halted.

"Nyx, you need to get away from it."

"No shit. I don't know why it's just standing here, but I'm trying not to excite it into playing chase-the-human-squeaky-toy. Can you get Jevryn?" Nothing like needing your absentee father to save you from your psychotic uncle's murder attempts twice in one day.

"He passed out again after you woke him up. He's alive but he's not an option."

Fuck. *Fuck, fuck, fuck.* "You worked for Kiev. What do you know about this thing?"

"I only ever saw the snakes. I didn't know he could make autonomous constructs." Kaden paused. "Can you step back again? See what it does?"

She did. Again, the construct moved with her. "What are you thinking?" she asked.

"If you can get to the doorway, the Meerkin have shielding against active death magic. It shouldn't be able to follow you inside the den." That's right—Vidrin had said they'd managed to weave their shields to defend against death magic. It made sense they would guard their entrances with them.

Okay then, so just…slowly back up all thousand or so feet to the den entrance and hope the giant death dog didn't decide to eat her between here and there. Somehow, she didn't think it was going to be that easy. Especially when, all around her, the well-fed unda began jetting spores into the sky. But she took another step back, and another, and another. The dog remained eerily in sync with her. It was all the creepier because, unlike an actual animal, no emotions showed on its face. No anger, no curiosity, no fear. Nothing.

Its patient stalking of her shot her adrenaline into overload with no outlet. Just controlled steps backward. Over and over and over. By the time she was within ten feet of the den she was practically vibrating with energy.

"Nyxi?" Seth asked from the doorway, his voice tight with tension.

She didn't dare take her eyes off the spectral dog to look at him. "What the fuck are you doing outside? It's raining magic-eating spores."

"Entrance overhang."

Oh, sure, because there was a two-foot overhang covered in chitin ore, he was perfectly safe. What if the wind decided to blow? Or he breathed too deeply and inhaled a spore? "Go inside."

"Just as soon as you come with me."

"Not sure how this thing will take that." It wasn't like the Meerkin entrance was particularly easy for a human to get through. The dog would have plenty of time to leap onto her while she climbed the rock face to the horizontal shelf.

"What is that thing?"

"Kiev's pet death dog."

"Can you portal in?"

She shook her head. "I'd need line-of-sight." Given the way the opening was constructed, she couldn't see in even if she was standing right beneath the overhang like Seth was. "The two of you get inside. Then I'll see what it does if I try to go."

"No." Seth said. "And Kaden? If you leave her out here I will murder you myself."

"Wasn't planning on it."

Nyx could have growled in frustration. "You'll only be in the way if it decides to attack. There's nothing you can do against it."

"And what are *you* going to do against it?" Kaden asked.

"I don't know, but it hasn't killed me yet and I'm the one it's fixated on." What was it doing? Why hadn't Kiev come through with it?

She took another step back. Another. Only a few more to the door, and—

The construct snarled and launched itself into the air. It leapt clear over her head, landing in front of the doorway between her and Seth. So that was a *no* on it letting her walk away, then.

"Do *not* touch it, Seth," she snapped.

As if the dog had been learning from her this whole time—or as if it had simply grown tired of waiting—it advanced on her, snapping its teeth and forcing her to retreat or come into contact with it. In a mimicry of her long walk here, it began marching her backwards, away from the entrance.

She heard a whistle as Kaden's sword cut through the air, into the beast's side—and went through it as if the construct were made of smoke. He barely managed to correct from the lack of expected resistance, dancing back to avoid his momentum throwing him into the creature's side.

He *had* succeeded in gaining the beast's attention. Judging by the quickness with which it whirled to face him, Nyx didn't think the dog intended to ignore him any longer. She did the only thing she could think of. When Kaden lunged again, she threw a portal into his path. The spores fell on it, dragging at her magic, but she didn't have to hold it open for long. She'd placed it too close to Kaden for him to avoid running through it. She deposited him at the most distant point within her line-of-sight and snapped the portal closed.

The dog's careful stalking of her ceased. As if her use of portal magic had snapped some tether of the construct's control, it lunged for her, jaws gaping.

She reacted on instinct, opening a portal behind her and jumping backwards through it. She stumbled as she landed, catching herself just as the dog materialized beside her.

It could portal. The autonomous death construct could *portal*. Suddenly, she understood why the blue of its eyes had looked so familiar.

It lunged for her again and she jumped through a new portal, the dog following her within the blink of an eye. From that moment on, her world narrowed to a single focus: jumping from place to place, staying one step ahead of the construct.

She lost track of how many doorways she opened and the strain of it quickly set in. This ability was a muscle she didn't flex often, and never this much, this fast. Between her hastiness and the spores feeding on each gateway, she burned through two bracelets in record time while fatigue ate at her. If the construct was likewise strained, the creature didn't show it, tirelessly arriving at her side less than a second after she portaled to a new location.

Where was its portal magic coming from? Was its supply finite? If she kept going, could she outlast it?

Every time she managed enough focus to jump through close to the den's doorway, it always managed to appear between her and that doorway too quickly for her to have any hope of reaching safety. And the more doorways she opened and jumped through, the more certain she was that outlasting it wasn't an option. She was too tired. If she kept pushing, sooner or later she would open a portal and it would close before she was fully through it. The *best* case scenario, if that happened, was that she lost an extremity, but not enough to kill her.

It never came to that. The next time she opened a doorway she was too slow, the dog too quick. Before she could move through, its jaw clamped on her right forearm. The dog dragged her back, away from the portal. She let it collapse, too exhausted to hold it open.

Fear shot through her and Constance warmed in her left hand, as if reminding her that she had a weapon. Kaden's sword hadn't done him any good, but the pain lancing through her arm felt a hell of a lot more real than something that could be delivered by a smoke creature, and through the daze of pain, she realized the spores were attaching to the dog where they hadn't before. Nyx gripped Constance and drove one of the now-bladed ends into the construct's side.

She half-expected her blade to pass through without resistance, as Kaden's had, but it embedded itself in flesh. The construct did not yelp or whine as a true animal would. Of all the things to be grateful for in that moment, that was probably the least of them, but she was. It did unlock its jaws from her arm, snapping to bite at Constance's length dug into its side.

Nyx didn't waste any time. Gathering the tattered remnants of her strength she opened one last portal, directly by the den's entrance. "Seth, get in!"

She thanked the stars when he listened, scrambling up the wall ahead of her as she dashed to it. This time, with the construct slowed from its injury, Nyx was fast enough. She launched herself at the wall and climbed. She choked back a scream as the muscles in her bitten arm protested. Seth leaned out of the opening, grabbed her arms, and hauled her inside just as the construct materialized below.

It lunged for the shelf, jaws snapping—and hit an invisible barrier. Magic sparked and sizzled as it hurled itself over and over at the den's entrance. Each time it impacted, she flinched. Seth pulled her against him, both arms locking firmly around her stomach, as if afraid that if he didn't hold onto her, she would be sucked back outside.

Nyx didn't know how long the construct railed against the magic blocking it, but eventually it stopped trying to batter its way through. Then it simply vanished, as if it had never been there at all. For a moment, she just sank against Seth in relief. Then a fresh wave of adrenaline surged through her and she bolted upright.

"Shit, Kaden."

Seth's arms around her waist tightened, holding her back. "Nyxi, no."

She jabbed an elbow into his ribs. He took it with a grunt. She broke his hold but he was fast, grabbing her and pinning her against the wall, like he'd once pinned her to a tree at her Station's boundary.

"That thing is locked onto you," he said, voice low. "If you go out there it might come back."

"And what if it didn't go far and it goes after Kaden because I'm not there? I left him stranded." It had felt like sending him to safety at the time, but now it felt like she'd left him as a lone, convenient secondary target.

"Kaden can take care of himself."

As if to prove the point, she heard the scrape of boots on rock and a moment later Kaden heaved himself up and into the den. He was sweaty, he was glowering, he was holding the metal canister she'd forgotten all about. He must have started making his way back the second she'd portaled him away.

His gaze flicked past them—at which point she realized she and Seth had had an audience of curious Meerkin for their entire argument—then settled back on her. His glower intensified.

"Don't give me that look," she snapped. "What were you going to do against it? The damn thing turned to smoke when you cut it. And *you*." She glared at Seth. "Let me go before I knee you in the balls."

He gave her that look and that grin that said he loved to live dangerously, and held her a moment longer before letting her go.

Kaden handed her the metal canister, and she took it reflexively. "What makes you think it's for me?"

He rotated it so she could see her name etched into the metal. Who the fuck did Kiev have sitting around just waiting to engrave her name into things at his whim? Then again, she supposed he *was* in a mountain full of metalsmiths.

"What's the likelihood it explodes when I open it?"

"None," Kaden said levelly. "It's a message container."

Right. Because she was obviously supposed to know that. She went to unscrew the lid and stopped, wincing as the muscles in her right forearm protested. When she looked at her arm, Seth took it and ran his hands over it, inspecting.

"It didn't pierce the armor, but it dented it."

She could see that—pointed indents pressing into her skin. Seth's fingers slid up to the juncture of her elbow and pushed. What she'd thought was a single sleeve of armor proved to be segmented, the forearm sleeve separating from the rest. He found another hidden seam, pushed again, and it snapped apart like a bracer.

Relief was instantaneous as the pressure was removed. Angry red spots marred her skin, but none of the teeth had driven the armor deep enough to puncture. She flexed her hand, closed it in a fist, flexed again.

"Okay?" Seth asked. She nodded. It was probably going to swell a bit, but she was fine. Seth frowned at the piece of armor, then looked at Kaden. "Do you have a repair kit?"

Kaden nodded and Seth tossed him the piece of her armor. He then swiped the tube from her and popped the end cap off. Nyx grabbed for the letter within, taking possession of it before he could.

Dearest niece—that is, assuming your blood runs true and you are alive to read this. Otherwise, my condolences, dear brother, but she could never have been left alive to stain the family name.

Ugh. In addition to being an absolute piece of shit on about every other level she could think of, it appeared Uncle Kiev was also a eugenics man.

If you are here, Nyx Fortuna, then welcome to the family, such as is left of it. I do not know what my brother has told you of our history, though I am sure that, between him and Arradin, they have already thoroughly poisoned you against me.

As if they would have needed to—he'd done all the work on that himself.

Nevertheless, I am an opportunist and would be remiss if I did not make you an offer. You may only be half an A-Morridahn, but our blood runs strong. Your signature on so many interesting planets proves that. Tell me, what did you think of the Kumir's origins? Was it my dear brother, or you, who killed Koral? More importantly, what do you think would happen to you should someone other than family discover you were there at the time of her passing?

Nyx's fingers curled into the paper at the obvious threat, dimpling the edges. She forced them to relax. Jevryn had said that A-Morridahns didn't bring outsiders into family matters. Kiev might have a twisted view of family—one which included him having absolutely no issues with killing her off if she proved unworthy—but since blood was the only thing that mattered to him, that meant she *was* family. And if she was family, he wouldn't tell anyone where she'd been. He was simply counting on her not knowing that.

So, here is my offer: Return to me with Riven by the dawn after tomorrow, and I will consider everything you've done, from the scar on my face to the tunnel Jevryn so recently dropped on my head, to be youthful misadventures. Knowing my brother, he has been remiss in teaching you about the family legacy. I will tell you anything you wish to know.

Your ability to possess a Station and yet leave it is a fascinating one, and we could do much with it, together. I could even be persuaded to stop interfering in this planet's squabbles, as you obviously harbor some fondness for the Meerkin beasts. Now that the Dwarves have lost Riven, my agreements with them are void, though they do not yet realize it. If I remove myself from the equation, your little pets may yet have some chance of survival.

What was with Kiev's assumption that any emotional attachment she or Jevryn had to a person or group of people meant they viewed them as pets? He'd referred to Griff as Jevryn's pet the first time she'd met him, as if he couldn't fathom a deeper emotional bond.

And I am not unkind. Bring your boys with you, if you like. The silent one could yet prove useful, and your attachment to the Illusionist is obvious, if unwise, given his immaturity and instability. Though I do hope you understand that neither are suitable for breeding. Fuck them if you like, but offspring are out of the question.

Bile rose in Nyx's throat and she crumpled the paper into a ball, stomach in revolt.

"What is it?" Seth tried to tug the wad of paper from her hand, but she refused to let it go.

"Nothing, he's just a dick." She smoothed the paper back out, batting away Seth's second and third attempts to grab it from her.

Make your decisions. If you are not at Eravendrin's border with Riven within the time allotment I have given, I will have no choice but to retrieve her with force. Should that happen, I will not spare your Meerkin any courtesies and I will, for the inconvenience, take something precious from you as well.

The first thing you should know about being a member of this family? Ruthlessness is not merely encouraged, it is required.

P.S. Oh, and try not to worry too much about your father. It is easy enough for an A-Morridahn to swallow one of our own deaths.

It is how we are born, after all. But swallowing a death meant for another is a nasty business. It would have been far easier for him to allow you to do it, but he always was a sentimental fool. He will be out for several days, so I am afraid you will have to make this decision without his fatherly advice.

—Kiev Sahren A-Morridahn

This time, Nyx folded the paper into squares and shoved it into her pocket. "Come on," she said to Seth and Kaden. "I need to talk to Jevryn."

Whatever it took, she was waking him up.

<h1 style="text-align:center">41</h1>

Nyx turned from the entrance and was immediately met with a wall of Meerkin. The letter had angered her so much she had once again forgotten they were there. That, and because they could be unearthly quiet when they wanted to be. Seeing them, still in armor, was when it really sank in for her—this entire battle that had just happened? It was her fault.

She half-expected for her, Seth, and Kaden to be driven out of the den for bringing Kiev's wrath down upon the Meerkin. Yet no one was looking at her with hatred, or suspicion, or blame. No one seemed upset.

Jori stepped out of the mix. "Uncle Vorex is still waiting to speak with you."

Nyx swallowed down her self-loathing and nodded. "Of course."

She stumbled twice on the walk to the large meeting room. Too much had happened in a single day and she was spent. But she didn't get to choose not to have this conversation, so she dug a little deeper and kept walking.

They reached the meeting room, its walls echoing with the sounds of voices raised in debate. Nyx wanted to curl into herself as she walked in and the room went silent, all eyes turning to her. She wanted to ask if anyone was hurt, if anyone had died, but it was a stupid question. It might have been a short battle before Seth's dragon put a quick end to it, but it had still been a battle. Of course people had been hurt.

She approached Vorex, forcing herself to meet his gaze. "I'm sorry," she said quietly. She needed to explain fully what she was apologizing for, to let him know the contents of Kiev's note, of the added danger she'd put them in. But she couldn't do that in front of everyone. The Meerkin might be a fairly open society that was comfortable discussing important matters in a lively debate setting, but while she admired that, it was too foreign to her. Especially given how she'd been raised. She wasn't comfortable in crowds. "Would I be able to speak with you alone?"

"That might be best." And though he was agreeing with her, it made her heart sink further into her stomach. Especially when he added, "There is a matter I would broach with you that you may prefer to keep private."

Vorex rose stiffly to his paws, raising his voice to address the others. "I would speak with the kin who is not of our kin alone, for a moment. Discuss matters civilly amongst yourselves until I return."

At the room's exit, Vorex paused, indicating Kaden and Seth who flanked her. "If your friends would not mind remaining behind? The others will undoubtedly have questions for them, and it will expedite matters if they are here to answer them while we speak."

Nyx hesitated. She felt she owed Vorex whatever he wanted in this moment, but she didn't want to leave Kaden and Seth in the position of responsibility. None of this was their fault—it was hers.

"Go on," Seth said, "we'll be fine." He gave her a reassuring hug, and she swatted his hand away when it wandered too close to the pocket Kiev's note was in. The man was an incorrigible pick-pocket, and she wasn't ready for anyone else to see those words just yet.

She followed Vorex to a suite of rooms. Once inside, the boundary spell flaring to life across the doorway, Vorex lowered himself onto a new bed of furs. He looked so tired, and her heart ached at seeing him like this, at having brought more trouble to his doorstep than he'd already had.

"I'm so sorry," she said again, wishing those useless words could do more than just express her regret. "I had no idea when we went for Seth that we would find Riven, or that Kiev would return. If

Jevryn wasn't so injured, he could have taken us off-planet and none of this would have happened."

Vorex considered this for a moment, the claws of his right paw tapping lightly against the stone floor, like a human might drum their fingers on a tabletop. "Do you know why I asked to see you, before we were attacked?"

She shook her head.

"I believe Jori informed you of the hard path my people have walked in my absence? Of their attempts first merely to eke out lives under Dwarven rule, and then later to attempt to reclaim what is rightfully ours."

She nodded.

"The numbers we brought from Arkadia turned the tide of our revolt. We are no longer a soft race, we Meerkin. No longer so trusting or kind as we once were."

They had been trusting and kind to her. And look what grief she'd caused them in return. What grief her *family* had caused them.

"I mourn the loss of our gentleness, even as our newfound hardness has led us to reclaim almost all of what we have lost. There are no more Dwarven outposts beyond the city of Eravendrin. They do not control a single Meerkin dwelling. They do not control a single Meerkin.

"But they remain on our planet. Since Kiev has joined their forces they attack us in the night, collapsing portions of our dens with their sorcerous metalwork and then fleeing through his portals, like cowards. They refuse all attempts at negotiation and, now they have seen we will not be easily conquered, they refuse to meet us in open battle unless Kiev is with them.

"I am *old*, Nyx Fortuna. Soon my spirit will pass beyond these lands, and while I have no fear of death, I have great fear of leaving my people a life in which the possibility of attack is a constant companion. I would see an end to this conflict, before I find eternal rest.

"For there to be such an end, we must have a decisive victory over them—nothing else will bring them to a place of negotiation. Bringing our own forces to Eravendrin is unwise, as it would be too easy for Kiev to simply portal theirs to surround us. Entering Eravendrin would also be unwise, and we will not seek to destroy their city as they attempt to destroy our dens. Me and my people will not be responsible for the deaths of children of any species, nor those who have chosen not to fight.

"Therefore, we need a battle *here*, where we are strongest. One in which the Dwarves field leaders of high enough rank to open negotiations after a defeat. We needed what you brought us before your well-meaning Seth put a quick end to it with his... What was that creature?"

"A dragon," she answered on autopilot, trying to wrap her brain around what Vorex was telling her. "You wanted this to happen?"

"It must seem brutal, I know, but yes. I knew, when you told me your friend was in Eravendrin, that your reclaiming him would have repercussions. We all did, and we were prepared for them. But when you returned with Riven as well, and the Dwarves among us explained her importance to both their people and Kiev? I asked to see you then because I hoped there might be a way to use that to provoke the response we needed.

"And even had none of that occurred, I was already fighting an inner battle with myself to determine what it was fair to ask of you. Whether I could ask you to use your own father against another of your family."

Her head snapped up. "How did you know?"

"Your scents are too similar for you to be anything but a direct relative. Even a granddaughter would be too far removed."

So that was why he'd asked Jevryn to come close to him in the meeting room, why he'd smelled him. She wasn't ready for this, to be tied to Jevryn publicly by that familial bond. Elena had taunted Nyx by asking her if she thought Jevryn would ever publicly acknowledge her. It had stung, at the time. But Nyx finally understood that Jevryn hadn't been wrong when he'd told her that being related to him was a dangerous thing. She was slowly starting to realize that maybe *she* didn't want to acknowledge *him.*

"Does everyone know?" she asked. She'd never considered that her lineage could be ferreted out by *scent,* of all things.

"If any other of my kin have discovered it, they have made no mention of it. Scenting a familial bond among our own people is second nature to us. We do as much without conscious thought. Determining those similarities or differences among other species is not something the others have much experience with. For my kin who were born here, they can distinguish a Dwarven scent from a

Meerkin scent, but they are not adept at untangling the finer points of it.

"I learned to do so on Arkadia almost by accident, when I realized those of the same species bore such different markers from each other, because it was rare for anyone on that planet to share a familial relationship."

Everything about Arkadia had been horrible. Nyx had been both glad that children couldn't be born into that place, and horrified by the forced sterilization of every person imprisoned there. But as she hadn't lived there, she hadn't given consideration to what it must be like to exist in a place where genetic relationship was an anomaly, rather than a norm. She would be the first to choose the family she had made over the one she had been born into, and yet there was a kind of horror to having no chance at a biological family at all.

"I am sorry if I have upset you," Vorex said, after the silence stretched between them too long. "I gather your relationship with your father is a complex one."

Nyx managed a short bark of laughter. "You could say that. I only found out he *was* my father recently, and he doesn't exactly want to be." She waved her hand. "But my family drama isn't your problem. But if you could keep this to yourself, I would appreciate it. I've been informed it's hazardous to my health for that relationship to become known." Though, so far, she was doing a bang-up job of keeping it secret.

"Should my people become aware of it, they will take the same vow of silence I now promise you. In truth, there will be little opportunity for it to pass beyond this planet. Given what we have seen of the universe, my people wish only to be left in peace. To which end I must now ask you what I am not sure it is fair to ask of you—do you believe that you, either on your own or through Jevryn, can orchestrate the confrontation we need? Would you be willing to?"

She shoved her emotional problems into the deepest pit in her brain she could find, and smiled at him. "I *did* come here because I wanted to help. I wasn't lying. And as fate would have it, I don't have to orchestrate anything." She couldn't bring herself to let Vorex read Kiev's letter, for anyone else to see that much casual bigotry and violence directed at her as if she should find it normal, but she recapped the highlights about Riven for him in broad strokes. "I was going to see if Jevryn thought he could get Kiev away from the planet, but if you *want* them to come here…"

"It is the course of action my people have decided on."

Worry nagged at Nyx. "I don't know how invested Kiev has been in this fight against you up until now. I got the impression that he's kind of been offering the bare minimum of support. Since I've pissed him off and now he has a personal stake—I don't know the extent of what his magic is capable of, but I don't think there are many moral boundaries he's not willing to cross."

"This is a risk we will accept. We have those capable of shielding against his magic. Those shields will not survive a sustained, targeted onslaught, but they have been mostly sufficient for the type of attacks he has made when he takes to the field."

"Jevryn and I will handle him. He's our responsibility."

"I am…not sure your father will be capable of much, in less than two days' time. Any and all attempts to wake him have been unsuccessful."

"I'll get him to wake up." She had to believe that she could, because she needed to believe that something could work out for her the way she needed it to. "Can I see him?"

"I will take you." He rose, and she winced at the creaks and pops that went through his limbs.

"If you give me directions, I'm sure I can find him on my own."

He gave her an indignant look. "I am *old*," he informed her. "I am not yet incapable of walking. You might recall I carried you some fair distance not too long ago."

"You did. Sorry."

"*Hmph.*" He bent his head, bumping it affectionately against her cheek. "Enjoy the youthful healthiness of your body while you have it. Once you reach a certain age, your favorite pastime will become cataloging your aches and pains, and growling whenever anyone else dares to mention them."

Her lips twitched upward. "I'll try to remember that."

She memorized the turns they took, so she could find her way back to the meeting room later. It wasn't a terribly long walk, and she wasn't prepared for the sight of Jevryn, lying on his back on a bed of adika furs, unearthly still, his hands crossed over his chest as if he had been arranged for his funeral. He looked vulnerable, in a way he never did while awake.

Black veins still spiderwebbed across the corners of his eyes and mouth, and her hand went reflexively to her cheek and the thorns embedded there. "Can I ask you something about these?"

Vorex nodded.

"You said they heighten emotions, especially anger. I *have* noticed that. But...do they cause this as well?" She didn't have to do much for her anger to surface. Merely thinking about Kiev's letter was enough to send black spreading through her veins, along with the by-now familiar surge of strength.

Vorex shook his head. "Sheathed in fur or armor as we are, our veins are not visible, as yours are. If such a thing occurs, we cannot see it."

"What about strength? Does it make you stronger?"

"No," he said gently. "They only upset the emotions. I am sorry if that is not the answer you wished to hear."

"It's okay." It was the answer she'd expected. "Thank you for bringing me."

She waited until he disappeared around a bend in the tunnel to actually walk into the room. She thought she might never have gone in, had it not been for the fact her legs were about to give out, and she was once again thirsty and hungry.

There was a table in the center of the room, bearing a flask of water, which she drank, and more strips of the adika jerky, which she ate. It took the edge off her hunger and exhaustion, and she walked over to Jevryn, settling cross-legged on the floor next to him. She turned her hands palm up in her lap, staring down at the black lines that still criss-crossed her flesh, then staring at the matching ones on his face.

"What exactly am I?" she asked his unconscious form. She felt like a chimera, patched together out of different things. A clump of Hidden here, a dash of portal witch there, and now this probable string of death magic tying it all together. Maybe it would feel natural to her if she'd grown up knowing all of it, being taught all of it. Instead, it was like her biology was a surprise bag of tricks, and something new might choose to pop out at her at any moment.

"I wish you'd been a real dad," she said softly. "I wish you'd been there when I was growing up. Maybe we wouldn't have gotten along. Maybe I would have hated you. But I don't think I would have. Because if Griff can still love you, after all this time and everything he's been through, I have to believe that there is something worth loving in you. Then and now.

"And I'm pissed off that you never gave me the chance to find out. I'm pissed off that if you had your way, I wouldn't know about any of this. I'm pissed off that before I knew who you were, I was starting to think I could rely on you. I'm pissed off that you almost died and left me here to deal with all this bullshit alone. I'm just… pissed off."

She laughed, short and sharp. "Story of my life, right? Maybe that's why I've always been so good at *repressing*. Maybe that's why none of this"—she wiggled her black-lined fingers at her unknowing audience—"came out of me until something forced it to." She sighed. "But it is coming out now, so I need you to wake up and tell me what to do with it."

She placed her hand over his chest. He didn't stir, but she hadn't expected him to. Because in retrospect, she was pretty certain she knew what had woken him outside the Meerkin den, and it hadn't been twenty minutes of chest compressions. It had been that moment when she'd felt something flow out of her, into him.

She focused on remembering what that had felt like, where the rush of power had stemmed from. If she was right, it was death magic in her. While she might not know how to wield it, at the end of the day, magic was still magic—Viktor and her mother had taught her enough to know *that*—and most magic was will-based.

So she found her will and that feeling and she latched onto it, pouring it out of her and into Jevryn. Funneling anything with a death label into another human being was logically counterintuitive, and yet it felt right on an instinctual level she couldn't deny. It moved through her like a current, this hidden piece of her. She had expected it to be awful—dark and consuming—but it was peaceful, like floating on a river in the shade of overhanging trees, no worries or demands to distract her.

She forgot what she was doing. She forgot *why* she was doing it. Lassitude stole over her, heaviness dragging at her eyelids. Stars, she was tired. So, so tired. If she only rested her eyes for a moment…

It was the last thought she had before she slumped forward, carried on the current of that beckoning oblivion.

Nyx woke to a cold rush, like IV fluids being pumped too quickly into her body. Her teeth chattered as someone shook her violently. She grabbed at the hands on her shoulders, trying to stop herself from being thrown about like a rag doll, her eyes opening to Jevryn's livid face.

"Impetuous, foolish child." He punctuated each word with another shake of her shoulders. The cold spilling through her cut off. "What were you thinking?"

Nyx wanted to respond. She really did. She thought she might be angry. Or maybe relieved. She couldn't focus long enough to decide which it was. Her head felt so light that the room was shifting back and forth. Nausea roiled in her stomach, and the furious Jevryn in front of her split into two furious Jevryns.

Her eyelids, heavy and sluggish, dragged down. Unable to hold herself upright, she slumped forward. The last thing she knew was the roughness of armor against her skin, and the strength of her father's arms closing around her.

42

For one of the rare times in Nyx's life, she woke up to Seth still asleep beside her. Or, rather, wrapped around her like a boa constrictor, as was his usual way. She couldn't remember how he'd gotten there with her or, for that matter, how *she* had gotten onto the bed of furs in the small, dimly lit room they now occupied.

But as her brain creaked back into operating condition, she remembered passing out while trying to—and apparently succeeding in—waking Jevryn up. She wondered what she'd done for their positions to end up reversed. Had he looked worried about her, when she'd woken to him shaking her?

Her head still felt muzzy, but the rest of her felt refreshed, as if she'd finally had a good night's rest. A glance at her watch and a quick calculation—she'd determined that Kyvren had a roughly nineteen-hour day—confirmed it was now the next morning. She shifted slightly, waking Seth, who squeezed her tighter.

"Correct me if I'm wrong," he said sleepily, "but I thought I reminded you about all the trauma I have surrounding you passing out, and how we agreed you wouldn't do it anymore."

"I'm pretty sure people don't get to choose when they pass out. Also, I think I was just tired."

He made a *hmph* noise in his throat and didn't say anything.

"Where are we?"

"An unused family suite Vorex let us have while we're here. You hungry?"

"Starving."

He stood, giving her a hand up. "Come on, I can make breakfast. The Dwarves' nutrition requirements are more compatible with ours than the Meerkin's are. Beren and a few others shared some staples and basic prep with me last night."

Nyx shook her head in amazement. "Where did you even find the energy?"

"I had nerves to dispel, on account of my girlfriend being unconscious and Jevryn being worried about it. Had to do something to keep my mind occupied."

The suite had a small kitchen, where the scent of cooking food soon drew Kaden and Jevryn. The first came in and wordlessly handed Nyx the repaired piece of her armor. The second glided in and studied her as if she were a museum specimen.

"How are you feeling?" he asked.

"A little fuzzy but otherwise fine."

He inclined his head sharply. "We will eat, and then we must talk. In private."

They ate—some kind of nutty porridge with berries and honey— seated on the floor around another low table. When they were finished, Seth and Kaden left for the den's central meeting room because, according to Seth, "That's where everyone hangs out in the morning." Man was a social butterfly.

Alone with Jevryn, Nyx waited. He steepled his fingers on the cleared table and repeated his question from the previous night, his words sharp. "What were you thinking?"

The clear disapproval in his tone hit her like a slap, and she remembered him calling her an *impetuous foolish child*. No amount of rest could change the fact that she'd been through a long two days, in which she'd been afraid Seth would die, then afraid Jevryn would, and now here he was admonishing her for doing the best she could in the situation.

"I was thinking that I needed you to wake up," she snapped. "Because your brother's a psychopath who attacked the den, tried to kill me with a death dog, and wants me to come join his side of the family even though I'm of 'impure blood'. But hey, he'll let me keep Seth and Kaden as sex slaves, because apparently that's an enchanting option that's his to offer, and if I don't accept it he's going to storm the castle in two days and destroy everything I love. So excuse me for trying, but I didn't have time for you to keep impersonating Sleeping Beauty."

Jevryn blinked. She'd stunned His Immortal Awesomeness into silence. He recovered quickly enough. "Please explain in fuller detail."

She was sure he would have interrogated at least Kaden—if not Seth too—last night, but then maybe he had been tired as well. Either way, she recapped the battle and her fight with the spectral dog. "He also left this." She pulled Kiev's note from her pocket and handed it to him.

He read it with none of the horror that had pervaded her at the words. At best, she would classify the expression on his face as one of mild disgust. "This is typical of Kiev, I am afraid."

"Why is he alive?"

"There are reasons."

"You said that the last time I asked, but it doesn't actually tell me anything."

He folded the letter and returned it to her. "Because those reasons are not yours to know or to bear, and nothing will be gained from your learning them."

She considered pushing, but he wasn't going to tell her. And he was right that she wouldn't really gain anything from the knowledge. She wanted to know, because she wanted to understand how Jevryn could allow Kiev to be out there in the universe, perpetrating the harms he did. But even if she knew that answer, it wouldn't help her stop him.

"Fine. Keep the family secrets to yourself. What are we going to do about him? Vorex wants to allow the battle to happen, and I promised him you and I would do what we can to neutralize Kiev during it. Is that manageable?"

"Yes."

She couldn't let it go entirely. "Why is everyone a pet to him? Griff is yours, Kaden, Seth, and the Meerkin are mine. What the fuck is his problem?"

Jevryn sighed. "Kiev has…never quite understood emotional bonds outside of the family. Even within the family, I am not sure the bonds are emotional, so much as he views us as the only people who are his equals and therefore worthy of his notice."

"What is—you know what? Never mind. I don't really want to know what his problem is." She had bigger ones to deal with. "You said he can't come to Earth without you, but that thing I fought out there? It's been hanging around my Station, following me whenever I go into Earth Between."

Jevryn's face took on an expression she would have called murderous, except he'd already explained he was never going to kill his brother. "Has it? Whatever loophole Kiev is exploiting in our agreement for that to occur, rest assured I will close it. In the meantime, do not engage with the creature again."

"I don't exactly choose when to do that. It's the one following me."

"Then remain within this dwelling where it cannot enter."

Her fingers clenched. "Are you asking me to not be involved in the pending battle that is partially my fault?"

"Yes."

Well, that wasn't going to happen. "No. I gave Vorex my word that you and I would both do what we could to neutralize Kiev. I can't do that if I'm in here. And if that thing's fixated on me, I don't put it past him to single out every person who can shield among the Meerkin and eliminate them just to get in here to me."

The look on Jevryn's face told her she was one-hundred percent right about the path Kiev would take if she decided to hide in here.

"If you want to help me, explain what it is."

Jevryn rubbed wearily at his temples, as if she was giving him a headache. "Your choice of 'construct' as a description for it is an apt one. It is a shell, inside which a portion of his magic resides."

"Can he see through its eyes? Control it?"

"Not precisely. It will follow a set of directives when gone from his side. Once it returns to him, he will then be able to see what it has seen."

"Is that something you can make, too?" Was it something she could make?

His face darkened. "The creation is within the limits of my ability, yes. But what he has done to create it is not something I am willing to do."

What was so bad that even Jevryn wouldn't do it? "But you made the snakes. In Eravendrin."

"That is not the same thing. Asking our magic to take a visible form that bears the likeness of a creature is no difficulty within our sphere of influence. It is severing it and sending it out into the world that requires something that ought not be sacrificed."

And that didn't sound ominous at all. "You said it follows a set of directives. Before today, it never attacked me. Even today, it only followed me until Kaden attacked it and I portaled him out of its range." She paused, following that through to its logical conclusion. "It was the portaling. That was what triggered it to act. Kiev wanted to know what I could do, so once I started doing something, the construct pushed me to keep doing it."

Jevryn inclined his head. "Most likely."

"And…how bad is that for me?"

He gave her a pointed look. "Kiev is not your concern. Once we leave this planet, he will no longer be an issue for you."

Nyx wished she could believe that as much as Jevryn seemed to. Rather than argue with him, she went back to understanding everything about the spectral dog that she could. "The construct—why didn't the unda or the spores destroy it? They couldn't even touch it most of the time, like Kaden couldn't. It wasn't until it bit me that they started having an affect on it." Even then, they hadn't seemed to bother it much.

Jevryn allowed the return to their previous subject. "Most of the time the creature—A-Lethe, it is called—is in a state of constant portal flux, existing not entirely here or somewhere else, but simply *between*. Kaden's attack failed because he cannot enter that flux state. Yours succeeded because A-Lethe exited flux in order to attack you."

She had so many questions. "Can it be hurt when it's in flux?"

"Only by someone who can also enter that state."

"And this flux state—you're telling me it's *constantly* portaling?"

"In a manner of speaking. It is balancing on the *cusp* of portaling, on the possibility of it."

She couldn't entirely grasp that, but she supposed she didn't have to. The more important question was: "How could it possibly carry enough magic to sustain that? How can it even use portal magic if Kiev's not actively controlling it?" It made sense to her, on some level, that it could be born of death magic and thus access some element of that. It didn't make sense to her that it could also portal.

"That would be due to the monstrous nature of its creation."

"Will you just tell me what he did?"

Jevryn sighed, readjusting the cross of his legs. "Very well. I suppose you know enough already that this will hardly matter. He used a portion of a soul for its creation. A very old, very powerful, soul."

The guess that leapt to her lips would have felt absurd, had it not been for the dog's name. "Lethe-Alihana's?" She had thought all the souls the Harvester had reaped had been chained within Stations. But what if some hadn't?

Jevryn gave her a piercing look. "Where did you hear that name?"

"Kaliaris told me that was what your planet was called. But he also said Lethe-Alihana's soul belonged to you."

"In part, it does. Lethe-Alihana is a sundered soul, half in my keeping, half in Kiev's. Planets give birth to life. That potential, that need, lives within every soul. It is how the Stations create and rearrange themselves as they do. As Lethe-Alihana was a planet with a portal well, the potential for endless portal magic creation lives with in it. Kiev thought he could harness that creation. I suppose, to some extent, he did. A-Lethe was an experiment. One that nearly cost Kiev his life, and did cost him Lethe-Alihana's regard. Hope that you never learn what it is to have your planet turn its back upon you, *na'tria*. As much as I have lived with, in my lifetime, I would not wish to live with that."

As if Nyx even had a planet to call hers. What would it be? Earth, where she grew up? Lethe-Alihana, who didn't even know her? Same for whichever planet her mother was from? But then… she *did* have a planet to call hers: Kaliaris. Maybe she wasn't born from the same cosmic wonder-dust that had made them, but she'd chosen them. And Kaliaris might not have liked her in the beginning, but she'd earned their trust. She'd earned their respect. And that meant more to her, in the end, than calling a planet hers simply because she'd been born to it.

"So what do I do if I encounter A-Lethe again? Can it be killed?"

"I do not know if it can be killed. I have never tried. If you insist on participating in this battle, then you will remain with me. I can keep A-Lethe from reaching you, so long as you are physically close to me. Should you encounter it at a later date—run. Or, preferably, portal. Either to my home, where it cannot follow, or to the bounds of your Station where you can be safely ensconced in its protections within a footfall."

Ordinarily, run away and fast was a battle strategy Nyx was actually quite fond of. But there was something about her uncle that got her hackles up, made her want to dig in her feet and refuse to budge. "Will it try to kill me?"

"Given the contents of Kiev's note, I find it more likely it will attempt to retrieve you and deliver you to him."

Hardly a better outcome. "Well, then I'll just have to make sure that doesn't happen." She stood, dusting off the bottoms of her pants. "In the meantime, we should go talk to Riven. I've read enough books to know that if we put that off for too long, she's likely to disappear before we can ask her anything."

Jevryn did not follow her cue, remaining seated. "I believe that highly *un*likely, and while we have relative privacy, we should discuss what you did to wake me." He held out his arm, indicating the floor she'd vacated. "Sit."

Nyx did not. "You mean, discuss that I obviously inherited more from you than the ability to portal? But I gather you already knew that, right? That's what you meant when you said I'd 'repressed' my heritage?"

"I suspected," he said calmly.

She fought back the urge to shake him like he'd done to her earlier. "Since when?" If this was another thing he'd been holding onto for months, she might scream.

"Since you picked up my sword in your Station."

Nyx remembered the odd sensation of holding it—her desire to be rid of it followed by the immediate desire, after she'd put it down, to have the hilt once again in her palm. "You put death magic in your sword?" No wonder it had been able to sever bits of her Station.

"Many blades are capable of channeling their wielder's abilities. It is not an unusual feature."

"Wait, Griff was really worried when I picked it up." She could still hear the panic in his voice. "If I *hadn't* had your ability, would it have killed me?"

"No."

She crossed her arms, not quite believing him.

"It would, admittedly, have been highly unpleasant. Arradin experienced it once. It left a mark on him."

"You let your boyfriend pick up something you knew was going to cause him excruciating pain?"

The corner of Jevryn's mouth was trying to curve up. "He and I were not so well acquainted at the time. There were communication issues and extenuating circumstances involved."

"Would this be shortly after you broke his wing as an intrepid explorer?"

This time Jevryn lost the battle, and his lips formed the barest of smiles. "He told you about that?"

"Only in the service of explaining to me that you can be an insufferable ass," she lied. "So was that when it happened? Right after you met?"

"Yes. Given the lack of a common language, he was under the mistaken impression that I was holding him captive. He intended to use the sword to escape. But that is not relevant to this conversation." He waved his hand, as if shunting aside the subject she'd distracted him with. "While I am not ungrateful to be awake—"

Trust Jevryn to be "not ungrateful" as opposed to actually expressing gratitude.

"—I must caution you against ever repeating what you did to wake me."

"That shouldn't be a problem, since I have no idea what I did."

He bestowed upon her an expression that somehow managed to convey that he hardly believed that, and also expected better of her. She remembered she was not supposed to be engaging in small sullenness, was further irked that she now felt reprimanded by a parental figure who had done nothing more than look at her, and thus she was tricked into sitting down across from Jevryn and being a good student.

Especially since it was information she did, after all, need. "Kiev's note said that swallowing someone else's death was a bad idea, but that it was easy for us to swallow one of our own. I assumed that meant that his attack was magically tailored to me, which is why you had a more violent reaction to ingesting it.

"Which is weird, by the way. The whole swallowing magic thing is weird." She paused, inviting a response, but Jevryn didn't seem to feel her words warranted one, so she continued. "Anyway, when I woke you up the first time, I didn't mean to use magic, but I figured out that was what it was after the fact, and it made sense that if you were struggling with something more easily overcome by my magic, specifically, that giving you some of mine would help. How did I do?"

"Quite well. A key point to remember in the future? Death is endless. You are not. The well inside you will never empty, but should you pull from it too quickly or for too long, you will collapse upon it. You opened a transfer to me with no boundaries, no restrictions. Never do so again. Had I not awakened when I did..."

He didn't need to finish the sentence.

"Each time you touch death, you risk joining it. There were many of my people who never did so. Many others who did so recklessly and to their own detriment. Only the A-Morridahns, famously, never lost a single member to over-expenditure, a feat the other families believed was due to the inherent strength of our line.

"But while our lineage afforded us more capacity for error, it was not the true reason behind our survival. That lay in Ilera A-Morridahn—and every matriarch before her—ensuring that her children knew precisely how razor thin death's ledge can be. She would perch us there for weeks, until the edges became ingrained in our memories.

"Decide if that is an experience you want for yourself, before you decide to continue using this magic. I do not need to teach you how to lock it away—you have been doing that instinctively your entire life—but you will require instruction if that is not the path you choose. You already find me unpleasant. Your current feelings will be nothing compared to those you will develop should you choose to embrace this part of yourself. Think upon it. There is no need to rush your answer."

He drew his knees up and stood. "Come. Let us speak with Vorex, and then see to Riven." He turned away, moving for the threshold.

"Wait."

He did.

Why did you do it? Why did you step in front of me if it would have been easier for me *to take Kiev's attack?* The words were on the tip of her tongue, but she ran from them at the last moment. "The black veins. When that happens, does it make you stronger? And why?"

He considered her a moment, as if he knew that wasn't what she'd stopped him to ask. But he only said, "It is the power of death in your veins. Nothing is stronger than death. As its bearer, it grants you what strength you can channel."

This time, when he walked out, she pushed to her feet and followed in silence.

43

The meeting room in the morning, rather than being a place of adults discussing matters of war and social welfare, had turned into a gathering place for community relaxation and socializing. At first, she thought it odd that they could simply carry on as normal, given what was to come in two—well, now one, she supposed—days. Then again, clinging to routines and habits was what made people able to keep going under adverse conditions. It was when those routines broke that life became truly chaotic.

Jevryn left her, striking out for where Kaden stood by himself to one side of the room, brooding. Nyx felt comfortable labeling it as brooding, considering he wasn't observing anything around him, wasn't engaging in conversation with anyone, and his face was exemplifying the textbook definition of a furrowed brow.

She scanned the room, looking for Seth and Vorex. One of the most notable transformations of the area from meeting hall to socializing hall was the addition of Meerkin cubs, a large cluster of whom were climbing over each other—literally, in some cases—in an attempt to get closer to Seth. He'd created half-a-dozen miniature dragon illusions, each in a different jewel-toned color. They were about the size of basketballs, and they darted and swooped in between the Meerkin cubs, exhaling puffs of smoke and leaving shrieking delight in their wake.

As she watched, one of the dragons looped around Seth. It flew up and an enterprising Meerkin cub scrambled up Seth's back, hind paws landing on his shoulders, left front paw on his head as the cub stretched up to swat the escaping dragon with their right front paw. The dragon fell dramatically, talons clutching an invisible wound, and burst into a puff of smoke when it hit the ground. Soon, each of the remaining five dragons met a similar fate at the paws of excited youngsters.

When the last one fell, Seth flopped dramatically onto his back. "I'm dead," he declared to the cubs. "You killed the Dragon Lord."

The cubs found this hilarious and pounced on him, quickly burying Seth beneath a sea of furred bodies. Something in Nyx's throat constricted. She'd never seen Seth around kids before. With Tobi, yes, but he was *a* kid, and more like a very small adult in his behavior.

The Meerkin cubs dashing about Seth now were very much *children* children. He was good with them, endlessly patient as they pounced and mock-attacked, paws digging into his sides, a tail or two thwacking him in the face and making his eyes scrunch up. He would be a wonderful father. Watching him, there was a part of her that wondered if maybe she wouldn't be as good of a mother. She wasn't that patient. She wasn't that kind. She was Elena Fortuna's daughter.

Before he'd brought up kids, she'd never really thought about it before. There hadn't been space to think about it. She'd had an emptiness inside her—a need to belong to a family in the way that she now belonged to Griff and Morgen and Evra—that hadn't left any room for what she could give outside of that. When he'd first said it, it had sounded like a pretty picture. But the more she thought about it, the more it opened the door to a lot of uncomfortable questions.

She didn't think it was possible to be a perfect parent, but she didn't ever want to make a child feel the way her mother had made her feel, even for a second. She also didn't want to throw up her hands, like Jevryn had, and say she would be a terrible parent so she wasn't even going to try.

Due to the time she'd spent without her memories, having them back had had the odd effect of making her feel like she was frozen at eighteen, at that point where everything that was *her* had been erased, and she'd had to start over as a shell. Now the shell had been merged with the original foundation, and the two never quite felt like they added up to twenty-six years of experience.

Either that, or no one ever felt as experienced as they thought they should. Either way, none of it made her think she was ready to be responsible for another human being's existence.

A large form came up beside her. "They have taken quite the liking to him," Vorex said, nodding at Seth and the cubs.

Rather than make an agreeable comment like a normal person, she blurted out, "How do you know when you're ready to have kids?"

Vorex chuckled. "Generally, I would say that if you feel as panicked by the idea as you currently sound, the answer is *not yet*."

Heat rose in her cheeks. "Right."

"My advice? He will make an excellent father. That will be as true two or five or ten years from now as it is today. Try not to put too much pressure on the situation."

"Yeah. Thanks." Pressure was definitely the last thing she needed right now. She had more than enough of it to go around from other areas of her life. She didn't even know why she was thinking about all of this, except that he'd put it in her head and now he was *right there*, literally covered in cubs.

"You may wish to go rescue him," Vorex suggested. "Meerkin young can play for hours. They *do* know not to bite adults, but sometimes their excitement does get the better of them. Small teeth, but quite sharp."

He ambled away before she realized she'd forgotten to ask him anything important, like where Riven was being held and if Nyx could talk to her. Well, it wasn't as if he was difficult to find. Left with nothing else to do, she went forward to rescue her boyfriend. She stopped a foot away and leaned over him, her face above his.

He cracked one eye open. "I'm dead," he informed her. "I was once a mighty dragon lord, but lo, I and my entire flight have been felled by these fierce warriors."

"I may need the mighty dragon lord to find it within himself to come back to life."

"As my lady commands."

She rolled her eyes, then smiled as a cub leapt straight at Seth's face. He caught them gently around the middle before they could make contact and set them down between Nyx's feet. The cub looked up. Their eyes went wide and without a single word they darted across the room for the safety of their parents.

Well, that didn't bode well for her motherhood prospects. "Am I that frightening?"

Seth grinned and stood up, dislodging half-a-dozen cubs who decided that, if there were to be no more dragons to slay, there were more interesting things to do. "That was Eilee. She watched your portal chase with the construct from a scrying pool and thinks you're *very* cool. So much so that you're intimidating." He pointed two thumbs at himself. "Me, however, I'm approachable."

"Does Mr. Approachable want to come with me to talk to Riven, since you got to know her in jail?"

He winced. "About that, I might have already taken the liberty yesterday. It didn't go well."

"How not well?"

"She may or may not be convinced I work for Kiev. I tried name-dropping Valedan, at which point she basically informed me that if I was on such good terms with the Blood Prince, I could produce him out of thin air, and then she would decide if she was willing to talk to me or not."

Given that Valedan had predicted just such a response, Nyx wasn't surprised. It was the entire reason she'd wanted to bring him and Liya along in the first place. Still, she figured it was worth a shot to try one more time. *Without* Jevryn. Somehow, she didn't think showing up with Kiev's twin brother in tow was going to make Riven feel more comfortable, and since Jevryn was still talking with Kaden, she and Seth snuck away without him.

She didn't even get across the threshold. She tried knocking and received no answer. Since the boundary spell could inhibit sight *and* sound, had Riven even heard the knock?

Seth reached across her and traced a rune scratched to the right of the doorway. "Doorbell, basically," he explained.

A moment later a gruff female voice asked, "Who is it?"

"You don't know me, but my name is Nyx."

There was a pregnant pause on the other side of the door. "That doesn't sound like a Meerkin name."

"No, I'm human. From Earth."

"And I suppose you're here to tell me how sorry you are for

everything I've been through, but you really need to ask me some questions."

That had been Nyx's intention, but hearing the tone of Riven's voice, she could tell it wouldn't work. No amount of sincerity or explanation on Nyx's part was going to get Riven to open up, and Nyx couldn't really blame her. "I came to find out if I were to bring Valedan to Kyvren, and he were to vouch for me, if you would be willing to listen to what I have to say."

Another pregnant pause, and Nyx could tell she hadn't gotten through. If Nyx were Riven, what would she want? She'd been called away from the place she'd lived all her life, tortured for information, and now someone she cared for was being dangled in front of her like bait.

Well, Nyx hadn't handled this well. "Valedan won't be here under duress. It's a long story, but we met because his fiancé has been staying with me for a few months."

"Sarai was staying with you?" Riven asked.

Nyx let out a breath at having an easy test to pass. "No, Liya, who used to be Liyan, has been staying with me."

Riven's voice softened. "She finally aligned, then? Is she happy?"

"Yes. She and Valedan are both very happy. But since she ran away from the wedding, and he's been looking for her without leave ever since, they're worried the Blood Matron will be upset with them. They're hoping bringing you home will make her less upset. Also, I believe they miss you."

Nyx waited while Riven pondered it. Finally, the Dwarf said, "And what becomes of me, after?"

"Whatever you want. If you want to return to Alzherra with Liya and Valedan, I'll make sure that happens. If you want to stay here with your people, that's your choice too."

Riven made a sound on the other side of the door that made Nyx think Riven didn't really view the Dwarven race as "her people." "If Liya and Valedan come and I speak with them alone, and *if* I'm satisfied with what they have to say, then I will listen to what you want to tell me."

"Thank you."

Riven snorted. "Don't thank me. I've no intention of telling you anything I suspect you want to know"

"That's okay. Thank you, anyway."

They left. Once she and Seth were out of earshot, he asked, "Will Jevryn bring Valedan here?"

"He promised he would bring anyone I asked him to." She hesitated. "Would you go with him to the Station? To talk to everyone? I can't go"—she tapped the numbered tattoo on her hand—"without losing another trip, and I want to make sure Morgen and Evra don't feel like they have to come."

"I'll go," he said, "but you know they're going to come, right? And it has nothing to do with obligation. They're our best friends, Nyxi. Get used to it."

"I'm trying," she muttered.

"Now," he slung an arm over her shoulder and dragged her into an empty room, activating its boundary spell. "Before I go on a solo trip with my future father-in-law, you're required to fill me in on the family drama."

$$44$$

S eth was less than surprised when Jevryn, after obtaining
Vorex's permission to bring yet more humans to his planet,
announced that Kaden would remain behind to "keep an eye on
things". By which he obviously meant keep an eye on Nyx. Seth had
a feeling that if Jevryn was given the choice of his future son-in-law,
his decision would run more in the tall, silent, and golden-haired
direction than it would in the not-quite-as-tall, mouthy, and dark-
haired direction.

Fortunately for Seth, the approval of authority figures had never
been high on his list of needs. Or, really, on the list at all. It was that
lack of concern, as they portaled to the outskirts of the Station, that
led him to stop Jevryn from crossing over immediately.

Jevryn turned a long-suffering expression on him. "If you wish
to deliver yet another idle threat in my direction out of your concern
for Nyx, let us consider it delivered and move on."

"It's cute that you think the threats are idle," Seth said, "but
that's not what I wanted to talk to you about."

Jevryn made a go-on motion.

"Why don't you like me?"

"I was not under the impression you cared if I did or did not."

"Oh, I don't. I'm just planning ahead for what to tell my kid
when they want to know why Grandpa never wants to come visit."

Jevryn's eyes flew impossibly wide, officially making this the most emotion Seth had ever seen the man display. The color drained from his face. "Is she…"

It was everything Seth could do not to burst out laughing. "The word you're searching for is 'pregnant', and no, she's not. But you should really see your face right now."

"Is *everything* a joke to you?" Jevryn growled.

"No." He dropped the sarcasm that was almost always present in his tone. "My future children are definitely not a joke to me. Which is why I thought I'd give you enough advance warning to decide what you want out of life. Because if you can't start handling things better with Nyx, then you aren't going to know our kids when we have them.

"And maybe you don't care about that, but the thing is? I think you do." Jevryn still looked far too green around the gills from having thought his daughter was pregnant than he would if he didn't care. "And I get that maybe you don't know what you're doing or where to start, so let me help you out. You know what matters to Nyx? Showing up. So show up. With some kind of regularity. Take an interest in her life. You've set the bar so low, she's not expecting Father of the Year.

"Do that, or forget about your grandkids ever knowing who you are. Because I'm not subjecting them to your fickle indifference. Nyx and I had enough of that growing up." He clapped Jevryn on the shoulder and stepped across the boundary onto the Station's grounds. Jevryn remained where he was.

It took Griff all of twenty seconds to arrive, wrapping Seth in a hug that threatened to fracture his spinal column. He gave himself a moment to appreciate it—Griff's affection, the way the Station felt like home in a way nowhere else ever had.

"I was extremely worried," Griff informed him, finally deciding Seth no longer needed to be crushed to death. "Jevryn informed me of where you were. Thank the skies they got to you before Kiev returned to the planet."

"They…didn't, quite." At the look on Griff's face he quickly added, "Nyx is fine, but it got messy."

"Define 'messy'."

"Kiev knows she's Jevryn's. He wanted to know if she was 'a true A-Morridahn', said something ominous about her swallowing her own death, and threw some black smoke at her. Jevryn jumped in front of her and swallowed it instead, then dropped a tunnel on Kiev and managed to portal us out, but we all thought he was dead and Nyx took it pretty hard."

Griff closed his eyes. Seconds passed.

"Are you okay?"

"No. I am breathing deeply with the hope of being okay at some point in the near future." Griff opened his eyes. "How? How do these things always happen to her?"

"She's a trouble magnet. You get used to the stress of it after a while."

"No." Griff shook his wings out. "No, I don't believe I ever will grow accustomed to it." His gaze went beyond Seth, for a moment, to where Jevryn still stood just outside the Station's boundary. "I do not understand why Jevryn did not return her home now."

Seth scratched at the back of his head. "Yeah, she's refusing to go anywhere until the Meerkin have their shot at liberation."

"He is her father."

"And she's an adult."

Griff tried again. "He is a councilor."

"And she's stubborn as hell. Did Jevryn tell you how I got separated from them?"

"Not in detail, no."

"Resonant interference."

Griff drew in a deep breath and let it out slowly.

Seth felt for him. "So, yeah. He's not taking her anywhere she doesn't want to go."

It took a moment for Griff to come to terms with this before saying, "Very well. I must discuss this with Jevryn. Kiev's involvement changes things." Griff enveloped him in another brief hug. "I am glad that you are well. I do not know what I would do if I lost either of you." He released him. "You can find Morgen and Evra in the laboratory. I told them about Jevryn's brief visit earlier, and they were quite upset with me for allowing him to leave without them. Am I to assume you will be taking them with you this time?"

Seth nodded and they parted ways—Griff for a Jevryn who still looked unsettled, and Seth for Morgen's laboratory. He made his way inside, down the stone stairwell to the lab, Morgen's and Evra's voices floating up to him.

"A pinch of powdered alsom root is not a precise measurement,"

Evra said hotly. "Everyone pinches differently. I do not understand how you can consider that an adequate instruction."

"It's intuition," Morgen argued. "It doesn't come out right if you attempt to boil it down to precise numbers on a scale."

Seth hit the bottom of the stairs and leaned against the wall, watching as Evra and Morgen argued. They stood at the end of the nearest lab counter, Evra's back to him, Morgen facing her. Seth watched as she tossed her hair disdainfully. Then he did a double-take, because *Evra's hair was down.* It was the type of thing he wouldn't ordinarily be inclined to notice, except he'd never once seen it out of its plait the entire time he'd known her.

"I thought you were a scientist," she was saying hotly. "Isn't measuring numbers on a scale what scientists do?"

"First off, 'scientists' is a broad term lumping us all together, and second off—" Morgen's gaze went past Evra to the stairwell. "Seth."

"We are all worried about him, but do not think you can change the subject by—"

Morgen put his hands on Evra's shoulders and turned her to face the stairwell. "Oh. Seth."

He grinned, sauntering into the room. "Did you miss me? Also, why is your hair down?"

Morgen held out his hand to Evra, palm up. She growled, dug into her pocket, pulled out a handful of coins and slapped them into Morgen's palm.

"I missed you until you lost me a bet." Evra's hands dragged through her hair, smoothing it back, and she started plaiting it with quick, efficient movements.

"And I missed you all the more because you just won me a bet," Morgen said. He tucked the coins into his pocket and thumped Seth on the back.

"You betted on Evra's hair?"

Morgen nodded. "I said the first person to see it would comment on it in under thirty seconds."

"Where is Nyx?" Evra asked, putting the finishing touches on her plait. "As she hasn't recently lost me money, I still miss her. Though I assume from your usual, carefree attitude that she is in good health."

"Oh, no, she's in horrible straits, I'm just a terrible boyfriend, carrying on happily despite it."

Evra folded her arms across her chest. "You are not half so funny as you think you are."

"Counterpoint: I'm hilarious. She's safe in the Meerkin's main den on Kyvren. She sent me in her stead, so she doesn't lose another trip from her deal with the Station, and also so Jevryn can't trick her into staying."

"Kaden?" Morgen asked quietly.

"He's fine too." Seth caught them up on the relevant events, all the way up to Riven wanting nothing to do with them. "So it looks like the two royal wonders upstairs are getting their wish. We need to take them with us."

"'We', as in, Morgen and I are not to be rudely left behind for the third time?" Evra asked with what, for her, passed as false sweetness.

Seth held his hands up defensively. "You can blame Jevryn for the first two times. However, Nyx sent me to make sure the two of you don't feel pressured to come along."

Evra rolled her eyes. "I am offended. She ought to know us better by now."

"Deep down, she does."

Evra tapped her fingers against her biceps. "We will need Enforcer armor, then. Morgen and I have it, of course, and I've seen yours, though the cloak and mask addition is not something I possess. Liya and Valedan will be an issue as well."

At that moment, several bags rose up through the floor, a note pinned to the foremost one. Evra swiped it and read, her expression clearing. "It would seem that either Councilor A-Morridahn did originally intend to take us all with them, or he was very dedicated to ensuring no one realized he did not intend to do so." She unzipped the first bag—which Seth could now see had her name embroidered on it—and pulled out a cloak with armored scales sewn into the material. She sighed. "Cloaks are horridly impractical in a fight. All the swishing and flaring. I do not understand why it is not simply a *hood* and mask."

"I think Jevryn's fond of all the swishing and flaring," Seth said. He turned to Morgen. "Nyx also asked for Laiveran's journal. Riven's not keen on talking, and she thought it might help."

Morgen nodded. "I made a copy of it ages ago, so even if anything were to happen to it, it should be fine."

Evra snorted. "You made *four* copies of it."

"What else was I supposed to do with my time? *You* try solving a cypher without any idea what the key is."

"I would never bother. An Amazon always plays to her strengths, and mine are physical not mental."

Morgen gave her a suggestive look, which led to her punching him in the arm before she grabbed three bags and strode off with a casual, "I'll see to Liya and Valedan."

Morgen rubbed his shoulder.

"It's difficult loving violent women," Seth said in commiseration.

"And yet so hot," Morgen answered.

Seth held up his fist, Morgen bumped it, and he felt *home*. The only thing missing was Nyx. Speaking of... "Hey, so just out of curiosity, if Nyx and I have ten kids, will you be the godfather?"

Morgen blinked. "Ten?"

"More like two. Three tops." Seth leaned back against the lab counter, thinking. Three was his limit, but... "She didn't actually specify how many she was open to, so it might just be one. What do you say?"

"You're asking this now?"

"I like to get the important details settled before I go to war."

Morgen rubbed the back of his neck. "And you're serious? About the whole godparent thing? And kids?"

He nodded "I've been informed it's going to be a few years"— especially since something about seeing him playing with the Meerkin cubs had made Nyx go all deer-in-the-headlights—"but yeah, I'm serious."

"Then I would be honored." Morgen paused for a minute, then gave him a wary glance. "I think I would be honored. Any children of yours are going to be unholy terrors."

"Yes," Seth answered. "Yes, they most certainly are." And he was going to love every minute of it.

45

Nyx didn't realize just how much she'd missed everyone until Jevryn and Seth returned with them a few hours later. She'd taken a brief nap since jet lag—or was it portal lag?—was doing a number on her. Awake but still feeling lethargic, she was on the floor of her room, stretching out stiff, aching muscles when she heard familiar voices. She leapt to her feet and took off, running past Kaden in the common room and straight at Evra. She pulled up short about a foot away from the Amazon.

Evra's face took on an expression of long-suffering martyrdom. "You may hug."

Since it was rare that Evra granted hugging permissions, Nyx took full advantage. "I missed you."

Evra patted her awkwardly on the back, which was her usual response to physical affection. Though Nyx was of the opinion that the back pats were getting slightly less awkward, and that maybe Evra hated the hugging ten-percent less than she had when Nyx first met her.

"The Station is strange without you," Evra said, which Nyx interpreted as *I missed you too*.

She stepped back, and Morgen held out his arms. "You wouldn't have forgotten about me, would you, little Guardian?"

Nyx transferred her hug to Morgen. "You know I missed you

too. The quality of conversation has really dragged without you around."

"Hey," Seth protested, "I'm an excellent conversationalist."

Nyx rolled her eyes, letting Morgen go. "You don't count."

"Do the rest of us get hugs?" Valedan asked from behind Morgen and Evra. His charming smile was perfectly in place, one arm wrapped around Liya's waist, as if he was afraid she would vanish if he let her go.

Nyx eyed him. She didn't know him well enough to be in hug territory. "Hugs are an inner circle thing."

He clasped his free hand to his heart. "You wound me."

Nyx decided it was a good thing he was going back to Alzherra. She didn't think the Station could handle the combined theatrics of Valedan and Seth longterm.

"Perhaps," Jevryn interrupted, "it would be possible to delay a discussion of grievances and the distribution of hugs to a less urgent time?"

Whereas Nyx was tempted to roll her eyes again, Valedan straightened, going from charming rogue to respectful royal in the blink of an eye. "Of course, Councilor A-Morridahn. If you would lead us to Riven, I would be happy to speak with her. I am eager to confirm for myself that she is well."

Jevryn motioned to Kaden, who fell in step beside him. Nyx let Valedan and Liya follow first, then Seth and Morgen, and took up the rear of the procession with Evra, linking her arm through the Amazon's.

"What have I missed at the Station?"

"You have not even been gone a full three days."

Nyx glanced at her watch, confirming dates. "It feels like more." It was, technically, a little more on Kyvren.

"You did not miss anything of terrible excitement," Evra said. "Kalvar had what I believe would be considered a mild crisis about his departure from the Station, should he pass the Proficiency Exam."

"I don't think a crisis can be mild, technically. And *when* he passes his exam, he doesn't need to worry about leaving because he can come back whenever he wants."

"We did reassure him of as much." At Nyx's skeptical glance, Evra amended, "Griff and Morgen reassured him. I relayed facts in a way that should have been reassuring, but Morgen informed me was not."

Nyx patted her arm. "You just have a direct approach. I promise you that, having acclimated to it, I now find your borderline-hostile recitation of facts soothing in the manner you intend."

Evra made a mollified noise and said, "The Warlock also came by."

"Oh?" Nyx strove for a tone of disinterest. "What about?"

"Dropping off some samples of a new tea she thought you might want to try in the cafe. I believe it was merely an excuse to speak with you, as she was disappointed to learn you were unavailable. It is my suspicion that she wishes to apologize for her prior behavior and distance, but is unsure how to go about it."

The hopeful part of Nyx wanted that to be true. "What makes you think so?"

"Diana intimated as much a week or so ago, without crossing the bounds of divulging her wife's personal confidences. I expected the Warlock to approach you at Tobi's celebration."

Nyx recalled that hesitant step the Warlock had taken toward her, before Seth had pulled her into the badminton game. "Well, if it comes up in casual conversation, feel free to intimate to Diana that I'm open to apologies."

"I will do so."

They walked in silence a bit longer, before Nyx asked, "Did you hear from Tamrin?" At the look on Evra's face, Nyx hastily added, "You don't have to talk about it if you don't want to."

"No, it is…nice," Evra said, with some wonderment on that last word, "to discuss things with a friend. I have not heard anything further. I have written to her again. I have written to mother, asking that I be allowed to visit this one time. I have received no response from either." She paused a beat, then said, "I have asked Morgen to try."

"Writing to Tamrin or your mother?"

"Both. Tamrin is just spiteful enough—and Morgen interesting enough—that she might respond to my partner where she refuses to respond to me. As for mother, she was a long shot to begin with. Having severed my bloodline, she cannot acknowledge me without implying that she is open to repairing it. Morgen is allowed some leeway there, as he is not a blood relation, and he did train under her at the start of his Enforcer career. She could choose to speak to me through him. Due to their prior connection, she could choose to allow *him* to visit and bring me with him, without having to wound her pride. Since he did leave his last encounter with her alive, I believe she at least finds him amusing, and there is some small chance she might allow it."

"Don't take this the wrong way," Nyx said, "but it's honestly comforting to know I don't have the only fucked-up family out there."

Evra snorted indelicately just as they arrived at Riven's door. It was Beren who answered the doorbell, then disappeared inside to speak with Riven. A minute later Valedan and Liya were ushered inside, and the rest of them were relegated to the room across the hall to wait.

Nyx honestly didn't understand how people waited for anything without access to a timepiece. Perhaps her obsession with time was a crutch born from too much solitude, or from the sense that time was the one thing that could be expected to reliably behave in the same manner, at least on Earth. Or, you know, when observed via a watch that kept the seconds and minutes as they passed on Earth. The point being, if she hadn't absolutely known that twenty-three minutes and forty-one seconds passed before Valedan reappeared and told her Riven would talk to her now, she would have sworn she'd been waiting for three hours. She stood.

When Jevryn made to go with her, Valedan winced. "I am sorry, Councilor A-Morridahn, but Riven is only willing to speak with Nyx."

Jevryn had that look on his face that said he was about to remind Valedan—and through Valedan, Riven—precisely how very important he thought he was.

Nyx drew him to the side, out of earshot, preempting that response. "You can't just force your way in there."

"Of late, people seem to frequently conflate what I cannot do with what they do not wish me to do."

"Fine, I don't want you to force your way in there. Obviously, if you want to play the High Councilor of the Universe card, you can. But I don't think you can make Riven talk to you, even if you cross ethical boundaries I'm not okay with you crossing. Kiev tried it that way and clearly didn't succeed."

"Yet you believe you will?"

She shrugged. "I'm going to try. And before you argue with me, think way back to yesterday when we were at your house and you promised we would work together and you would take my concerns seriously."

Jevryn's face said that he didn't like it. "You will inform me of everything that transpires."

"You got it." She left before he could change his mind, towing Valedan out the door with her. Valedan, for his part, managed to throw an impressive number of contemplative glances in her direction during what was an objectively short walk across an objectively short hallway.

"What?" she finally asked, when he paused outside of Riven's door.

"Two things. One, I was under the impression that Guardians didn't leave their Stations."

The good news for Nyx, in this situation, was that it wasn't publicly known that Guardians *couldn't* leave their Stations, only that they didn't. "We usually don't. I did have executive approval for this trip, though." She jerked her thumb across the hall at Jevryn.

"Which brings me to the second thing. What is your relationship with Councilor A-Morridahn?"

Considering that, thus far, every time she tried to pretend she had no relationship with Jevryn she failed, she decided to try a different tact. "I'm his secret love child," she said brightly. "He doesn't want anyone to know about me, so he's attempting to buy my silence with small favoritisms." She winked for good measure.

Valedan shook his head. "Very well, don't tell me. I suppose it is none of my business."

"That's the spirit." She clapped Valedan on the back and followed him into the room, where Liya was sitting next to Riven, chatting as if they were old friends. Which, Nyx supposed, they were.

Nyx hadn't gotten a good look at Riven at any point thus far, only a brief glance in the prison, before Kiev had come in. The Dwarven female was as solidly built as her male counterparts, with black hair sheared close to her skull. Her face was bruised and her lower lip split, which no doubt contributed to the wary way she eyed Nyx. "I agreed to listen to you because Valedan asked me to, and because I want to see Constance. It's unlikely I'll answer your questions."

Nyx decided to take it as a hopeful sign that Riven had said *unlikely* as opposed to *you can pry my secrets from my grave* or something equally cheerful.

"I understand. I'd like to tell you a story, and if you still don't want to talk to me after, I'll leave and won't bother you again."

Riven nodded and held out her hand. "Constance first."

Nyx did not want to part with Constance. Constance did not want to be parted from Nyx. She had to extract another promise of the weapon's return before it would leave her fingers for Riven's, the necessity of which seemed to please the Dwarf, as if it were a crucial first step in confirming authenticity.

"How did you bond with it?" Riven asked, rolling the collapsed staff gently in her hands. It had not, yet, shifted form.

"My friend Morgen—he's very smart—thought that it wanted a commitment. After that, Constance and I found ourselves in a not-great situation where its habit of getting stuck to my hand almost got me killed, and I made it some promises and we came to an understanding."

Riven looked up at her, an incredulous expression on her face. "You merely spoke to it?"

"At length and with great vehemence. And with magic involved. Morgen said that was important."

"Indeed. I am beginning to think I should speak with this Morgen at some point."

"I'm sure he'd be happy to. Like I said, he's very smart, and though he's too polite to say it, I think he needs more stimulating technical discussions from time to time." Griff could and was providing a lot of that intellectual companionship, but he was about nine centuries behind on current magical theory.

Riven had clearly decided this was enough conversation, as she closed her eyes and Constance morphed in her hands. Valedan and Liya leaned forward, watching as Constance began to change. It did not morph into anything new, but remained nebulous, in some in-between state that was full of nascent promise. It reminded Nyx a little of the state it had been in when Jevryn had held it, except that then it had been furiously attempting to take a form, but seemingly unable to settle on a specific one. Now it was quiescent, as if this was the state it had been made in and, in the hands of its maker's descendent, it was content to be as it had begun.

Riven and Constance remained that way for some time, and perhaps it wasn't the most absurd of ideas, given how Nyx had struck her bargain with the weapon, when she thought the two were talking in some way.

Eventually, Riven opened her eyes. "It likes being with you. It speaks well to your character." She handed Constance back to Nyx, who took it with a sigh of relief. She'd grown as attached to Constance as Constance apparently had to her.

The weapon returned to its typical bo staff form, already collapsed, and Nyx tucked it into her holster. She swallowed. She had a feeling this had been the easy part, and now she was to be taxed with the difficult one.

She gave a sidelong glance to Liya and Valedan, but they weren't leaving, and Nyx had a feeling they wouldn't unless Riven asked them to. "I'm guessing you know why I wanted to talk to you?"

Riven's face grew guarded once more. "The same reason Kiev A-Morridahn did. The same reason Jevryn A-Morridahn waits on the other side of that door for you to tell him whatever I tell you."

"The subject matter is the same," Nyx said, purposely vague, with Liya and Valedan still in the room. "But my reasons could not be more opposite."

"So you do not wish me to repeat the feat for you? To 'combat the threat' of the one that exists? That was his excuse."

"No." She took a risk, because she knew, in the end, it was going to come down to showing the Harvester to Riven, anyway. And she'd already told Valedan she had the creation Riven's ancestor had made, so... "I don't need you to make another one. I have the original."

Everything about Riven went still, her gaze sharpening. "Then you must be—"She broke off, then looked to Valedan and Liya. "Would you give us a moment of privacy?"

Valedan hesitated, looking between them. "If that is your wish?"

"It is. And no listening in with shadows," she added at Liya's back as the two exited.

"Do you think she'll listen?" Nyx asked.

"Liya has always been good about respecting the boundaries of those she values. I don't think I'm mistaken in saying she values me." The brief fondness that had crept into Riven's eyes while she talked of Liya faded when her gaze refocused on Nyx. "You're Hidden."

Nyx didn't answer. She didn't quite know how, considering everyone was supposed to think the Hidden were extinct. It must have shown on her face, because Riven snorted.

"I consider myself something of a scholar of my family's work. Of the ancestor who bound us to the Alzherran royals, in particular. I poured over every single one of his journals, could recite entire passages of them from memory. So imagine my surprise when, shortly after the eradication of the Hidden began, I was looking through his things and found a journal I had always managed to glance over before.

"In it, my ancestor spoke of a terrible creation. One so powerful that it had reshaped the course of the universe. And I thought to myself, who has both the means of destroying the Hidden, and would want to do so? It seems to me that if my ancestor made something dangerous enough to shape history, it might well be one the Council would go to any lengths to reclaim."

Riven paused for a moment, then went on, her tone contemplative. "Did you know that Dwarves can feel our creations? We may not know where they are, but we feel it if they are destroyed, or if they yet live. Those of us who are strong enough are also attuned to the creations made by others in our family line. So I searched for a creation powerful enough to be the one my ancestor created, and I found it.

"For years, I felt it, and given my ancestor's writings, I kept waiting for something terrible to come of it. Then one day, my sense of it vanished. Not in the same way it does when a creation is destroyed. It was more that I simply could not feel it. That was when I understood the Hidden were not fully gone. That at least one of you remained, and you had taken over the Hiding of the object."

Again, Nyx said nothing. She had the distinct impression that saying nothing was in her best interests, because saying the wrong thing might make Riven clam up.

"Do you have it with you?"

An unsettled feeling spread through Nyx. This was the first time it had occurred to her that, while sending Valedan from the room protected her own secrets, it also left her vulnerable. But...she was a portal witch, possessed of portal magic. If she needed a quick escape, she always had her trusty fallback of portaling to Jevryn's library and waiting for him to come get her.

She could lie and say she didn't have the Harvester with her, but if she did, Riven might not tell her anything more. "Yes."

"I would like to see it."

"See it," Nyx agreed. "But not touch it. Don't take this the wrong way, but I don't trust anyone with it."

There was an odd look in Riven's eyes, but even Nyx's suspicious nature in that moment wouldn't have called it hunger or longing. No, it was more like…trepidation. She didn't think Riven was very fond of this thing her ancestor had made. And that was, honestly, one of the highest recommendations Nyx could give in her favor.

Focusing on the web of Hidden magic surrounding the Harvester, Nyx added a single exception to the one that was already there for Seth, one that resulted in a sharp intake of breath when it took hold.

For a moment, the Dwarf only stared. Then her eyes fluttered briefly closed before she said, "There was a final entry in my ancestor's journal. The very last one, long after the others had been written. He said his creation had been used for a great destruction. Was that—is that true?"

"Yes."

"What was it used for? The journal he left was not one for his work. It was full only of his reflections and his guilt. And that guilt was endless."

Nyx swallowed. "Did your grandfather ever name his creation in his journal?"

Riven shook her head.

"Then I'll tell you the name it became known by, before it was wiped from collective memory. This is the Harvester of Worlds. And that is precisely what it did at the hands of its wielder. Many, many times over."

"No wonder he bound us in servitude," Riven said, more to herself than to Nyx. More directly, she said, "You told me your intentions were the opposite of Kiev's. What does that mean?"

Nyx tucked the Harvester back inside the shirt of her armor. "It means that I want to destroy it. And that I would like to find a way to free what it was used to make."

Riven frowned. "What it was used to make?"

"Did your ancestor's journal mention anything else? About what was made from what the Harvester destroyed?"

"No," Riven said, but she said it slowly, as if turning remembered words over in her head. "But he said our bondage was fitting, as his creation had led to the bondage of others." She met Nyx's gaze directly. "What did he mean?"

For a moment, Nyx considered telling her the truth of it. The Harvester was Riven's family legacy, her family's shame. And yet… the universe was built on the transit the Stations allowed. Nyx wasn't naive enough to think no one would have a problem with that transit disappearing, no matter the means by which it had been created.

Most people didn't want to see beneath the surface of their lives to the things which made them possible. If their conveniences were built on the silent suffering of others, well, the silence was the key part. If they didn't see it or hear it or know about it, they didn't have to feel guilty about benefiting from it. They didn't have to change their behavior. If Nyx somehow managed to shout the truth of the Stations' natures to the entire universe, very few people would thank her for it.

So she went, once more, with vague explanations. "The planets the Harvester consumed—they were pulled back out of it. Not as they once were, not the planets themselves, but more their essences." She had a feeling Riven might balk if Nyx told her planets had souls. "But what was left of them does feel, and they were magically bound in order to power something. I'm hoping you can tell me how to use the Harvester to unbind them."

Riven shook her head. "I don't know that I can. Aside from the fact that you haven't told me what you want to unbind, I don't know how the Harvester works or was built. My ancestor did not write that information down. I think he was afraid that if he did, someone would attempt to replicate it. He must have had a design journal when he was building it, which I assume he later destroyed, as it was not among his things."

"By any chance, is it something like this?" Nyx pulled the journal

—the one she and Morgen had been operating under the assumption was Laiveran's—and handed it to Riven. It was a risk, handing the Harvester's blueprints over to one of the few people in the universe capable of building something from them. But she believed Riven was sincere in having no intention of ever duplicating the Harvester. Besides, given their isolation, it would be far easier for Riven to simply try and take the one already in existence from her.

Riven frowned, flipping through the pages. "Yes, this is his handwriting. The cypher is one of his more obscure ones—I don't have it memorized." She continued flipping pages, flipped back, studied them for several minutes. "But I don't think I need to. I understand enough from the diagrams to tell you what you want to know. The device itself is a lure and a cage, designed specifically for the entity it holds.

"The cage, controlled by the wielder, can be set to allow the entity to consume, which appears to be its base nature. The alternate side of that is extraction—which is what you described—during which the condensed energy that was consumed could then be pulled out by the wielder."

Riven looked up from the journal. "It is a very basic idea on a grand scale—containment, with the allowance for intake and extraction. But that is *all* it does. If the extracted energy was bound in some fashion, it was done so by the person who extracted it, not by the Harvester itself. The only sense in which the Harvester could unbind it would be through a second consumption."

Disappointment bled through Nyx. She'd assumed, when the Council had made the Stations, that they had made them with the Harvester in a literal sense, not that they had simply used it as a materials source. And she had assumed that, she realized, because it was what Jevryn had let her believe.

Allowing the Harvester to consume the Stations again was out of the question. Even if she could discover how to untether the Avatars and Guardians from them so they were not likewise consumed, it wasn't what she had promised Kaliaris, who had an understandably deep hatred of the thing that had ended their original life.

Unless… The very fact that Kaliaris and the others still existed proved they had not been destroyed by the Harvester. They had been altered. Stripped down to a core essence. If they could be ripped from their current moorings by the Harvester, could she release that core essence without constraints? And if she could, would it allow the souls to finally find some measure of peace?

It wasn't a question Riven could answer. Nyx didn't know if it was a question anyone could, but *if* she solved the Avatar-Guardian issue, and *if* the Stations wanted to take that risk for a chance at freedom, she needed a plan for what to do with the Harvester after. One that ensured no one could ever use it again.

"Can the Harvester be destroyed?"

"The cage, or the entity within?"

"Either." She felt a stab of guilt as she said it. She didn't think the Devourer, as Kaliaris had referred to the entity, was evil. She thought it was simply its nature, and its nature was hunger. Perhaps, in the ecosystem it had been born into, in its original place among the stars, that hunger had served a function, had been held in check.

Contained as it was within the Harvester's cage, stripped from its original moorings, it had become an apex predator to be commanded at another's whim. She couldn't blame it for being what it was. And she lamented that it might need to be destroyed simply because humanity had placed it somewhere it ought never have been.

"I can only give you a best guess," Riven warned.

"I'll take it."

"There is nothing strong enough to destroy either—except perhaps themselves. And even then, they are equal in power. One may contain the other, but neither will succeed in destroying the other."

"If they're equal, how is the Harvester containing the entity?"

"Trickery. I told you it was a lure, as well as a cage. Consider that in a fight between two equally matched opponents, if one person does not see the attack coming, it is easy for them to be subdued. The Harvester contains the entity because the entity was lured to within its confines. If released and given the opportunity, the entity could likewise contain the Harvester.

"And that is precisely what I suggest you do with it. The cage cannot be destroyed, but the door can be opened." She flipped to a page in the journal and showed it to Nyx. "I don't pretend to understand what this entity is, or how it was taken from its place in the universe, but I am assuming you must, on some level, or you would not be asking these questions." She tapped a drawing on the page. "This is the entity's original location. Understand that I only under-stand that it *is* a location. I am familiar enough with my ancestor's notes to know that much, but I do not pretend that I could locate it or fathom how to reach it.

"But should you succeed in determining it, take the Harvester there. Open its cage, let the entity return to where it was born, and then feed the Harvester to it."

"That all sounds very simple," Nyx couldn't help but notice. "What aren't you telling me?"

"I would hardly call traveling to the far reaches of space, to a place I cannot understand how you would even reach, much less survive long enough to do what I have described, simple. But...yes. There is one other thing you should know. It concerns the opening of the cage."

Riven talked. Nyx listened. It was very simple, really, what the Dwarf explained. A curious kind of numbness spread through Nyx, and she decided then and there that she would never repeat what she had learned. Ever, to anyone.

46

Unsurprisingly, Jevryn was waiting for Nyx when she stepped out of Riven's quarters. Looking past him, she could see the room she'd previously been waiting in was empty.

"Where is everyone?"

"Their presence underfoot was unnecessary. I sent them to speak with Vorex's strategists to determine how they might best be useful in the coming battle."

"And I don't need to be a part of that discussion?"

"No. Your place will be with me." He held up a hand, forestalling argument. "That is not up for discussion. I have trusted you in this matter"—he indicated Riven—"as you asked me to, and you must trust me in this one. With Kiev's presence, and therefore A-Lethe's, a guarantee, your place is with me."

She decided if she argued with that logic it would only be out of stubbornness. She wasn't a soldier. Viktor hadn't trained her to fight as a part of a larger unit on a grand scale. He'd taught her to survive close-quarters encounters with one to five people.

Morgen, Kaden, and Evra did have that training. More importantly, they were all far more capable of taking orders than Nyx was. She wouldn't be much use, even if she did try to merge into a Meerkin or Meerkin-allied-Dwarf unit. Her friends would be and, if she had to guess, they would be assigned as a unit of their own, because they already knew how to work together. Under that scenario, Seth could fall in with them where he would otherwise be as difficult to control as she was in a regimented setting.

"Okay," she agreed. "I'm with you. We need to talk about what Riven told me."

Neither of them had to state the obvious need for privacy regarding that conversation. Since her friends were otherwise occupied, meaning their newly allotted quarters were currently empty, she and Jevryn made their way to them in silence.

"What have you learned?" Jevryn asked once they were inside.

"Well, before we get to the things you don't know, how about we start with the thing you did know and lied to me about."

The muscle beneath Jevryn's left eye twitched, and Nyx wondered if she was giving him a headache. She kind of hoped so.

"Do elaborate."

"You told me the Harvester was used to make the Stations, but that's not true."

Jevryn went completely still. "What do you mean it is not true?"

Nyx's righteous indignation wavered. "You mean you didn't know? How could you not know? You were there."

"No, I was not. Given the universe-wide disaster we were on the brink of because one man had lost his wife, the others were not going to let me anywhere near the Harvester given what had happened to Arradin. I cannot even say they were unwise in that decision. So yes, I did believe, given the fact they have always been adamant about keeping me, specifically, from the Harvester, that it was directly used to create the Stations. What makes you think it was not?"

"According to Riven, the Harvester can't manipulate what it contains. It allows the entity within it to consume, and then allows the Harvester's wielder to extract that consumed material. It can't do anything else with it. The Council may have taken the planets' souls back out of the Harvester, but however they made them into the Stations was achieved by another method." She had to ask the obvious. "You never questioned it?"

"Of course I questioned it. But by then it was too late. I intimated to you my fears for Arradin, after he first was bound. Let me be clear in them now—after it occurred, he wanted to die. I do not know if he can now be killed within the Station—I do know it would be exceedingly difficult to manage—but there was a time when his binding to that place was new, its roots shallow, and that was not the case.

"So I did not leave him. It was not until he had come to terms with what he now was that I felt it was safe enough to leave him, to turn my attention to undoing what had been done to him. By that time, the other Stations had already been created, the Harvester Hidden.

"And before you ask, no, *I* had nothing to do with the Hidden being killed off so that we might all remember where we had kept the Harvester all these centuries. I will fully admit that once we did remember, I had every intention of taking it someday. But the window of use for it would be small, and I wished to understand *how* to use it to achieve my goals before bringing the Council's attention upon me.

"Unfortunately, Alistair ruined all of that. Kaden had to take the Harvester to you, and I spent a few years enduring Psionics' pleasantries so that not a single member of the Council would doubt that I do not have it in my possession.

"By the time I was released, Kaden was on Arkadia, and I did not trust another Tracker with your mother's scent. I intended to retrieve Kaden from Arkadia once I was no longer so closely watched, but I had barely been returned to freedom a month before I received word there had been a prison break from Arkadia. Which led me to Earth, and *you.*

"You had the Harvester and, given your Hidden nature, you are one of the few people who could examine it—even use it—without drawing the attention of everyone who remembers the feel of its magic. I had hoped your connection to the Station might allow you to understand the bond between it and Arradin in a way that I have thus far been unable to."

Nyx…hadn't attempted to explore her Station bond through the lens of the Harvester. She had been so focused on finding its maker, both because she'd needed to know how to destroy it, and because she'd believed it would give her the answer to separating Griff from the Station, that she hadn't stopped long enough to think to ask Kaliaris if they remembered how they'd been remade into their current form. Given how they felt about their situation, though, she couldn't imagine they wouldn't have volunteered any relevant information, had they been in possession of it.

"I'll look into it once I'm back on Earth," she promised. "Until then...Riven was able to tell me how to destroy the Harvester. Sort of."

"Sort of?" Jevryn repeated, the words sounding as if he found them distasteful. No doubt he would have preferred something more flowery like *in a manner of speaking* or *but there is a caveat.*

She kept her tone matter-of-fact as she laid out what Riven had told her. She punched it up a bit, emphasizing the difficulty of finding the Devourer's original location to return it to, so that, even bad at lying though she was, he never suspected there was one key detail she was leaving out. And it wasn't really lying, was it? Not when she would find some way around what Riven had told her.

"May I see the journal?" Jevryn asked. She considered it progress that he didn't even chastise her for not having told him about its existence before now.

He examined the page Riven had claimed was a location, but after a moment his lip curled in irritation. "I had hoped for portal coordinates, but this is the type of puzzle Arradin would be far more adept at solving than I."

"I'll have him get with Morgen on it. They tried working out the cypher together without any luck, but while Riven doesn't know it by heart, she has the key on Alzherra and has agreed to send it to us, once she's returned." There wasn't actually any writing on that page—it was all numerical—but maybe knowing the cypher would give Griff and Morgen enough context to put the location together. "Supposing they solve it, how does that work, exactly? Can you portal into space? Like, just up there"—she waved in the general direction of outer space—"in the void with the stars?"

"With enough determination and the proper insulating atmospheric spells to survive the environment? Yes. Once we refined those spells that allowed us to survive inhospitable planets, it took shockingly little time for someone to decide that they would also allow one to survive space, and wish to try it."

"Who was it?" Nyx asked.

"Arradin, naturally. The idea had scarcely crossed his mind before he talked me into taking him. He found the vastness of space freeing. I found it...less so." Jevryn looked slightly seasick at the remembrance. "We never agreed on the matter."

Before they could discuss anything further, the doorbell rang, and Nyx found Jori waiting outside. He greeted her, but then looked past her to Jevryn. "You told Vorex last night that you would be willing to assist with the evacuation. If so, that time is now."

Nyx looked between them. "What evacuation?"

"We are sending the cubs to the outlying dens," Jori said. "Many of their locations remain unknown to the Dwarves, so even if they choose to attack more than our central den, the future of our people will be safe."

"And you're helping?" Nyx asked Jevryn.

"Portaling them will be far more expedient than sending them traipsing across the planet on their bare paws, and far safer."

"How are you going to know where to portal them?"

Jori said, "I will show him. He has explained to me about this sight portaling, and I must admit that skipping across the land sounds like great fun."

"Given the distances explained, I should be able to leave anchors at the six dens in question within the next four hours."

Nyx nodded. "Okay, let's go."

"You," Jevryn said slowly, "are not coming."

"I want to help. I *can* help. I can line-of-sight portal. I can make anchors. Let Jori take you to three of the dens and I'll go to the other three."

"No."

"But—"

He held up his hand. "Not while A-Lethe and Kiev roam this planet. You are not safe aboveground apart from my side, and to bring you with me now serves no function. Should A-Lethe catch wind of you, it might even hasten this battle before the Meerkin young are removed to safety. Would you risk that?"

She gritted her teeth. "No." Of course she wouldn't. "Is there *something* I can do?" Seth and the others were currently learning how they were going to be useful when Kiev attacked. She didn't even know what she was supposed to do when that happened, other than hide behind Jevryn's robes. Now the one thing she could do—assist with evacuation—she was being told she *couldn't* do.

"We will be bringing back other Meerkin from the outlying dens who wish to fight," Jori said. "If you want to help, many are setting up temporary accommodations and ration supplies for them, as well as medical rooms for those who may be wounded in the battle."

Her tension eased at having a task, something she could *do*. "Put me to work."

The Meerkin did. For the next four hours she cleaned long-unused rooms in the den, carried furs to set up communal bedding areas, assembled what felt like trail mix bags, given the amount of jerky and dried fruit she portioned, and generally fetched, carried, and relayed messages for anyone who asked her to. It took her mind off everything to come, and soon she no longer felt at loose ends.

But when Jevryn returned, work temporarily halted. Everyone in the den had heard that he was going to portal the cubs out, and everyone wanted to see it. As she followed the flow of traffic into the meeting room, Nyx wondered if Jevryn understood the measure of trust the Meerkin were placing in him. She was more than a little surprised they were letting him do this at all.

The Meerkin crowded in, packing against the back two-thirds of the room to give Jevryn space. He stood in the cleared front area, his back to the Meerkin, facing the empty wall. Without turning, he made a come-forward gesture with his left hand and said, "Nyx?"

The Meerkin parted to let her pass, and she came to Jevryn's side.

"Have you ever opened simultaneous portals?"

She frowned. "No."

"It requires the ability to split one's focus with equal attention, and first attempts are best done using anchors. It can be impractical without a ready supply of magic, especially depending on how long you intend to leave the portals open. These will be in use for quite some time."

Several feet above Jevryn, his first portal opened. It was not to a space on Kyvren, but to the portal well in his home. She could tell it was the one in his home by the way she was drawn to the magic, the headiness of it, though he'd portaled directly to its center and the only thing she saw was a two-foot diameter circle of purest blue above him, a column of magic funneling to him from it. Being an opportunist, Nyx took the time to refill her own bracelets from the magic drifting down.

"You must exercise extreme caution opening a portal to a well. Even *near* a well. You are opening a portal to a place of limitless potential, and as the match is already struck, it can be all too easy to burn everything in sight. The concentration required to hold this open with minimal risk takes years to develop. Do you understand?"

Nyx nodded.

"Good." He spun a tendril of magic from the column and looped it around her wrist, drawing her into his working. "Now, pay attention." That current looping around her intensified as Jevryn drew on the magic above. She felt his anchors as he found them, six points spread across the planet. He reached for them with simultaneous precision, six doorway-sized portals opening equidistance apart on the wall before him.

"Could you hold them?" he asked.

She hesitated. She couldn't open them—not as he had done—but hold them? "Maybe." She'd never tried to hold *two* portals open at the same time, much less six.

Jevryn made a noise in the back of his throat that she couldn't interpret. Then, to the Meerkin behind him, said, "You may proceed."

After Jori jumped through each of the six portals and returned, effectively soothing any concerns about safety, the Meerkin came forward in six orderly lines. An adult was at the head of each procession of cubs, reminding Nyx of nothing so much as a Dead Earth classroom, each teacher at the head of their students.

They had barely started through when Jevryn peeled off a single thread of portal magic—the one connected to the right-most portal —and held it out to her. "Take it."

She shook her head.

He raised an eyebrow. "I believe you said you wanted to help."

"I don't want to drop it, they're walking through." She'd never taken over a portal someone else had created, the way Jevryn had assumed control over the one she'd opened on Nethrayne. "Besides, aren't I supposed to be keeping this ability under wraps?"

"Word of your portaling during your fight with A-Lethe has already spread throughout the den. There is no 'under wraps'." He held the thread out again. "Take it. If you drop it, I will catch it, and none will be the wiser."

She shook her head again. She wasn't going to risk the cubs lives on her ability.

Jevryn released the thread. It hovered in the air and Nyx's worried gaze shot to the corresponding portal. It remained, whole and steady. "I have been doing this a very long time, *na'tria*. The threads are merely a visual guide for your benefit. You have my word no harm will come to the Meerkin. Try."

Hesitantly, she reached out and took the floating thread. The transition of control as she grasped it was bumpy, as if she'd jumped onto a horse that was already moving. But she *did* know how to ride, and it only took her a second or two to settle in, for her control to replace his.

There was an immediate difference in the flow of magic. Where he had needed only the thinnest of threads to hold the portal open, Nyx required something more along the lines of fine yarn. She'd barely grown comfortable with the control when he peeled off the second thread and handed it to her.

Once again it was like jumping on a moving object, finding her balance, and discovering the strength she needed to keep it was more than he required. Splitting her focus meant the magic required to hold two was more than double what she'd needed to hold one. Her fine yarn strings thickened.

No sooner had she gotten her footing again than he handed her the third. The fourth. The fifth. By the time he piled on the sixth, her yarn strings had grown into thick ropes that she could barely keep hold of. She staggered under the weight, striving to hold it as the last of the Meerkin cubs bounded through. She felt a moment of relief before she remembered that she couldn't let go yet. The adult Meerkin had to come through.

She struggled as they began to arrive, but it was too much—too much to focus on, too much magic funneling through her from the portal above Jevryn. The ropes were slippery in her hands. She gritted her teeth and clung to them, but as she tightened her grip, they slid like eels through her fingers.

The two outermost portals flickered at the edges, then stabilized when Jevryn deftly swiped the ropes from her hands. They immediately thinned, shrinking back to the almost gossamer threads he'd begun with. Nyx dragged the back of her hand across her forehead, wiping away sweat, staring jealously at the delicate strands of portal magic and the seeming effortlessness with which Jevryn held them. He hadn't opened the portal to the well for himself—he didn't need that added access to more magic—he'd opened it for her, knowing that she would.

"What is the lesson here, *na'tria*?"

She was bent over, hands resting on her thighs as she caught her breath, and he wanted to know what the lesson was? "I'm not as good as you?"

He shook his head. "The lesson is that magic is a muscle. You must establish a baseline before you are capable of greater feats. Attempt to do something more complex than you have the foundation to manage, and you will falter."

She didn't entirely mind Jevryn's teaching methods. She had never learned well by having things explained to her. She'd been too eager to *try*, and if an explanation droned on for too long, she quit listening. Far more helpful, to her, to attempt to do a thing first, and then find where her weaknesses were.

Eventually the adult Meerkin were all in the den, and Jevryn severed the portals. She watched them collapse in on themselves, determined that someday, she was going to be as good as he was. She glanced down at the tattooed number two on her hand. It just... might take a while.

The den was a flurry of activity with the arrival of the additional Meerkin. Everyone was busy settling in and receiving their orders on where they would be when the time came, and she and Jevryn were soon forgotten, which worked for Nyx.

One thing, however, didn't. "What am I supposed to do when Kiev arrives?" she asked Jevryn. "And please don't say 'stay behind me and keep quiet' because that's not helpful."

"No?" Jevryn clasped his hands behind his back and began walking in the direction of their suite. "It is a simple instruction with little room for misinterpretation. I should think it would be quite helpful."

Nyx followed him, her irritation getting the better of her. "That's not—" She cut off when she saw the corner of his lip twitch. "Are you putting me on right now?"

He frowned, his face a caricature of seriousness. "I do believe there must be an issue with translation on that one. I am not quite certain what you mean."

Nyx couldn't believe it. Jevryn A-Morridahn actually *did* have a sense of humor. It was even drier and more deadpan than Griff's, but it existed. And he was using it, for her. It occurred to her then that one probably didn't reach the age of nine-hundred-and-some-odd-change as a councilor by trusting people. Kaden had said Jevryn found people irritating, and Kiev had called him a recluse. But talking and interacting with people led to the possibility that you might actually like someone, and the moment you started to like someone was the moment it became easiest for them to stab you in the back.

Her father, Nyx realized, was likely a very lonely person. And maybe it was her bleeding heart tendencies, or maybe it was that he finally did seem to be trying a little, that made her say, "I don't think they're all that clear of instructions, actually. The opportunity for misinterpretation is endless. How *far* behind you am I supposed to stay? Two feet? Ten? Is this directly behind you? Behind and off-center to the left or right? If you could expand on the nature of 'keep quiet' that would also be helpful. If I'm possessed of the sudden urge to sneeze, I should know if that will ruin your delicate focus."

"Ah, I can see my error in thinking such instructions would be clear." He led them into their suite, his face returning to its normal unreadable neutrality. "As it so happens, 'stay behind me and keep quiet' were not the instructions I had planned to give you."

She perked up. "You mean I actually get to do something?"

"If Kiev approaches in the manner I suspect he will—and given that he believes I am still indisposed, I have no reason to think he will not—then yes, I have a role for you. Provided you can master one thing before nightfall."

"I can do it." Whatever it was, she wouldn't fail.

Jevryn's face took on that carefully neutral expression that, for him, passed as a pained one. "We may also require your Illusionist. Provided, of course, that he is capable of both the magical task and taking instruction. I have my doubts on the latter."

Nyx smiled. "What do you need?" She listened as Jevryn explained, then said, "Seth could do that in his sleep."

"And the part where he is required to take instruction?"

She crossed her arms. "You know, he isn't half as empty-headed or contrary as he acts."

Jevryn sighed. "Yes, I am aware. That is precisely what concerns me."

"He'll do his part."

"Very well. Let us discuss the role that you must play. Prepare yourself for much tedious, repetitive practice."

B y the time evening rolled around, Nyx was exhausted. Pleased and nervous, but exhausted. It was not the kind of exhausted that came with drowsiness, however. Not when she was worried about her friends, none of whom she'd seen for a single moment since they'd left that morning while she was talking to Riven.

Her practice with Jevryn finished, she decided they'd been gone long enough. "I'm going to go see if I can find everyone." She didn't make it more than two steps toward the doorway when the boundary spell dissipated. Evra, Morgen, Seth, and Kaden walked in on a wave of conversation. Seth spotted Nyx and made a beeline for her. He caught her in a hug that lifted her off her feet and spun her in a circle.

"You're in high spirits," she said when he put her down.

"Of course I'm in high spirits. I get to do *so much cool shit* tomorrow."

She laughed and smoothed an errant strand of his hair back into place. "We're going to be aiding in what may be the deciding battle for an oppressed people's freedom, the primary impediment of that freedom being my psychotic uncle, and you're excited because you 'get to do cool shit'?"

He nodded emphatically. "Nyxi, I haven't gotten to do cool shit in *months*. I can't even temporarily fool *you* anymore on account of your mystical Station powers, Evra threatened to murder me in my sleep if I mess with her—"

"It was not an idle threat," Evra assured them.

"—and Morgen just assumes that anything weird that happens in the Station is because of me, or will be handled by you or Griff, and doesn't worry about it."

"There is no point in worrying about things in a Station where you know the Guardian and the Avatar," Morgen pointed out.

Seth waved him off. "Point being, I can only get so much excitement out of jump-scaring Kalvar and bottling premade glamours for Griff. I need to stretch my wings." Illusory wings with black feathers sprouted from his back and stretched wide, underscoring his point.

A throat cleared. Jevryn had an odd look on his face, and his voice was slightly more tense than its usual level of tense when he said, "I believe I will retire for the evening. I suggest you all do the same." He left abruptly, disappearing into one of the side rooms and raising its boundary spell.

"Was it something I said?" Seth asked.

"I think it was these." Nyx ruffled the feathers that, while illusory, nonetheless held shape and texture beneath her touch. "Did Griff ever tell you he had wings in his human form?"

"No way, like an angel?"

"He doesn't care much for that comparison, but yes, exactly like that."

"Remind me not to break out the fake wings at home, then." He vanished them. "What have the two of you been doing all day?"

"Practicing. We may need you for something tomorrow." She drew him off to one side of the room while the others flopped down onto various piles of furs. Unsurprisingly, the Meerkin weren't exactly big on furniture. "Do you think you have time in your busy schedule of doing cool shit tomorrow to do one thing for me?"

"Nyxi darling, I don't know if you know this, but I always have time for you. What do you need?"

She outlined the plan in broad strokes.

"I don't like it," Seth said immediately, once she'd finished.

"I'm shocked," she said dryly.

"Your plan is to go out and talk to the guy who basically wants to kidnap you and indoctrinate you into the evil ways of his family."

"*My* family," she pointed out.

"And you're assuming he's going to walk right up at the head of his army like a cinema villain."

She shrugged. "Jevryn says he will. Considering he's known him for nearly a millennium, I'm going to go out on a limb and say he can accurately predict his twin's behavior."

"There are a million ways this could go wrong."

"And I have an exit strategy. But it doesn't work without a little sleight-of-hand from you first. So, what do you say?" She looked up and cartoonishly batted her eyelashes at him. "Please?"

He rolled his eyes. "Fine, but for the record, I still don't like it."

Nyx patted her pockets, frowning. "Oh no, I seem to have left the record book at home. Whatever will we do if your objections can't be recorded for posterity?"

"You're a brat," he muttered.

"And you're an ass. Now that that's settled…" She dragged him over to the others, a bright smile on her face. "What are the rest of you doing tomorrow?"

"Little Guardian," Morgen said, "you don't think you're getting out of telling us about your conversation with Riven *that* easily, do you?"

If Nyx were being entirely honest with herself, that conversation with Riven felt like it had happened days ago, now. But given how it had ended, she really didn't want to talk about it. "I do, actually, and—" She frowned, suddenly realizing her little group was missing people. "Where are Liya and Valedan?"

"Staying in Riven's quarters tonight," Morgen answered. "Valedan claimed it's because bringing Riven home is the only thing that might keep his mother from murdering him, but truthfully I think he views her as family and doesn't want to let her out of his sight. Now"—he pointed a finger at her—"talk."

"You first."

"You drive a hard bargain, but fair."

They settled in the common area, talking well into the night, despite Jevryn's suggestion they do the opposite. At some point Kaden left, quietly enough that she didn't see it happen. He'd hardly spoken, which wasn't precisely unusual, but it worried Morgen, if the tightness around her friend's eyes was any indication.

The rest of them parted ways soon after. Nyx hadn't really felt the reality of what was to come while she was sitting with them all, talking and laughing. Alone with Seth in their room, it hit. Even in the best case scenario, people were going to die soon. And while she couldn't entertain the possibility that some of them might be her friends, because if she did she would lose her mind, she had a visceral need to remind herself that right now her friends were still with her. That right now, Seth was with her.

She pulled him close. She didn't want to talk, so she didn't. Her lips met his and she drank him in, hardly stopping to breathe, hardly able to let go of him long enough for them to both fumble out of their clothes. She kissed him, and she held him, and she took him, and she told him without words exactly what he meant to her: everything.

47

Nyx had calculated the sunrise time on Kyvren, and set the alarm on her watch to wake her and Seth an hour before dawn. They didn't talk as they dressed, strapping on boots and weapons, tying on cloaks. There was a somberness in the air that left no room for levity, even from Seth. When she moved for the door he pulled her back, flush against him, covering her mouth with his own.

He cupped her face as they broke apart, his thumbs stroking across her cheeks. "I know being asked to be careful is your least favorite thing on any planet, but please be careful. For me."

She searched his eyes. They were dark and worried. "I'll be fine. I'm primarily a distraction. Jevryn is doing most of the heavy lifting."

"Promise me." His hands slid down to her waist, pulling her closer.

"I promise."

He kissed her again and then they were out the door, meeting Jevryn and the others in the common room, all of them making their way down to the meeting room together. Some of the Meerkin had been up for hours, keeping watch. Others were in the hallways with them, making their way to assigned outposts.

Vorex awaited them in the meeting room, motioning them over to where he looked into a six-foot-wide basin of water that reflected the exterior of the mountain. Viktor had explained to her the basics of scrying spells in her youth, but Nyx had never actually seen one before now. She took her place with the others and waited.

As Jevryn had predicted, Kiev arrived with the dawn. She watched through the scrying as he walked up to the edge of the chitin-ore field before the mountain. No portal yawned open behind him now. The attack of two nights ago had been a response made in anger and rashness, two things she was unsurprised to learn Kiev was prone to. Today's arrival was a calculated affair, and Meerkin scouts had reported Jevryn portaling in several miles deeper into the forest, stretching that portal to bring the Dwarven forces through before closing it so that now, his focus was not required to maintain that passageway.

A-Lethe stood at Kiev's side. The reason the construct could portal on its own—namely that the soul shard in its making powered it like an endless battery—meant Kiev could draw on A-Lethe as an endless source of portal magic. Separating A-Lethe from Kiev was crucial to their plan, and that was where Seth would be coming in.

In the scrying pool, Kiev looked straight ahead. "As I am certain you are listening, Vorex, allow me to make you an offer. I want two things that you have: the human Nyx Fortuna, and the metalsmith Riven Gare Ru. Bring them to me, and I will negotiate your surrender to the Dwarves without bloodshed. Consider your people. Consider their children. Consider how many of them will die this day if you refuse me. You have fifteen minutes to make your decision."

Vorex gave a short, low growl.

Jevryn looked at Nyx. "Are you ready?"

Her palms tingled and her chest felt too light. *No, no I don't think I am.* "Of course."

"If you have doubts, I will take your place."

"No." Jevryn on his own could distract Kiev from the regular battle, but their own would cause much damage in and of itself. If Nyx went out, if they contained him, *that* was the path that led to the least loss of life. "I'm good."

Jevryn nodded, his gaze sweeping past her to Seth. "Do not stumble, Hawthorne."

Seth grinned at him. "I never do."

As she and Seth left, she heard Jevryn talking to the Meerkin who was managing the scrying. "If you could focus in on the area directly surrounding Kiev—yes, perfect." Line-of-sight portaling, it turned out, could be done via a scrying image as well as *actual* line-of-sight.

At the den's primary exit, Seth's hand on her wrist stopped her before she could slide out.

"I know, I know," she said, "be careful. I—"

His lips crashed down on hers, fierce and hard and quick. "For luck," he said.

Head spinning, she slipped out the entrance. Seth slipped out behind her, invisible to sight. Walking confidently across an empty field toward her waiting evil uncle and his army, while the opposing army watched through various scrying pools, was not something Nyx had ever had occasion to practice for.

Shoulders back, head up, she told herself, because it felt like the advice she would give someone else in her position. Six feet from Kiev A-Morridahn, she halted.

"You are late, if you intend to accept my offer, niece. And you are lacking a certain required person."

She did her best to look like a nervous person trying to be brave, which wasn't all that difficult because that was exactly what she was, just not for the reasons she was pretending. "Is my dad going to wake up?"

Kiev's gaze narrowed. "Your 'dad'? Please tell me he does not allow you to refer to him as such. It is so…base. He is your father, child."

She flinched, as if his words had actually struck her. "Is my *father* going to wake up?" She let desperation creep into her voice, let her words tumble out one atop the other. "Nothing I've tried works. He doesn't have a heartbeat, he doesn't—"

Kiev cut her off with an upraised hand and a curled upper lip. "I cannot believe Jevryn has allowed you to continue on in this state. Look at you, blathering on about your fears as if you were *common.* A-Morridahns should always negotiate from a position of strength. Attempt to imagine you have some."

Nyx straightened her shoulders. "I *do* have some. I have Riven. Tell me how to wake up my father, and I'll give her back to you."

Kiev raised his eyebrows. "And your Meerkin friends? You will simply leave them to extermination?"

She hesitated. "If I go with you, you'll leave them alone?"

Kiev pretended to consider it. "Unfortunately, the original agreement was for you and Riven in exchange for the Meerkin. You cannot offer me the same payment and expect to get your father out of it as well."

"But he's your *brother*," she protested, as if she were naive enough to think that would matter to him.

Kiev's nose wrinkled in distaste. "Yes, it has long been an issue between us. He will pull through or he will not. But you, my dear—I am afraid you are out of time. And you do not seem to understand that you have already failed to deliver on the offer I made you."

Nyx tapped her fingers against her thigh and Seth overlaid an illusion of her in the space she'd been standing at the same time she Hid herself, stepping back behind him just as A-Lethe surged forward, jaws clamping on her arm. The illusion of her cried out—and then began to laugh.

Nyx whispered in Seth's ear, and her words, her voice, issued forth from her illusion. "I'm sorry, Uncle. You didn't actually think I'd come myself, did you?"

Seth dropped everything but sight from the illusion, and A-Lethe's teeth closed suddenly on empty air, passing through the fake Nyx. "I'm not even here," she whispered in Seth's ear. "But I might be over here," a second Nyx said, popping up twenty feet to the left. "Or over here," said a third to the right. "Or back here." A fourth appeared mid-way back on the field.

"I might even be *right here*," a fifth said behind Kiev, tapping his shoulder. This one, Seth gave the illusion of portal magic to before it disappeared, reappearing back toward the den's entrance with that same feel of clinging magic.

Kiev snarled and issued an order to A-Lethe. "Find her and bring her to me. By any means necessary." The construct flickered and was gone, chasing illusions of Nyx.

Show time.

Jevryn portaled directly behind Kiev. Magic split from him on either side, curving around his twin. Nyx, still Hidden, stepped up and seamlessly caught it, connecting the circle, just like they'd practiced. Magic flashed upward and downward, curving together to form a sphere that met aboveground and below. It formed a space much like A-Lethe inhabited when the dog was in-between realms —a demarcating line of *potential* that was not-quite-here and not-quite-there. Just as Kaden hadn't been able to injure A-Lethe in that state, the sphere they had erected around Kiev could not be crossed. If anyone tried, they would simply move through it and Kiev as if they were not there. Nyx and Jevryn, holding that potential, existed within the same space.

It *could* be portaled into or out of, which was why this plan had been dependent on two things. One had been separating Kiev from A-Lethe and the infinite portal magic the dog provided. The second had been divesting Kiev of all other portal magic he possessed. Watching her uncle's face go from smug to confused to furious as he tried and failed to draw on that magic was one of the most beautiful things Nyx had ever seen.

Seth, trickster class Illusionist and Nyx's favorite pickpocket, popped into visibility. He was wearing eight portal magic bracelets and had a single earring dangling from his fingertips. "Thanks for these," Seth told Kiev. "My girlfriend doesn't usually let me give her things I steal, but I think she's gonna love these." He glanced back over his shoulder, to where the Meerkin were streaming out of the den in droves. He winked, a gesture that looked like it was for Kiev but Nyx knew was for her. "Sorry, gotta go do cool shit."

Nyx hadn't thought Kiev could look any more disgusted until that moment. "Is *that* what the A-Morridahn bloodline is to be brought to?" he asked Jevryn. "I suppose I shouldn't have expected better of you than to let her associate with someone so wholly unsuitable, given your own choices. Though at least Arradin, for all his many faults, was intelligent."

Jevryn's response was drowned out as the line of Meerkin met the approaching Dwarves and claw met steel. It was everything Nyx could do to hold her focus, to not let go, to not panic as bodies clashed around her, then *through* her, as if she was made of smoke. For a moment, the edges of the working flickered before Nyx drowned out what was happening around her, focusing only on Kiev and Jevryn. The sphere re-solidified.

"Is that my niece, buckling under pressure?" Kiev asked.

Nyx didn't say anything. Jevryn had said that to hold the boundary against Kiev would take the two of them, so Kiev would know she was there. But since he couldn't communicate with A-Lethe to summon the dog back, it wouldn't matter. And since he wasn't looking for where, specifically, she was—likely because he probably thought it was Seth's illusions keeping her out of sight—his knowledge of her didn't strain too much the power required for her to maintain her Hiding. If it became too much of a problem, she could always weave Kiev in as an exception alongside Seth and Jevryn, but when he realized he could find her and A-Lethe still couldn't, he would likely put together that she was Hidden. And she was still hoping, for the time being, to keep that to herself.

Around them, the battle raged, and Nyx couldn't stop her focus from straying. From trying to find her friends in the chaos. And it *was* chaos, of a kind she never wanted to be in the midst of again. She wanted to close her eyes, but she would still be able to *hear* it all —the scrape of claws against steel, the thud of hammers against armor—and then she wouldn't be able to catch flashes of Evra here, Morgen there, wouldn't be able to reassure herself that they were still alive.

And yet every time she watched a Meerkin go down and not get back up, she felt like she was doing nothing, standing here, safe from the violence by virtue of not *really* being here at all. Rationally she knew that Kiev, if unleashed, could cause more devastation than she could prevent by physically fighting, but it didn't make her feel better.

And then, suddenly, Kiev came to attention. A dark laugh escaped him. "Being an A-Morridahn means making difficult choices, Nyx. It would appear your first one has arrived. I told A-Lethe to find you by any means necessary, and it is quite an intelligent creature, capable of the same strategy you and I might manage. I do believe it has determined, based on its observation of you on Earth, that if it cannot find you, it will have to draw you out via your friends.

"So here is your choice: continue holding me, or save *her.*" Kiev pointed. Nyx followed his gaze across the battlefield to where Evra was cutting a line through the Dwarven ranks. Far at her back, A-Lethe bounded toward her.

"*Nyx.*" Jevryn's short bark of her name was an order not to go. But he'd said he could keep Kiev busy on his own. He couldn't contain him as he now did without her, but he could fight him.

"I'm sorry." She dropped her Hiding, grasped Constance, looked to the empty space at Evra's back, and portaled.

Constance shifted in Nyx's hands as she landed, flowing into a shield she held up just as A-Lethe slammed into her. The force drove her back into Evra. "It's me, don't take my head off," she shouted.

At that Evra's feet dug in, effectively stopping their skid. "Nyx? What are you doing?"

"Saving you from my uncle's death dog. I gotta go though." If she stayed here, A-Lethe was going to crush them, Constance or no. Nyx was A-Lethe's target, its priority. Now that it knew she was here, it would follow. "I need you to dive left."

"I will not—"

"You can't fight this thing. Trust me. Please."

Evra made a sound suspiciously like a growl. "Be careful." She dove left. Without Evra to prop her up, Nyx fell backward. She opened a portal beneath her, as she'd once done on a planet when she'd been too cold to move. A small part of her had hoped A-Lethe might be destroyed with something as simple as Nyx closing the portal on him as it fell through with her. But the dog simply turned insubstantial as Nyx landed on the hard rock of a small landing on the mountainside.

She opened another portal, leaping through just as A-Lethe landed beside her. So it went as it had the first time, Nyx portaling, A-Lethe always a split second behind. Her heart thudded painfully in her chest as she jumped from point to point, watching the magic dwindle from her bracelets. If she kept going as she was, she would spend it all and A-Lethe, filled with endless regeneration, would catch her. It would drag her back to Kiev. With A-Lethe at his side, would he overcome Jevryn? Would he turn the tide of the battle and destroy the Meerkin?

Against Nyx's throat, the Harvester pulsed, a hot thump against her skin. *I know you,* it seemed to say to A-Lethe. *I know you and I once held you and I could yet hold you again.*

She thought about it. For a moment, she thought about it. And then she remembered that brilliant light exploding out of it when she'd allowed it to consume the Kumir in her Station. Remembered its hunger, and how it had wanted to reach next for her friends. If she allowed the Harvester to consume A-Lethe, she didn't know if she could hold it in check. Not here, on the outskirts of a battle where so much chaos reigned.

She jumped through a portal a hair's breadth ahead of snapping jaws. Another bracelet on her wrist ran dry. She turned as A-Lethe followed, striking the bladed end of Constance into its chest. The blade cleaved through empty air, the lack of resistance carrying her swing high as the dog vanished. Teeth clamped down on her right calf from behind, jerking her to the ground. Before she could do anything, her surroundings dissolved. They resolved into the ground between Kiev's and Jevryn's feet, her sudden appearance knocking the two apart. A blink and she was on her back, the dog towering over her, its jaws clamped around her neck.

Portal magic streamed from A-Lethe to Kiev. He had no bracelet in which to contain it, but it wrapped around him, coating him in a thin layer, as Nyx had once covered herself in magic from Lehine's well.

"If my brother moves," Kiev told A-Lethe, "tear out her throat."

Nyx's heart pounded into overdrive. She shifted her gaze to the left, all too aware of the way teeth pricked against her skin as she did so, and saw Jevryn, his sword held lightly in his hands, the tip pointing down. "She will be of no use to you without her throat," he said mildly.

"At this moment the only *use* she has is her hold over you." Kiev spat to the side.

Think, damn it, Nyx ordered herself. It was a surprisingly difficult task when razor sharp teeth were puncturing your skin, but she did it anyway. A-Lethe was powered by a soul shard, but it was Kiev's death magic, wrapped around that shard, that gave it form. That *made* it A-Lethe.

It is easy enough for an A-Morridahn to swallow one of our own deaths. It is how we are born, after all.

Given what Kiev had ordered A-Lethe to do, what was the construct, if not a death meant for her? This was either the smartest or the dumbest idea she'd ever had. Defiance spilled through her— she hadn't come all this way, hadn't done and survived everything that she had, to end up a mere pawn between Kiev and Jevryn.

The chaos thorns pulsed in her cheek. Anger spread through her, the rush of what she now understood was death magic spilling through her veins. In such close proximity as she was to A-Lethe, that magic in her resonated with the magic in the construct. She could feel the creation of A-Lethe, the potential. She could feel the shining shard of Lethe-Alihana at its center.

She reached out to the darkness in her, and then she opened her mouth and invited the darkness outside of her in.

"Nyx, no!" Jevryn shouted.

But it was too late. A-Lethe was a death, *her* death, and she was accepting it—inviting it, *wanting* it. Teeth and claws and fur dissolved into black smoke that flowed into her, down her throat to settle in a cool lake in her belly. For a moment, the silvery shard of Lethe-Alihana's soul shone bright, and then it too was swallowed down.

Two things happened at once. Kiev let out a sound of pure rage, magic emanating from him, and the bodies around them surged upward, burying Jevryn in a mound of reanimated corpses. At the same time, Nyx heard the voice of her father's planet and it—or at least this sliver of it—was utterly insane.

Hello, daughter. We are broken, yes, but happy. So, so happy. You have freed us from the son's fetters and we would repay you. Let us destroy. Let us kill. Let us sweep a mist of death upon the land let us feed let us kill let us—

Nyx blocked the voice out. The shard sat in her throat like ice, a cold that burned viciously. Her body vibrated with the force of its containment. Her head swam but she forced herself up, to face Kiev before he attacked. Hands that were too weak and conversely too strong gripped Constance as she gained her feet. The world was limned in a white haze, as if it were nighttime and all the people and objects had been painted in glow-in-the-dark white.

Kiev met her gaze, and she saw the last thing she would ever have expected to see in his: fear.

He should *be afraid,* the soul shard chattered. *He who dared to sunder that which came before him he who—*

Nyx shut the voice out again. It was too much, too raw. Kiev drew on the portal magic he'd taken from A-Lethe and vanished.

Nyx immediately turned, looking for Jevryn. He'd broken free of the horde that had engulfed him, and as she watched he slashed at the nearest bodies, severing limbs and torsos. He struck out with a kick, knocking another back. In the moment of space it bought him, his hands clasped together around the hilt of his sword. He thrust it into the ground. A pulse of power radiated from him in all directions, and the corpses went still.

Safe. He was safe.

Through the white haze clouding her vision, she could see the battle nearly finished, the Meerkin on the verge of victory. Heart pounding in her chest, she searched the battlefield, found Evra and then Kaden. Morgen and then Liya and Valedan. All alive. All safe.

Seth. Where was Seth? Panic clawed at her as she felt for that spark, that unerring sense that could lead her to him anywhere. But even here at the end, everything was so *loud*, and she couldn't feel it. Couldn't feel him.

Her heart thudded faster, faster—*there*. Her head jerked to the right, following that feeling, and she couldn't see him, but she knew he was there. Relief flooded her veins, her lips breaking into a smile.

A flicker of portal magic came to her right and Kiev reappeared. His mouth opened, that torrent of black spilling out, but not at *her*—at the point where she was looking, where her gaze terminated.

No. She portaled across the battlefield. It took her a second, two at most, to land in front of Seth. It had taken Kiev less. Seth was visible, now, the familiar feel of his magic gone, his expression wide and astonished.

She caught him as he fell, crashing to her knees, down, his torso heavy on her legs as she clutched him to her. "Seth?"

Another flicker of portal magic. "I told you that if you defied me, I would take something precious from you."

Nyx's head jerked up. All that rage and darkness that lived inside her, every black impulse she had ever shoved down and ignored, the ones Seth had always dragged her back from the depths of, tore out of her. She screamed a banshee's wail and that power—the one that was promise and absolution, peace and terror—rode out alongside her scream. It carried with it the shard of Lethe-Alihana's soul, and together the two struck Kiev like a hurricane.

And then she was pulling on a different power, on the magic in the portal bracelet's lining Seth's wrist, reaching for her anchor on Earth. The world disappeared only to resolve moments later into the clearing behind the Station. Another wave of magic, pulled desperately as she envisioned the Warlock's shop, heedless of the danger of portaling to within four walls, and then they were *there*. Around her, people startled at their sudden appearance.

She locked eyes with the Warlock. Her voice, raw and desperate, pleaded, "I need Tobi."

Seth was so still in her arms. Too still. She couldn't feel him breathe, couldn't find a pulse beneath the fingers she pressed to his neck. But he wasn't gone, he couldn't be gone. Tobi could fix him. Doctors brought back people who flatlined all the time, right? This was something like that. Less than a minute had passed since she'd caught him, brought him here, and it would be enough. That pitying look Ankira was giving her didn't *mean* anything, and when Tobi came up behind his mother, relief crashed into Nyx.

Fine. Everything was going to be fine.

Tobi approached, put his small hand on Seth's face and closed his eyes. Her heart hammered so hard in her chest it was almost all she could feel. She waited. And waited. And waited.

Tobi opened his eyes. They held that gravity that was the weight of the Congregation speaking through him. "We are sorry, Nyx Fortuna. He is gone."

"No." Her arms squeezed around Seth. Her voice broke. "No, he's not gone. He just needs help, you need to help him."

"That which Death takes cannot be returned. Each life ends when it must." He turned away.

It was the emptiness in his voice, the finality of his retreat, that made it real. Tobi always helped. If something could be done, he helped. But now he was leaving.

A high, keening wail left her throat. The world grew fuzzy and distant, the only real thing the body in her arms and what it meant: Seth was gone. His eyes, once so vibrant and filled with perpetual laughter, stared lifelessly up at her.

She was supposed to close them. That was what you did for the dead, wasn't it? Closed eyes that could no longer see?

But she couldn't. She pressed her forehead to his and curled around him as she sobbed, convinced that if she just didn't let go, if she held onto him, he would come back to her somehow.

They were Nyx and Seth, Seth and Nyx. He was her constant and she was his. Neither was meant to exist in the world without the other. But no matter how closely she held him, no matter how hard she cried, no matter how many times she said those three words she'd never said to him in life, he did not come back.

Time passed. Eventually her body ran out of tears, leaving her with swollen eyes and a raw throat it hurt to breathe through.

A shadow fell over her. The hem of a black cloak pooled on the ground, and then Jevryn crouched before her. His hands closed over hers. They tried to pull her fingers free of Seth but she refused to let go. She was never supposed to let him go.

"It is time, Nyx." Jevryn's voice was gentle in a way it never was.

She shook her head. It would never be time.

"I am sorry." Jevryn's hands left hers to settle on Seth. Magic flowed from his fingers, and when Nyx realized what it meant, panic flooded her.

"No, don't. *Please* don't." She clung tighter even as Seth's body disintegrated. She made a desperate grab, her hand clenching around his raven's feather earring. In the next blink he was gone, reduced to ash that condensed into a sphere and then hardened into a small black stone that clinked onto the floor.

Nothing left of him but rock, and a raven's feather earring.

Everything in her shut down. Her emotions, her thoughts. Her hopes, her fears. She was an endless black ocean and the waters were calm and vast, the gentle lapping of their waves beckoning her to remain within them forever.

She didn't hear the words Jevryn spoke. She didn't resist when he lifted her into his arms. She just curled into him, because he was an easy place to hide from the world, and he carried her as if the burden of her was slight. She barely noticed when they reached the Station and he handed her to Griff, who carried her upstairs and placed her into her bed.

She rolled onto her side, away from them both, and waited for the blissful emptiness of sleep.

It was a long, long time in coming.

48

Nyx didn't know how many days passed. For the first time in her life, she didn't care what the day or the time was, had removed her watch some time ago and shoved it in the nightstand drawer.

She didn't care. She just *hurt*. She kept waiting for it to get better, but it didn't. It was a festering wound in the core of her being and all she could do was curl around it and ache.

She kept expecting to wake up and discover it wasn't true. That the anxiety she'd been mired in for months had taken her into a nightmare, and when the dawn's light came through the windows, she'd realize Seth was right beside her. That he'd never been gone.

But it never happened, so she shut the curtains. And when Griff tried to open them, she walled the windows over entirely. She ate and showered to keep Griff at bay, but she didn't do either often. At some point, she learned Kiev had survived, but it didn't really sink in through the fog in her brain. It didn't matter.

Evra and Morgen came to see her. Multiple times. She couldn't really remember what they said. She knew when Liya and Valedan left, because she was too tired to shut the Station out.

At some point, Evra lost her temper. Nyx couldn't recall the exact words the Amazon had shouted at her. Something about how they'd all lost Seth, and were they supposed to sit around and watch her die too.

Evra had tried to drag her out of bed, and that was when Nyx had found the energy to reach through the Station and throw Evra out. Her control had been sloppy, fueled by grief and a rage that had nothing to temper it. Evra had hit the wall on the other side of the hallway, knocking the drywall out to either side of the support beam where she hit.

There had been an awful kind of crack, like maybe she'd broken a rib, and Nyx had known that she should care. When Evra had pushed to all fours and given her a look that was a potent mixture of shock and disbelief and hurt, Nyx had known she *did* care, and she'd tried to latch onto it.

Tried to swim her way up from that black ocean, to say she was sorry, to say she wanted to try, she *did*, but she was drowning and she couldn't find the surface. The words wouldn't come. Her face wouldn't change expression.

Evra had shoved to her feet and limped down the stairs. She hadn't come back.

⸻

One morning came differently than the rest. It came with a push from Kaliaris, the Station reaching out with the small freedom their differed bond with Nyx and Griff allowed them.

She would have ignored them, too—they couldn't *make* her do anything—except she'd realized what they were pushing her towards. The garden. Seth's garden. She didn't need to look at her watch to know what day it was now. Her birthday.

Her heart contorted itself in her chest. She hadn't been to Seth's room since she'd returned, didn't think she could, but this was different. She found herself walking outside, shuffling like a zombie into a torrential thunderstorm. She sank in mud up to her ankles, and managed enough control to firm the ground so she could walk to the edge of the Station where the ugly wall kept Seth's garden secret.

She sucked in a steadying breath and shoved the gate open. The storm calmed to a quiet drizzle as she latched the gate closed behind her and stared at the entrance to a maze. One path branched to her right, the other to her left. Directly ahead of her, a pedestal waited.

An envelope rested on it, dry and in place despite the rain and wind, kept safe by Kaliaris. Her name was scrawled across it in Seth's familiar handwriting. Her hands shook as she tried to open it, slicing her finger on the paper before managing to extract the letter.

There were two pages. The first said:

If someone else takes the best, what do you get?

The answer to that was a little too obvious—you got what was left. She looked at the path that branched to her left. He'd built her a puzzle maze. One she could navigate by coming up with the answers to the clues he'd left her. Because he knew her, and he'd known how much she would love it.

Her knees buckled and she clung to the pedestal to keep from dropping into the mud. This wasn't fair. He should be here. She shouldn't be standing in what he'd built for her, alone, reading letters from his ghost.

But she couldn't stop. Gathering her strength, she slid the first page behind the second.

I know, I know, that one was too easy, but I'm starting slow. Being clever isn't as easy as everyone thinks, and you have to let me pace myself.

She folded the letters, tucked them into her pocket, and turned left. As she walked, the hedges to either side began to flower, small, white blossoms of delicate star jasmine opening in her wake. This continued until she reached a dead end covered in rose briars.

Another letter was tucked into the vines, and she plucked it out.

Were the motion-activated flowers too much? Morgen talked me into those. So if they were too much you should totally blame him.

Okay, okay, moving on. To move forward, you'll need the answer to the following riddle:

When all is well, I am not seen
My appearance can cause quite the fright to some
I carry all day, but I never grow tired
I die every second, and am born just as often
If you want to draw me out, the price is pain

What am I?

She didn't have to think about it too long, mostly because Seth never let an opportunity to even the scales pass him by: blood. She'd pricked his finger in the Shadow Market to get blood for Veritas to use, and now she pricked her own on one of the sharp thorns barring the way forward.

"Guess this makes us even, baby," she whispered as the vines curled back. It didn't feel even. It felt heavy. She shoved down the weight of it and moved forward.

It took her the better part of two hours to work her way through the maze. Sometimes, answering a riddle or solving a puzzle opened a treasure box, where Seth had left her some small gift. A sketch. A book. A coffee mug. One extremely filthy original poem that made her laugh and then made her cry.

She dragged her feet on completing the maze, because when she read his words she could hear him speak them, could see his face with its perpetual half-smirk, and it was almost like he was here.

Except he wasn't here, and as soon as she finished the maze, that certainty would sink into her again. Her world had a Seth-shaped hole in it, one his letters and his gifts and his memories were trying desperately to fill, but the second they ran out she would be alone again, with nothing left to blunt the pain.

By the time she reached the final question, her heart felt like lead. She knew it was the last one, because of the question:

A word that combines Seth's favorite thing with Nyx's chronic obsession.

It was too *them* for it to be anything but the last. The letter containing the question had been set on top of a final treasure chest that had a set of wooden rollers on the lid, like the kind you might find on a combination dial lock, except instead of numbers, the rollers had letters. One word, nine letters.

She put the last four letters in first, the answer to her half of the question: time. It left five letters for Seth's half. It took her a few minutes before she could put them in, not because she didn't know the answer, but because what would have once been sweet now only reminded her of what she'd lost.

When they'd been younger, when they'd been on the precipice of crossing that bridge from friends to lovers, he'd kept making weird, intentionally nonsensical jokes about night being his favorite thing. He'd eventually gotten tired of waiting for her to figure it out, and she'd come into her room one night to find her encyclopedia on Greek mythology open to the page on Nyx. The goddess of night.

Slowly, she turned the rollers to the correct letters, spelling out *nighttime*, and heard the click of the lock disengaging. Inside was a black sports watch and another note.

You're still wearing the one I stole for you—I mean, bought you, DEFINITELY bought you—when you were twelve. I thought it was maaaybe time for an upgrade. Sure, the compass only works in Dead Earth, but you can recalibrate the altimeter on the fly, and I don't really know how a barometer functions, so it has potential on both those scores.

I promise I paid for this one.

Her old watch was still sitting in her nightstand drawer. Part of her wanted to throw this one in there too, but she slipped it over her wrist instead, clipping the band in place.

In the very bottom of the chest, beneath where the watch had been, was a button that said: *push me.* She pushed. The hedges in front of her peeled apart, revealing a stone path that led into the very heart of the maze.

It was a large, circular space, with two small ponds to either side of the path, which led straight to the maze's centerpiece. The hawthorn tree towered twenty-five feet above her, its branches spread wide, white flowers in full bloom. Given the color of the blooms, it took her a moment to realize another plant grew with it. Twining up the tree, crawling over the branches, entwined with it on every level, were white queen of the night flowers.

Something told her not to open the letter waiting at the base of the trunk. That nothing good would come of it. If she'd been a different person, maybe she could have walked away. But she wasn't a different person, she was Nyx, and she had to know, no matter how much it hurt.

It only took the first five words for her to wish she hadn't.

I love you, Nyxi darling.

She closed her eyes, sucked in a breath past the sudden constriction in her throat. Three words he'd never said in life, that she hadn't either. But at least he'd gotten the chance to, in this way, and now she would never get to say it back.

She opened her eyes and made herself keep reading.

I know I've never said it, but then, you never have either. It never felt necessary before. Before your memories, before I left, before everything. I tried to tell you before I left for Nethrayne, but you didn't want me to.

Because she hadn't wanted the first time he'd said it to be when he was leaving. Because part of her had been afraid that if he'd said it, he wouldn't come back. Now he was never coming back and she could have heard him say it, she could have said it back, if she hadn't been so fucking stupid.

So I'm saying it here, where you can't shut me up. I love you. And because I do—and okay, realistically, because I'm an impatient bastard—I'm not waiting another two years to ask you again: Marry me.

I don't need a legal contract where we sign on the dotted line like they do on Earth. I don't need a magical ceremony where we're blood-bound on pain of death like they do on Areve, because don't even get me started on how fucked up that is.

I don't need to chain you to me by magic or legality. That's not what I want. But every culture in the universe has some form of marriage, whatever they want to call it and however many people it involves, and I want to call you my wife so that everyone knows that there is nothing I wouldn't do for you.

So marry me. Because I'm selfish and I want to call myself your husband.

But if you say no, if marriage isn't what you want, it doesn't change anything. Because I can still call myself yours.

Happy birthday, Nyxi darling. I will love you as long as I breathe.

It was the last line that did her in. That drove home that he *had* loved her, and never would again. Because he wasn't breathing anymore, and dead people didn't love.

She pressed her back to the trunk of the hawthorn tree and slid to the ground.

She didn't get up again.

49

Nyx was barely aware of being lifted, of the black of Jevryn's robes beneath her cheek. She wondered, vaguely, why it was him and not Griff. If Griff thought sending her biological father to get her would make some difference, he was mistaken.

But then she was also vaguely aware that she wasn't by the hawthorn tree, that she wasn't being carried *to* her room but from it. But she couldn't remember how she'd gotten there.

The part of her that was still *Nyx*, the part buried deep, deep down, tried to rear its head and snap at Jevryn to put her down. That she didn't need to be carried, that she didn't need to be treated like…like she was broken. But it was a passing inclination that quickly faded.

At least until she lost touch with Kaliaris and realized Jevryn had taken her outside the Station's boundary. But by then, it was too late to do anything. She had no portal magic left, and before she knew it Earth was gone, replaced by the thalacite walls of Jevryn's home.

She managed the energy, then, to struggle until he put her down. To talk. "What are you doing?" Talking hurt, her voice raspy and her throat dry and sore.

"Attempting to save you from yourself."

She took in the sparse room. Windowless, doorless walls. Bed. Small table. Archway leading to what she assumed was a bathroom.

Icy understanding trickled through her. She was in Jevryn's home. "You can't mean for me to stay here."

His head dipped briefly in a nod.

"Take me back," she demanded.

"No."

"When Griff finds out—"

He interrupted her. "It was by Arradin's request that I brought you here."

Hurt and betrayal stabbed through her. "He wouldn't."

"I believe it pained him greatly to do so."

"Then why did he do it?" she snapped.

"Because he does not wish to see you die."

"I'm fine," she said, fully aware of how ridiculous—and untrue—the statement was. "I just need time."

"You have had time. Do you know how long you remained by that tree?"

She shook her head. She didn't remember leaving it.

"Two days. Arradin nearly went out of his mind leaving you there, but he thought perhaps if you were left alone, you might come back to yourself. Instead, we had to bring you in, and summon the Warlock to combat your dehydration, and you remained unresponsive even while seemingly awake.

"So, yes, Arradin asked me to take you. Because he cannot be harsh with you, and harshness is what you need."

"I don't need anything from you."

"On the contrary, you clearly do."

"You can't keep me here. Kaliaris won't allow it, my bargain with them—"

"Has been suspended, as even your Station recognized the need for intervention."

A flash of rage burst in her, that they would all turn against her, but then it died just as quickly. She turned away from him and dropped onto the bed. She was so fucking tired.

"You have the night," Jevryn said, "to pull yourself together. You need to do *something* constructive with yourself, so I think it is time you finally learn what being an A-Morridahn means. We will begin lessons in the morning."

He portaled from the room, leaving her no chance to reply. She stared at the space where he'd been. A small spark of that rage returned, a tiny ember that didn't quite die.

He thought she needed to learn how to be an A-Morridahn? She would *love* to see him make her try.

She rolled over, seeking once again the emptiness of sleep. It refused to come. Jevryn had succeeded in waking her from the protective numbness she'd wrapped herself in, and now all the memories were creeping back in, bringing so much pain with them.

People died. She knew that. She wasn't the first person to lose someone, but she couldn't just let it go. She couldn't just let *him* go and move on with her life like he'd never been there.

Not when it was her fault. Because she always knew how to find Seth, and it had gotten him killed.

As she sat with that thought, her mind finally connected it to another. A lone one that fanned the embers of that spark of fury inside her, kindling it into flames that felt like something more akin to wrath. A thought that provided a single focus for her pain: Kiev A-Morridahn.

Kiev, who had imprisoned Griff.

Kiev, who had killed Lana and Fari on the ley lines.

Kiev, who had wanted Koral to violate Nyx's mind.

Kiev, who had thrown Temerex to the wilds of Amentia Furor.

Kiev, who had taken Seth from her.

She stumbled out of the bed, through the archway and into what was indeed a bathroom. She stripped out of her clothes and showered, and when she came back into the room and found a bowl of soup waiting on the small table, she ate it.

Jevryn thought she needed to learn to be an A-Morridahn? Then she would. She would take everything he had to teach her, and she would be well-behaved and competent. She would do whatever he wanted and she would convince him and everyone else that she was fine.

Because Kiev A-Morridahn had to pay. And if no one else was going to make him do it, she *would*.

BONUS SCENES

I have two bonus scenes for this book from Jevryn's POV—one near the beginning of the book, and one at the end. They are available exclusively to my newsletter subscribers, and you can get them by signing up for my newsletter at:

https://michellemanus.com/newsletter/

If you enjoyed the book, it would be beyond super awesome of you to leave a rating and/or review at your retailer of choice. Reviews really are one of the best ways you can help support authors.

Thanks so much for reading!

Do you need something to tide you over until the next Nyx book comes out? Do you enjoy fantasy and female characters with a lot of pent-up rage? *A Song to Wake a Thousand Sorrows* is available now!

A woman with unimaginable power. A king hellbent on ruling the world. An ancient force that could mean salvation or destruction.

The survivor of a brutal childhood, Clare Brighton craves the kind of wealth and notoriety that will mean the horrors of her past can never again touch her. With nothing but a battered guitar and a Songweaver's talent, she comes to the capital of the Faelhorn Provinces, determined to gain her place.

But there is another, more dangerous power that dwells within Clare. An entity she calls the Song, it is ancient and fathomless…and no longer content to be held in the cage she has trapped it in. It is a power the ruthless Jackal King has long been searching for, and should he discover she possesses it, the cost will be far greater than her life.

Clare has sworn that she will never again let anyone control her. But escaping the Jackal King's notice will require the one thing she never wanted to need: help. It will come first from the two lords who have taken her under their wing. Next from the second prince of Faelhorn, who Clare alone knows is not what he seems. And finally, from the Song itself.

The Song has the strength to save her—if it doesn't destroy her first.

ALSO BY MICHELLE MANUS